G000244837

RILEY CAIN was born in Dublin. An avid reader, Riley loves collecting classic ghost stories, and watching scary old movies at Halloween – in the dark! These interests led to 2020's *The Halloween House*, a poetry collection of fun and frights for younger readers. Riley haunts the internet at www.rileycain.com

BANSHEE RISING

RILEY CAIN

CURRACH
BOOKS

First published in 2021 by

CURRACHBOOKS

Block 3b, Bracken Business Park,
Bracken Road, Sandyford, Dublin 18, D18 K277
www.columbabooks.com

Copyright © Riley Cain 2021

All rights reserved. Without limiting the rights under
copyright reserved alone, no part of this publication may be
reproduced, stored in or introduced into a retrieval system,
or transmitted, in any form or by any means (electronic,
mechanical, photocopying, recording or otherwise) without
the prior written permission of both the copyright owner and
the above publisher of the book.

ISBN: 978-1-78218-9145

Set in Linux Libertine 13/16
Cover and book design by Alba Esteban | Currach Books
Illustrated by Alba Esteban

Printed by L&C, Poland.

For Caitlyn,
My proof every day there's magic in the world

'OUR PEOPLE MOVE
AMONG MORTALS,
BUT THEY CANNOT SEE US...'

The Mythological Cycle of Ireland

ONE

The phantom horseman raced the moon and midnight witches.

The chase was headlong, thundering up from darkest reaches. The rider's cape whipped like black fire in the charge from horrors pursuing along country lanes. The way was north, beneath autumnal stars and tumbling leaves to reach the city, its river and the haunted miles beyond to the rendezvous.

The first dreaming suburbs were disturbed as horseshoes clattered from grassy pastures to rattle and spark on ancient cobbles. Echoes crashed between unlit dwellings to unsettle their restless souls. The horseman strained at the reins and allowed no pause, driving his mount on with snarled curses. Together they raced to the crossing point, that place of merging between fluttering gas lamps and garish neon signs, where the irregular roadway surrendered to ordered tarmac in demarking the border between realms.

Without pause, the phantom horseman lashed his mount and drove through.

Shrieks of merciless fury pierced the division and the horseman looked back to see his pursuers bursting through. Cast up from dragging shadow, the twin witch riders hurtled on. They were hellish silhouettes, black veiled and flowing. The diaphanous material of their masks pulled taut in the wind against skeletal features and hissing lips. Cadaverous hands curled from ragged lace to haul the reins of frothing horses, steering them in reply to their quarry's every racing move. One pale hand extended, jagged nails deftly flicking to send a sharpened missile the way of the horseman. His cloak was cut but the target was missed. The sleek arrowhead passed on to burst a shop window, and its display of television screens erupted into a million speckles of falling starlight to shower hunters and hunted alike.

The horseman reacted to the attack, swapping the reins to one hand while twisting to extend the other and the flintlock pistol it held. A crash of light and smoke hurled his brutal answer at the witches and the flying ball struck the lead figure dead centre. The rider was blasted from the saddle with a black-lipped screech. The demonic form tumbled to the roadway as nothing more than a pile of smouldering rags.

The horseman turned away just in time to catch the full flare of headlights ahead. A taxi flickered through the curtain between worlds and turned unknowingly into the horseman's path. The rider acted instantly and spurred hard. With a snort the mount responded, rearing to clear the vehicle in a bound and leaving a howling witch and her panicking steed behind.

The river!

Ahead the waters coursed, timelessly rolling beneath a bridge leading north. Flaming torches danced along the balustrades, ancient lamps to mark the shimmering way, but only to the mid-point where the sodium lights of the mortal sprouted. They cast a soft glow against the windows of a tram snaking through the spectral divide. The phantom's horse shied in fear from the intrusion of mortal engines but was soothed by its master and cantered on.

Mounted witches sat waiting on the road ahead.

Black veiled like their partners, the dread assembly of three clopped into view at the northern end of the bridge, and hooves striking behind announced the arrival of the surviving witch. The demon sisters offered a chorus of poisoned hisses for the horseman trapped between them and began to close on him, drawing forth together blades of keenest cruelty.

A sound reached the watching phantom and carried hope with it. From deep within the spirit realm and tumbling to the borders of existence, a church bell sounded the quarter hour to midnight. The distant ghostly chimes remained inaudible to the hustle-bustle of the mortal world but came clear and rousing to the horseman. Inspired by the promise of time yet in hand, he reached to draw a glittering sabre and sent his horse into a renewed charge.

Horse and rider swept among the harridans. The opposing beasts reeled in panic from the violence of the advance. The sabre struck left and right in a desperate song of colliding metal. A break in the ranks was created and the phantom spurred through, galloping past the blockade amid loathsome screeches hurled into the land of the living.

The pursuit weaved on. Riders steered between lumbering buses and cars. Traffic signals turned furious red against the horseman, but he ignored all and charged for the junction, urging more of his mount. The witches raced fatally close, gaining steadily. Whitened hands reached to produce new arrowheads.

The truck came from nowhere, a howling mortal behemoth storming the junction. Its motorised snout roared at the unseen phantom horse and passed within a hair's breadth of the beast's flank. Continuing its manoeuvre, the gigantic vehicle swept into the path of the speeding witches.

The collision was a whinnying blast of vapour and silver light. Hunters and horses smashed unprepared and headlong into the belly of the mechanical beast. Solid forms burst to night mist tripping over the cold frame of the truck's container and for a brief spell all was silent. An instant later the witch riders erupted from the truck's opposing side in a confounded mêlée. Disrupted by their violent passage, the demon hunters railed and hissed, fighting for control of their startled rides. Veiled heads swept angrily in every direction for a glimpse of their prey but found nothing.

The horseman was lost to the bustling streets of the mortal realm.

Midnight came chiming as the horseman at last reached his destination. Beneath the shadow of a towering gateway whose arch offered the promise of '*Requiescat in Pace*' for weary souls, he gently urged his mount to advance on the cemetery gates. Horse and rider slipped as vapour between the bars.

The way forward was an avenue lined with memorial stones and their shadows. Slowly the pair progressed, hemmed in by urgent whisperings from behind the fog-shrouded headstones and every mournful vault.

Sackimum Brody is waiting, the night said.

Preserve us from all harm, the shadows replied.

The spirit world rippled with rumour and fear.

After a short distance, the monuments divided to reveal a car waiting in dark silence among the graves. The automobile's vintage design - round carriage lights and spoke wheels under sweeping arches – set it at odds with the modern world, and yet, old fashioned and funereal as it was, it was real and of the mortal realm.

Similarly, the figure who stood patiently nearby was a tangible presence, a man of living flesh and blood, albeit one who chose to stand in blackness amid the graves of a midnight cemetery. Proof of the shadow-man's mortality came in a soft plume of breath from his unseen lips as he leaned casually on his walking-stick and closely considered the headstone that had been set as the meeting place.

'Professor Brody,' the horseman's greeting came grimly from under his concealing hat.

Polished shoes crunched on gravel as Professor Sackimum Brody turned his angular features to the pale light of the moon. He steadied his slender form on the stick and faced the horseman with grey and thoughtful eyes.

'Tell me,' he said, and his tone was soft but insistent.

'The rumours are true,' the spectral informant confirmed.

'The old enemy?'

'Yes,' the spirit agreed, and his horse shied from the truth of it. 'The ancient realm is stirring. There is fire and conjuring under the mountains. The Pooka has been seen, near and far.'

'They are still searching,' the Professor said hopefully.

'No. The search is complete. The grave of the lost King is found, by a mortal man, and the Pooka makes preparations.'

A mortal man. Brody was aghast.

'But the spear,' he reminded his ghostly companion, 'the spear is *not* found, and their King is nothing without it.'

'What you say is also true for the girl who is our hope and the sword she requires,' the horseman warned.

'That hunt continues.'

'Too slowly.' The phantom extended a finger towards the headstone. 'It is time to set promises aside. Send for the girl.'

The Professor caught a breath and closed his eyes firmly against the suggestion. 'Not yet. What if I am wrong about her?'

Orbs twinkled with fearful vision.

'If she is not who you say she must be, the lost King will come unchallenged, and his army behind. He will destroy all for his sport and none will be spared, not mortal, not spirit. You *must* send for the girl.'

'I might be wrong about her,' the Professor said weakly. 'I am not certain yet.'

'Belief in her is all we have left,' the spirit declared as he began to withdraw to the night. 'Only one thing is certain, Brody. If you do not seek her out, the ancient enemy surely will.'

Left alone and cold at the graveside, the Professor turned again to the stone. He allowed himself the briefest of smiles and a flowering of memory as he read the inscription once more.

Barry McCabe,
Father & Scholar, 1978 – 2012

'My friend,' he said sadly to the memorial. 'I'm sorry, it's getting harder to protect your daughter from what's coming.'

Weighed upon by doubt and guilt, the Professor turned for the car, its engine growling to life at his approach, its lamps flinging smoky beams against the night and its hidden fears.

TWO

Caitlyn McCabe squeezed her eyes shut against the coming of the ghost.

'I don't see you,' she whispered tightly and with insistence, knowing full well her protest was a futile exercise.

She *could* see, and no recourse to sense or science or the fierce clamping of her eyes could change that inexplicable fact.

As always, her gift manifested as feeling before sight, a chill on her skin as a foreshadowing signal just ahead of a slight shift in her senses, like wind-chimes caught in a spectral draught, and finally the inevitable electric tingle from tips to roots of her long black hair. She blindly set her brush on the dresser and waited.

The spirit drifted into her room and drew near.

The shudder Caitlyn offered in response was due merely to the cold the spirit brought. She was not afraid of ghosts, far from it. Caitlyn had seen enough phantom knights, gliding ladies and shrouded forms in her fifteen years to know how harmless they were.

The simple truth was that while accepting the restless dead as an inconvenient truth in the fabric of her world, Caitlyn's uncanny and unexplained gift of seeing them was apparently shared by no-one else and that was the unsettling element. It made her different and she hated it.

You're such a freak, Caitlyn McCabe.

'I don't see you,' she tried again. The lack of conviction in her voice made her sigh despondently.

She compromised and opened her blue eye.

She was not afraid of ghosts.

Or phantom mice.

The tiny rodent, covered over with the silver hue of the spirit world, peeked nervously back over the memory box on her dresser.

Caitlyn opened her green eye and regarded the mouse with a smile. She tracked where the creature progressed un-reflected along the base of the dresser's mirror, from box to bottle to bracelet to bauble, and she was amused at the feverish investigation offered to each by its twitching nose.

'You found Gran's trap, didn't you?' she asked the mouse, currently distracted by a thorough, snuffling examination of a framed photograph. The mouse saw a landscape of summer green where Caitlyn's Dad smiled and posed between two happy companions, one with muddied knees and the other with a vivid yellow flower in his lapel. Caitlyn reached her hand slowly for the ghost's consideration and the mouse deserted the picture-men to approach her. Its tiny nose tickled at her fingertips and she giggled.

'Caitlyn!'

Gran's voice, shrill with excitement, broke the moment and drove the mouse to cover behind the photograph in a skittish flash. Slippered feet on the stairs announced her eager approach.

'It's okay,' Caitlyn assured her frightened guest. 'She can't see you.'

Gran appeared in the doorway, her face a mix of agitation at the news she carried and weariness from the climb. 'Them flippin' stairs,' she said breathlessly and fumbled for the handkerchief she always carried in her housecoat pocket. She dabbed at her brow as she recovered her breath. 'Guess what.'

'The trap in the kitchen worked,' Caitlyn said idly. 'You caught the mouse.'

'I did,' Gran replied happily. She leaned wearily against the doorframe.

'Gran, you know you shouldn't be straining yourself,' Caitlyn cautioned.

'I know, love, I know,' Gran said, waving her handkerchief like a flag of surrender to her granddaughter's good sense. In the act, however, connections were made in the old woman's head and she fixed Caitlyn with a narrow stare. 'How did you know I was coming to tell you about the mouse?' Her eyes darted about the small bedroom, filled with urgent knowledge. 'He's in here, isn't he?'

'Yes,' Caitlyn said and smiled at her Gran's agitation. She stretched her hand to the old woman. 'Do you want to see him?'

Gran shook her head at the offer. 'No thanks, love. I'd only get annoyed. I'm two weeks trying to catch the little...,' she considered the most acceptable insult..., 'the little *fizzer*, and he's gone and turned into one of your ghosts. Now we'll never get rid of him. We're haunted by a ghost mouse, oh my.'

'They're not *my* ghosts,' Caitlyn protested sullenly, and she pulled back her hand.

Regretting her words in an instant, Gran moved to Caitlyn's side. She reached for the girl but caught herself in the motion, hesitating awkwardly. 'I'm sorry, love,' she said, 'that's not what I meant...Anyway, I suppose there's no harm in having a ghost mouse, is there? He won't raid the biscuit press, will he?'

'No,' Caitlyn said and smiled behind her hair despite her annoyance.

'Grand, so,' the old woman said. Relieved, she picked up her granddaughter's brush and began to tend Caitlyn's long black tresses. 'For a second I thought I might have to kill a cat.'

'Gran,' Caitlyn protested, laughing, and the moment of tension faded away.

'Where is the little pest anyway?' Gran asked.

'Behind Dad's picture,' Caitlyn replied, and she sensed at once the slowing of the brush strokes. In the dresser's mirror, Caitlyn spied the momentary sadness in her grandmother's eyes as they fell on the face of her son.

Gran caught her granddaughter's gaze and collected herself, returning hastily to brushing. 'I've said it before, and I'll say it again,' she declared busily, 'but you have the greatest head of hair in creation. Your mother's gift, I imagine. You certainly didn't get it from our side.' She gestured to the photo. 'Your Dad was on the way to being a baldy-locks just like your grandfather, Mr Lollipop-head himself.' Laughing to herself, she laid the brush on the dresser, wary of invisible mice.

'I haven't ever seen Dad,' Caitlyn offered. 'Not once.'

Gran smiled. 'And that means he's in a better place, right?'

'Right.'

'You're a good girl, Caitlyn,' Gran said. She bent to offer her granddaughter a gentle kiss. 'School night, missy,' she said. 'It's bed for you and a plate of chips in cranberry sauce for me.'

' 'night, Gran.' Caitlyn watched her pull the door

behind and she turned her attention once again to the mouse where it re-emerged from hiding and crept close to the dresser's edge. 'Well, 'Mr Fizzer',' she addressed the phantom, 'you have a choice to make, and I can't help. Do you stay, or do you go?'

In apparent response to Caitlyn's words, the mouse shifted itself to sit on its hind quarters and regarded her. In this position it sniffed the air it no longer breathed and looked into the giant face above as though contemplating deeply the question posed. At last, and all at once, the choice was announced in a brief flaring of the ghost's silver light which obscured all vision for a moment before dwindling to leave no trace of the tiny spectre.

Alone again, Caitlyn smiled behind her mane of hair and looked through the light fading on the image of her father's forever smile.

'Why did you not stay?' she asked quietly.

THREE

Some stay, some go. That's the way of it with spirits and that's all Caitlyn knew.

One clear example was Mr Patrick Byrne, 1929-1994. Resting in peace according to his headstone at Glasnevin cemetery, Mr Byrne had been in life a postman, and after forty years ferrying letters to doors in Dublin city, Caitlyn reckoned he must surely have earned his eternal rest. And yet, by error or design, here he was again this morning, passing her as she stepped out for school, having reappeared promptly a day after his funeral to resume postal duties in the hereafter. Precisely who was writing and why were enduring mysteries Caitlyn did not need to add to her own unanswered questions.

Another case in point was Poppy the cat. The feline lay in its usual spot on a gatepost near the McCabe house. Late and lamented by the O'Hare children at Number 15, Poppy had been claimed by a speeding van six months ago. She now tended her silvery fur in the bright October sunshine and stretched lazily and just long enough to track Caitlyn's passing with a self-satisfied air.

For all her spectral sight, Caitlyn could explain none of it, neither the 'why' nor the 'how'. Weaving her daily path between the solid living and wispy departed, she knew no more than the reality of her gift of 'seeing' while spending the greater part of her days trying to ignore it. And so, while the rest of the daytime world only glimpsed blacksmith Thomas McMurray in historic photographs at the local library, Caitlyn saw him bending eternally to his work over a blazing forge. By a rush-hour street thronged with cars, the glowing spirit continued the hammering of shoes for horses long gone. And while Constable McCarthy stood nearby, crystal clear to her as he busily directed traffic in the centre of the road, the same vehicles drove straight through him in oblivious haste.

Caitlyn was haunted by ghosts and questions in irritating measure.

She had long since given up trying to figure out the peculiarity of her ability. Gran had been unable to offer any clues other than to deny the source lay with her father. 'Nothing like that among the McCabes,' she stated with certainty.

That suggested the ability came perhaps from Caitlyn's mother. But she being a mystery as deep and dark as Caitlyn's hair, the question joined those others she wilfully pushed to a corner of her mind every day: Why do spirits walk the mortal world? How was it she and no-one else saw them? What did it mean that she *could* see? Who was responsible? Why was that man driving the old-fashioned car only wearing one glove?

Caitlyn's head snapped towards the fresh puzzle, that and the car's distinctly old-world aspect drowning out the day's other questions. The vehicle swept by in a vision of rounded headlights atop flowing arches, the engine-hum a refined purr beneath a long and polished bonnet. The gleaming distraction allowed her no more than a momentary glimpse of the gloved oddity at the wheel. That and confirmation the driver was a man of the mortal world. Any passenger he might be conveying in the car's sleek interior remained obscured behind, of all things, drawn curtains in the rear compartment, a feature that rendered the car altogether hearse-like.

The car passed with a whispered fading of its motor and Caitlyn dismissed it. She crossed the road, pausing just long enough to allow a phantom coach and horses to pass in the opposite direction. More a regular part of her morning, she followed the shimmering vehicle's progress, anticipating its turn to an overgrown path where it led the way to the gates Rosehill House. Without slowing, the carriage passed smoothly and with a puff of silver essence through the decaying, padlocked barriers.

Caitlyn stopped to peer between rusting bars, tracking the coach's slow climb to the tumbling ruin that was Rosehill. Still imposing, the once grand residence never failed to impress her. Shattered windows sagged beneath a caved-in roof to offer grim welcome to callers at its bricked-up door. Creeping ivy that spilled heavily over the structure threatened to ensnare and hold them there forever. Visits by local children to Rosehill were strictly by double dare only, and never, ever, on the full moon. Ironically, Caitlyn knew that was the best time to visit.

Sniggers, mocking and harsh, drew her abruptly about. Caitlyn stiffened as she faced a more troubling figure than anything in the spirit world. The mortal form of Debbie Walsh glared maliciously back.

With perfect hair and skin tanned from another sun holiday, Debbie Walsh regarded Caitlyn with a twisting sneer of glossed lip. This was the look she reserved for everyone at school whose daddy did not own two cars and a holiday home. Except, that is, for the Kelly twins who flanked her now, tittering like evil but useful minions. 'Well, if it isn't creepy Caitlyn McCabe,' she said, drawing closer. 'Did you miss me?'

Caitlyn knew better than to answer the girl's leering tone. Any response to Debbie Walsh was to invite further derision at the very least, and more than a risk of physical reaction. She watched the girl slink dangerously close and braced as Debbie examined her with keen and cruel regard.

'Do you actually like having witch's hair?' Debbie asked at last and with a measure of distaste, all to the squealing joy of the Kellys.

'Witch's hair,' one of them repeated, dutiful and delighted.

Caitlyn felt blood rush hotly to her cheeks, but she held her tongue and Debbie Walsh's gaze.

'Which eye are you hiding today?' Debbie asked. Her head bobbed sharply for a better view past Caitlyn's fringe. She thrilled as Caitlyn angled her head away. 'The blue one,' the bully announced with mock disgust. 'Different coloured eyes. You're such a freak, Caitlyn McCabe.'

'It's called heterochromia,' Caitlyn informed her defiantly. 'Can you say that?'

Debbie Walsh bristled at the challenge and her mind searched behind flaring eyes for a punishing response. 'You should go live in Rose Hell,' she declared to eager nods from her supporters. 'You'd fit right in with the other witches. Here, I'll help you move in.' Her hand lashed forward like a striking snake and gripped Caitlyn's satchel. Tearing it from her, Debbie tossed it high and over the gates. The bag thumped on the muddy path beyond the bars, spilling pens and notebooks out of reach.

Amid ecstatic cackles from the Kelly twins, Debbie Walsh cast a final hateful look to her. 'Freak,' she said and swept away.

Left alone on the path, Caitlyn struggled with simmering rage and bunched her fists against it and the violent thoughts she entertained for Debbie Walsh. A phantom gentleman on his morning walk, dismayed by the rage in her face, stepped cautiously past, tipping his hat politely before hastening away. She blinked against anger and switched her attention to the fallen satchel, mentally tracing the long path she would need to follow to reach it from the broken fence at the rear of Rosehill.

Caitlyn sighed at the realisation she was going to be late for school.

Fifteen minutes and one long walk later, Caitlyn stooped to recover her soiled bag and turned to make her way carefully back through wild undergrowth. She cursed under her breath as brambles and branches reached to toy with her, slowing her progress even more. There was no way she could make first period maths at this rate.

'Maths,' she grumbled. She abruptly halted as the word brought her up from the gloom Debbie Walsh had imposed on her. 'Who wants to do maths anyway?' With a bold 'the hell with that' she changed course and pushed through the vegetation.

Rosehill sagged on the rise, lifeless but for a cloud of ravens above its crumbling façade. Gliding back on the air from their nests in the ruined upper reaches, the birds' caws were a harsh protest at Caitlyn's approach.

She entered by the usual route, crossing the buckled terrace before reaching a jagged hole in the decaying brickwork. The frames of the French windows that had once stood here were now just a pile of rotted wood by the hole. Caitlyn ducked cautiously through and stood to survey the decrepit remains of the grand ballroom.

Lost to a chaos of vegetation and collapsed plaster, the ballroom stretched away from her, its scale a testament to great and colourful celebrations that once played out between now splintering walls. Cracked remnants of an ornate dance floor lay amid groping roots under the gaze of frameless windows. On high in one far corner, a last surviving section of the viewing gallery that once hugged the circumference of the room fought a losing battle with dragging ivy. Tendrils of the clawing vine stretched over walls, the fallen balcony and hanging doors to attack the wide staircase, adding to time's decay in pulling its structure to a buckling ruin of its former self.

Caitlyn made her way between tall ferns and flourishing weeds to the space she called her own. At the centre of the ballroom where a small oasis of discoloured floor remained untouched by all but sunlight from the punctured roof, her seat of fallen stone waited. She would sit, she decided, and just long enough to forget boring maths and bullies. School could wait. She eased onto her rough seat and, after a moment's pause to prepare, laid a hand to the stone. Her skin prickled and senses shifted to the familiar electric tingle in her hair. With eyes wide, blue and green, Caitlyn smiled.

Sometimes seeing ghosts was good.

FOUR

On any other day, Caitlyn's late arrival in class would have drawn a tardy slip and the prospect of detention. As she slipped sheepishly through the door, ten minutes into Higher History, Sister Mary Immaculata offered a disapproving glare from her seat at the head of the room. Thankfully, the old nun had not been in a position to punish a student since 1892, while Miss Farrell – 'Biscuit Barrel Farrell' to the pupils seated before her - was far too excited with news to deal with timekeeping today. In mid flow, she absently waved Caitlyn to her desk and raised aloft a newsletter without interrupting her address to the others.

'The flyer for the Halloween dance will be on the notice board later today,' she announced and moved hurriedly to her next, and preferred, item. 'Now, remember, everyone,' she said through an excited smile, 'it's nearly time for the trip to Newgrange.' She drew a breath for added dramatic effect. 'Tomorrow, thanks to sponsorship from the faculty of archaeology at Trinity College no less, we step back in time, five thousand years into Ireland's Neolithic past.' Smiling more broadly, and clearly undaunted by the flurry of groans and a whispered *'boooooring'* from Debbie Walsh, Miss Farrell swept to the whiteboard where she had already sketched out the important details for the excursion. With arms whirling in demonstrative fashion, she continued. 'The key when we arrive is not to be overcome by the wonderful exterior of the burial mound,' she said, and traced a hand rapidly about her circular diagram, complete with arrows to indicate the standing stones and entranceway. 'Don't worry, we will of course spend time examining the area immediately to the front of the structure and the mysterious carvings to be found there.' More groans sounded, accompanied by a quietly despairing *'noooooo'*. Sister Mary Immaculata tried in vain to silence the class with her deathly stare. 'However,' the oblivious Biscuit Barrel continued, 'you will recall from our earlier classes the real magic begins once we proceed *inside* Newgrange itself.'

With a breathless flourish, the teacher drew attention to another diagram. This showed, in jagged outline, a roughly cross-shaped area, pierced on all sides by the teacher's explanatory arrows. 'The passage tomb,' she said, her voice quavering with reverence, 'with its three burial areas.' She pointed to each of the cross's tips unnecessarily. 'Here, in small groups, we will follow the narrow corridor taken by our ancestors as they brought their dead for burial. We will see the great stone bowls known as....anyone, anyone...?'

No-one.

'...ossuaries, which received the bones, and...,' here it seemed Miss Farrell might actually faint with excitement, '...we will see the path illuminated just once a year by the rising winter sun and which ancient peoples believed lit the way in guiding spirits back to the land of the living.'

Sr Mary Immaculata shook her head in disapproval and crossed herself protectively against talk of pagan spirits.

Miss Farrell whipped delightedly from the whiteboard to face the class, offering hope to the students that she was done with the subject of Newgrange. But the teacher was clearly intent on sharing one final detail with them. Her gaze fixed Caitlyn and she smiled proudly as she made to speak.

Oh, no, no no, Caitlyn silently pleaded, *please don't*.

'I am sure the class might be interested to know that we have our own local link to Newgrange here today,' Biscuit Barrel said. 'It took an army of archaeologists working over many years to uncover the history of Newgrange and restore the site to glory. One of them happened to be Dr Barry McCabe. He was your father, isn't that right, Caitlyn?'

Caitlyn flushed and felt the eyes of her classmates on her. 'Yes, Miss.'

'Yes, Miss,' Debbie Walsh scoffed under her breath, and her eyes promised vengeance.

'Without researchers like Dr McCabe, the secrets of Newgrange might have remained buried forever. I know that I for one am grateful for his work and the work of his colleagues. You should be very proud, Caitlyn.'

'Yes, Miss,' Caitlyn said, and buried her head in the history book on the desk.

FIVE

'Roll up, roll up. Ladies and gentlemen, Magic Man's gonna do his thing!'

Luke Goslin's announcement rose above the din of the cafeteria, demanding immediate silence. Arms held wide for attention, the sixth-year class captain - and all-star footballer - turned about to draw curious faces up from lunchtime meals to him.

'That's right,' Luke proclaimed loudly, 'it's time for another Magic Man challenge.'

Pupils raised a cheer and streamed riotously to the call. Abandoning pasta and half-eaten sandwiches they closed around Luke Goslin's table in a mass of jostling for an event that never failed to entertain.

Caitlyn drifted along the fringes of the throng, peering over shoulders in search of the figure at the centre of attention. Magic Man Danny Joyce, a third-year like her but a relatively new arrival in the school, was revealed by a parting of bodies, seated quietly amid the crush. Caught like a prisoner among Luke Goslin's crew of sixth-years, he sat in quiet resignation, his new challenge lying before him on the table, tantalisingly covered by a stained football jersey.

'What's the *brainiac* going to do today?' someone taunted, prompting a chorus of mocking laughter.

'Make himself disappear,' another chimed in, increasing the volume of hilarity.

Danny sat, not laughing. Seemingly oblivious to the taunts – though Caitlyn wondered how - his face had become an emotionless space of quiet contemplation for the mystery beneath the jersey.

'Please, *please*,' Luke Goslin called with feigned impatience, recapturing the crowd's attention. 'If you'll all be quiet, I'll explain today's epic challenge.' He waited for his audience to fall dutifully silent, and when the room was hushed, he reached forward to snatch the jersey aside. Exposed by the action were three Rubik's Cubes, set in an orderly line with their individual squares twisted to a disarray of colours. Whispers of anticipation rippled among the gathering. 'Today,' Luke Goslin declared, 'Magic Man will break the record for the Rubik's Cube, three times over in a single sitting.'

'Can't be done,' a Goslin stooge protested on cue.

'It can,' Luke Goslin shot back, 'and it will.'

Caitlyn eyed Danny, watching how the boy screened out the theatrics around him for an intense focus on the cubes. Quickly but precisely, he examined the visible sides one after another in the time afforded by Luke Goslin's showmanship.

'What's the record?' a spectator chimed in. 'Someone check it.'

'Four-point-five seconds per cube,' Luke Goslin replied to doubtful hisses, 'but look it up, please do.' He paused momentarily, preparing the final phase of his scheme. 'And if you still don't believe it can be beaten, I'll bet ten to each one placed against Magic Man.' Here he produced a note and snapped the money crisply between his fingers.

'It can't be done,' the stooge cried again for effect, but the cry was lost against howls of acceptance for the bet and the metallic rain of coins onto the table.

'We need an official timer,' Luke Goslin said.

'Oh, me, me,' Debbie Walsh squealed, elbowing through the crowd to offer her phone and a winning smile to Luke Goslin. 'It's top of the range, brand new,' she cooed.

'Thirteen-point-five seconds is the time to beat. Let's get started.' The crowd erupted with cheers of encouragement and shouted insults as Luke Goslin leaned close to Magic Man's ear. His jocular tone dropped to a harsh whisper. 'Don't mess this up, weirdo,' he said.

If Danny heard, he did not show it from the depths of his consuming focus.

From Caitlyn's position to the rear of the mêlée, Danny the Magic Man became a form barely glimpsed over butting shoulders and bobbing heads. She caught a last sight of the boy, rolling up his sleeves as he maintained his concentration and, as a hush of anticipation descended, the crowd became a solid barrier, and he was lost to her.

Debbie Walsh keyed the timer. 'Go.'

Danny's hands whipped forward to capture the first cube, fingers pulling and flicking even at the first touch of the moveable surfaces. Clicks from the plastic mechanism sounded with furious rapidity as colours aligned in rows, columns and blocks, dizzyingly faster than the capacity of the assembled spectators to follow.

Smack! The first re-ordered cube touched down. Magic Man grabbed for the second, his hands a blur of activity beneath his steady, unwavering stare. Green side, red side, white side, blue, and *smack!* went the cube.

Debbie Walsh turned the timer to Luke Goslin where he stood, chewing a thumbnail and scowling. It was impossible to tell which was quicker, Danny's hands or those digital numbers.

Magic Man whirled on, accelerating through the final challenge, fingers and cube as one, chasing time and colours.

Smack!

Three cubes in a row, the multi-coloured squares on all sides uniformly arranged. Silence reigned as faces agog swivelled from cubes to Debbie Walsh to find her features no less astonished.

'Oh, wow,' she breathed, 'oh....wow.' She turned the phone timer for all to see.

Thirteen seconds.

The student body exploded to a wall of sound, cheering, wailing, and howling at the result. Scarves and hats, and a bowl of pasta, were sent flying by jubilant pupils. Luke Goslin breathed again and flung his arms around Debbie Walsh, who beamed delightedly in return. The sixth-years high-fived and raked in the coins from the table while dreams of riches melted from the faces of those who had doubted.

Becoming visible to Caitlyn once again as the crowd dispersed, Danny remained unmoved, his face holding the same flat, indifferent expression. Oblivious to her gaze, he reached out once more, this time to bring further order to the cubes, their straight arrangement seemingly more important than the celebrations for his talent. She watched the action and how afterwards he calmly massaged tired fingers and rolled his sleeves back into place. And as he did, she saw the fresh bruises on his forearms, a circle of blots discolouring his pale skin.

Caitlyn recognised the signs and knew in an instant what they meant. The bruises signalled with dark certainty that Danny Joyce would not turn for home after classes today. Instead, at the school gates, as before, he would turn left. From there, she knew, he would take the path he walked whenever the bruises showed, the way that led into the arms of the ghost.

She would need to be ready.

She would be, she vowed to herself. She would be waiting to watch the boy who haunted himself.

SIX

With the end-of-school bell clamouring in her ears, Caitlyn hastened across the yard. Weaving impatiently through the growing tide of students, she pursued her theory. She reached the gates, exited and side-stepped quickly to a spot a short distance along the fence from where she could begin her discreet vigil.

From this vantage point Caitlyn was afforded a clear view through the bars towards the science block. It was Wednesday, so it was from there Danny's class would eventually emerge at the end of 'double bubble', Mr Dee's two-period chemistry class. On any ordinary day, Danny would progress alone through the gates to cross the road and turn right for his route home. But Caitlyn was willing to bet this was no ordinary day. She had seen the bruises so clear and angry on his arm.

They seemed to be the signal, though it had taken her some time to see a link. Twice previously and by chance she had witnessed Danny's strange route and his phantom encounter, only later realising they occurred when Danny appeared in class bearing new marks. The first time he had carried them on his neck, a small cluster of dark patches he couldn't quite hide with his shirt, the second time as a single discoloration on swollen cheekbone. Luke Goslin had joked loudly at break that the bruise looked like a map of France and everyone laughed. Caitlyn did not join in. Her mind had already begun to make connections.

Her attention was drawn abruptly to the science block where doors burst open to release the first of those escaping Mr Dee. A mass of delighted students emerged to join the homeward rush and for an instant Caitlyn feared she would miss Danny among the hundred bustling heads. She caught him at last, partially hidden behind a group of chattering teenagers. Craning her neck, she tracked his path through the gates and watched his progress towards the kerb.

A squeal of laughter pierced the air behind Caitlyn and she froze, recognising at once the shrill tones of Debbie Walsh. Her mind raced in panic and she was certain she was caught in the act of watching Danny. She braced for a sneering humiliation just a moment away. With flushing cheeks, she glanced sharply back, only to find Debbie caught delightedly by the attention offered to her by Luke Goslin. The sixth-year's clear interest in her sculpted hair was apparently the cause of the girl's hysterical laughter and she patted the waving curls as the pair walked close together, trailed by the Kelly twins who glared jealously at them. All remained unaware of Caitlyn in her place by the fence.

Releasing the breath she had held unconsciously, Caitlyn turned in search of Danny. At the kerb, the boy's place had been taken by a girl from the second year and he was nowhere to be found. Caitlyn cast her gaze about, dismissing clusters of pupils who jostled along the pavements until she spotted him again, moving among the throng and conspicuous in his solitude. Caitlyn's heart skipped. Danny had turned left and was walking steadily away from home.

She was right. Danny Joyce was on his way to the spot where the ghost surely waited. She set off to follow.

Why are you so interested in Danny Joyce, anyhow, Caitlyn McCabe? The question in her head mimicked the sneering tone of Debbie Walsh and she grew angry at it for that. *Is it because of how he reacts when the ghost comes? Do you hope you're not the only one?*

Shut up, Caitlyn hurled back, instantly unsettled by the flowering rage she felt. It had surfaced so raw and swift she feared the words had been forced past her lips by it. But when she looked at those nearest her, expecting to be met with disturbed glances, she saw indifferent faces passing by.

He's weird like you.

'Shut up,' Caitlyn ordered, and this time she did catch the darkly confused glances aimed her way. She quickened her pace, blushing.

Metres ahead, Danny had reached the turn he must take for events to play out as she anticipated. Sure enough, and even as she willed it, the boy slipped around the corner and continued along his way, drawing her quickly on. She halted at the corner and peeked to find him still moving along. In the next few seconds, she knew, he would cross the road, carefully looking both ways. She would follow, but not until he had ceased looking back and was safely on the opposite footway. Precisely as expected, the boy angled to the kerb, checked both ways and proceeded to cross.

Caitlyn broke cover, working hard to appear causal, strolling lightly as she followed to the same footway as Danny and fell into step behind. The street continued straight and long, flanked to the right by the open expanse of football fields while immediately to Caitlyn's left the rusting fence which contained the overgrown boundary of Rosehill traced the footway. Were she to look up and between the trees she would catch sight of the crumbling ruin brooding on the low rise. But this was not the time to take her eyes off Danny. And as she watched, it happened.

The spirit came. From nowhere, and in a shimmering of light directly ahead of Danny, the ghost emerged as through a curtain shifting on the surface of daylight. Caitlyn faltered and watched breathlessly as the spirit's face emerged from the light, its shape and features an *exact* mirror image of Danny's. Ghost Danny stood in Danny's way where he continued to walk, unperturbed, unseeing. It was the face of the phantom which altered at the encounter, shifting to become one of recognition and of joy on seeing the boy, and, as ever before when Caitlyn watched, the spectre's arms became outstretched for him, circling to embrace as their forms met only to fail and pass through like smoke. Joy became anguish and ghost Danny looked to his empty hands.

Caitlyn kept watching, seeking anything new in the incident. The ghost's part was played. The next move was Danny's.

Unaware of the spirit form and its actions, the boy strode on, lost in his own daydreams. But after a few steps he slowed visibly, and after a few more he came to a stop. Like someone stalled by the resurfacing of a faint memory, Danny paused and became quite still but for a slight tilt of his head as though listening to some internal voice. A phantom whisper.

He feels it, Caitlyn knew for certain and with a thrill, he senses the spirit. She gazed on with clenched fists, waiting for more than there had been before, some sign of increased knowledge, anything, willing it just like the spirit willed it with imploring and out-stretched fingers. At the edge of his own phantom's touch, Danny half turned, drawn towards knowing. But then, just as on previous occasions, he shrugged off the vague feeling and walked on. Empty hands fell away and the spirit drifted alone and downcast.

Caitlyn stared after Danny, sharing the phantom's disappointment as she fought a desire to immediately pursue the boy, to walk right up to him and make him see. A single touch is all it would take, a grasp of his hand for just a second and he would...what, understand? He would see the array of spirits moving through the mortal world and he would understand and happily accept her and what she revealed to him?

Caitlyn gave up the idea with a sigh. No, he wouldn't understand, and it was foolish to think so. Danny would flip out and recoil from such a vision, and from her, just like anyone would.

But he wasn't just anyone. He was the boy who haunted himself and that had to mean something. But what? Caitlyn sighed wearily for another question to add to her list.

With nothing more to learn and nothing new to teach, Caitlyn shifted on her heels to turn for home. Taking her focus from Danny's receding form, her attention was drawn to the far end of the street and her eyes narrowed in suspicion at what she saw there.

The hearse-car sat by the kerb. Its engine idled as sunlight flared on the polished bonnet. Caitlyn slowed to take in the sight. Squinting, she looked past the vehicle's ornate grille and sweeping arches in search of the driver's face. The low afternoon sun played against the windscreen, obscuring whoever sat behind, but did nothing to blot out the keen sensation Caitlyn felt that the driver's eyes were firmly locked on her.

The car roared forward as though spurred by her attention and Caitlyn caught the same sidelong view as before of the man at the wheel, that one-gloved figure accelerating away.

She swung to track the vehicle's hasty escape and gasped when she saw in that moment the ghost Danny crossing into the roadway. The shimmering form was too lost in grief to notice the car bearing down. Despite her knowledge, she steeled for a collision that would hurt neither the living nor the dead.

The car swerved. A second before it must surely plough through the spirit, the brakes of the vehicle squealed, and the vehicle slid precariously around the drifting boy to come to a shuddering stop. Caitlyn looked in wonder as a slender hand pulled at the curtain in the rear compartment and revealed a pair of startled eyes. A second later, the car sped on, driving hard to the end of the street where it turned quickly into the passing traffic and sped away from Caitlyn's astonished gaze.

'He *saw*,' she said, her voice a bare, stunned whisper. 'He saw.'

She staggered back from the realisation, her head spinning. She looked for ghost Danny towards gaining some explanation, but he had already faded away. She spun next towards Danny, but he too had vanished.

Caitlyn stood alone in the street, beset by new and dizzying questions.

ॐ ॐ ॐ

'She saw,' the driver gasped as he steered the car on. He scanned the rear-view mirror and sought a response. 'Professor?'

'She saw *us*,' Sackimum Brody said. 'That was clumsy, Marcus.'

'I'm sorry, Professor,' Marcus replied sheepishly. He pulled the glove free and found his hand shaking through a mixture of fright and excitement. 'But I really do think she saw the ghost.'

Within the curtained confines the Professor offered a long sigh for his young assistant's theorising. 'You *think*. That means you do not *know*. How often have I schooled you against guesswork?' He shook his head. 'I remain unconvinced.'

'There was no way of knowing for sure on the way to school,' Marcus admitted. 'Caitlyn seems to be well

48

practised in not reacting to the ghosts around her, although there were clues. Take the old house, for example. But I was sure when she followed the boy. She saw what we saw.'

'Haunted houses fascinate children,' Brody retorted, 'and the boy, well, perhaps she finds him attractive. Would you call it all definitive?' He watched Marcus shake his head in the mirror. 'No, it is not enough. We need more than conviction, Doctor.' After a moment's reflection, his tone softened. 'We are dealing with a situation of such unusual provenance. I do not doubt your observations, Marcus, but we must have *proof.*'

'That's why you organised the class trip,' Marcus deduced.

'Precisely,' Brody said. 'It will be a controlled experiment for us to observe. If there is anything to learn, we will know it tomorrow. I am sure of it.'

'At Newgrange,' Marcus intoned, almost reverently.

The Professor nodded darkly. 'Newgrange will tell us what Caitlyn McCabe holds to herself.'

SEVEN

'Caitlyn! Caitlyn, you'll be late!'

Gran's urgent voice from the bottom of the stairs dragged her from dreams of ghosts in old cars. With a groan against the morning, Caitlyn struggled up to sit at the edge of the bed, the motion one of dizzying effort. Through a mass of hair cob-webbing her face she croaked, 'I'm up.'

Sleep had come, but only after hours of tossing and turning, and then in form so disjointed as to offer no meaningful rest from the events of the day. The watching eyes in the curtained window came again, and again, and again, through fitful sleep and wakeful memory, the gaze turning her way repeatedly an instant before the engine's roar.

'You're going to be late for the trip,' Gran chirped.

Newgrange. Caitlyn came fully awake with a start and leapt from the bed, the combination of speed and alarm making her head swim dangerously once more. Her clothes, neatly folded on a chair, were retrieved in a flash. Together with the gymnastic challenge of dressing at high speed she hunted for a wayward shoe which had seemingly wandered under the bed in the night.

Gran waited with tea, toast and a reproachful look.

'Thanks, Gran,' Caitlyn offered as she wolfed her breakfast down and aimed for the door.

'Packed lunch in your bag,' Gran instructed hurriedly, 'fruit, too. Make sure you eat that, no swapping it for junk. I'll be making stewed apples and cabbage if you want some later.'

'Yes, Gran, no thanks, Gran' Caitlyn said dutifully, gaining the driveway, 'I'll see you later.'

'Enjoy yourself, love, and...,' Gran faltered, swallowing the words.

Caitlyn paused, understanding. 'If I see Dad, I'll tell you,' she promised.

'Thanks, love,' Gran said, and quickly got back to shooing the girl on. 'The bus, you'll miss your bus.'

She made it, just. The bus was already loading as she arrived at a jog, and she fell into step behind the remaining students as they were ushered forward by the ever-enthusiastic Miss Barrel. 'No pushing,' the teacher ordered with good nature, 'I'm sure you are all as eager to get there as I am.' She caught Caitlyn's eye over the jostling throng. 'High spirits,' she said with a wink.

Caitlyn ascended the steps and moved through the aisle between occupied seats. With eyes fixed on a cluster of vacant spaces towards the back, she studiously avoided Debbie Walsh's daggered gaze and made her way there through the student clamour, dodging an impromptu game of catch-ball. She ducked a paper airplane arcing past her face. The projectile distracted her as she sat and came suddenly face to face with Danny Joyce in his window seat.

'Oh, ah,' Caitlyn stammered at him over the book of puzzles he held. 'I'm sorry, I thought...well, I didn't... but you're here, I can...I'll move, I'll move.' She felt her cheeks burning, dangerously hot.

Danny stared calmly back as she jabbered, scrutinising her as though she were a mystery to be fathomed. He said softly, 'It's okay, you can sit here.'

Caitlyn was already retreating, awkwardly escaping. 'No, really,' she blurted, almost falling into the aisle, 'you're busy, reading and all, and I'm...there are so many nice seats.' She bolted, hurling herself towards an unoccupied row on the far side of the vehicle. There, hidden between the high seat backs, she wilted and rolled her eyes.

There are so many nice seats???

Her groan of despair was lost to the vehicle's starting grumble and it pulled into morning traffic to nudge along in a line of slow-moving cars, a line that included a car of vintage, funereal appearance following the bus closely.

EIGHT

M1 North. Next Exit.

The motorway sign promised release at last from the rush-hour trudge and the students raised a cheer for freedom as the bus swept along the on-ramp and accelerated. The stone and glass of Dublin faded quickly to a rolling of green fields hemming both sides of the slender black line on which the bus travelled. The serene expanse coupled with gentle motion served to gradually ease loud voices in favour of a restful journey. Only class-clown Rodney Kavanagh defied the peace, continuing with self-amusing impersonations of animals spotted from his window until one grating 'MOOO!' was cut violently short by an audible punch to the arm, after which he too fell silent. The motorway coursed on, and whispering motion drew on heavy eyelids and tilted lazy heads.

Caitlyn regained some of her own lost sleep, drifting down to engine murmur between trails of her tumbling hair. There were no ghost cars this time. She dreamed of white horses and laughter, and flashing blades and weeping.

She snapped awake in her seat, chased by a sudden vision of cat's eyes leering in darkness. In the jolt of waking, her knees struck the seat in front and she hissed against the pain. She reached to rub the tender areas and, looking outside, saw the bus was passing through a curtain of rain. The cloudburst sent great drops pattering against the window to create a shape-shifting view of the landscape. As she watched, the engine moaned down through the gears, slowing the bus for the off-ramp and the final leg of the trip.

The journey became a swaying passage over country roads winding ever deeper between hedgerows and over-arching trees. Leaves of darkest green thickened on all sides to keep the world at bay, reducing light and sound but for wild branches which slapped the windows as though objecting to the vehicle's smoky growling amidst nature's blissful peace. The noises, sounding harsher in the enclosed cabin, served to rouse the heaviest sleepers and brought attention abruptly to the beauteous change in the world. Concrete and steel on the one side of sleep had yielded to nature's wonders on the other and the students looked on, keeping to the quiet of the place.

Newgrange appeared to them in equal silence.

With the parting of the trees it rose, shining and resplendent on the hillside. A triumphant construct of the ancients, the glittering white mound, a crown of quartz for the head of a giant, blazed against the sky in reply to the worshipping sun. Its encircling wall gathered the rays to surge with visible power, demanding to be seen and its magnificence revered.

Among awed whispers, Caitlyn heard neither the soft gasp of wonder that was her own nor the feeling of cold glass against her hand where she pressed it unconsciously as though seeking to touch Newgrange itself.

'Here we are, children,' Miss Farrell gushed deliriously, 'please be ready to exit the bus in an orderly manner. And for those who have your field notes, don't forget to bring them along.'

With a hiss of brakes, the bus glided to a halt and a less than orderly movement of students began into the rising warmth of the morning. To repeated urgings from Biscuit Barrel to 'mind the road, mind the road', the children milled towards the entrance gate of the Newgrange enclosure in a jabbering mass.

Across the heads swivelling furiously to sights and sounds, Caitlyn looked again towards Newgrange where it stood imperiously above the throng. Her gaze roved over the glittering façade to locate first the hulking marker stone at its front and behind it the shadowed doorway offering passage to a place beyond history, to Ireland's secret past. She was suddenly filled with a clear though inexplicable impression that the entire site was...waiting.

Enveloped by the exuberant tide of students, Caitlyn was carried on.

NINE

Newgrange burned like white fire.

Caught by the fully risen sun, the mound blazed gloriously and cast its gathered rays on the students where they tramped up the hill, forcing one and all to shield eyes against the glare as they advanced, their hands held as though saluting the tomb's glowing magnificence.

'Keep together, everyone,' Miss Farrell instructed, shouting to be heard above her pupils, whose chattering added to another, more distant sound.

Trailing the group, Caitlyn turned her attention in the direction of that sound, coming to her on the air from a site lower down the slope and just outside the Newgrange enclosure. Beyond the hedgerows, amid thin marker poles of red and white and areas bordered by fluttering tape, she saw a team working busily in precise trenches, digging, brushing and heaving buckets of earth away. Caitlyn recognised at once the signs of archaeology and the workers as researchers in pursuit of new discoveries in the ancient landscape.

This must have been how it was when Dad was here, she mused, and she saw clearly in the actions of the researchers his own as he sought the past beneath the cut surface, his eagerness in digging, his precision with the trowel in teasing up artefacts, and, as some lost treasure resurfaced, his broad smile at discovery.

'Exciting, isn't it?' Miss Farrell gushed all at once at Caitlyn's shoulder, jolting her from daydreaming. 'Imagine. How the thrill of the hunt must feel, the anticipation of ancient discoveries at your fingertips. Oh, it's all so exhilarating.'

'Yes, Miss,' Caitlyn said.

'No dawdling now, Caitlyn,' the teacher chastised softly, 'we are so near the best part.' With that, she strode away to break up a wrestling match between two boys that was diverting attention from the tour.

Caitlyn followed, looking once again to Newgrange as the sounds of digging filled her ears. Drawing level with the mound's dark portal, she peered into its inky shadows. The way of the dead. Even from her place in the sunshine, Caitlyn could perceive how cold it was in there. She shivered at the thought and turned her attention up to the area immediately above the door, to the spot that made Newgrange famous. Miss Farrell was already urging the other students to do the same.

'Note,' the teacher said with breathless wonder, 'the rectangular opening that we have seen in photographs.

You are looking at the lightbox where the sun shines only once a year during...anyone, anyone...?'

No response.

'...the winter solstice. As the old year shifted towards the new, our ancestors marked the occasion by sending light from the rising sun into the burial chamber, perhaps to wake the resting spirits.'

Caitlyn heard the words through the digging that was a persistent refrain in her head, and she turned her attention to the mammoth standing stone set at chest height some metres in front of the entrance portal.

'Note the swirling patterns,' Miss Farrell instructed the class, 'three spiralling designs that remain a mystery to us. Why are there three? Were they etched to represent the seasons? Are they an ancient star chart, perhaps? Or, as some have suggested, do they represent hidden paths, routes from the mortal world to those of spirits and gods?'

Drawn in by the circling patterns, hypnotised by them and the increasing rhythm of the digging, Caitlyn felt herself reach out, driven by an overwhelming desire to touch the swirls and trace the paths, to go where they led.

A new sound washed past and caused her to stop, to leave her outstretched hand floating on the air as she looked for the source. Soft yet urgent, the sound came as an expulsion of breath, like a great gasp betraying expectation, and she turned towards it. She found herself looking once again at the dark portal of Newgrange. Unsettled, she withdrew the hand that had grown inexplicably cold. She bunched a fist against the stinging discomfort and glanced down at her fingers, releasing a breath against the harsh chill they felt. And then she was not looking at the flexing fingers at all, but at her stream of breath, smoky on the freezing air that defied the morning sunlight. Confused, she looked through the rolling plume to the grass beneath her feet where frost particles were growing in time to the dying of the light, spreading about her shoes with a crunching and unnatural rapidity to transform green to white even as she watched. The air, suddenly frigid beneath thickening clouds that cast wisps of snow, became icy against her skin and Caitlyn turned urgently to seek an answer among her classmates and Miss Farrell.

They were all gone.

In the piercing winter landscape, Caitlyn was alone in the shadow of Newgrange. Alarmed, she spun this way and that in search of mortal life, finding none, not even at the site of digging. Where there had been diggers and markings, there was now just open countryside. The trenches so distinctly visible just moments ago had been reclaimed by the gentle sweep of snowy landscape. With a rising panic she pivoted away from the biting wind to look down the hill, searching for the path back and her escape.

The funeral procession blocked her way.

It moved in eerie silence up the slope, led by maidens with burning torches whose flames were buffeted unkindly by the wind. The warriors followed, fur cloaks and thick beards providing some comfort, but against the chill alone, not the pain of loss. The grief of all was given voice by the mourners crowding about the bier carried above downcast heads. Soft lamentations rose on the air as blooms were cast up to the lifeless figure being carried to his resting place.

Caitlyn looked on the scene, her eyes wide at the impossibility of it. She watched the maidens pass and saw tears on cheeks and saw too how the warriors leaned on their spears against the weight of grief. She stepped back to make way for the greater part of the funeral, and, as the bier was lowered at the top of the hill, she strained to see the face of the one whose passing was mourned by so many.

The man was an old, old King, the lined features beneath his crown swathed in a thick grey beard and framed by locks of hair grown white as the falling snow. Caitlyn looked on the face in wonder and was stilled by it, and by the certainty that she recognised in the elderly form a much younger man who somehow existed in a deep recess of her memory.

Punished by the wind, Caitlyn watched those in mourning step aside to make way for one who walked solemnly in her crown of bones to reach the head of the procession. The holy one turned and spread her flat palms over the body in a moment of blessing before reaching to the sword clasped in the old man's thin fingers. All who witnessed the separation of sword and King cried out against the pain of it.

The priestess held the sword aloft for all to see and proceeded to the standing stone. Held high, the gently curving blade and gold-touched handle were clearly visible to Caitlyn where she followed events, the cold forgotten in her amazement. She looked on and saw the priestess grip the sword's handle and point the weapon directly at the portal of Newgrange. She saw how the holy one next touched the reflecting blade to the surface of the standing stone at a point to the left and drew the metal with a harsh scraping across its breadth. The blade continued its jarring note in being drawn back to its starting point.

Silence fell on the gathering as the metallic sound was carried away on the moaning wind. Caitlyn examined the assembled faces, all now turned towards the portal of the mound, and she detected in each one a keen watchfulness for something expected and eagerly anticipated through the ceremony just witnessed.

What came was a pitiful weeping, carried by the voice of a solitary mourner whose pain outweighed all others. Her keening despair cut like a knife through the storm and drifted untouched amid buffeting gusts in its heartfelt clarity. A silvery flow of pain that reached to chill the blood, the woman's unending anguish did not emanate from the depths of Newgrange or from among the watchful gathering. Caitlyn squinted into the storm for its origin, her scalp prickling to the woman's relentless aching. She realised all at once the anguished lament came from somewhere behind her position and she turned to see. Caitlyn's breath stopped in her throat as she saw the coming of the woman.

Tall and terrible in bearing, the weeping figure seemed to form from the icy waste itself, spinning up through whirling flurries. Swathed in a pale winter cloak of Celtic knots and gold braiding, the woman shifted behind driving flakes, a phantasm lost and weeping ceaselessly. Her unending agony was communicated by this sound alone, as the features of her face remained obscured by the profusion of black hair cascading from beneath a tiara of gold far past her shoulders, hair that parted but slightly despite the wind, and just enough to reveal one tear-filled eye where it overlooked the burial ceremony and then turned to fix a world of pain and rage on Caitlyn.

Caitlyn reeled, driven by terror plucking at her heart. Transfixed by the woman's glare, she stumbled, her every instinct crying out against it. To see one glistening orb was terrible but, somehow Caitlyn knew, to see both would be the promise of death. She felt a blow at her back and the air drove from her lungs in a cry that was at once pained and terrified. She tumbled towards the icy ground, falling past the standing stone she had blindly struck. The earth rushed up to meet her and she landed heavily, rolling across the green grass and the glaring autumn sun that burned the vision away.

Miss Farrell appeared, hovering against the blue sky, her face a mask of concern for Caitlyn. 'Oh, my goodness, my goodness,' she squealed. 'Are you all right? Caitlyn? Are you injured?'

'I'm fine,' was all Caitlyn could manage through deflated lungs. She felt the teacher reach for her and recoiled at once from the act.

'Oh, yes,' Miss Farrell blurted awkwardly, 'no touching, so sorry, I forgot.'

'I'll be okay,' Caitlyn assured her. She was keenly aware of the student faces massing about, drawn to the 'accident'. She offered a weak smile to Miss Farrell. 'Thank you.'

'Well, all right, then,' Miss Farrell said doubtfully. 'You take your time, sit up slowly.' She faced the others and clapped hands for attention. 'Okay, everyone, let's move on. There is much more to see.'

The onlookers moved away slowly, bored by the episode and ready to be bored some more by the tour. Soon the last of the stragglers drifted off, leaving only Debbie Walsh behind. She looked down on Caitlyn with undisguised contempt.

'You're such a freak, Caitlyn McCabe.'

A shadow fell between the girls, and they looked to find Danny standing on the edge of matters. As ever, his face held to its calm, almost emotionless setting.

'What are you looking at?' Debbie Walsh demanded of him.

'Oh, sorry,' he said with no evident regret in his voice, 'I didn't mean to stare. It's just in this light, well, I think your roots are showing.'

Debbie Walsh blanched. A panicked hand darted unconsciously to her head against the awful possibility an instant before her brain warned against mind games. Her eyes became hostile slits for Danny.

'You're a smart one, aren't you, Danny Joyce?' she hissed and wished him harm with a malignant glance. 'I'll tell my boyfriend what you said.'

She spun on her heel and stomped away, missing the ghost of a smile that broke across Danny's lips.

Caitlyn saw it, though, and how briefly it lasted before he recovered his emotionless bearing. She watched him consciously gather himself, like an actor slipping expertly into character before he turned to her with his face a blank canvas offering no clue as to his thoughts or feelings. But there *was* something, and it was in how he looked at her, still sitting there on the grass with the sun on her face. She would recall it later, that split second extra he took in looking at her, like a puzzle he wanted to understand.

Danny nodded politely and left, breaking the moment without further word.

⚬ ⚬ ⚬

'It's over, Professor.'

'Indeed,' Brody said. He shielded his gaze from the sun and tracked Caitlyn's progress where she rose to rejoin her classmates. 'That was illuminating,' he whispered to himself and noticed how his shielding hand trembled.

'It was incredible,' Marcus added. 'What in the world did we just see?'

'Something neither of this world nor the next,' Brody mused. 'I believe we have just witnessed the funeral of King Lug.'

Marcus gasped. 'King Lug? I don't believe it.'

The Professor chuckled. 'You didn't believe in ghosts before I gave you that glove,' he reminded the Doctor.

Marcus passed a hand vigorously through his thick hair. 'This is incredible,' he said, 'Caitlyn McCabe just showed us an event that shouldn't exist outside folklore.' He leaned on the car to support his quaking legs.

'No,' the Professor said thoughtfully, 'and I don't think it was Caitlyn who showed us.' He met his assistant's startled gaze. 'She was a witness too. Something quite beyond the girl was at play here. It reached out to her.' His eyes roved to Newgrange and examined the structure hulking inscrutably on the hill.

'You accept that she saw what we saw,' Marcus said.

'That I do,' Brody acknowledged. He turned towards the car. 'There is no denying her sight now. It may therefore be time for the next step.'

'Who was the weeping woman?' Marcus asked idly.

The Professor whirled back, and his features lit with sudden alarm. 'Don't ask that!' he commanded sharply. Collecting himself, he softened his tone. 'You'll sleep better.'

Struck by Brody's harsh and bizarre response, Marcus slipped behind the wheel and gunned the engine. He caught the Professor in the mirror and noted with concern how pale and drawn the man's features had become. 'What next, Professor?' he asked.

Brody gathered his senses and nodded in decision. 'It is time to face the inevitable,' he declared. 'It is time to meet Caitlyn McCabe.'

TEN

The letter was delivered by hand the following morning.

Followed across the schoolyard by the jealous spirit of Mr Byrne the postman, the courier arrived promptly at 8:50am as instructed, fully ten minutes before class time. Headmaster Flood, Flood-Flood-Suck-Your-Blood, took less than five minutes to absorb its exciting contents before hurrying to find Miss Farrell's first class. There, a further silent reading brought a squeal of delight from Biscuit Barrel.

'Great news, everyone,' Miss Farrell gushed to the class, and she fought to contain herself and hush the students. Even the shade of Sr Mary Immaculata paused in glaring at naughty children to pay attention. 'I have just received a letter. It is from Trinity College Dublin and I want to read it to you.' She held up the single white sheet for all to see and unfolded it fully and reverently.

"Dear Miss Farrell,

'Allow me to convey greetings and felicitations as Dean of the Faculty of Archaeological Remnants and

Treasures, TCD. I touch pen to paper this October morning in communicating news I trust will be the occasion of joy among your student body.

'The excursion undertaken by your class yesterday to Newgrange was, I hope, an overwhelming success and stimulating to one and all. Trusting that to be the case, I, on behalf of my faculty now extend an invitation to you, those in your good care and their parents to visit Trinity College two days hence with the twin aims of discovering yet more of the rich heritage of Newgrange and exploring options for those students interested in gaining a scholarship to the Faculty of Archaeological Remnants and Treasures. Refreshments and treats will be available to all.''

Refreshments and treats. Heads popped up attentively across the classroom.

Scholarships. Miss Farrell smiled to bursting point at that.

'Boys and girls, this is momentous,' she said, barely able to form the words. 'This is an opportunity not to be missed.' Debbie Walsh scoffed loudly. 'Now, now, Debbie,' Miss Farrell corrected her softly, 'not everyone is offered a chance like this. We should welcome it.'

Debbie rolled her eyes. 'What, a scholarship in digging holes? No thanks. I'm going to be a footballer's wife after I leave school.'

Miss Farrell shook her head and folded the letter.

'May I see, Miss?' Caitlyn asked and the paper was handed over.

'I knew you would be interested,' Miss Farrell whispered happily with a wink.

While Biscuit Barrel clapped hands to draw attention to the top of the class once more, and Sr Immaculata beamed proudly, Caitlyn carefully unfolded the paper and viewed its contents. From the official university seal in green and blue at the top, she retraced the inviting words from paragraph to paragraph and at last to the swooping signature at the base of the message.

Professor Sackimum Brody.

ELEVEN

'Oh, isn't it exciting, love?'

'Yes, Gran,' Caitlyn said. She helped the old woman from the bus, amused at her child-like enthusiasm for their surroundings while secretly sharing it. Taking a moment to ensure Gran was safely grounded on the cobblestones, she looked to the morning light.

The grand Front Square of Trinity College hemmed the visitors.

Caitlyn turned through the sculpted elegance of the broad courtyard, her eyes roving over artistic gables and rising columns. She faced manicured greens lying in the shadow of the college's giant bell tower. Gazing up to high perches there, she found whitened angels captivated by their own forms reflected in the tall windows of the teaching blocks whose capped doorways offered Caitlyn paths to higher learning on all sides. And set above all on the arched entranceway, the college clock marked the hour of her arrival with golden hands.

Miss Farrell moved busily through the scene where

she worked to shepherd parents and pupils drifting from the assembly point.

'So exciting,' Gran repeated. She stepped forward as though to embrace the whole of the sun-washed campus.

With sudden concern for the old woman's sleep-walking progress towards a bike rack, Caitlyn darted to offer a guiding 'This way, Gran' and a gentle hand.

'I haven't been here since your Dad graduated,' Gran sighed. 'If he knew you're following in his footsteps, love, he'd be made up, proud as a peacock he'd be.'

'I'm not following yet, Gran,' Caitlyn cautioned. 'The invitation was for everyone.'

The woman waved a dismissive hand for the others. 'Rot and snot,' she said. 'Just look around, you fit right in here, love.'

Caitlyn grinned at the unintended irony in Gran's words, knowing the old woman saw only a fraction of what surrounded them.

To Caitlyn's gaze, the population of the square was at least trebled by those others gathered in this meeting place of phantoms. They moved in their shimmering hundreds to mingle with the unseeing visitors and pass un-captured by tourist cameras. Norman warriors suspiciously eyed big-wigged gentlemen as shoeless flower girls stepped between. A troop of redcoat soldiers marched in perfect formation, cheered on by handkerchief-waving ladies in bonnets. Behind them, a 'cut-purse' thief in medieval garb ran from an armoured knight astride his galloping horse. Spirit astronomers peered skyward with telescopes and excitedly compared findings in leather-bound journals. Standing aloof, a gentleman in a top hat wound his pocket watch in time to the college clock, marking eternity's slow but steady passage. A flash of light, dazzling and sharp drew Caitlyn's attention and she was in time to see the spinning flight of a huge axe through the air close to Gran's head as a Viking demonstrated his weapon skills to delighted spirit children in ragged clothes.

'What did I miss?' Gran asked as she noticed Caitlyn's momentary alarm.

'You don't want to know,' the girl replied.

Any further query was cut short by the reappearance of Miss Farrell with a breathless 'This way, ladies', to which a dandy spirit in silk stockings bowed and helpfully added guidance with a wave of his lace kerchief.

Caitlyn and Gran rejoined the others in passing through a column-flanked doorway, beside which a large brass plate set into the stonework announced: The Faculty of Archaeological Remnants and Treasures.

'Here, now,' Gran whispered abruptly. She nudged Caitlyn as she poked a finger at the lead letters on the plate. 'FART,' she whispered and took a fit of giggling.

'Gran,' Caitlyn snapped, trying not to laugh.

Entering from bright sunshine, the school group found itself within the softer atmosphere of a wide marbled hall, and the babble of voices fell at once to hushed tones in keeping with this new and cloistered place. Cool air carried every sound to a vaulted ceiling where high windows on either side filtered light towards a floor of chequered tiles. The hopscotch pattern ran past a broad staircase to one side and beneath a massive velvet curtain which cut the visible space in half.

'Welcome, one and all.'

Everyone jumped to the voice reverberating near and far, and heads turned in unison to a figure descending the staircase, thin and straight as the walking-stick he held.

Caitlyn's mind flashed. *Muddied knees*, she thought instantly as she recognised the man from her father's picture. She watched closely as the new arrival paused at the mid-point of the stairs and met the upturned faces fixed on him with a knowing air and a smile.

'It is said,' Professor Sackimum Brody declared, 'that visitors to the palace at Newgrange would partake of a great feast in honour of the old gods. It is good to keep tradition alive.'

The Professor raised his stick towards the curtain and the barrier drew back for all to see.

The hall resounded to gasps of amazement.

The invitation had promised refreshments and

treats but this...this now lying before the gathering was beyond such descriptions. Along two immensely long tables a feast, no, a cornucopia of delights had been set. 'Treats' could not hope to sum up the array of cakes and buns rising in cream-topped mountain ranges, 'refreshments' did nothing to prepare for the sight of cascading chocolate fountains set amid multi-coloured beverages fizzing in punch bowls as wide as the eyes regarding them. Stacked sweets in wrappers, in shells and in glaze abounded, threatening avalanches of sugar at the slightest touch. Taste buds ached for the banquet.

'Please,' Brody urged his guests, 'ingest, imbibe.' When his words were greeted with blank stares, the Professor swept his stick up again. 'Enjoy.'

The charge began.

Shielding Gran from the cheering rush of bodies, Caitlyn watched parents and classmates as they fell upon the spread of delights. Left in their wake, she felt all at once the weight of a gaze on her and looked to the stairs. The Professor looked back, his smile replaced by a look of intense curiosity which, when spotted, he hid from her in turning back up the steps.

'Victoria sponge-cake!'

Caitlyn faced her Gran. 'What?'

'There,' Gran exclaimed and pointed, 'they have Victoria sponge-cake. I wonder if they'll give me their recipe.' Without further ado, Gran broke away and headed for her target treat.

Concerned for the old woman as she plunged into a chattering storm of eating and drinking, Caitlyn was about to follow when she felt a gentle tap at her elbow. She turned to find a well-dressed man of middle years who offered a disarming smile. Caitlyn found herself unconsciously glancing at his hands in search of a single glove.

'You must be Caitlyn McCabe,' the man said. 'I'm Dr Marcus. I studied with your father.'

Caught unprepared, Caitlyn could only reply, 'Oh.'

'He was an amazing student, the best,' Marcus recalled, and he gestured to the stairs as he guided her gently that way. 'Professor Brody always said that. He's delighted you're here today.'

'He knows I'm here?' Caitlyn asked warily.

'Of course,' Marcus exclaimed. 'He and your Dad were close. You should go up and see him.' He offered a wink. 'I'll make sure your grandmother gets her cake recipe.' Before she could respond, he left her alone at the foot of the stairs.

Caitlyn peered a moment after the insistent Marcus and then up the grand steps the way they led to a tall, panelled door, shut firmly against the sounds of celebration in the hall. Curiosity wrestled with caution and she took a half-step forward, only to compensate with a full step back.

Under her breath she cursed her doubts. *What the hell are you afraid of?* Up there might be all the answers she wanted, and more. And down here, well, down here there was cake.

Debbie Walsh's shrill laughter rose above the rest and Caitlyn shot a glance to where the girl stood, greatly amused at a dab of cream she had just plonked on the nose of one humiliated Kelly twin.

Resolved, she shifted her foot wilfully towards the first step. She yielded fully to the motion and slowly ascended. Halfway up, she hesitated again with a frown of confusion. She had come to a point where the party noise ebbed and reached her from far behind, almost as though the sound was held at bay by some unseen force. She passed through and on, dimly aware she had bunched her fists.

Clearing the last step, she faced the door and caught an image of herself, a distorted reflection in the varnished wood. Her twisted other seemed to peer back fearfully, and not from the surface of the panelling but from haunted depths beyond it. Caitlyn was seized by an urge to flee from knowing what lay further past the barrier and struggled to keep her place.

With a steadying breath, she put a hand to the door and pushed.

TWELVE

The room was a midnight museum.

Made immeasurable by a staining gloom on every surface, the 'office' beyond the door was a maze stretching from Caitlyn between opposing bookshelves. Volumes towered to a railed walkway and beyond to a ceiling of ornately decorated plaster. A single light suspended in offering forlorn opposition to an onslaught of dusty shadows. Between the shelves, the placement of numerous tall display cabinets and wide tables completed the labyrinth. Nowhere Caitlyn looked could a straight path through the office be found.

Taking a tentative first step between the cabinets, she discovered they contained an array of oddities and objects made misshapen and unsettling behind the refracting glass. The tables she approached played host to a disarray of loose papers and leather-bound books with warped covers, collections yellowed and worn by time, covered over with scrawling of ancient languages and symbols that could not be discerned as any language.

'Hello?' Caitlyn squinted uneasily into the darkness.

Teeth. Hard by her face and grimacing white, Caitlyn saw a row of clamped teeth. She reeled from the sight with a gasp and saw a human skull wearing a rusty crown. The monstrous vision grinned through glass, sightlessly amused in its resting place of crudely piled and polished bones. Unsettled, Caitlyn retreated from the grisly display and progressed cautiously between the tables.

'Do you like my collection?' the smooth voice of a man asked from nowhere.

Jolted by the unseen presence, Caitlyn looked all around between glass walls, to jewelled goblets and dusty daggers.

'It's very interesting,' she tried, hoping to locate her host through his next response. At a point farther off she spied movement close to one of the bookshelves and discerned a figure engaged in some busy activity. She edged past a case to gain a better view and slowly perceived the silvery form of an old woman whose back was turned as she worked a feather duster on the stacked volumes. 'Hello?' Caitlyn ventured and stepped closer.

'Hello.' The polite reply echoed about but had not come from the busy ghost.

Caitlyn turned in a renewed search for the speaker but found no-one wherever she looked. A collection of masks leered with ancient and blind malevolence on her confusion. Swallowing hard against rising nervousness she stepped on.

After a few paces, the edge of the maze was reached, and Caitlyn found she had come close to the limits of the room. Through a single tall and arched window directly opposite her position, weak autumn sunlight glimmered and fell on four items placed together in this area left free of the crowding museum. At its heart sat a broad desk, another riot of spilling papers. Behind and before sat twin chairs, high-backed and ornately carved; the one facing her was made a pool of deepest shadow by the angled light. Finally, and close to the desk, a glass cabinet stood, half in size to those others she had passed. What lay within gathered the feeble light washing over it and multiplied it to glittering rays of colour. Caitlyn felt drawn towards the hypnotic display and saw a large book, its old cover bedecked with jewels numerous and brilliant and clustered about a huge ruby at the centre which burned like fire at her approach. Caitlyn could almost feel heat rising through the glass to her face from the stone.

'Do you know what it is?' the same voice tested her.

She detected movement from the inky depths of the chair and watched as a face of pale and thin features eased into the light to peer at her over the pages of an opened book.

'Professor Brody,' she said, her voice fallen to a whisper.

'Caitlyn McCabe,' he replied. With a flick of his book, he guided her attention back to the shimmering display. 'Well, do you know what it is?'

Transfixed by the Professor's intense stare, Caitlyn struggled to turn once more to the object of his inquiry. The red gleam illuminated the memories she held of her father and his books.

'The Chronicles of Ireland,' she said reverently and without effort, 'a collection of every story and poem from spoken tales and ancient songs. The author is unknown. The cover is elk hide. The precious stones were gathered from all corners of the island.'

'Precisely,' the delighted Brody confirmed, and then, almost too casually, he added with a twinkle, 'it is one of a kind.'

'One of a pair,' Caitlyn corrected him automatically. 'There's a copy in the History Museum. That one has an emerald on the cover instead of a ruby.' Abruptly aware she was being tested, Caitlyn faced the Professor.

'So like your father,' he beamed.

'You knew my Dad,' she prompted him and drew closer to the desk.

'My late colleague Professor Alexander Gilbert and I agreed your father was the best student we ever worked with,' Brody recalled fondly. 'As a team we made some of the greatest finds in Irish archaeology. It was a pleasure to know him.'

'You worked with him,' she said, hoping for more.

Brody nodded, his mind flooding with recollections.

'Were you at Newgrange on the day he died?' she pressed.

Brody snapped his book shut and the noise of it rolled through the room. 'Ravens,' he said cryptically.

'What?'

'Ravens,' he declared again and laid down the book to reveal its cover. It was dominated by a bird of menacing form sweeping on black wings towards the viewer. 'I have been studying them. The raven is a most fascinating creature. In all cultures where they exist, the raven is afforded a special place in legend and folklore, and imbued with powers, magical abilities. For some they were messengers of the gods, for others they are portents of death. Some believed they see the dead.'

Caitlyn's eyes narrowed at the Professor's words, which had come slowly and deliberately. There was no reading the man's face, however, because as he spoke, he had withdrawn ever so slightly into the darkness that seemed part of him. His eyes were pinpricks studiously watching her.

'Why am I here?' she asked.

Her demanding tone seemed to amuse the Professor and he took time in focusing his thoughts. Caitlyn wondered if he liked long games of chess.

'Why indeed,' he said at last. For the first time he shifted his gaze from her and gestured to the empty chair. 'Please, be comfortable.'

'Thank you,' she said crisply and moved to sit. In doing so she was forced to angle past the spectral cleaning lady who had progressed from the book-shelves to begin dusting the Professor's desk. As ever, Caitlyn made her actions and reactions subtle, casual, not wishing to draw curiosity.

'So, to business,' the Professor said. He set his hands flat on the surface of the table as one would in prepar-ing to play a piano. In the half-light Caitlyn was startled at the sight of jagged scars on the skin of both. All at once conscious of her stare he hastily withdrew them.

'What business?' Caitlyn was becoming exasperated.

Brody was abruptly irritated. 'Excuse me,' he said and turned to the ghost. 'Mrs O'Toole, really, must you do that now? Please come back later.'

Dumbfounded, Caitlyn looked on, wide-eyed. She peered into the Professor's face and its undeniable acknowledgement of the ghostly presence. She stared at the ghost of Mrs O'Toole as the spirit nodded curtly in response to the Professor's request and departed. Open-mouthed, Caitlyn's brain scrambled at what she was witnessing. It was all she could do to point in a feeble attempt to communicate her question through the shock.

Brody caught her look of wonder. 'Mrs O'Toole?' he guessed. 'Yes, I see her. I see all spirits, just as you do, Caitlyn. I have had sight for the past nine years. But you, well, you were born to see, weren't you?'

Shock assailed Caitlyn's senses and the room seemed to lurch beneath her. 'I can't...,' she tried, fighting her breathlessness, 'I don't...'

'You don't understand,' Brody finished for her. 'But of course, you don't. You have spent your young life believing no-one else possesses your gift of seeing, that you are alone with it. Rest assured, Caitlyn, you are not alone.'

She tried to stand, but for what reason her addled brain could not immediately decide. Perhaps it was to escape. Yes, she eagerly agreed, escape. She would run away from the madness of this meeting. That was the best response. The greater part of her fevered mind gained some focus and she worked to recall the path back through the maze which now tilted wildly across her vision. In the grip of panic, and even as she found her feet, a smaller voice within struggled to be heard.

The answers don't lie that way. Shutting your eyes doesn't help.

Caitlyn wavered, struck by her inner voice and its daunting truth. She fell back into the chair, grounding herself there as her toes and fingers tingled and her head whirled.

'Are there others who can see like we can?' she asked.

'To the best of my knowledge, no,' the Professor admitted. He flicked a finger between them, 'Just us.'

'The man driving the strange car,' Caitlyn said, 'that was you?'

'Good heavens, no,' Brody protested with a smile. 'I never learned to drive. No, that was my assistant, Dr Marcus. He sees, but not through himself, not naturally, only because I allow him to.'

Caitlyn's confusion increased. 'But you have to touch,' she argued, 'he can't see spirits unless you touch him.'

'Not entirely correct,' Brody explained, and again he chuckled. 'It's a funny story really, a cold winter, Marcus borrowed my gloves, huge shock, some screaming. We laugh about it now. You see, touch does not have to be limited to physical contact for a glimpse of the departed. A shared item of clothing, a hat, or in Marcus's case a glove, worn first by a seer, is sufficient to offer the gift.'

Caitlyn's mouth flopped open under a flood of responses, each tumbling and clamouring to be the first uttered. It was all too much, too soon, too crazy! She mumbled incoherently and forced her lips back together.

'Questions,' Brody deduced, and he grasped at the air as though to catch them. 'I quite understand but we should proceed slowly. Anyway, there are more important matters to attend to first. We should perhaps begin with...'

'How did you find me?' Caitlyn asked with sudden clarity, already knowing in her heart the answer. 'My Dad?'

Professor Brody's smile faded. He patted the desk awkwardly. 'Yes,' he said, 'he shared the first hint of your gift with me. We were trusted friends as well as colleagues. His loss was a terrible blow.'

'Did he talk about my mother?'

'No,' Brody said too quickly, and Caitlyn noted his speedier rapping on the desk. 'No. He would not talk about her beyond saying how she...,' he faltered, catching the unguarded comment. 'Caitlyn, this is not the way we should begin.'

'Tell me,' Caitlyn demanded.

It pained the Professor to say it. 'She left you. When your gift became apparent, when she touched you, she left. That was when your father came to me.'

Though the Professor continued to speak, his attempts at explanation were lost as Caitlyn took the blow of his revelation. Her fingers dug deeply into the arms of the chair against a surge behind her eyes and the tears they offered. She would cry later, in the folds of the pillow in her room, but not here in front of Brody. She fixed him determinedly.

'Tell me what you know,' she said.

'Actually,' Brody said, 'it would be better if I simply showed you.' He rose and crossed to the window. He looked down on the main square, already lying under shadows creeping from the sun's western descent, and saw the last students and visitors departing for the day. Absently he tugged an old-fashioned pocket watch from his waistcoat and looked to consult the college clock. He set his timepiece by its golden hands. 'Excellent,' he said and smiled. 'It will be dark soon.'

THIRTEEN

'Our chariot awaits,' Professor Brody announced dramatically.

With a flourish of his walking-stick as he led Caitlyn onto the college square, Brody gestured to the waiting car, that same hearse-like vehicle with its strange obscuring curtains. The vehicle's engine purred steadily.

At the leading end of the car's tomb-like bonnet Caitlyn caught sight of a tiny silver figurine set there, shaped as a woman leaning forward, arms swept back with silver sleeves billowing in some imagined wind.

'This is a Rolls Royce,' Caitlyn gasped, recognising the silver lady.

'A Rolls Royce Silver Wraith,' Brody added fondly. 'Marcus will drive us.'

'Drive us where?' Caitlyn demanded. 'Where are we going? Where's Gran?'

'Oh, yes,' Brody realised, 'Gran. Where is the lovely lady? I have been most eager to meet her.'

As though on cue, Dr Marcus slipped from his place

behind the wheel and opened a rear door, allowing Gran to emerge into the evening glow.

'Here I am, love,' she piped up cheerfully. 'Dr Marcus has been very kind. We've had a great chat, haven't we?' Her words came pointedly and with a dark glance at the Professor.

He met her look with a warm smile.

'Mrs McCabe. Professor Sackimum Brody. I am delighted to meet you at last.'

Gran offered a thin copy of his smile. 'It's lovely to meet you, Professor.'

'Oh, do call me Sackimum, please.'

Gran put on mock airs. 'Oh, I shall,' she cooed before darkening her tone. 'And let me tell you what else I shall do. My son respected you, Sackimum Brody, and said long ago you were a man to be trusted, a man Caitlyn could turn to if the time ever came. So now that we're here, and Dr Marcus has explained everything to me, I hold you responsible for my granddaughter's safety. If anything happens to so much as upset her, I'll take that walking-stick and make you into a human lollipop.' She smiled like a mother shark.

Caitlyn sucked in her lips as Brody wrestled speechlessly with his own startled imagination.

Dr Marcus broke the moment. 'We should get going,' he suggested and leaned close to the Professor to whisper sharply, 'Dr James is coming.'

'Aha,' Brody replied, almost glad of the distraction from Gran's withering glare. Straightening, he turned calmly and quietly to regard a figure who hastened across the square towards the group. Brody whispered softly to Caitlyn, 'Dr Matthew Remington James, talented, jealous. Give nothing away.'

'Professor Brody,' Dr James called urgently as he rushed to close the distance, 'Professor Brody!'

'Good evening, Dr James,' the Professor replied with practised courtesy.

The Doctor stormed up, and in a manner so animated that Caitlyn believed for a moment he might strike the Professor. Dangerously close to Brody, the man halted and thrust forth a clear bag for him to see. 'Look,' he demanded triumphantly, 'look.'

Everyone gazed at the bag and saw a black dagger contained within the plastic. The weapon was chipped and soiled from years in the earth but retained its lethal appearance. Extending from a thick bone handle, its cruelly curved blade was evidence of the work of furious hands amid a crazed forging. Etched markings, indecipherable along the length of the blade, hinted more to agony than art in their flow to a tip of jagged sharpness.

'Most curious,' Professor Brody acknowledged grimly. He studied the weapon closely.

'This was found today at *my* dig,' Dr James proclaimed for all to hear.

Brody caught Caitlyn's eye. 'The latest excavation at Newgrange, you might have seen it.'

'Yes,' James said, casting a dismissive look at the girl, 'my dig. The dig you advised against, Professor. The dig you said would yield nothing worthwhile. But what's this?' He shook the bag for effect and the dagger nipped at its plastic prison.

'I said the excavation would lead to no good,' the Professor corrected him.

James scoffed. 'No good for you. Look at these markings. This dagger is going to re-write the history books, yours included. This changes everything.'

'I wish you well with your inquiries,' Brody said coolly. He turned to lead Caitlyn and Gran to the car.

'I'll be sure to keep you updated,' Dr James sneered after him as Marcus joined the Professor.

'That's a Fomorian blade,' he whispered.

'Not now,' Brody replied sharply, noting with concern how Caitlyn heard. He ducked quickly into the vehicle.

'Well,' Gran said, eyeing Dr James as they pulled away, 'he's not very nice.'

'No, Mrs McCabe, he is not,' Brody agreed. 'Dr James rates himself more highly than the examining board of this college ever did.' The Professor reflected sadly as he watched James receding behind. 'I have always taught my students to dig for knowledge,' he said. 'What Dr

James seeks in the earth is his own glory. It will be his undoing.' He waved the topic away. 'Enough of such matters, the sun is down, the adventure begins.'

'Mrs McCabe insists you can speak freely of Caitlyn's abilities, Professor,' Marcus said as he steered the car through Dublin's darkening streets.

'Oh, yes,' Gran laughed, 'Dr Marcus tip-toed all over the place until I came right out and said that I know all about Caitlyn and the ghosts. Sure, didn't I see many a spirit myself when I was changing her nappies?'

'Gran!' Caitlyn protested.

'Splendid,' Brody cut in. 'In that case you understand why I contacted Caitlyn.'

'No, I don't,' Gran said, growing stern. 'I don't know why you couldn't just leave her be. Maybe you'll get some grand research, Professor, but there isn't any good in this for Caitlyn as far as I can see.'

'Caitlyn has a right to know where her talent leads,' the Professor argued gently.

Fed up with adults talking over and about her, Caitlyn said, 'I want to do this.'

'Well, that settles it, I think,' the Professor concluded.

'Where are we going?' Caitlyn asked again. She looked out on the city draped in streetlight and shadow.

'Mrs McCabe is going home,' Dr Marcus explained. 'She has promised me some banana-and-beetroot cake when we get there.' The mirror caught his delighted smile.

Brody blinked with confusion and made to ask about bananas and beetroot.

'And where are *we* going?' Caitlyn cut in to distract him.

Brody smiled. 'You and I, Caitlyn, are bound for the heart of this haunted city. We are going to Temple Bar.'

FOURTEEN

'One ghost.'

Caitlyn was totally unimpressed.

Alighting from the car with the Professor after instructions to 'mind yourself, love' and 'be home early, pet', Caitlyn had peered expectantly left and right along the narrow length of a cobbled street to find exactly one, single, solitary ghost. The spirit, clearly a pleasantly weary drunkard from the 19th Century by his long coat and battered top hat, was at pains to stand upright. He clung valiantly to a street-lamp and offered Caitlyn a watery smile as his feet began to slide from under him across the stones.

Caitlyn shook her head and joined Brody where he was standing at a small safety barrier set about an area of recent digging. The Professor mused silently, lost in closely examining the site with a professional eye, though Caitlyn just saw a hole.

'This is not what I expected,' Caitlyn said flatly.

'Oh?' Brody said. He looked momentarily at the girl as he moved past the barrier. With the aid of his stick, he bent to play his hand across a long granite block. The shaped stone had been exposed at the base of the building's wall by the dig. 'Tell me,' he went on, 'what did you expect?'

'More than this,' she said, jabbing a disappointed thumb towards the drunk who was forming a pyramid with his backside as he tried to stand up again. 'I see more than one ghost every day.'

'Oh?' Brody said distantly again. He traced his hand upwards over the plaster work. 'How many?'

Caitlyn shrugged. 'I dunno,' she said after a time, 'three, four, five. It depends on the day. I see more if I visit Rosehill.'

'Who is Rose Hill?'

'Not who,' she corrected. 'Rosehill is a place, an old mansion, a ruin. I see a whole gaggle of ghosts there.' She leaned against the wall and allowed visions of Rosehill to replace the clownish efforts of the spectral drunk.

'A 'gaggle of ghosts',' the Professor repeated, enjoying the phrase on his tongue. 'I do like that.'

She thumbed to the drunkard again, 'This is a bit of a let-down to be honest.'

The Professor smiled and turned to her. 'Ah, young Caitlyn,' he sighed indulgently, 'to see you must look.' He allowed the tip of his walking-stick to strike the granite block, so out of place among cobbles and bricks. 'What do you see?'

Caitlyn sighed and looked. She saw cobbles, turned earth, the wall, the granite block. And what her eyes took in, a quietly probing area of her brain played with and assessed. Prompted by it, she pushed from the wall and stepped back for a broader view of the site and the building. She saw more this time, though she missed Brody's smile for her growing awareness.

'There was a door here,' she said. 'The block is a step.'

The Professor's smile grew broader.

'Correct,' he said.

Slowly and carefully Brody raised the rounded head of his walking-stick and with a precise aim he struck the metal against the plaster work. Spider cracks ran instantly from the blow and a rough segment of plaster tumbled away. He struck again, harder, and more of the wall's covering fell away. Ragged fault lines sped from the Professor's blow and the lost doorway emerged fully through rolling dust.

'For most of your life, Caitlyn, you have let seeing prevent you from looking. You have been peeking through a keyhole, settling for mere glimpses of what is really there.' Brody shielded the girl from the gritty avalanche and led her to stand directly before the granite-framed entrance. 'Here you see the surface world, and there is what lies beneath when you *look*. Archaeologists spend their lives searching for it. But none of them has your ability.' He pointed with his stick into the dark space of the portal. 'There is something deeper, that which lies beyond hidden doorways. That is what you and I see.'

'This is definitely not what I expected,' Caitlyn breathed.

'There is more to your gift, Caitlyn, so much more. But it is not enough to see. You must *look*, and you must learn.'

The Professor's words seemed to reach her from far away as she strained to peer through crushing shadows. 'Unbelievable,' she whispered as she drew nearer the doorway. She felt a soft draught play through her hair from within the space.

Brody threw up his hand sharply. 'Listen, do you hear it?'

Intrigued, Caitlyn edged closer to the entrance and inclined her ear. The cold blackness of the route pressed round and the night itself worked to blot out sight and noise but for a far off and elusive sound. It was one that grew a little more distinct with each step farther she took. Caitlyn heard...singing. It was a woman's voice, soft and whispering as a night breeze in its song.

'Alive, alive oh-oh.'

'It can't be,' Caitlyn gasped to the darkness.

'It is,' the Professor said from nowhere.

She felt his hand grasp hers and pull her through.

Shadows fell away in a silvery eruption and the ghost world of Dublin rose before Caitlyn's eyes. Shimmering figures swept in a hustle-bustling throng in a square surrounded by high-windowed dwellings of the departed. Carriages, carts and horses conveyed gentlemen, ladies and warriors from every age, while old automobiles chugged after the rest, hooting impatiently for passage. A line of hooded monks, candles in hand, attempted to process with dignity amid the multitude, watched by shawl-wearing women puffing on clay pipes. A prisoner, confined by hands and feet in a wooden stock, sat and grumbled as passers-by took howling merriment in assailing him with jeers and rotten vegetables. Overhead, a biplane of yesteryear rumbled with stalling mechanical coughs. Redcoats chased a roaring caveman through the streets. The pursuit crossed another, a pack of dogs after a butcher's boy on his bicycle. Drunks laughed at the sight and sang, and in the windows about, candelabras flared to spread golden light on masked balls and gala dancing. Near and far the night was transformed to a vibrant festival of phantoms.

'Welcome to the spirit realm,' Professor Brody said as he released her to it.

Caitlyn wandered in a daze, greeted at each step with joyous waves and smiles. She was offered flowers, ribbons, beer, tobacco! Drinking warriors raised a cheer at her passing for no other reason than to have cause for fresh drinking. The prisoner in the stocks paused in his grumbling to offer a restricted wave. Likewise, a genteel lady passing in her stately carriage fluttered a kerchief in greeting as she swept on to one of the many noisy parties surrounding the square.

'Ha-Ha!' A caped highwayman, tall and terrible in mask and tri-corn hat leapt from the night into Caitlyn's path and thrust forth twin pistols. 'Your purse, young Miss, or your life,' he demanded menacingly.

The Professor intervened quickly and with good nature. 'Henry Cassidy,' he said, 'is that you, you old devil?'

With a delighted cry the highwayman shoved his pistols away and pulled aside his mask. Caitlyn saw strong features give way to a handsome smile. 'Professor, you've come back to us. Well met, sir, well met indeed.' Hands of friendship grasped vigorously between living and the dead.

'The young lady is in my care this evening, Henry,' Brody explained. 'Please say hello to Caitlyn McCabe. Caitlyn, this is Captain Henry Cassidy, the notorious Phoenix Park highwayman.'

'It's nice to meet you,' Caitlyn said uncertainly.

'The honour is mine, young Miss,' Cassidy replied, taking her hand and offering a courteous bow. His face turned to hers with sudden concern. 'Why, you wear no rings, Miss, and no pendants, no adornments at all.'

'Err...no,' Caitlyn confirmed.

'This must be remedied,' the highwayman insisted, rising tall. 'To mark our first meeting, I shall this night secure a diamond ring for your finger, or a band of precious stones for your dainty neck.'

'Oh, no, please,' Caitlyn blurted, 'you shouldn't.'

''Tis done,' Cassidy declared, and he darted swiftly into the shadows, his cape whipping behind.

'Mad as a bag of badgers,' the Professor said, gazing fondly after Cassidy, 'but a true friend in a tight spot.'

Caitlyn looked curiously after the highwayman. In the act of watching his racing form her attention was drawn to a spot he passed at the edge of the square. In the shadow of a looming doorway there, Caitlyn thought she glimpsed a small face with wide and hopeful eyes that sparkled briefly as they met hers. The vision was indistinct and momentary. The harder Caitlyn looked, the more it blended with the shadows and, an instant later, it was gone.

Shall we continue?' Brody invited. 'We must not be late.'

Caitlyn hastened after the Professor and found him checking his pocket watch as he moved nimbly through the crowd.

'Late for what?' she asked, jostling in his wake.

'Night Court,' Brody replied simply and pressed on.

FIFTEEN

The Night Court was a place heard long before it was seen.

Beyond the western edge of the square, where the sounds of festivity dwindled, a fresh, though muted bedlam filtered through the snaking streets. Like a battle heard far off, or a disturbance under water, it came dimly to Caitlyn where she moved with the Professor to reach broad steps leading up to towering doors.

'Brace yourself,' was all the Professor could offer and he reached for the doors' huge brass handles.

The tumult of the place erupted like a wave through the opened barriers. The scene presented to Caitlyn was a deafening mayhem playing out on all sides in a chaos of spirits passionately arguing. Clouds of legal paper fluttered over a sea of heated contests to the accompanying shrieks of those in angry dispute. Professor Brody valiantly pushed a weaving path through the madness of shouting towards the unoccupied judge's bench. Caitlyn fought to follow and looked where wigged lawyers bellowed back and forth, negotiating the sentence for a guilty witch. They waved sheaths of documents to sustain their arguments while the hag cackled her mad merriment at the dispute. A passing witness stepped accidentally on the tail of her black cat and the animal added its tortured wailing to the cacophony as it scurried amid bustling feet. On high, the visitors' gallery thronged to bursting with hysterical merrymakers who shouted mock judgments of their own for those charged while offering a chorus of jeers for the lawmakers below.

Caitlyn felt a hand on her shoulder and found Professor Brody signalling for her to take one of a pair of empty chairs he had somehow located. She joined him in escaping the storm of ghosts.

'This is a madhouse,' Caitlyn said, barely audible above the din.

'All courts are,' Brody returned with a grin. 'Not to worry, calm will be imposed shortly.'

As though cued by the Professor's words, a great light surged up to fill the area about the judge's bench. It spilled glowing tendrils across the surface of the desk and coursed into the fine carving of the throne-like seat behind. And with the light came the judge. Furious of face and gigantic in stature he emerged through the rear of his seat, glowering from beneath an imperious wig which tumbled to the waist of his crimson robes. The fury he conveyed with gargoyle-twisted features increased in the failure of those before him to cease their caterwauling in his very presence. A claw-like hand reached for a gavel lying upon the desk and the judge wielded it to a hammering for order, each furious strike casting a dance of sparks.

'SILLLLENCE!'

The command was met instantly, obediently, fearfully and with a collective spectral breath.

Brody whispered through the side of his mouth to Caitlyn. 'Lord Norbury of Cabra, Judge of the Night Court.'

With piercing eyes roving yet across the assembly in search of any who would defy an order in his court, Judge Norbury cast his gavel aside and slowly took his seat.

'Bring up Ned Feathers,' he rumbled gravely.

The spirits allowed themselves whispered gasps for that name. They exchanged fretful glances and turned expectantly to the dock where, from a place deep below, came a rattling of chains and a whine of rusty hinges on cell doors dragged open. As the crowd watched, thin fingers appeared like spiders over the edge of the dock to haul forth manacled hands, and the skinny form of Ned Feathers came into view. The old ghost rose and met the gazes upon him with rat-like cunning and a defiant scowl.

A caped lawyer drifted from the gathering to nod politely and nervously to the judge. 'My Lord, I am

Quentin Caldecott for the prosecution. May I call my witness?'

'Meh,' Lord Norbury grunted.

The lawyer turned to the assembly. 'I call Professor Sackimum Brody.'

With a wink for the startled Caitlyn, the Professor stood and approached the witness box. There he was met by a medieval warrior who moved to produce a long dagger which he pointed dangerously at Brody's throat.

'Do you swear,' the warrior recited, 'by all that is right in the three realms to speak the truth and only the whole truth this night?'

'I do,' Brody agreed and took his place in the box as the somewhat disappointed warrior withdrew the dagger.

'Professor Brody,' Caldecott stated loudly for effect, 'were you, or were you not, the primary investigator of the charges levelled tonight against the prisoner, Ned Feathers?'

'I was,' the Professor said.

'Will you sum up, therefore, for my most gracious Lord and those gathered here the nature of your findings?' Caldecott requested.

Professor Brody cleared his throat. 'Through inquiries among both the living and departed, I have established that Ned Feathers haunted a house which was occupied by mortals with the aim of driving them from that house.'

Uproar. The court assembly howled outrage to the rafters and hurled deafening streams of abuse at the prisoner. The visitors' gallery erupted to cries of 'poltroon!', 'rapscallion!' and demands for all manner of gut-wrenching punishments for the 'scoundrel!'

Caitlyn shielded her ears against both the noise and the swearing.

The gavel sparked and thundered for 'SILLLLENCE!' and Lord Norbury's burning glare promised fierce chastisement.

'If it please the court,' Caldecott said through the renewed hush, 'may I ask Professor Brody if he established precisely *why* Ned Feathers chose to engage in this illegal and most despicable of acts across the dark winter nights the year just passed.'

Lord Norbury cocked a dourly interested eyebrow in Brody's direction.

'My Lord,' the Professor began, 'it is useful to understand that Ned Feathers once lived in the house he came to haunt, and in that very dwelling he amassed a great sum of money over many years of life. This he hoarded into old age, hiding the fortune within the walls of that part of the building now serving as a playroom. It appears from my investigation that Feathers, once departed, vowed to drive out all and any who might stumble on the money and claim it for themselves.'

'It's my money,' Ned Feathers shouted angrily. His words were met by bitter hisses from the gallery.

'But hold a moment,' Caldecott said, throwing up a dramatic hand. 'What was that you said, Professor, just now? Did you state that the dwelling today contains...a playroom?'

To the court's rising horror, Brody nodded. 'Yes. Ned Feathers haunted a household containing two children.'

Pandemonium. The crowd cast off all sense of civility and spewed a torrent of furious denunciations at the prisoner. A mass of raging spirits surged to the dock and fought in clawing at the terrified Ned Feathers. From the midst of the throng, someone flung the witch's screeching cat. The judge's gavel banged and flashed in outraged futility against the howling tempest. Lord Norbury directed constables into the court to restrain those climbing into the dock and force 'ORDER! ORDER! ORRRDER!' on the proceedings. Only after what seemed an eternity of roaring struggle was the crowd pushed back, all the while shooting poisoned glances at the shaken prisoner.

'I will have silence in my courtroom!' Lord Norbury snarled. He turned angrily to the prisoner. 'What say you to these allegations, Ned Feathers?'

The prisoner's lips quivered bitterly. 'I want my

money. If I can't have it, no-one can. I'll chase every-one from my house, I swear it.'

Lord Norbury growled. 'I have heard enough. Thus, I offer judgement. Professor Brody, I am grateful for your efforts in this matter and asks one final service of you. Will you assist the court in revealing the location of the Feathers fortune to the mortal occupants of his former home? This to be secret restitution for all they have suffered.'

'Very good, my Lord,' Brody agreed with a courteous bow.

'That's my money,' the prisoner argued shrilly.

'As for you, Ned Feathers,' Lord Norbury continued, and here the court held a collective breath, 'you will be taken from this place to the place of detention set aside for crimes such as yours. You will be consigned to the Glasnevin tombs, there to be chained among the bones of the silent dead. Their empty eyes will witness your haunting for the passage of three hundred Halloweens. Take the prisoner down.' The gavel banged to reinforce the sentence.

Jubilation. Shouts of praise for Lord Norbury mixed with further abuse heaped on Ned Feathers, drowning out his anguished cries of protests as he was dragged rattling to his fate.

Professor Brody rejoined Caitlyn. 'That went well, I must say.'

His words were lost on her in that moment. Distracted by a movement in the gallery, she strained to catch again the little face she was certain this time she saw. The same wide expression had appeared between the railings there only to vanish when the crowd rose to hail Judge Norbury. Searching further became useless and slowly the Professor's voice reached her. 'I'm sorry,' she said. 'What did you say?'

'I said the outcome of the case is a cause for celebration,' the Professor repeated, and he began to push his way through the crushing throng. 'But perhaps somewhere a bit less hectic.'

He summoned Caitlyn through the sea of spirits.

SIXTEEN

'Questions.'

The Professor's word slipped across the glinting tip of his walking-stick as he toyed with it and studied Caitlyn through reflected moonbeams.

Having returned to the square, they sat together, their café table ideally placed for viewing the endless whirl and rush of spirits. Caitlyn looked high and low at the spectral rumpus, captivated still by the wondrous spectacle of the ages united in the glowing hereafter. A clanging tram pulled up to deliver passengers, their varying costumes of fur, wigs, bonnets and capes identifying figures from across time moving busily through this single realm. The Professor's question was as a phantom too, drifting only slowly to reach her.

'Yes, I have questions,' Caitlyn heard herself say. 'I have so many questions I don't know where to start.'

The Professor smiled indulgently. 'You have seven questions. You simply need to place them in order.'

'What?'

'That's one.'

'I'm getting annoyed.'

Brody set his stick aside and began the lesson.

'In any field of inquiry,' he said, 'be it science or the supernatural, it is sufficient to be armed with seven questions: Who, What, When, Where, Why, Which and How. The world's greatest minds have succeeded in the pursuit of knowledge through beginning with any one of the 'simple seven'. How old is the earth? Why do objects fall down and not up? Where do rainbows come from? When did seasons begin? Why does the moon sometimes blot out the sun? How deep is the ocean? Which question do I ask first? There is no mystery in the universe to endure against the 'simple seven'.'

He fixed her with a penetrating stare.

'Decide on the question of most importance to you at this moment and begin with that one. Simple.' He considered the night and moonbeams while he waited.

Caitlyn looked at the Professor as though seeking more but detected nothing in those fixed thin features. She turned instead to the square and its occupants, taking in again the silvery multitude of forms.

'Why do I see ghosts?'

Caitlyn sensed the importance of the question immediately in the tightening of Brody's lips. He hesitated, seeming to falter as the question weighed heavily on him. For an instant, she thought, he appeared to be on the point of turning with the intention of delivering an answer, but the next and with a shift of his shoulders, he spoke without meeting her gaze.

'The mortal and spirit worlds are distinct realities. In the one, the living do not see those departed, in the other, the dead do not ordinarily see the living. That is the order of things and has been for so long. Yet the realms overlap in places and ways no-one quite understands. Total separation is apparently impossible and there are...,' he searched for the clearest term, '... crossroads, places where souls meet and see, and join. You, Caitlyn, were born at such a crossroads between worlds and therefore you see.'

'That doesn't tell me anything,' Caitlyn argued. 'That can't be the answer.'

'I'm afraid it is,' he said with a shrug.

A chilling thought struck her. 'Is my mother in the spirit world?' she asked.

'No,' Brody replied, and a little too quickly.

Caitlyn let the moment pass while she slowly absorbed the information she had gained. Like segments of excavated pottery, she examined and considered the Professor's words, so decorative but with so many pieces missing, and set them against what she already knew. In the process, and despite her own desire for answers, she made no emotional assumptions on the path to the whole truth.

In the silence of her reasoning, and with her gaze roving idly over the square, Caitlyn suddenly caught again those wide eyes fixed keenly on her. Between the trundling vehicles, past flowing gowns, eyes in the open and hopeful face of a little girl peeked from corner shadows.

'Why do spirits remain?' Caitlyn asked with renewed focus and care.

Brody nodded his approval for this most sensible query. He passed a hand before the surrounding phantoms.

'There is no single reason why some of the departed do not pass on,' he said. 'Each spirit has his or her reason. For many, they simply like being ghosts. For others, fear of the unknown beyond holds them here, while for others unfinished business in the mortal world keeps them, though, as you saw tonight, tampering in the mortal world is prohibited in law. Wilful haunting is a serious transgression from the supernatural order of things. Finally, there are those who sincerely wish to depart but cannot. Through confusion or unknowing, they missed their moment to journey on and simply remain, lost in the spirit world.'

Caitlyn listened and learned, all the while watching the watcher until, in a swish of skirts between, the little face vanished.

SEVENTEEN

The night's lessons concluded, they walked between worlds in silence.

Caitlyn followed Brody where he led the way from spirits and their revelries to the quiet flow of the river. There, and with a ha'penny each for the phantom bridge-keeper, the Professor handed Caitlyn her ticket as they crossed the arching span beneath lamps flickering on gliding waters. At the mid-point, Caitlyn felt the familiar rush of electric tingle in her hair, and she watched the lights of the mortal world flare. She saw Dr Marcus where he waited by the idling Silver Wraith at the far side of the bridge.

The journey became a lulling drift where the silver lady in her forever flight drew them on, and Caitlyn grew tired with the car's whispering miles, and of thinking and speculating. Too much information and yet not enough weighed on her and caused her feet to drag at last up the garden path to Brody's 'Goodnight' and Gran's 'It's late'.

There would be no memory of falling into bed, only of tumbling along the spectral path of dreams. She followed ghost lights and tinkling laughter, once more past shimmering smiles where she walked, all the while observed by hopeful eyes. In a place beneath all worlds, and darker than the rest, she drifted to doors huge and cruel. She pushed the blackened portals to access a cavernous interior and frowned on a crowned woman kneeling before a blazing hearth. Lost to consuming and dark practices with bloodied knife and stained fingers, the figure traced spirals in the ashes and whispered urgent and babbling incantations. Straining to hear, Caitlyn drew reluctantly closer. In her fearful curiosity, she did not at first see the weeping shadow which rose behind her. But at last she heard the figure's weeping and felt the air chill at her coming. Frozen by fear, Caitlyn could not turn, even in the certain knowledge that a single cruel eye watched and a pale hand with sharpened nails reached through tears to grasp coldly at her shoulder.

჻ ჻ ჻

'Wakey wakey, cakey bakey,' Gran chimed maddeningly with her hand shaking Caitlyn's shoulder.

Language was impossible through the shock of waking. Caitlyn offered her best effort, a cavewoman grunt of greeting for her grandmother and the harsh morning light. Only slowly she rose, through the warm duvet and her sleep-blasted hair and with a snort for her wild-girl reflection in the mirror. Her brain ran addled, wrestling between sleeping and stirring, and dreams of the living and departed. They were just dreams, weren't they? She mused on what had been real or unreal and the thinking hurt, demanding a balm of focus. She found confirmation of the truth through squinting. Lying on the dresser beneath the mirror she saw the evidence and reached for it. Between her fingers she held up and inspected the Ha'penny Bridge ticket the Professor had handed her.

'What's that, love?' Gran asked as she busily arranged Caitlyn's school uniform.

'It's real,' Caitlyn said as much to herself as Gran. Focus was coming at last.

'That's nice,' Gran replied absently and handed Caitlyn her hairbrush. 'Best you get busy before crows make a nest in your head.' Greatly amused, Gran laughed her merry way from the room.

Fortified with Gran's 'flu-beater' brew of porridge and onions, Caitlyn made her way to school, pushing through leafy gusts to join the flow of students more eager for the building's warmth than the morning's first period.

Inside she weaved between jabbering groups, dodging sniffles and sneezes as she aimed for the classroom where, she was sure, Miss Biscuit Barrel would already be waiting, no doubt burning with fevered anticipation for a report of her meeting with Professor Brody.

Have you ever seen a ghost, Miss? I saw lots yesterday. The Professor was so kind, and we talked about ghosts and went together into the spirit realm. It was like a field trip. He told me lots.

And yet he told less than he knew, Caitlyn recalled through the myriad images of the night playing in her head.

All at once she stopped, pulled up short as she focussed not on anything Brody had said, but on a single moment from elsewhere in the night. She mentally replayed it, watching again how the Professor stepped confidently through the Night Court to the witness box, again the medieval warrior raising his dangerous blade as he spoke. *'Do you swear by all that is right in the three realms to speak the truth and only the whole truth this night?'*

He did say it, Caitlyn realised, he did. *Three* realms.

A group of students jostled loudly by, drawing her back to the present. Abruptly conscious of daydreaming in the middle of the corridor, she eased to one side and found herself under the gaze of a trio of leering pumpkin faces. Hand-drawn, garishly orange, the faces peered blankly from a flyer for the Halloween dance pinned to a notice board. Beneath date and time and an insistent 'Don't Forget!' boy and girl silhouettes twisted in a cartoon-approximation of dancing, their efforts the apparent cause of pumpkin smiles.

Debbie Walsh smiled for her own reasons as she crept up. 'You're not really thinking of going to the dance, are you?' she asked, appalled, and fixed Caitlyn over sneering lips. The Kelly twins tittered nearby, fuelling Debbie's taunting. 'Like, I mean, how do you even get a dress to match those eyes?' Caitlyn moved to go but Debbie anticipated her and blocked the way as a further thought occurred, this one so wickedly delicious it lit up the bully's face to a laugh. 'Are you hoping for a kiss on the dance floor? I'd give up on that idea. Who'd touch you, Caitlyn McCabe?'

She left you. When your gift became apparent, when she touched you, she left. That was when your father came to me.

The words burned like fire, stiffening Caitlyn's shoulders. Its power bunched her hands to fists, and she spun on Debbie Walsh to reveal a scorching fury in her eyes.

Debbie Walsh scoffed at the show of defiance and she made to offer another cutting remark. But derision tripped at her lips when she looked deeper into those eyes of blue and green and she faltered under a vague but unwavering knowledge they offered something worse than harm, a fate much, much worse if she dared open her big dumb mouth again.

Debbie retreated from Caitlyn's glare and from the warning voice shrilling from deep where fearful superstitions lie. Her feet moved of their own accord and carried her quickly between the shoulders of the twins. Swallowing hard, she collected herself enough to seem uncaring, to shrug and force the impression of a painted smile for all to see. 'Such a freak,' she offered as her parting shot and she hurried away without looking back.

⸬ ⸬ ⸬

The tears came later. In the ground floor toilets and at a time she was sure everyone else was in class, Caitlyn locked herself in and released her stifled weeping to the tiled walls. Aching and pitiful, her sobs came up and through fingers clenched to catch the pain, a last futile attempt at control. Through the tears she caught her image refracted, swimming misshapen in the mirror and she cursed her huddled and pathetic form and slapped the sink top against bullies and cruel questions. Harder she struck the porcelain, harder, and harder until the stinging made her catch a breath against crying and she found strength in the pause. Dashing moist cheeks with fierce palms she beheld herself, wounded but renewed, and searched for the glare that had driven off Debbie Walsh. She found the embers of it in the glass, a trace fanned by lingering anger. With slow control she reached to let the water flow and washed away those traces, for now.

The questions remained, but in the mirror, Caitlyn saw the one to find the answers.

EIGHTEEN

Rosehill would be the antidote to the day.

Home and homework could wait, Caitlyn determined as she turned left from the school gates. The whole mortal world could wait, in fact, while she would sit in the ballroom at Rosehill and lose herself to the sights and sounds there.

Thoughts of the visit put a spring in her step, though she remained alert for another Debbie Walsh ambush. She chastised herself for that, behaving like a frightened rabbit in the hawk's shadow. After all, she knew what would happen if the hawk touched its perfectly manicured claw to this particular rabbit.

Caitlyn chuckled at the notion of Debbie Walsh meeting spirits and glanced about self-consciously. The only witness to her merriment was a spectral rag-and-bone man leading his horse and cart the way home towards the setting sun. She hurried on.

Past the hidden gap in the fence that was her access to the grounds, Caitlyn pushed easily though bushes and brambles along the familiar path and on towards Rosehill's twilight welcome. Buckled stone steps demanded a careful pace but she picked her way expertly and gained the ruined terrace. The ivy-clad space in the brickwork stood ahead and she walked to it, already smiling in anticipation of the vision beyond.

A sharp clicking noise from within stalled her and she frowned at the alien sound. Cautiously she edged to one side and peeked into the shattered ballroom.

There was someone in there!

She pressed against the wall and listened over her own booming heartbeat to a fresh bout of clicking in the gloom. There was someone inside Rosehill, and from her obstructed glimpse through the ivy, it was not a spirit linked to the place, *her* place. The figure within was a mortal intruder.

The clicks stopped briefly, and she detected a voice softly but insistently muttering until the sounds began once more, faster this time. Once more they ceased and again the intruder's voice came, more bitterly this time before the clicking recommenced.

Caitlyn tilted her head and started at the realisation she recognised the sound. Slowly she eased closer to the gap to look.

Danny Joyce sat in the ruin of the ballroom. Angled to Caitlyn's gaze through the darkening interior, his face was lit by the screen of the phone he had placed carefully on a fallen stone. His unseen hands were a flurry of shadow, whirling and twisting in urgent clicks as he concentrated on his task. The hands stopped and illuminated eyes darted to the phone's timer display. Danny muttered angrily, 'Too slow.'

Caitlyn watched the boy reset the timer, and by its light saw the completed Rubik's cube he placed aside in favour of another, this one randomly arrayed and ready to test him. She followed his finger to the phone where it hovered a moment. He jabbed and the timer was reactivated. The cube's furious clicks came anew. Bare seconds later the task was complete, and the timer consulted.

'Too slow.'

Danny slapped the cube down next to its partner and exhaled angrily, and at the sound the spirit came. Easing from the darkness behind, phantom Danny emerged and with a look of such anguish that Caitlyn almost cried out. The spirit's tortured features drew near and with wavering hands it reached for Danny's bent shoulders only to falter as the mortal boy restarted his practice. The clicking drove shimmering hands to cover the phantom's ears as though the noise was torture to endure.

Danny howled and bolted from sitting. Furious at the timer, at his slow pace, at everything, he ground the cube in his fist.

'Too slow!' he cried and with venom enough to drive his unseen other back a frightened step. 'Stronger, faster, higher, do it, son, do it. Go, go, go.' He spun about, whipping his arm back to fling the cube blindly and unknowingly through phantom Danny. The puzzle erupted in a clatter of plastic hail against the wall. 'You do it!' he challenged the darkness.

Phone and surviving cubes were snatched up and Danny fled through Rosehill from his anger and frustrations.

Caitlyn shakily entered the space he left and watched for signs of return, but the boy had gone, leaving his phantom self to look pitifully on the cube's shattered remnants. She stepped cautiously around the ghost and bent to pick up a broken square as though it offered a clue to the bizarre events of moments ago.

'This is my fault,' the ghost boy lamented, and he began to withdraw.

'What's your fault?' she asked, but the spirit had exchanged words for tears.

Even as Caitlyn reached for the truth, the spirit drifted away in mournful silence until the shadowed corridors of Rosehill swallowed him up and left her alone.

NINETEEN

The Wraith waited, rumbling by the kerb.

Caitlyn saw the vehicle through thoughts of Danny as she turned into her street, catching the gleam of its metalwork where it sat in the last of the afternoon light, shedding the mortal wash of a dying day.

She slowed as she approached and angled for a view inside but gained merely a reflected view of sky until a door swung to reveal Professor Brody rising to meet her with his warm smile.

'Perfect timing,' he said and turned to watch the sun fall at last below the horizon. 'It would not do to be late.'

'Late for what?' Caitlyn asked with a frown.

'We have an appointment,' Brody replied simply. 'You should change, the night will be cold.'

Searching the Professor's face in vain for more information, Caitlyn rolled her eyes and turned to the house. 'I'll get changed,' she muttered.

Night pressed fully round when she returned to the car, and as Marcus carried them away, Caitlyn eyed the Professor where he sat quietly with a small notebook, poring over its scribbled details, immune to her staring. Her frustration grew to fill the silence.

'What was my father like?' she asked suddenly.

Brody felt the question more than heard it, his face softening as he mused and looked to her.

'My goodness, how do I begin? He was a brilliant young man, by far the best student of his year. His thirst for knowledge was like nothing I had known, so many questions demanding answers, and every answer leading to yet more questions. Do you know he taught himself to read Ogham, the hieroglyphs of the ancient Irish? Yes, I expect you do. Do you know also how popular he was among the female students? Oh yes, elbows nudging whenever he passed, "here comes Barry McCabe". Not as popular with some of the males as a result. Weaker students were jealous of your father for many reasons. Students like his class-mate, Dr James.'

Dr Marcus offered a scornful grunt on hearing the name.

'Your father outshone them all,' Brody recalled with a dismissive wave. 'He lived for his studies and his work, hardly ever talking about anything else, until you came along, that is. Overnight he became rather like someone who has spent a lifetime searching only to happily discover the answer in an unexpected place. Once, I remember, he described to me how he had seen his face so many times reflected in golden caskets and precious stones, but never as clearly as when he looked at you. You were his greatest treasure.'

With a satisfied nod for his words, the Professor left Caitlyn to her thoughts and ruffled through the pages of his notebook.

The sound was paper skeletons, falling like leaves.

She tightened against the memory and almost gave in to it when a tingling at the roots of her hair drew her back.

'We're almost there, Professor,' Marcus announced as they crossed seamlessly over.

'Let us out at the corner, thank you,' the Professor replied, already reaching for the door.

They emerged into the still night of the spirit realm. Far from the raucous surrounds of the previous evening, Caitlyn followed Brody into a deserted side street to the lonely sound of his walking-stick tapping on the stones.

'It's not far,' he assured her.

He pressed on as she regarded the gloomy stretch, a cavernous route of black windows and blank lamps winding between inky buildings. More than once Caitlyn looked nervously over her shoulder in expectation of some horror stirring in those deep and lightless pools. And something did move there, a form slight and swift, betrayed only in the briefest flash of eyes set in a hopeful face.

'We're being followed,' Caitlyn whispered urgently.

The Professor chuckled. 'I don't doubt it,' he said and led on.

Caitlyn made to say more but her voice trailed away amid sounds rising at the corner ahead. When she looked to the Professor for some explanation, she caught only his growing smile.

They emerged into a courtyard of indistinct dimensions, contained all about by ancient dwellings of jutting gables and leaded windows. The structures, haphazard in design and size, crammed tightly together to lean over the small square while reducing the night sky above to an irregular patch of lonely stars. The noise reaching the new arrivals, made louder in the confined space, clearly had its origin in a building on the opposite side of the courtyard, the lamplight within dancing in time to the motion of countless figures giving over to uproarious singing and revelry. As Caitlyn and the Professor looked on, a single pane of frosted window shattered under the force of an object flung from within and followed by delighted cheers.

'The Half Moon Inn,' Professor Brody announced with obvious delight.

'More celebrating,' Caitlyn noted tiredly, 'do spirits do anything else?'

Brody shrugged. 'Irish ghosts are a particular breed,' he admitted and invited her to proceed. 'Shall we?'

Pressing through the creaking door of the Half Moon, they found the party in full smoky swing. Ghosts of all times and tribes filled every corner of the space, jostling for room as they surrounded tables and assailed the bar in their droves. In one side area, singers regaled the throng with the news 'there's whisky in the jar-oh', though even with electric guitars they were forced to compete hard with howling revellers chiming in with songs of their own.

Caitlyn stuck close to the Professor where he led her between tottering souls. At one table she discovered monks of old in the company of swilling Vikings, all amusedly engaged with a game of cups and dice. The group gave way to another, a collection of wigged gentlemen who listened drunkenly to one of their number poetically reciting his 'need to fart at Gogarty's art' before collapsing with delighted guffaws. The sights and sounds were altogether enough to distract Caitlyn from the inn door which eased open once more and just enough to admit a tiny figure who scurried quickly to the shadows beneath a table and tracked the girl with eyes wide.

'Professor Brody!'

The happy call came from a point near the bar, and Caitlyn strained to catch sight of a portly ghost in rolled sleeves and apron who pressed forward. The spirit thrust a meaty hand for the Professor to shake.

'Mr Kavanagh,' Brody replied with a smile.

'Professor Brody, as I don't live and breathe,' Mr Kavanagh said. 'It's only wonderful to see you again.'

'Mr Kavanagh,' Brody said, 'may I introduce my young companion. Miss Caitlyn McCabe. Caitlyn, Mr Kavanagh is the proprietor of the Half Moon.'

'Good evening, sir,' Caitlyn said.

The spirit beamed happily. 'Another with the gift of seeing, Professor? Well, janey-mac-me-shirt-is-black, who would have thought it? A pleasure, Miss McCabe, truly and welcome, a table for you both?'

'If at all possible,' Brody said with a doubtful glance at the crowd.

'All things are possible in the Half Moon,' Mr Kavanagh declared proudly, and he led the pair to a vacant table overlooking the revelry. 'Can I bring you playing cards or dice this evening, Professor?' he added as he quickly wiped surfaces clean.

'Not tonight, thank you,' Brody replied. He sat and placed his hands at rest on his walking-stick. 'We are waiting for someone.'

'And for the young lady,' Mr Kavanagh inquired. 'Perhaps I can offer some scaltheen, by way of welcoming you to the Half Moon. We don't stock mortal drinks, but I can send out.'

'I don't think ...,' Caitlyn began, doubtful of the offer. She turned to Brody. 'Scaltheen?'

'Butter and boiled eggs melted in brandy,' the Professor explained, failing to see Caitlyn's look of disgust as he scanned the inn and its guests closely.

'No, thank you,' she quickly informed Mr Kavanagh.

'Very good,' Kavanagh said with a bow and he departed for the bar.

The noisy celebration continued unabated as they looked on, and in the act of looking, Caitlyn noted how keenly the Professor observed the room and how he repeatedly surveyed a trio of ghosts seated towards the centre of the inn engrossed in a game of cards.

She took the time to look around, examining the spirits at their fun until her gaze was caught by a figure seated alone in a booth. Hooded and shaded from full sight, he did not partake of the merriment on all sides, choosing instead to watch just as she did, and from behind a candle whose flicker created obscuring shadows to shield the watcher's features.

'Well, well, well.' The voice cutting through the din was smooth and female. Caitlyn saw Professor Brody become quickly alert to it.

The lady spirit weaved through the crowd, striking and tall with a dazzling smile. Dressed in fine lace and, impossibly for the inn's confines, a grandly hooped dress, she swept delicately yet majestically through the chaos, trailing a collection of droopy-eyed admirers who elbowed one another competitively.

'Laetitia,' the Professor said, clearly flustered in his delight. He rose quickly and almost upended the furniture where he struck his knees on the table.

Amused by her effect on Brody, the lady whipped open a hand-fan and concealed her smile.

'I should be offended, Sackimum,' she toyed with him. 'You visit the spirit world and do not call on me, and here I find you in the company of a young lady.' She snapped the fan shut and offered her gaze, candle-dancing and full. 'You must be Caitlyn McCabe,' she said, and her eyes probed knowingly.

'Yes, Miss,' Caitlyn replied.

'Oh,' Laetitia exclaimed joyously, 'a lady of manners. We are the rarest of persons in the spirit realm, my dear. I do so hope we shall be friends.'

'Caitlyn,' Brody coughed, trying to collect himself, 'this is Laetitia Pilkington. Poet, diarist, and lady of merit, 1709 to...'

The lady's finger shot to Brody's lips to silence him, twisting them ridiculously out of shape. 'Don't you dare disclose a lady's age,' she teased him.

Caitlyn tried not to laugh. 'How did you know my name?' she asked instead.

Laetitia leaned close and whispered behind her fan. 'I keep a close check on Sackimum and his business. He's so sweet.' The lady resumed her posture and addressed her male followers. 'I need a seat. Who will be a darling and fetch me a chair?'

The entourage of fawning admirers rose to the challenge immediately and bolted to action. As one they sprinted madly for a nearby stool, shoving and tripping all the way, much to Laetitia's amusement. In the calm left behind, Professor Brody quietly presented his own chair.

'Miss Pilkington,' he said with a suave tone.

Caitlyn rolled her eyes.

'Darling Sackimum,' Laetitia cooed and took her place with a swish of skirts.

The moment was broken by an outburst at the table Brody had previously kept under watch. All attention turned to a wigged gentleman who leapt to his feet in a blizzard of playing cards. With a cry of 'I'm no cheat, sir, how dare you,' the man reached for his sword just as a second individual, sporting a thick moustache and black attire sprang up and reached under his coat to produce a flintlock pistol. The opponents struck together, the one driving his rapier clean through the other as he in return fired a shot at point blank range. The smoke of the thundering volley cleared to reveal the pair, unharmed and still glaring murderously at one another while the gathered spirits bellowed with laughter at the scene.

'I received your note,' the Professor said quietly to Laetitia, his gaze resting on the dispute.

'I was correct in sending it,' Laetitia said, also staring. She gestured to the quarrelling men with her fan. 'This is all very strange.'

Caitlyn was at a loss. 'Why is it strange? They're already dead.'

'No,' Brody said, 'the argument itself is not so curious, but the presence of one of those men certainly is.'

Laetitia leaned to Caitlyn's shoulder to direct her attention. 'Look carefully,' she instructed with pointed fan, 'directly before you, that is the writers' table. The man in black is Sheridan Le Fanu, the famed author of dark fiction. Seated beside him and shuffling the cards, that is Mr Bram Stoker, likewise a writer.'

'He wrote Dracula,' Caitlyn said.

'Correct,' Laetitia replied. 'The writers always game together. But look again to the man with the sword. That is Buck Whaley, a most disgraceful character. He, my dear, is leader of the notorious Hellfire Club, a collection of rogues and wastrels. He is certainly no writer, and I dare to suggest he has never even read a book.'

'And before tonight he never set foot in the Half Moon Inn,' the Professor added sombrely.

The Professor and Laetitia exchanged suspicious, concerned glances.

A piercing scream cut through the inn's hubbub to shatter the observers' curiosity. All turned and saw a little figure who sprang with alarm from her hiding place beneath a table. A young girl with eyes wide in fear pointed through the waves of her shriek to the candle-lit booth at the wall, and the shrouded figure sitting there.

'THE POOKA!'

The accused burst from his booth to the shrill unmasking of his name. The action caused his hood to tumble back. The dread face of the Pooka was revealed and all who saw cried out. Caitlyn caught a horrified breath at the sight of cat's eyes set into a barely human face that leered upon the terrified spirits already retreating before its murderous glare.

The Pooka hisssssed.

The sound washed across sharp teeth and black lips to drive the spirits further back, creating the space the demon creature required. He darted forward on spindly legs and vaulted a chaos of fallen chairs and wailing ghosts to land on the table where the writers sat. A clawed hand shot through a storm of playing cards and coins and passed under the tunic of Buck Whaley. The Pooka clutched fiercely at something there as the ghost reacted with a cry of 'Not here!'

Through a collapsing wall of spirits who went howling from the struggle, Caitlyn jostled and strained to see. For the briefest instant she caught a glimpse of the opponents' hands where Whaley and his attacker grappled for a circle of gold, upon which was set a large but misshapen emerald jewel. A crown, she realised, the violent contest was for possession of a crown.

The wrestling figures heaved and spun in their struggle, upending table and chairs as the writers scrambled away from them. Bottles shattered underfoot to create a pool of glass that undid the opponents. Heels skittered on the moving layer of slivers and they fell together, their combined weight driving the crown hard against the floor. Caitlyn watched the emerald stone erupt from its setting and she tracked its bouncing progress across the room towards her. Unconsciously she snatched up the jewel and held it close.

The Pooka struck out at Whaley, landing a fierce blow to his opponent's face and wrenching the crown from his grasp in the same motion. The creature rose and launched forth, sailing over heads to crash onto the table from where the small girl had emerged. There he paused just long enough to cast a look of dripping hate on her and sprang for the window. The Pooka erupted into the night in a hail of diamond shards.

The Half Moon became a tumult of rage in the Pooka's wake. The earlier fear gave over to a collective fury and the gathering surged for the door to give chase. Spirits charged, tripped, fell into the street and skidded across the cobbles as they looked to regain sight of the fleeing offender.

Professor Brody grabbed his walking-stick and made to follow. 'Stay here,' he instructed Caitlyn sharply. He quickly skirted the throng at the door in favour of the Pooka's own route. In defiance of his years and thin frame, Brody leapt nimbly onto the same table and jumped into the night.

Disregarding his words, Caitlyn was already rising, her face transformed from the initial surprise she felt to an expression of solid determination.

'No, Caitlyn.' The warning was uttered by Laetitia Pilkington as she read the girl's intentions in her face. But, hemmed in and surrounded by overly protective suitors, Laetitia could do little else but swat irritably with her fan at the pesky gentlemen.

Caitlyn dived for the window and sped hard after the Professor.

The courtyard was a scene of spectral riot. Spirits milled about frantically, crying aloud and seeking the Pooka in every corner with jabbing swords and readied pistols. All at once a voice more urgent than the rest bellowed 'Look there, the roof!' and attention turned skyward. Caitlyn looked with the rest and saw the creature's silhouette against the starlight where he progressed along the jutting line of the buildings. A crash and tinkling of glass nearby caused her to turn and she was in time to see the Professor smashing his way into a darkened building where he quickly vanished.

'Give chase,' a voice cried, and Caitlyn was swept up on a tide of charging ghosts. Pulled along, she worked hard to stay on her feet and keep track on the fugitive above.

The Pooka turned on his pursuers below and hissssed.

A pistol shot, thunderously loud, sent a bullet to shatter brickwork close to the creature's head and he was driven on, pursued by a flight of whistling arrows.

Vikings cursed, gentlemen issued threats, nuns invoked the Almighty's vengeance, and all jostled Caitlyn in the flight to overtake and trap the detested Pooka.

A troop of soldiers joined the fray, sprinting to bring the creature within range of their muskets. To their officer's shouted command, they formed a disciplined firing line at the double. Weapons cocked and levelled upwards, tracking the racing target closely.

'Don't shoot,' a voice in the crowd shouted all at once in alarm, 'for pity's sake, hold.'

There was a second figure on the rooftop. It rose from the gloom to cut the Pooka's escape route and smoothly drew from the walking-stick it carried a thin and secret sword.

'Pooka,' Professor Brody said where he appeared from shadow.

The Pooka's teeth gleamed with joyous hate. 'Sackimum Brody,' he whispered bitterly and drew from his cape a sword in answer to Brody's. 'Nemessissss.'

'Trickster,' Brody snarled in reply, 'liar, cheat.'

The words angered the Pooka, and he hissed again. 'Don't test me, Brody,' he warned and cut the air, 'I gave you those scars and I will give you more.'

The Professor scoffed. 'You gave me more when our blood mixed, remember? Now I walk the spirit world in search of you. What evil business are you about tonight?'

The Pooka threw back his head and cackled with wicked delight. 'You are so far behind the game with all your questionsss,' he taunted. He turned his sword to the crowd milling below, seeking out and finding Caitlyn. 'You will fail, even with a new apprenticcce. Oh, yes, I saw her tonight, your talented little ssseer. Too little, too late, Brody, she will be destroyed with the ressst. Puzzles and poetry can't save your world. The King is coming and the Fomorians with him. They will take everything.'

'He comes empty-handed,' Brody retorted. He smiled, pleased how the words angered his opponent.

The Pooka struck with a curse but the attack was clumsy, fuelled by blind rage, and the Professor easily met the swinging blade with his own to deflect it. The Pooka tried again, this time swiping backhanded with a snarl, and Brody leapt back from the arcing tip. The distance between the adversaries increased and the Pooka seized his chance. In a flash he had gained the rear edge of the building.

'Another night, Brody,' the creature growled as he retreated. 'I will watch you sssuffer.'

With a last baleful look for the Professor, the Pooka dived into the night and was gone.

TWENTY

Roars of protest rose from the spirits for the Pooka's disappearance. Not ready to give up the pursuit so soon, the crowd milled to cries of 'this way!' and 'that way!' until indecision broke it abruptly into small groups which raced in all directions to continue the chase.

Caitlyn was left alone in the suddenly quiet street. She ignored the rapidly fading cries and peered to the rooftop where Brody's silhouette lingered a moment to regard her and then blended once more with the surrounding darkness. She stood with only bewilderment for company.

'You're Caitlyn McCabe.'

The little voice, soft and whispering, came from behind and Caitlyn turned sharply. She found the night cobbles empty and silent.

'I am,' she confirmed, scanning hard through black doorways for sign of a reaction.

It came not from the portals, but from a tiny corner hidden by stone steps and railings. From the afforded cover, the features of the spirit girl who had cried out her warning in the Half Moon peeked furtively between the bars and regarded Caitlyn doubtfully.

'You really are her?' the girl whispered, hardly daring to believe.

Caitlyn approached the railings carefully, seeing in those wide eyes a readiness to flee. 'Yes. Who are you?'

'I'm Mia,' the child replied.

'Have you been following me, Mia?'

The little ghost nodded sheepishly. 'Can you help me find my mother?'

'Is she with the others chasing that terrible man?' Caitlyn asked.

'The Pooka,' Mia said helpfully. 'No. I fell asleep and when I woke up, I couldn't find her.'

Caitlyn began to understand. 'Oh,' she stammered, hunting for the best response. 'I don't think...'

'You're Caitlyn McCabe,' Mia reminded her softly. 'I heard the Professor say your name. I listened when he talked about you.'

Caitlyn frowned. 'What did he say about me?'

'Mia.' The Professor's voice was firm, his face dour as it appeared at Caitlyn's shoulder.

With a frightened gasp the spirit girl fled, vanishing into the night in an instant.

Caitlyn rounded on Brody, her mind racing.

'Questions,' he guessed.

'Lots of questions,' she replied darkly.

The Professor sighed. 'Your education is moving far more quickly than I anticipated, Caitlyn McCabe.' He mused for a time, tapping his cane rhythmically between his feet. Finally, he nodded decisively. 'Very well, let's return to the Half Moon, shall we?'

He led the way, carefully sidestepping the pool of glass created by the Pooka's escape. He forced re-entry to the ruined inn through a door hanging on one squealing hinge. Inside, Mr Kavanagh despaired at the carnage wrought to his establishment as he worked his broom against it with patient resolution.

'What are you not telling me, Professor?' Caitlyn demanded. She folded her arms and peered sternly at Brody where he walked further through the now quiet inn.

'That there are three realms, not two,' he said, 'though I suspect you already deduced that much.' He watched her nod. 'I wanted to bring you more slowly to that knowledge but the Pooka has put paid to my best intentions, it seems.' He walked amid the destruction of wood and glass and kept his focus to the floor as he scanned the debris closely.

Caitlyn leaned against an undisturbed table. 'The Pooka is from the third realm,' she said.

'He is.'

'Who is he?'

'He is many things. He is a messenger, a thief, an assassin. He is a monster, the willing slave of an ancient evil rising in the third realm.' Irritated, the Professor jabbed with his walking-stick and drove a shattered chair from his path.

'Go on,' Caitlyn prompted. She watched the Professor square his shoulders for the telling.

'The ancient realm is a place reserved for creatures like the Pooka and the gods of old, those the living world now chooses to forget. We think of them as stories and myths, but once upon a time, before time, they walked the earth. Then, the realms were not separate, they were one. Spirits and gods moved freely among the living and there was enough magic in the world to create the stories you've read. Dig deep enough and you find the truth of it all.' His shoes crunched on broken glass as he drew near the writers' table.

'Greed undid everything. The greed of a single, demented king with ambitions to rule all others led the ancients to war among themselves. Their battles spread over the world and what had existed in perfect balance was destroyed in a storm of violence. The old order was wiped away and never restored, even after the selfish king was struck down and his army scattered across the sea. From the ruins a new balance was sought and eventually found, though not in unity but separation. One realm became three, with ancients, mortals and spirits divided, each vowing not to interfere in the affairs of the others. That remains the highest law.'

'Ned Feathers,' Caitlyn said, recalling and understanding.

'Very good,' the Professor said, impressed. 'In haunting the mortal realm, Ned Feathers breached that law which above all others must not be broken. The Glasnevin tombs are filled with spirits like him.' Here Brody squatted to closely examine items scattered on the floor.

'And the Pooka is doing the same in the spirit world?'

'Yes,' Brody said. He lifted a playing card from a puddle of wine. He held it to the light for closer inspection. 'However,' he continued, 'the aims of the Pooka go much further than Ned's petty desire for money. And what he seeks is not for himself but his master, King Balor.'

'The selfish king.'

Brody nodded and turned the card, the King of Spades, for her to see. 'One-Eyed King Balor, tyrant ruler of the Fomorians. Together with the monstrous army raised by his queen, the sorceress Cethlinn, it was Balor who sought the whole world only to gain an unmarked grave on a lost battlefield.'

'Fomorian,' Caitlyn repeated. 'It was a Fomorian dagger Dr James showed you.'

'Yes.'

'Has he found Balor's grave?' she gasped.

'Not yet,' the Professor said, 'but the dagger suggests he is not far from it. That must be why the Pooka is so busy in his own search.'

Caitlyn frowned and gestured to the upturned tables. 'What is he searching for?'

The Professor pursed his lips against the question and offered one of his own. 'What did you see the Pooka and Buck Whaley fighting for?'

'It was a crown.'

'Be precise,' he instructed.

Caitlyn focused on the memory of it. 'It was gold, with sweeping bands etched around the headpiece. They were early Christian, I think, Celtic knots combined with religious symbols.' She caught the Professor's slight smile. 'What?'

'You sound like your father,' he said and watched her blush. 'Go on.'

She refocused. 'The crown was topped not with tips but with circles of gold, each containing...circles within circles. There was a jewel, just one, it was big and set on the main band.'

The Professor stared hard. 'What colour was that jewel?'

In response, Caitlyn drew the glittering emerald into the candlelight.

Gently, almost reverently, the Professor reached to accept the stone. He turned it in his fingers, admiring the craftsmanship that had so precisely smoothed one hemisphere, and he carefully noted the damaged edge which spoke to a lost half of the precious jewel. He forgot himself in a moment of deep remembering and his lips went unguarded.

'Balor's golden spear,' he whispered.

'Wait, what?' Caitlyn asked, confused. 'What are you talking about?'

Brody eased into a chair which creaked under the weight of his knowledge.

'The earliest records,' he said, 'the Erin Metrical and the Book of Tara, relate how King Balor possessed a great and magical spear. The weapon was filled with power enough to sweep all enemies aside while controlling the Fomorian army. It is recorded that Queen Cethlinn exhausted her magic in its creation and was forced to rest for an entire year afterwards.'

'You mean a kind of giant magic wand,' Caitlyn said.

Brody nodded, satisfied with the comparison. 'Precisely. Balor requires it if he is to be anything more than a hollow king.'

Caitlyn frowned. 'You said Balor is in his grave. He was struck down, you said, dead and buried.'

'I did. But I did not say he had passed on,' Brody cautioned, 'and I did say his queen is a sorceress.'

Caitlyn's mind surged with cold possibility. 'Are you saying Queen Cethlinn can bring him back? If the King's grave is found, she can raise his spirit?'

'She has been waiting ten thousand years in the caves of the ancient realm for that very opportunity,' the Professor said with a sombre nod. 'Clearly she has sent the Pooka to locate the spear in anticipation of a successful search by Dr James.'

The Professor offered Caitlyn the damp playing card.

She turned the coloured face up and examined the profile of the King of Spades and the headpiece he wore.

'But a crown is not a spear,' she said.

'No,' Brody said, his mind far away. 'But the old texts also offer some detail of Balor's weapon.' He worked to recall the precise wording:

'A golden shaft, infused with curses,
Dipped in poisoned light,
Forged to hateful sharpness,
In the fires of a witch's might,
Metal pulled from a midnight sky,
To torture skin and bone,
With tip of piercing madness,
And pommel of emerald stone.'

'Emerald stone,' Caitlyn repeated softly and looked again to the jewel. 'What does this all mean, Professor?'

Brody remained silent as his attention was drawn inward. Lost in thought, he sat and looked on the dial of the pocket watch he could not recall tugging from his waistcoat. His drifting gaze fell between the delicate hands of time, searching vainly for answers to the questions that plagued him now.

'It's late,' he heard himself say and the sound drew him up sharply from his daydreaming to a fresh vitality. Snatching up the emerald, he leapt upright and snapped shut his watch. He turned to face his apprentice. 'Research,' he declared, 'this entire evening gives cause for further inquiry and examination of the historical texts. From there we can proceed.' He aimed for the door.

'Research?' Caitlyn blurted as she followed. 'Do we have time for that? What if the Pooka gets to the spear first? Shouldn't we be looking for it too?'

Brody halted and turned again to Caitlyn. 'We don't need to,' he said with a wink. 'I already know where it is.'

TWENTY-ONE

The Pooka wrapped himself in shadows.

With diamond eyes glistening, and keen ears listening, the creature traced his escape route through the paths of the phantom city. More than once he stopped abruptly to a new clamour of spirits charging past with their curses for him. The hunt was still afoot, and the Pooka was wary.

He progressed on, creeping through darkened streets and alleys, from one safe pit of gloom to the next until the great shadow he sought was gained. The sight of it stretching forth from the high walls of Dublin Castle confirmed he was halfway home. The knowledge brought his sharpened smile twinkling.

Up the Pooka clambered, the stone of the old battlements offering easy purchase to his claws. Over he went, into the silent precincts of the castle, abandoned at this hour by ghost and guard alike. Ever watchful for traps, the Pooka took time to scour the night, sniffing its cold air before committing to the next leg of the journey, the route beneath, the crossing point, one of the secret ways remaining. He allowed himself a whistling chuckle for mortals who had made the way a tourist attraction, their dull brains ignorant of the truth.

The foolsss.

He reached the hidden well without incident, and without hesitation he eased into its burbling waters. Light reflecting on its broken surface danced across his cat-like orbs as he descended and sank below. Feeling the stream bed under his feet, he kicked off to break free of the shimmering from the well mouth and he swept into enveloping darkness. He followed by memory more than sight the stream where it snaked beneath the worlds of mortals and spirits. With fingertips extended to the stone walls hemming the water, the Pooka propelled himself forward against the current until and at last the walls parted at the edge of a greater body of water, a crushing void immeasurable and black.

The breaking surface of the Pooka's rise echoed through a cavern of incalculable dimensions. The sound and white water he created rolled quickly to a hollow void of night and were lost. He sought at once for one of the many lurking threats here, finding as ever the limits of Dubh Linn, the Black Pool of Dublin, beyond even his sharpened vision. Treading water, the demon allowed his senses attune. Not all dangers in this dripping space betrayed themselves to vision.

Quickly then he pulled towards shore and away from the hungry depths of Dubh Linn.

On the Pooka swam, driven harder by pursuing splashes and ripples that lapped at his feet where he scrambled ashore. On up the bank side he moved, carefully using the rocks of the shore for cover as he eased past a shapeless figure patrolling gigantically through the permanent night. On past the silken door of legend he travelled, and down towards a place where the light of the world was cursed and forbidden. Corridors of ornately carved stone plunged now to ever darker levels in escaping the realms of silver and sunlight, bringing the Pooka closer to his destination.

It lay in waiting at the end of one final twisting path.

A vast columned space opened up and caused the Pooka to look on in breathless wonder. Despite his countless journeys through this place, he faltered on its threshold, overawed again by the chamber and the forgotten ones who had shaped its gigantic design.

Night-shrouded on every side, the chamber's huge walls and flanking columns gave mute witness to labours relentless. Across every surface shadow poured into carved and swirling art, a record of former beauty deadened by the blind wear of time and forgotten by web-soiled candelabras. High above, from impenetrable recesses cut into the rock, stone-carved beasts clawed with monstrous features holding promises of foul destruction on intruders. The Pooka shivered as he detected whispered currents of air swimming from the depths of those recesses, cold breathing that seemed to come from the very jaws of the glaring statues.

Casting off irrational fears, he stepped forward. In the distant dark ahead, the end of his journey emerged. Twin arched doors towered between the columns. He hastened towards them and his footsteps became unnaturally loud through the resounding emptiness. But the sound betrayed the involuntary slowing of his pace when he reached the heart of the chamber and what stood there, more terrible than all the rest. His steps dwindled into the crushing silence as the Pooka halted between two gigantic statues standing eternal vigil over a massive sarcophagus.

The dizzying scale of the figures offered testament to their importance among those who had fashioned them from whitest marble. The one, in warrior stance, held forth his sword of mystical design, its blade bearing the same interlocking artistry as the surfaces of the corridors that had brought the Pooka here. The figure was portrayed in a charge, frozen as he hurtled to battle, his cape sweeping behind in flight and tied at a neck that had been rendered headless. The demon looked without pity to the base of the sculpture and past its ancient inscription to where the severed head lay in its crown. The upturned face of battle communicated the agony of its fall, and the Pooka sneered at the transformation.

'King Lug,' he scoffed, translating the inscription without needing to look.

The other statue was harder to look upon, more dreadful to the Pooka's sight, and as ever he sought to disregard it in his passing, lowering his head wilfully to avoid her gaze. Yet, despite keeping the stone tomb protectively between him and the statue, the icy fear he always felt in its presence came creeping and drew his eyes up to look upon the woman.

She stood in mourning for all. Tall and straight, the shining marbled form of the young woman refused the darkness as she inclined her crowned head to weep into cupped hands. Long sculpted tresses flowed from beneath her tiara to become one with the decorative cape she wore and to conceal further her sad aspect. Almost all the royal face was hidden save for a single feature which transfixed the Pooka again where he circled the form with his unwilling head upturned. Between spreading fingers, one eye of the woman looked down to seize his vision and still him in his tracks. For this was not an orb made heavy with mournful tears, but one sharpened to pierce with a burning rage.

'Aoife,' the Pooka breathed. His reverent translation boomed in every dark corner.

'Do you never tire of looking at her?' a female voice rang with mockery from the black.

The startled Pooka spun about, drawing his sword in a swift movement. His cat orbs probed the sightless void, and he became angry as he recognised that voice. 'Morrigan,' he whispered bitterly. 'Show yourssself.'

His command was met with tinkling laughter to his left and he spun there, in time to catch the fleeting silhouette of a woman passing between columns. The fluttering of a cape in rapid motion directly behind turned him sharply. He was an instant too late to catch her where now, bizarrely, she moved on the opposite side of the chamber. She was everywhere and nowhere all at once. The Pooka snarled, tired of this old game and the Morrigan's single pathetic gift.

'You're late,' the Morrigan's voice chastised him.

'So late,' the Morrigan said from a second place.

'Very late,' she said from a third.

The Morrigan strode towards him from the direction of the twin doors. Drawing forth in blackness, the shadows clung to her raven hair, her war dress of links, her cape of feathers. A hand with black painted nails rested on a sword glinting in tune to the cruel smile on her lips. The warrior halted to study the Pooka with ill-disguised contempt.

Scowling in return, he re-sheathed his weapon pointedly. 'You are not the one I answer to.'

'You seek an audience with the Queen,' the Morrigan said, gesturing to the giant doors. 'She's busy.'

'She awaits my report,' he said and brushed past.

'She is conjuring,' the Morrigan warned casually, though her smile was impish. She watched and was amused at how the Pooka hesitated at her words.

He held his face from hers and kept hidden his sudden rush of fear. 'I will see her,' he insisted and pressed on.

Entertained still, the Morrigan followed with her wicked smile.

TWENTY-TWO

Flame and heat rose to the opening of the doors.

The Pooka was blasted by the storm within and almost driven back by the burning wind flying at his skin and piercing light erupting in his eyes. Screwing up his features, he stepped further into the room. At his first footfall, blacked-veiled figures swept from left and right to intercept him, blocking his path and circling angrily against his intrusion with chipped claws holding arrowheads at the ready. The Queen's handmaidens, each a stooped and faceless witch, stood firmly in his way and breathed threatening hisses.

'Let him come,' a regal voice commanded. But only slowly did the sinister guard retreat.

Seeking his mistress by her voice, the Pooka looked towards the head of the chamber and to the thrones which sat there, unkempt and threadbare. He found them unoccupied. The command, he realised, had come from a spot to his left, near a mammoth fireplace carved from the rock and currently the source of all violent illumination and burning within the space.

Blinded still, he sought the Queen but in vain. Instead, at the edge of the gaping fireplace he found only a veiled witch who feverishly operated a gigantic bellows to maintain the scorching inferno.

'Majesssty,' he uttered respectfully into the light and, in time with the Morrigan, he bowed.

'Returned so soon, Pooka.' The Queen's voice, so cold in the fire, was surprised and laden with menace.

'I return in triumph,' her servant proclaimed, and he reached beneath his cape. The Queen's guard of hags instantly closed in once more, claws raised against hidden weapons. The Pooka cautiously withdrew the gold crown he carried for all to see. 'That for which you sent me, Majesssty.'

Queen Cethlinn drew up from caressing fire, a dread goddess forged by its heat and carried on its dancing flames. The crown of torturous spikes she wore reflected the blaze and lit a face untouched by time yet not entirely without blemish. From forehead to cheek, a livid scar glistened like a molten stream past eyes unblinking and forever cruel. She fixed what measure of joy she could pretend to on her servant.

'You gained the crown,' she noted as she pressed between the ranks of her guard. 'Good. Were you seen?'

The Pooka's breath caught in his throat and he bowed lower, terrified to look directly at his mistress.

'I was, my Queen,' he admitted as he listened to the hisses rising about.

'Excellent,' Cethlinn responded, perplexing him. 'Witnesses are useful to us.'

'I...I don't underssstand.'

'No surprise in that,' the Morrigan jeered under her breath.

'Brody was there,' the Pooka offered, ignoring his rival.

Queen Cethlinn's head snapped up from her inspection of the golden prize. 'Brody.' She uttered the name as a curse even as it brought a smile to wrinkle her scar.

'Yes, Majesty, and a girl.'

The Morrigan frowned. 'What girl?'

'Brody saw you,' the Queen pressed the Pooka. 'He saw you seize the crown?'

Her servant squirmed. 'Yes, Majesssty.'

Queen Cethlinn rose to full height, drawing back her shoulders at the news imparted, and as her head fell back, she cut the air with icy laughter. 'Perfect,' she howled to the stone ceiling. 'He was there to see it. Oh, the gods play on my side.'

Clutching herself against the delicious pain of merriment, the Queen thrust forth a hand to demand the crown so eagerly offered by the Pooka. She beheld it in its glory and examined the crafted designs delightedly, only for her smile to wither as her fingers ran to the empty setting.

'Does it please my Queen?' the Pooka asked, too stupid to see the gathering storm in her face.

She rounded on him, her eyes blazing with fury and the lightning fire that surrounded her. She thrust the crown like a weapon, aimed directly at her clumsy servant. 'Where is it?' she shrieked, and the witches shook and nattered. 'Thief,' she accused him, 'you would steal from me. Where is the emerald stone?'

The Pooka flung up his hands in supplication and fell wailing to his knees. 'No, no, my glorious Mistressss,' he wailed, 'I steal for you, not from. The stone, the jewel, it was torn away. I thought nothing of it, so broken a thing.'

'You thought,' she sneered enraged, 'you thought, and you lost. The emerald *was* the prize, our path to the spear. And you lost it!'

Cethlinn's wrath played out in her hands. Clawing and twisting, she mashed the crown between her fingers as though it was a paper toy. The action distracted her from furious visions of torture for the Pooka and she gathered herself, allowing the storm within to pass. She stepped to the fire, the Pooka still fixed in her terrible vision, and held the crown to the flames, maintaining a grip on it even as the golden lump began to melt and pour in burning rivulets between her fingers.

'My Queen!' the Pooka cried out in horror. He darted for the treasure, pursued by grasping witches.

With a cry against the flames torturing his hands he strained for the liquid crown until Cethlinn seized his throat in a crushing grip.

'The crown is nothing,' she declared through her fury. 'Watch it burn and see the truth in it. The whole world will be thus when Balor regains his spear.'

'How can we find it now?' the Pooka gagged, his protest cut by the Queen's tightening grip. His eyes rolled helplessly.

'Morrigan,' the Queen snapped.

The warrior bowed. 'The other half of the emerald is still in its place. I have seen it for myself.' She cast a contemptuous glance to the Pooka. 'All that is required is a clever thief to seize it.'

'You will be the one,' Cethlinn instructed her.

'No, Majesssty,' the Pooka wheezed jealously and he fell to his knees before her. 'Let it be me. I will redeem myssself.'

'No,' the Queen barked. She looked down on him, and at the same time through him to the dark heart of plotting within herself where the seed of an idea grew. 'You will play another part.'

The Pooka blinked in confusion. 'But the emerald is the only way,' he argued.

'It is not the only way,' Cethlinn mused, her thoughts churning to a foul design. 'Brody saw you. And through that I see him.' She peered to the stone ceiling, imagining her enemy in the realms above. 'He moves through the spirit world even now in pursuit of clues. Later he will fall asleep in his library for want of answers in paper books. He is thinking hard, growing suspicious, racked by doubts. He will seek knowledge, and we must make sure he finds it in the places of our choosing. A little knowledge can be a dangerous thing. And because of that he will surrender the spear to me, only then to realise he has done it. The King will come in glory and I...,' Cethlinn shuddered under the strength of her own desire, 'I will be Queen again.'

'Yes, Majesssty,' the Pooka agreed dubiously.

Cethlinn peered deeply into the fire, lost in the ecstasy of her grand plan and its magnificent conclusion. The flames danced in celebration of it, but all too briefly. Abruptly they lessened and began to fall back, denied their sustaining air.

Robbed of her vision, Cethlinn turned her furious attention to the witch at the bellows. 'Who told you to stop?' she demanded and jabbed a ringed finger at the offender. Her signal was understood at once by all present.

The witch retreated, her clawed hands held forth in useless surrender to her sisters who already advanced slavishly to pounce and punish. She tumbled beneath them and issued pitiful screeches where they fell on her and used raking fingers in a sundering chaos of hissing. Torn to silence and to nothing but the rags that gave her form, the offending witch was lifted and cast as fuel to the Queen's waiting fire.

Cethlinn directed her words of judgement for the Pooka's ears.

'The price of failure.'

Amid the violence, the Morrigan approached the Pooka quickly and pulled him to his feet, not to help, but to utter again her question. 'What girl?'

Oblivious to the query, Queen Cethlinn swept towards her throne and took her place in one ragged seat. Yet possessed by her own racing thoughts, she addressed the Pooka once more. 'Speak to me of our unwitting friend,' she demanded, 'talk to me of the talented idiot Dr Matthew Remington James.'

The Pooka sagged visibly. Burdened by the news he carried, he chose his words carefully, seeking to avoid a fresh onslaught. 'I have added to his successes as you commanded. Clues have been left, instructions sssubtle. By my plotting he thinks the trail to King Balor is uncovered by his own clevernesss. The man is vain, easily led, yet he remains unaware of my help...'

The Queen shrugged, unimpressed. 'So, he digs?'

'Yes, my Queen,' the Pooka agreed, though awkwardly.

The Morrigan smirked, anticipating the truth.

'And?' Cethlinn's lips tightened.

The Pooka squirmed.

'He digs in the wrong placcce.'

The Queen brought her scream from the throne and carried it to the Pooka with bunched fists and blazing scar. She drove him before her very presence and towards the waiting hands of the witch guards. She towered where he crumpled weeping and pleading at her feet. 'Idiot,' she accused him, and caught him cruelly by the hair. 'Dolt of a servant,' she spat and dragged him squealing to the witches. 'How much time have you wasted?' she demanded and cast him to eager, scrabbling hands.

Bony fingers ensnared the Pooka's limbs. The razor nails of witches stroked his neck and cheeks, and their reeking corpse breath sighed from behind stained veils. Sinking into their skeletal arms, he called pitifully to his Queen. 'He is closer than he knows, near, very near.'

An unspoken direction from Cethlinn stayed her servants. 'Go on,' she said, stretching her own fingers impatiently and with loud cracks.

'Where the Doctor digs,' the Pooka explained frantically, 'is of a distance from the King no greater than that which separates me from your glorious Majesty even now. A final clue, one last prompt, and we will have King Balor, this I ssswear.'

'Clues and prompts,' Cethlinn mocked him. 'We do not have time for more childish games.' She peered again to the fire in search of a new plan.

The Morrigan drew near.

'Majesty,' she began softly, 'I have a suggestion. Where soft tactics fail, it has been my experience that there is only one true alternative, and that is fear.'

Queen Cethlinn turned to the black-clad warrior and eyed her closely. 'Do you suggest you visit the dim-witted Dr James? You would rise up to put fear in one hand, and a last clue to my King in the other?'

The Morrigan humbly bowed. 'Such a visit yes, but not one from me.' She cast a mischievous glance towards the Pooka.

'Do not dare say it,' he whispered coldly as he read her intention.

'Release the Banshee,' the Morrigan dared.

Queen Cethlinn considered long. The flames caught features in search of a decision and ran to the slow twisting of the scar where her smile grew wider.

'No, my Queen,' the Pooka implored, 'the Banshee is death. She is treachery.'

'All men fear her,' the Morrigan countered, 'they know in their weak hearts what she is. Dr James will dig in the right place or he will dig his own grave.'

The flames surged, catching Queen Cethlinn's smile as it touched her eyes.

'Let us visit my granddaughter,' she agreed.

The Pooka shuddered within the bony embrace of the witches. 'Oh no,' he whispered.

TWENTY-THREE

There came a woman's weeping. Beyond the darkness of the stone passage, behind the dungeon door, from the depths of a broken heart, the Banshee wept.

Plaintive and soft the keening lilted. Past all comfort, it seeped under the door to crawl along the damp walls of the passageway to reach the visitors, bearing anguish unbearable to their ears.

'For whom does she weep?' the Morrigan asked.

'For usss,' the Pooka whimpered at the rear of the group.

Queen Cethlinn shook her head tiredly. 'Fool. It is always like this, and for ten thousand years past since falling into my trap. They are tears of mourning for her dead brother and their failed treachery against me. This,' she rounded on the others and drew a finger along her angry scar, 'this is a granddaughter's kiss.'

The Morrigan shrugged. 'Well, you did poison her brother.'

'He slew my husband and beheaded *my* brother.'

'Quite a family,' the Morrigan said.

'May I remain here?' The Pooka asked feebly.

With a scolding look, Queen Cethlinn reached beneath her garments and drew forth a large key which she thrust at the Pooka. A finger's flick made her instruction clear.

The Pooka accepted the key meekly and advanced.

The weeping.

It found him, reached out and caressed him. The lament offered chill tendrils for the Pooka's neck and icy needles for his heart, and for his lips the luring promise of death's sweet kiss. All of this he felt with a shiver, all, even before looking into the eyes that watched behind that door.

He hesitated, almost failing, and the key became a dead weight in his shaking grip. For a moment he surrendered to the temptation to flee, to avoid what waited in the dingy cell, and he took a step back. *That way Queen Cethlinn lies*, his inner voice warned, and that was just as bad as continuing. He willed himself forward, pushing fear down deeper into himself until it rolled coldly in his stomach. Close enough to reach the door, he offered the key with a hand so shaky the metal scraped loudly across the lock to find its place.

The weeping ceased.

Through the deathly silence the Pooka heard his own whispering fear and the broken rhythm of his breath, the blood pounding in his ears, the boom of his faltering heart.

The key shrieked in turning. The Pooka hauled on the door, moving aside with it to shield himself against harm, and admitted Queen Cethlinn.

In the slimy confines of the cell, the Banshee knelt, dark and brooding as a spider. The cape she wore was tattered black and it spread far and wide to form about her an island where light and love were alien. From torn shores, the material rippled towards the dark interior and rose, higher, higher, to meet on all sides the midnight waterfall of her hair, through which no part of her face could be seen, only felt as she regarded the visitors entering her space.

'Hello, Aoife,' the Queen said.

The realm held its breath.

'Grandmother,' the Banshee's voice was like air from a crypt.

'How long has it been, my sweet?' Cethlinn said with mock affection. 'It must be, oh, fifteen years since last we spent time together, is it not?' She waited for a response and was agitated when none came. She proceeded quickly to business. 'I have use of you,' she said and snapped her fingers.

There was power in the action, all in the cell felt it. And they saw how it pulled the Banshee from kneeling and unwillingly to her feet. The motion came in a clatter of shackles restraining the woman's pale hands. The Pooka whimpered and fell back from the rising while the Morrigan reached slowly for the comfort of her sword.

'Perhaps this was a mistake,' the warrior ventured.

'Calm, Morrigan, calm,' Cethlinn said, 'this will work. Under my command, the Banshee has long served my needs. She will serve once more, and well.' She snapped her fingers again.

The shackles crashed to the floor. Banshee fingers flexed to claws.

The Pooka's resolve failed. He drew back, crying out as the doorpost struck his back in fleeing.

'Say you will serve me, Aoife,' the Queen commanded.

'Yes, Grandmother.'

Satisfied, Queen Cethlinn smiled but her eyes remained vigilant as she turned to leave.

The Banshee struck. With dizzying speed she launched forward, hands whipping out to grasp for the Queen's exposed face. Nails sharpened to points would have her eyes this time. A mere fragment of space remained when the wall-mounted chain restraining Aoife's neck drew violently taut and hauled her crashing back to the floor.

Cethlinn stepped to leer over the fallen prisoner. 'Oh, my wayward love,' she mourned through gritted teeth, 'how bitter you are yet. Defiant you remain, and so slow to sense.' The Queen reached to bring from her garments the snaking coils of a whip. 'The lesson must begin again.'

The whip cracked, and in the shadows of the passageway the Pooka covered his ears against the Banshee's tormented wails.

TWENTY-FOUR

What does this all mean, Professor?

Caitlyn brought the memory of her question up from sleeping. From deepest dreams, lost yet somehow unsettling, she came awake all at once to early morning light angling across her room. Through a gap in the curtains an autumnal beam inched its way along the wall, already clear of the wardrobe and currently tracking towards the edge of the mirror on the dresser. She watched as the light seeped over the wooden frame bordering the glass to find the reflective surface. Like fuel to a fire, glass and light combined to burst in a dazzling eruption that burned off the last of shadows and sleep.

Well, Professor?

Light alone does not illuminate all things, Caitlyn concluded, such as the questions she had thrown at Brody in the ruin of the Half Moon Inn. It served only to re-ignite the recollection in her mind of his face, later, in the car on the way back. She had watched his brow furrow deeply and his lips twist in struggling for answers to all she demanded to know. Finally, with the aid of a fine silver pen and his small notebook, he offered guidance. He tore out a page and handed it over.

Read this.

Casting aside the duvet Caitlyn reached hurriedly for the jacket worn and so wearily dropped to the floor the night before. She rummaged in the pockets to locate the paper scrap and brought it into the light to quote the Professor's sweeping text aloud.

'Palace of the Gods,' she read, 'Rediscovering Newgrange, by Professor Sackimum Brody.'

Time to begin your studies, she heard him again.

Caitlyn dressed quickly.

Gran was already busy in a sizzling kitchen, working to her own enthusiastic version of 'Shake, Rattle and Roll!' as Caitlyn bounded downstairs for the front door.

'Morning, love,' the old woman called cheerfully, 'ready for breakfast?'

'No time, Gran,' Caitlyn replied as she pulled on the door, 'I have to get to the library.'

'The wha'?' Gran's startled face appeared in the kitchen doorway. 'But it's Saturday.'

'I know. Back later.'

'I was making fried bread and liver, enough for two.'

'Ugh, Gran! Love you.'

The walk to the library ordinarily took fifteen minutes. Caitlyn marched it in ten. Pausing just once, at the garden gate to stroke Poppy to a burst of silver sparkle, she strode along her way in search of knowledge. With a quick wave to a somewhat bemused Constable McCarthy, she reached the pedestrian bridge over the main road and followed its rise where it snaked past the ruined monastery of St Canice. Between leaning headstones, she caught sight of Mr York the phantom gravedigger at his tending, and beyond the monastery's glassless windows the shimmering monks where they gathered for prayer under roofless arches. She hurried along to the crest of the bridge and over to feel the downward slope beneath her feet as the route dipped to its journey's end at the edge of what locals still referred to as 'the village'.

Caitlyn made her way past the shops, bank and post office, and swiftly across the village car park, where a ghost encampment of Irish warriors rested around high fires, timelessly ready for battle with spear and sword. Through military ranks and parked cars she raced to gain the steps of the library, chased by skittering October leaves.

After the chilly bustle outside, the library's interior was a welcome oasis of heat and hush. She pushed through the door to cross the foyer, passing before the hawkish, bespectacled gaze of Mrs Brennan, the elderly librarian under whose reign the library adhered to its strict rules of warmth and whispers. Both were policed, ironically, by her frosty stare and the loudest 'SSHHH!' in Ireland. Thankfully, Caitlyn noted, there would be little to test the librarian's patience this morning. The only other patron in the building appeared to be the spirit of Squire Whitehead, once the owner of all land around the village, here always and forever seated in his place in the Reference section, keenly reading as ever the newspaper account of the 1969 Moon landing.

Caitlyn paused just long enough to return Mrs Brennan's curt nod of greeting and walked on. Leaving the main floor, she moved swiftly between shelves as she mapped her shortcut past Fiction A-F, through Sciences, and on to History. Here she narrowed her search, unconsciously leading with a guiding finger as she bypassed World War II, Irish Independence, World War I, Rome, Greece, to finally arrive in the Ancient World. The hunt became alphabetical and ended quickly.

'Brody, Professor Sackimum,' she read past her finger, 'Palace of the Gods: Rediscovering Newgrange.' She slid the book quickly from between its neighbours.

The thick volume weighed heavily in her hand as Caitlyn brought it to a nearby study table and sat. Flicking to the contents page, she rolled her eyes at the chapter listings: Societal Structures of Old - Interpreting Ceremonial Underpinnings.

'Blah blah blah,' Caitlyn heard herself mutter, thumbing the pages towards the centre-bound illustrations.

Nestled between the swathes of text, Brody offered a varied collection of prints and photographs for the reader's consideration. Old black and white pictures detailed the earliest examinations of Newgrange. Men with pipes hanging under ridiculously big moustaches posed in front of the ancient mound with shovels and trowels in hand. A lady shielded by a brimmed hat and parasol looked to the triple swirls carved into the face of a great standing stone. Beneath the picture ran the text: 'Three realms in harmony.'

A thumb-flick brought up the centre pages and the illustration which spread dramatically over both. Caitlyn felt a tingle across her skin as she read of "Lug and Balor - The Fomorian invasion". She examined the scene.

Across the breadth of the illustration, the slopes of Newgrange burned. In an epic battle, warriors arrayed in purest green held fast against the ugly and deformed brutes who were their invading opponents. Black arrows flew over war banners to strike shields engraved with Celtic knots while spears, their tips catching the high sun, flew in reply. Curved swords crossed with blades smoothly gleaming where the furious struggle for Newgrange unfolded.

Towards the bottom of the picture, and brought to the foreground by the artist, the competing kings broke from their ranked armies to face in single combat. At a distance from the main fight, a young ruler bedecked in robes of green and gold uttered his battle cry as his sword cut the air, its carved blade shedding in its wake a trail of blood from the target it had just struck. Directly opposite, the Fomorian King with his golden spear fell back from the blow, his hand cast in agony to one injured eye in his snarling face. Blood seeped between groping fingers, red as the cape through which the wounded King fell.

Caitlyn shuddered at the bloody encounter and turned the page. Her breath caught involuntarily as her gaze fell on the next picture.

Kneeling eagerly at his work, Caitlyn's father smiled broadly at her. Trowel in hand with his sleeves rolled up for work, Dr Barry McCabe looked up from a shallow trench excavated some distance from the Newgrange mound, allowing the light of a summer's day to catch the fullness of his handsome features. No great treasure lay within the trench, not even a gold coin protruded from the dirt to cause him to smile so, but Caitlyn knew why he did. The joy lay in the dig itself and in the ongoing search for answers. She knew because that was the smile he so often brought home when there was nothing in his hands but the clay stains of a long day.

The faces photographed on the opposite page watched her unsmiling. "Dig leaders Professor Sackimum Brody and Professor Alexander Gilbert" posed together before a detailed map of Ireland. Gilbert wrote a buttonhole flower, just as in the picture on Caitlyn's dresser, while Brody peered back at her with folded arms. He looked like a man holding tightly to secrets.

'Let's see what you have to tell me,' Caitlyn whispered, and she began to thumb through the chapters.

The Professor responded from the pages over the course of the morning.

> *At its simplest, the story at the heart of Newgrange is one of good against evil. That in itself is a story told and retold in all societies ancient and modern, a time of peace and plenty is disturbed by a jealous or greedy warrior who brings darkness and want. The coming of the tyrant leads to dreams of a saviour, the dream itself becoming a prophecy whispered to worry the tyrant who nevertheless believes that he can defy its telling and rule forever.*
>
> *So it was with King Balor.*

In a world of plenty, the evil King made his bid for power, overcoming all with his Fomorian army and the assistance of the sorceress Cethlinn, whom he made his Queen in order to sustain his power.

Then, a prophesy. Balor's own grandson, as yet unborn, is proclaimed the hero who will come and end his reign. To deal with this, the King orders his only daughter imprisoned in a high tower. But love overcomes all, and the princess is discovered by a warrior of the Clann Dé Danu – the Tribe of the Goddess Danu.

Lug is born of the union, and a twin sister, Aoife, who possesses her grandmother's gift of magic. Sister and brother forge the Sword of Lug to counter the Spear of Balor. Battle is joined, the evil King over-thrown and order restored. Finally, Newgrange is built to contain the honoured remains of the fallen Dé Danu.

Truth or tale? Scholars today see only an ancient myth. It hardly matters, for what we have in Newgrange is proof in stone that those who built the giant structure believed, and they believed without doubt.

'And I believe it's time for a break,' Caitlyn muttered. She wearily placed the book aside. Missed hours had slipped by, tiring her eyes and stiffening her neck. She flexed tight muscles and wondered if the weight of new knowledge in her brain was at the root of it. She rotated her head slowly to iron out a stubborn kink and watched as the book's pages rolled lazily to the warm air circulating through the library. A turn to her left and the outside world of shoppers and spirits pressed against the window. A slower turn right, that's where the muscle was tightest, and Caitlyn found herself looking along an avenue of shelves towards a bank of computers beyond. An idea formed, and she winced as her neck finally popped free, allowing her to relax blissfully in her chair.

Brody watched from his portrait, silent, arms folded.

Caitlyn brooded. 'You write a lot, but you don't give much away, do you, Professor?' she grumbled to his silence.

She looked to the computers again.

TWENTY-FIVE

Caitlyn typed quickly.

Search: Sackimum Brody.

Professor Sackimum Brody, born 1958, is Dean of the Faculty of Archaeological Remnants and Treasures at Trinity College Dublin. Born the first son of Tristan and Mirabell...

'Blah blah blah,' Caitlyn muttered and sent her fingers clattering once more across the keyboard.

Search: Brody and Newgrange.

She scanned the list of offerings from the thrumming machine: *2004, Professor Sackimum Brody leads an all-new team for the latest excavation at Newgrange. Expectations are high...2005, June, Newgrange yields a wealth of new finds. According to team leader, Professor Sackimum Brody, a vast collection of previously unknown artefacts has begun to emerge from the area around the ancient mound. The Professor described shields and arrowheads as being among the latest discoveries...2006, August, Excavation team refuses to discuss major Newgrange find. Professor*

Brody suggests that a mysterious artefact (pictured) is nothing more than a construction pillar, though witnesses describe 'a golden pole'.

Caitlyn clicked on the story's linked picture. The scene expanded to reveal workmen gathered busily below a covered object which was suspended by straps from a small crane. The workers' arms extended upwards, captured by the photographer in the act of guiding the cargo aloft. In the same instant, however, it looked as though they reached in hopeful adoration and to touch the hoisted object. The subject of their attention was almost totally obscured within padded wraps but at one end the covering sagged to reveal the hint of a sharpened tip to the shining artefact, offering not a golden pole, but a golden spear.

Search: Sackimum Brody and Archaeology.

2007, September, Sackimum Brody receives prestigious honour for Newgrange work...

Caitlyn scoured her mind, hunting through the recesses of her memory as her fingers hovered above the keyboard.

Search: Sackimum Brody, Scars.

2012, October 19th, Eminent scholar may not survive vicious attack. Professor Sackimum Brody was found gravely injured in his offices today after what doctors describe as a life-threatening attack. Apparently assaulted with a bladed weapon, the Professor suffered multiple stab wounds and lacerations. Investigators believe the Professor only survived by using a sword from his own archaeological collection to defend himself during the frenzied attack. Doctors state that if he lives, the Professor will bear the scars of his ordeal for the rest of his life.

With a gasp, Caitlyn re-checked the date, 2012, October 19th.

Her Dad.

The memory surged up rebelliously, hot against her cheeks.

She was six, hauling eagerly at the box lids despite Gran's laughing appeals to 'go easy'. The containers were laid out around the room, and in the excitement for Halloween she didn't know where to begin as she sprang eagerly from one to another. She squealed to the vivid bursts of colour pulled out, the unwrapping of pumpkin lights, ghostly silhouettes and plastic witches, and how this was just half the fun. Gran would get a chair to stand on and call down for the right decoration for the right place, insisting all must be done by the time dad got home. But the doorbell rang early that day, drawing Gran down the hall with a line of paper skeletons in hand, their jointed legs dancing to the call. The policeman took off his cap as soon as the door opened, and something in the motion and his haunted expression caused Gran to release the string she held. The skeletons fell like leaves.

Caitlyn shut off the computer. That was enough for today.

She decided wilfully that she was hungry and distracted herself with choices for lunch - *fried bread and liver, bleh.* With a host of tastier alternatives running through her head she retraced her steps towards the shelves of the Ancient World, easily spying the gap for Brody's book just beyond the halfway point. Fifteen minutes, she calculated, yes, fifteen minutes after replacing the book, she would be tucking into... hmm...a chicken wrap, lotsa mayo, excellent choice.

Danny Joyce almost collided with her as he rounded the end of the shelves.

Caitlyn's cry pierced the sanctified quiet of the library and she threw a hand to her lips too late against it and the enormous measure of embarrassment that followed.

Danny reared back in alarm and he tottered dangerously, almost losing the stack of books in his arms.

'I'm sorry...,' Caitlyn blurted, 'I didn't think anyone else...'

'No...,' he tried, 'I thought no-one...'

'SHHH!' came the librarian's hiss.

Silence. Total, enveloping, eye-to-eye silence.

Ohhh hellll.

Danny's lips moved. 'I was borrowing...,' he

whispered haltingly, and when his voice failed, he lifted the books helpfully.

'I was replacing...,' she responded, and tapped her book. A dread quiet threatened to overtake matters once more and she raced mentally to counter it. 'Ancient Mysteries,' she read quickly from the top book in Danny's stack.

'Oh, yes,' he said and shrugged awkwardly, 'my thing, I suppose. Newgrange?' He gestured to the Brody book.

'After the school trip,' she explained lamely, 'extra research. Bit nerdy, yeah?'

'No,' he said, and blushed at the sincerity of his answer.

The returned silence was less ominous this time.

'Well, I should get going,' she said. She slid the book into its place.

'Oh, yeah, me too,' he said, nodding. He watched her turn to go. 'I was going to get something to eat,' he blurted and held his books as a shield.

Caitlyn paused just long enough to avoid sounding over-eager.

'Sounds good,' she said.

TWENTY-SIX

They chose Dario's by the bridge.

'Heeey, Danny.' The loud and effusive greeting came on a wave of vinegar and sizzling burgers. Behind the counter as they entered, a man in kitchen whites hailed Danny with a salute of one meaty hand. It was Dario, proud owner and operator, who insisted his establishment was a 'diner' and not merely a 'café'. Dario's Diner. Apparently, that sounded more American and so, in Dario's thinking, far more trendy for his young customers. Not that any of the youngsters currently filling booths and tables with their noisy chatter ever chose to go to 'Dario's Diner' or 'the diner'. To them it was just Dario's. They chose Dario's.

'Hey,' Danny called back to the chef as he led Caitlyn to a vacant side booth.

'Your usual, Danny boy?' Dario asked. He vigorously shook hot oil from a fresh basket of nuggets.

'Go for it,' the boy agreed, 'with a cola.'

'And for your girlfriend?'

Danny squirmed.

'I'll take a minute,' Caitlyn said quickly, lifting a menu from its place.

'Lady wants a minute, awriight,' Dario drawled good-naturedly. He went to deliver the nuggets to a table of babbling girls.

'I'm sorry about that,' Danny said.

'Chicken burger, fries, and same as you to drink,' Caitlyn selected, cutting through his discomfort.

Danny smiled and turned to relocate the chef, and Caitlyn caught sight of a large bruise behind his ear. 'Dario. Number thirty-one with a cola, thanks.'

'Lady wants chicken, awriight,' Dario translated and set about his work.

The space between them filled with burbling conversations and hissing grills.

'So,' Danny fumbled, 'how did your visit to Trinity College work out?'

'It was okay,' she said carefully, 'it was...interesting.'

'I'll bet. Will you go there, after school, to study?'

'Probably.'

'I'm sure I'm not supposed to say, "that's great". Y'know, college and study and all, but it is. You're lucky.'

'Will you go?' Caitlyn asked.

He shrugged awkwardly. 'I wasn't the one in my house picked for that,' he admitted. 'I don't know, maybe.'

Dario arrived with a fresh 'Awriiight' and a tray of food. 'Here we go, best in the village, enjoy, tell your friends.'

After he departed, Caitlyn and Danny swapped the misplaced orders with amused smiles. Organised and set, they reached simultaneously to the pair of drinking straws on the table between them. Fingers brushed and Caitlyn whipped her hand back in alarm.

'I forgot,' Danny said, 'you don't like to be touched. I heard that about you.' He scooped up the straws and offered her one.

'It's not...,' she tried to explain, all at once *wanting* to explain, 'it's complicated.'

'That's okay,' he assured her, 'really, no problem.' He placed her straw on the table before her.

'I should say sorry,' Caitlyn said abruptly.

'You don't have to, really.'

'Not for this.'

Danny frowned. 'For what?' he said and watched her carefully as he slugged his drink.

'On the school trip, you were trying to help, and I didn't thank you. I should have.'

'Debbie Walsh was the one in the wrong, not you,' he corrected her.

Caitlyn balled her fists at the mention of the name. 'I don't know why I don't just get her and...I don't know, just...,' she fumed.

'It's never that easy, though, is it?' he said. 'Bullies always know how to pick their moment somehow, when there's no quick answer or a way to fight back.'

'Luke Goslin,' she guessed. 'He beats you.'

Danny shook his head. 'Luke's never laid a hand on me. Lame, isn't it? He doesn't even have to touch me.'

'It's not lame,' Caitlyn replied even as her mind struggled with the information. *Where do the bruises come from?*

'It's something,' he brooded over his fries.

Caitlyn sighed and shook her head. 'Look at us. Why are we letting 'Plebbie' Walsh and 'Puke' Goslin put us off the finest food in Dublin when they're not even here? Let's talk about anything else but them, agreed?'

'Agreed,' Danny replied with a raised glass. He made to bite his burger and paused to allow a smile to cross his lips. ''Plebbie' Walsh, she'd hate that.'

'Maybe I'll say it to her face one day,' Caitlyn was smiling too. She lowered her voice. 'Or maybe I'll just send her this chicken burger. It's awful.'

They laughed together and the sound became familiar and relaxed as it drifted to mix easily with the chorus of others in the diner.

TWENTY-SEVEN

'Okay, my turn,' Caitlyn said. 'Cats or dogs?'

Danny scoffed. 'That's not even a question. Dogs, every time.'

They strolled from the village into a late afternoon chill, the autumnal sun losing its weak power as it sank towards the horizon ahead of them. In place of heat, the reddening orb compensated by offering the couple a last dazzling display of light to make stark the monastery trees, turning brown leaves to gold and drawing sparkling winks from the granite headstones.

'Chocolate,' she suggested next, working hard to ignore the silvery monks who crowded at bare windows to hug themselves childishly and blow exaggerated kisses towards her and Danny. 'Dark or dairy?'

'Dairy,' he replied, oblivious to the scrum of phantom holy men even as they were driven back to their duties by well-aimed clips and swats from the angry abbot. 'You?'

'Oh, eh, the same,' Caitlyn said, holding in the laughter she felt at the chaotic scene. 'Gran likes dark, says "it's good for the oul ticker".'

'You live with your grandmother?'

'Yeah, since Dad died there's just her and me.'

'Superman or Batman?' he challenged.

'Wonder Woman,' she countered.

'Oh, yeah.'

They left the bridge and moved on, tracking the pavement slowly home as the day gave over to filtering twilight. At a sheltered stretch they saw their breath become suddenly visible on the cooling air, though only Caitlyn saw the waiting Constable McCarthy and the sharp salute and cheeky grin he presented as they drew level. Nearby, a pair of spirit women in shawls paused in collecting firewood to nudge one another and point knowingly at the boy and girl.

'Do you live with your parents?' she asked him.

'Yeah,' he said simply, and then quickly, 'New York or Vegas?'

'New York,' she replied, 'in the winter when there's snow in Central Park.'

'Wow,' he was impressed, 'you've thought about that one.'

She nodded. 'And you?'

'Vegas,' he said. 'The best magic shows are there.'

'Not New York?' she asked with a despondent tone.

'Oh, there too, yeah,' he added in a hurry. He looked and found she was smirking, teasing him.

Reassured and entertained, the spirits jabbed one

another and went back to gathering wood for their phantom fires.

A bus lumbered by, outbound from the city. It rumbled past the fence hemming Rosehill before slowing towards the school. The highest windows of the building caught the full and final brilliance of the sun.

'It looks as though the school is on fire,' Caitlyn noted with a laugh.

'Wouldn't that be great?' Danny said as the bus pulled in. 'Dario's or somewhere else?' he asked and looked everywhere but at her.

She read his motions. 'Are you asking...,' she tried carefully, 'I mean, is this...?'

'Truth or dare,' he challenged abruptly.

'Truth,' she said.

'If, if I was to ask, invite, you for lunch again. Would you come?'

'Yes,' she said and without pause this time.

'Oh, no,' Danny replied, his voice filled with dread.

'What?' She rounded on him.

'What?' he spluttered in his panic. 'No, no, not what. *That.*' He pointed. 'Debbie Walsh just got off the bus.'

Together they watched in horror as Debbie Walsh struggled happily onto the pavement with a multitude of shopping bags. Distracted by her purchases, she had not yet begun to look around.

'We'll front it out,' Danny suggested. 'We'll walk right past her and ignore anything she says.'

'We will *not*,' Caitlyn shot back. 'She'll have the whole school after us on Monday if she sees us together.'

The happy shopper moved to the kerb. Her attention was diverted in scanning for a safe moment to cross.

'Thirty seconds,' Danny estimated, 'she'll have us spotted in thirty, twenty-nine...'

'Stop that,' Caitlyn snapped. 'Turn back.' She spun on her heel to lead the way and issued a harsh breath as she came face to face with ghost Danny. The spirit boy looked directly into her face, his sad features longing to be read, his hands reaching up to gesture towards Danny, to silently implore a moment, begging for communication. 'Not now, not now,' Caitlyn whispered desperately, as much against the unfolding crisis as the sad phantom. 'We'll cut across the playing fields.' She made that way and signalled for Danny to follow.

'No,' he cried and reached to stop her. The phantom boy threw horrified hands to his mouth as Caitlyn whipped from Danny's touch, angered and flustered in equal measure. 'Sorry,' he said, 'but look, it's all open ground. She can't miss us if we go that way. Follow me.'

The ghost Danny understood immediately. Urging hands pleaded for her to hurry after his mortal mirror image.

Debbie Walsh skipped across the deserted roadway humming a happy tune.

Danny raced to a spot nearby, dangerously over-grown with brambles and wet nettles. Gingerly, but with practised skill, he clasped two long stems and pulled them aside. A greater part of the bramble growth followed and revealed a gap shorn through the fencing behind. 'Let's go,' he said, indicating with a jerk of his head that she should go first.

Caught between a prickly path and the threat of barbed comments, Caitlyn shot a final glance towards Debbie Walsh and plunged for the break in the fence.

A riot of neglected undergrowth swallowed them up. With the bramble curtain eased carefully back into place as Danny slid through the fence, they stood hidden from the roadway and listened to the busy *clip-clop* of Debbie Walsh's heels approaching on the pavement.

Danny could not help himself. 'It sounds like we're being hunted by a tap-dancing donkey,' he whispered.

The laugh was halfway to Caitlyn's lips before she could clamp a suppressing hand over her mouth. She stabbed Danny with a warning elbow against any further humour.

The clip-clopping halted.

Caitlyn squeezed her fingers tight, cutting off the very breath that might betray their hiding place. Through the shield of foliage, she detected the paper rustling of shopping bags where their owner turned slowly, and with a chill she sensed the enemy's attention coming to rest on the bramble bush.

The vegetation erupted with sound and motion. Startled in the twilight, a blackbird sprang to flight through the leaves to issue its shrill, chattering protest against the dying of the light. Flapping violently into the air, the bird drove crackling bags and rapidly clopping heels ahead of itself.

Caitlyn breathed again, and in the time it took for Debbie Walsh's footsteps to move beyond ear-shot, she examined her surroundings. From the bramble covered gash in the fence a rough path cut between untended ferns and bushes to wend across an unruly landscape. She lost sight of the path after a stretch, but as the land rose farther on, she spotted it once more, curving from the undergrowth to lead to the crumbling side of Rosehill.

So, this was the secret to Danny's after-school vanishing act, she realised. But of course, it struck her all at once in peering from the damaged fence to the route it obscured. 'This is how you do it,' she said aloud, unguarded, and she bit her lip against the revelation, but too late.

His eyes locked on hers momentarily and she saw the same appraising look he had offered her at Newgrange. 'I think she's gone,' he said simply.

'Good,' she said and avoided his gaze by turning towards the fence. The streetlamps across the playing fields twinkled distantly to life as she looked.

'Are you afraid of ghosts?' he asked.

'No. I mean, wait, what?' she spluttered and faced him.

Danny flicked a thumb at the darkening ruin. 'Now that we're here,' he suggested with a wink, 'unless you believe in ghosts.'

'You have no idea,' she scoffed with a grin and stepped towards Rosehill.

TWENTY-EIGHT

Rosehill glowered on the trespassers.

Altered by the oncoming dusk, it hulked on the crest, rearing against the sky with chimneys upraised to offer its darkness and rot to the night. Windows of bottomless gloom paused in envying the far-off city lights to peer disapprovingly on those who avoided snagging branches and clinging ivy to draw ever nearer. In vain the house sent forth a tumbling flight of bats to dissuade them, and from one of its many cold hearths pushed a formless spectre of soot to moan a warning through corridors bleak and dripping.

'Do you hear it?' Danny asked. In the lee of the house, he stopped to peer upwards at the brooding edifice.

'It's just the wind,' she said and made for the collapsed doorway. Though they had approached from an angle unfamiliar to her, Caitlyn quickly regained her bearings to step nimbly across the fallen masonry and enter Rosehill. The broad space opening up on all sides as before was hung with the deepest shrouds of night. Robbed of their daytime colour, the invading roots and ferns stood dimly, seemingly frozen in shock at Caitlyn's entrance at this the very witching hour. Beyond the inky forest, the grand staircase sagged under a terrible weight of shadows lying on it. At the higher end, the shadows rose to become massive drapes concealing what terrors might lurk on the upper floors.

She heard Danny's footsteps behind and his soft whistle for the scene.

'Is this the coolest haunted house in Ireland, or what?' he breathed.

'You think it's haunted?' she asked, her amused smile shining in the dark.

'Oh, yeah. There's no way it's not. It just wouldn't be right for a place like this not to have ghosts.'

'You believe in ghosts, then?' she pressed him.

'Well,' he replied with a shrug, 'not really, not in that way. I like a ghost story, who doesn't? I just mean, if a ghost from a story had to be somewhere, it would be here, wouldn't it? If someone wanted to write a ghost story, it would be here, and the ghosts would be here. I don't know what I mean.'

'I know what you mean,' she assured him and chuckled softly.

'Exactly,' he said pointlessly and added his laughter to hers.

The sound echoed like a memory through the sad chambers of Rosehill.

'I should get home,' she said, and was that a hint of reluctance in her tone?

'Yeah,' he agreed and turned to go. 'I'll show you the way back to the road.'

'I know the way.'

'But my way is much shorter than your...,' he cut himself off sharply, awkwardly. 'Shorter than other paths,' he fumbled.

Even in the dark she saw how he turned his face away.

'Truth or dare,' she said.

He spun to her, and with fearful eyes wide enough to offer pinpricks of weak light.

'I've seen you here,' he admitted quickly, 'but I wasn't watching you, I swear, I wasn't. I've just seen you coming here, that's all, like I do. I'd already be here, and I'd see you on your path. And I'd hide, no wait, hell, not hide, I don't mean that, like some creepy stalker. I'd just clear out, you know, so you wouldn't find me here and think I'm all weird and all.'

'I don't think you're weird,' she said. 'But I could give you a kick for not telling me about the shorter path before.'

She was joking, not angry, he could tell, and he sighed through a faltering smile at that.

'I'm going to be late,' she insisted and made for the doorway.

'You didn't answer my question,' he called after her.

She paused and frowned back at him. 'Which one?'

'Dario's or somewhere else?'

'Somewhere else, definitely,' she said.

'How about here,' he suggested and raised his arms in the darkness.

She mused over the ruined surroundings. 'Fine,' she said. 'Daytime. You bring the food.'

'I'll get takeaway from Dario's,' he promised.

'No!' she protested, but when she looked, she saw he knew how to tease as well.

She left him and his shining smile in the gloom and plunged back along the overgrown path. Picking her way carefully towards the bramble bush, she remained wary of hidden roots and potholes waiting to ensnare misplaced ankles. Only once did she pause, straining briefly to navigate by the distant streetlights beyond the wild flora. Satisfied, she kept her vision towards the guiding lights and set off again, easing through thickening scrub, oblivious to the figure who studied her with keen suspicion amid the branches.

At one with the shadows, the Morrigan watched Caitlyn go.

TWENTY-NINE

Caitlyn reached home at a trot and saw the Professor's car already waiting.

Dr Marcus was behind the wheel, a hand hanging lazily from the open window. The other brought one of Gran's steaming cups to his lips as he watched Caitlyn approach.

'He's inside,' he informed her as he savoured his tea.

Inside meant the parlour, Caitlyn knew as she stepped through the front door, the room Gran reserved for extra special guests. Her voice flowed from there now in an uninterrupted stream of one-sided conversation.

'And so much like her father you wouldn't believe, so curious about things and wanting to learn, her head always in a book, she was in the library all day actually, I expect they had to kick her out though it's not like her to be late when she has to be somewhere.'

'Hi,' Caitlyn said as she looked round the door frame. She saw Professor Brody, politely seated with a cup of tea in his hand and, on a delicate plate perched in his lap, a thick square sandwich, very much untouched.

'Ah, there y'are love,' Gran cooed. 'The Professor's been waiting for you.'

'Sorry, I got caught up with things,' Caitlyn said.

'No need for apologies,' the Professor said graciously, 'your grandmother has been a wonderful hostess.'

Gran beamed. 'Good job I had the shopping done or I'd have had nothing to offer. You haven't touched your sandwich yet, Professor.'

Brody held up his plate for Caitlyn's benefit. 'Sausage and parsnip,' he said, working hard to force his grimace to a grateful smile.

'With mango chutney,' Gran happily reminded him.

The Professor's features were politely tortured.

'You should wrap that for the journey,' Caitlyn said with a helpful wink, 'we're late enough already, aren't we?'

'Splendid plan,' Brody agreed, and he sprang from his seat. 'Mrs McCabe, my fulsome thanks for your hospitality this evening.'

'Aw,' Gran sighed, 'and I had cake.'

'We should get going,' Caitlyn insisted, trying to suppress the urgency in her tone.

'Marmalade tart with a beetroot topping,' Gran offered hopefully.

'Thank you, no,' Brody said, and then, as a mischievous afterthought, 'a slice for Dr Marcus, perhaps.'

'Done,' Gran said with delight and whipped the sandwich away to prepare all.

Minutes later and back at the car, through Marcus's polite protests to Gran for the food parcel she forced into his hands, Caitlyn and the Professor clambered in, waving farewell as the driver hastened to be gone.

'Where to, Professor?' Marcus asked in the mirror.

'The Winter Fort, if you please, Doctor,' Brody replied as he opened his small notebook. He looked briefly to Caitlyn. 'We have a busy night ahead of us.'

'The Winter Fort,' Caitlyn repeated, her mind firing with knowledge, 'the ancient Viking base of Dublin.'

'Very good,' the Professor said, clearly impressed. 'Tell me more.'

Caitlyn searched her memory of learning. 'The Vikings established Dublin around the year 841. The Winter Fort was their first town, built on high ground above the River Liffey and close to the Black Pool, the Dubh Linn, where they moored their boats. The pool lies somewhere under the modern city now.'

Brody smiled. 'You are quite correct.' He dug into his pocket to produce the shattered emerald stone. 'If my research is accurate, the Vikings will provide us with an answer to this shining riddle.'

'What do you think the answer will be?' she asked, watching closely how the gem winked in response to the passing streetlights.

'I'm not sure,' the Professor admitted. 'There are still gaps in my knowledge despite all. I confess I fell asleep at my desk last night searching for clues.'

'Oh, wow,' Marcus exclaimed happily from the front, 'marmalade and beetroot.'

Across the green hue of the stone, Caitlyn and Brody exchanged quizzical glances.

THIRTY

Dr Matthew Remington James worked late.

Alone at his desk he pored with obsessive curiosity over trinkets and shards, the newest artefacts pulled from the earth for his consideration. From the pile of labelled finds, he drew item after item to his desk lamp for closer inspection, willing each to be the final clue he needed. With keen precision he isolated ancient arrowheads from the collection. These he set carefully on his map of the Newgrange dig, and he gasped at how they seemed to point towards a find greater than all the rest.

He was close, so close.

Through the great brilliance he felt within himself, James knew with unshakeable certainty he would succeed in the search. Only he could. A treasure of staggering proportions was yet to be found at Newgrange and it would take a mind as great as he knew his to be to locate it. The evidence before him was undeniable, so many artefacts, uncovered by him at the battle site he had found, not by idiots who settled for rock markings and stone walls.

'Brody,' he whispered bitterly, hardly aware of his own voice as his hands ran across the treasure-strewn map.

The arrowheads, yes, he remembered and picked again at the metal shards. They had been the first find, the first sure indicators he was correct in labouring with shovel and trowel on the hillside. Given up by the wet earth, they had surrendered to the dogged intelligence whissspering in his ears, pushing him towards ever greater discoveries. Discoveries like the crushed helmet and its clay-encrusted artwork that he touched, and the remnants of a shield torn apart by a devastating force, pieced together again by his stag- gering skill. Then, of course, there was also the dagger.

The weapon of strange design and stranger mark- ings passed beneath his fingers, dangerously sharp in hinting at a history he would surely uncover, pointing the way to a treasssure only Dr Matthew Remington James could reveal to the world.

It was so close, as close as the weapon he lifted to play through the lamp light. Though carefully freed from the layers of dirt which had held it underground for so long, the washed blade was still unsettling to look at. It was a dagger made for agonising death and communi- cating the vile curses of its timeless markings. The desk lamp flickered as the blade passed near it. A power surge somewhere within the university, James guessed, but the illusion of mystical power brought a smirk to his lips.

'Show me the way,' he whispered to the blade. He allowed its weight to draw the tip down to the map with the circular image of Newgrange. From there he drew the weapon gently in a random direction, amused by thoughts of his great mind divining through powerful magic. The lamplight danced to the moment.

'Idiots,' James cursed, railing against the campus electricians. He smiled once more at thoughts of what he could do to such fools with his dagger.

The smile dropped away as a sound reached for him. Faint, almost beyond the limits of hearing, it came thinly and from an unknown direction through the office walls. Drawn by curiosity, he set the dagger aside and rose, the weapon's thump on the desk seeming to cause another interruption to the power of the light.

James crossed to the windows and looked through each in turn to survey the deserted university grounds. The night was still, no breath of wind disturbed the trees, and even as his lamp flickered again, the lanterns dotting the cobbled walkways remained bright and true.

The sound came again, closer, and this time distinctly within the building. James walked to his door and pulled it open to peer along the darkened corridor. No lights showed beneath the doors of neighbouring offices. His lazy colleagues had left him alone hours ago. The night pressed heavily on the windowless passage, even more at the far end, and he stared harder there, where the shadows seemed somehow thicker than the darkest night should allow.

The sound came again, this time clearer, unhindered by locked doors, and his senses identified at once from the heart of darkness the soft weeping of a woman.

She rose in deepest black from the night. Born of the gloom, the Banshee seeped from it with no more sound than the crystal keening she issued and followed her own voice the way it led towards Dr James.

His features drew rigid with fear and the Doctor fell back, hands pressed out in voiceless denial of that which approached. Beneath a prickling scalp his mind shrieked as the unbelievable became undeniable and he watched the gliding advance of the woman between the walls of the corridor. To the border of light and dark she came, and faceless beneath cascading hair but for a sliver of parting as her voice continued its tortured lament. Mesmerised, James saw in the parting a single eye, moist with cruelty and swimming with death.

The desk lamp burst to shards, a victim of the invading dark.

The Doctor retreated blindly, but his leaden steps were insufficient to outpace the floating nightmare. An understanding deeper than mortal learning demanded a shrill scream against the vision, but his lips quivered to a perfect O of horror and remained helplessly mute. He could only watch as the Banshee pressed through the doorway to reach for him with hands pale and clawing.

'You're not real,' he heard a voice protest and realised it was his own, dried up to a croaking whisper. 'You're not real.'

She wept in mourning for his lack of belief.

The sound sent him reeling further and his legs struck hard against the desk. He tottered as pain shot to sting his frozen mind. In panic he cast out a hand to steady himself and found sudden hope in the handle of the dagger. He snatched desperately for it and moved to level the blade against the Banshee.

Her furious reactions were faster. The Fomorian knife was struck aside, the blow of metal against metal creating a shower of sparks to light the pallid shape of her cheek and she drove him back against the wall. The edge of her blade to his throat held James upright as his legs at last failed him.

'You're not real,' he wept pitifully. 'You're not real.'

'I am real and cruel as the night,' she assured him with cold breath against his lips.

'Please,' he whimpered, 'I'll do anything you ask.'

'You must choose,' she sighed from the veil of her hair. 'Choose to dig or choose to die.'

He blinked at the words and struggled frantically to perceive what sense they contained. 'Dig,' he gagged at the prompting of her knife, preferring that word over the other.

Her hand rose to reveal a parchment scrap, a discoloured page rolled and bound with frayed string. She pressed it to him.

'Dig here,' she whispered and released the page to his grip.

The Banshee retreated, holding the knife edge to his throat and afterwards its tip, and after that her single terrible, unblinking glare to keep him in his place. She poured away with receding shadows, her anguished lament slowly fading to a dreadful echo until only the dark corridor remained.

Unsupported, the Doctor's legs buckled under a combined weight of terror and belief. He tumbled to the floor and buried his head in his arms against the weeping he could still hear, pathetic sobs he recognised bitterly as his own.

THIRTY-ONE

Caitlyn watched the nightscape change.

Through the window, she peered in silence on the hypnotic pulse of streetlights, their regular beat created by the car's steady progress. Oncoming vehicles flared brilliantly through her vision and sped on like comets breaking from the galaxy of lights that was the city ahead. The happy homes of the mortal world, arrayed in uniform ranks along the route, sparkled with illuminated life and the flicker of television screens.

The light pulse abruptly skipped a beat as she watched, losing a single spark to a pool of black sky, and Caitlyn guessed at a blown bulb in need of replacing. The rhythm began again but only to be interrupted by another dead light, and just as quickly by another, bringing her from her lazy reverie. With a frown she looked through the windscreen at the thread of lights but saw no more breaks in the line of sodium dots coursing ahead. Traffic signals jumped from green to amber to red and Dr Marcus slowed the car to a stop.

With the vehicle idling at a junction, Caitlyn divided her time between looking at the cars zipping from left and right and the routes on either side. She frowned once more as she saw, far off to the right, another lamp flicker and fade, and then, inexplicably another and this one in precise time to the extinguishing of its opposite number. Taking up the pattern the lights began to vanish in pairs, creating a two-by-two march of darkness ever closer towards the car.

Caitlyn turned to Professor Brody where he sat, engaged with scribbling pen and notebook. Opening her mouth to warn him of the bizarre occurrence rapidly approaching, she was struck dumb to find that the same electric outage was accelerating towards them from the left.

The Professor, drawn up from study by her movements, took in the sight and was pleased.

'Good,' he said, 'we're crossing over.' He gestured to the road before them with his pen.

Caitlyn looked as directed and found the way there also plunging steadily to black, until the only lights remaining were those of cars waiting at the traffic signal. A flash of green pulled the vehicles forward and their headlights surged to a blinding intensity until, and in an instant, they burst and vanished.

The Wraith shuddered over the darkened ghost road and its tyres fought momentarily for purchase on a surface altered from smooth to rough. The head-lights weaved to reveal trees where houses once stood, while the previously dazzling cityscape had receded to a pinprick scattering of weak embers.

One of the lonely beacons apparently stronger than the others caught Caitlyn's gaze. She quickly perceived this to be an optical trick caused by its proximity to the car and as the vehicle swept on, she saw a lantern's glow and by it the black-toothed smile of a dishevelled peasant with one hitchhiking thumb cocked hopefully to the sky.

A parting in the trees further on revealed a fresh and violent luminescence. Set back from the road, a fire blazed in a clearing to warm the metal of a cauldron. Around all, bedraggled witches danced with abandon and hailed the spectral night. Some turned at the passing of the car and with rolling hands invited the travellers to join them.

'I shouldn't care to break down on this stretch of road,' the Professor admitted.

The car braked violently.

Thrown roughly forward, Caitlyn and the Professor looked over the seat-back to a scene of confusion outside. In the full glare of the car's lamps, two caped figures hurried to regain control of a handcart they had upended in the road. Frantically they worked to recover a crudely wrapped and irregular form which had tumbled free in the accident. With desperate efforts they struggled to replace the uncooperative shape on the cart.

Dr Marcus cursed under his breath. 'Damned body snatchers.'

With a final heave, the phantom figures restored order to their grim business. Pulling and pushing, they hauled their cargo quickly away from exposing head-lights, and Caitlyn watched in stunned fascination as they vanished between the trees.

A thunderous clamour rose on the car's opposite side. Caitlyn spun there in time to see a pair of horses galloping into view. These leaders of a team of four drew a juddering coach which overtook the car to the bellowed urgings of the driver and the cracking of his whip. In a flurry of spinning wheels, the coach bounced dangerously on, offering a brief glimpse of the hitchhiking peasant where he clung secretly to the back of the speeding vehicle with his lantern swinging madly. His crooked smile of delight was lost to swallowing night.

Dr Marcus eased the car forward, leaving the witches to peer hungrily after it from the roadside.

'Why do you see all of this?' Caitlyn asked the Professor abruptly. 'You said you weren't born with the gift like me.' She caught a nervous glance from Marcus in the mirror.

The Professor grimaced, stung by the pain of remembering. 'No, I wasn't,' he said, 'I gained it later.'

'Nine years ago,' she prompted him gently, 'on October 19th.'

His smile was grim but impressed for her learning and as he went where she led, it tightened against unwelcome memories.

'I was already aware of Queen Cethlinn and her ancient realm by that date,' he recalled. 'Your father brought that terrible knowledge up from the earth to me with Balor's spear six years before. Since then, and with the help of Professor Gilbert, I had worked to hide all traces of the excavation and its dangerous artefacts. We thought we had done enough.' The Professor faltered as events replayed in his mind. 'It was not nearly enough. I was at my desk when the call came about you father, and I realised then Cethlinn would never be deterred by the efforts of three mortal men. But the call prepared me, and when she sent her assassin, I was ready.'

'The Pooka,' Caitlyn whispered.

'We fought,' Brody said, nodding as he clenched his scarred hands, 'and we bled. Blood mixed with blood and that was the beginning. When I came to in my shattered room, the Pooka had gone and in his place, I saw those who came to help me, and the spirits walking among them.'

'It takes some getting used to, doesn't it?' she said.

'At first I thought I was dying,' he confessed, 'then I thought I had gone mad. Then I saw Laetitia. That was a beautiful madness.'

The Professor smiled again beneath faraway eyes.

'There's the bridge, Professor,' Marcus announced.

'Splendid,' Brody said, self-consciously breaking from his dream, 'we're almost there.' He gestured for Caitlyn's benefit to where the headlights caught a rough wooden span offering passage across black waters.

Caitlyn examined the structure of rope and beam warily. 'Will that hold us up?'

'Oh, I expect so,' the Professor said, 'solid Viking engineering, perfectly sound.'

'Vikings don't drive cars,' she warned him.

The Wraith's wheels passed the first timbers and the bridge groaned alarmingly beneath the vehicle's weight. The night mist filled with squeals of tortured wood and creaking ropes, and the bridge swayed off kilter on its posts. Somewhere unseen, a portion of the span detached violently and plunged splashing to the hungry waters. The noise was answered by the car's grinding gears as it worked all the harder for the opposite bank. Splinters flew from spinning tyres and engine's roar.

After what seemed an eternity, passengers sighed as they sensed firmer ground and the smoother roll of the vehicle.

'Perfectly sound,' the Professor concluded again.

The car eased to a halt amid the mist. 'This is as far as I can go,' Marcus said. 'I don't want the car covered with arrows.'

Brody agreed with a nod and scanned the night, probing the swirling fog for a bearing. 'Do you see it?' he asked of Caitlyn.

'If you mean fog, yes, I see it,' she replied dryly.

'Follow me,' he instructed. He popped his door gently.

Stepping into the night, Caitlyn shivered as the mist rushed to test her skin with icy caresses. Smoky tendrils licked at her face and hands as though to sample her, a foreign presence in this uninviting place. Distracted, she peered in search of Brody.

'Professor?' she called out. The word froze in a rolling plume and was answered by frogs croaking at the hidden river.

'This way,' he called back at last, his voice made miles away by an impish trick of the blanketing murk. She moved to join his waving silhouette.

'What are we looking for?' she asked as they trudged forward.

'That.' He pointed to a slow parting in the smoky veil.

They came into the shadow of a broad gate of stout wooden trunks, flanked by a pair of watchtowers. Caitlyn looked in wonder at the barrier and along high walls running from the spot to follow the line of the hill rising behind, an encircling shield for those within. Burning torches inside the enclosure revealed tracks snaking between straw-roofed dwellings which gathered themselves about a central structure, long and bigger than the rest. This dominating building sat at the very heart of the fortress.

'Do we knock?' Caitlyn whispered.

Her low tone was met with a similar whispering on the air, and her head jerked towards it in time to see an arrow, fired from the Winter Fort to bury itself in the mud at her feet.

'Who approaches?' a gruff and threatening voice demanded.

The Professor stepped forward with his hands held visibly from his sides.

'Sackimum Brody and a fellow traveller from the mortal realm,' he declared officiously.

The Professor's announcement became the subject of muttered exchanges along the high walls.

'What do you want here, Brody?' the same voice demanded.

'I seek an audience with your leader,' Brody explained. 'I have come to see Ivar the Boneless.'

THIRTY-TWO

'Listen carefully. There are some crucial ground rules here.'

Brody's instruction to Caitlyn was an urgent whisper as they walked behind their burly guard and to the seats he indicated with a gruff thrust of his axe. The Professor worked to avoid eye contact with the Viking and his fearsome brothers assembled in the great hall. On all sides, in half-shadows created by a crackling fire pit, the cruel, bearded features of a Viking horde lurked behind circular shields and watched.

'What did you say?' Caitlyn whispered. The volume of her words was enough to cause an unsettling ripple of shields.

'There are some things you must be mindful of here,' the Professor warned softly once more. He shifted closer to her and pointed secretly through the flames to a raised and empty platform. 'King Ivar doesn't like me very much, so remain polite at all times, be respectful. Don't call him 'Boneless' or you'll be headless. And above all else don't utter the name of Brian Boru.'

'Brian Boru?' Caitlyn's brow furrowed.

'Please!' Brody whispered urgently. 'Don't say his name!'

'Why not?'

'Do you really have to ask?'

Caitlyn's mind worked quickly and fixed on the truth. 'He was High King of Ireland. He beat the Vikings for control of Dublin, but he died in battle as the Vikings retreated.'

'In 1014,' Brody added. 'Viking power never recovered. They do not really accept that fact of history, so for heaven's sake, avoid the subject.'

Caitlyn stored the information as another question formed itself. 'Why doesn't Ivar the Boneless like you?'

'BRRRROOOODY!' The roar came from without and with power enough to rattle the shield wall.

The fire-lit procession swept into the hall, feet thundering over the boards in marching grandly towards the raised platform. An advance guard of four men led the way, fully armed with axe and spear, and prepared the path for those who followed. Four more Vikings, armed likewise, came on and carried on broad shoulders twin longboat oars, each rigged and strapped to contain between them a throne of heavy beams. Seated there in war cape and helmet, King Ivar the Boneless was conveyed above the heads of his warriors, his gaze roving over all from an unruly mane and beard.

In his elevated place, the bearded monarch glared closely at his guests, maintaining his manic gaze as he passed. The procession turned to the platform and the throne came to rest with a loud thud.

The King shifted in his seat, using his mighty arms to settle crippled legs. Thus prepared, Ivar accepted a huge wooden tankard brought to him and he supped deeply, staring all the while at his guests as ale ran in streams to soak his beard.

The Professor braced himself and rose.

'Your Majesty,' he greeted his host.

Ivar released a monstrous belch in return and the shield wall clattered with laughter.

'Why do you intrude on my home, Brody?' The King demanded for all to hear. 'Why, grave burglar, thief of skulls?' He shot a fiery glance at Caitlyn. 'Does he still keep my bones in a glass case?' As an afterthought he pointed at her and looked across his men. 'Who is this girl?'

'My name is Caitlyn McCabe,' she said defiantly for herself, drawing again the King's furious attention across the flames.

'Careful,' Brody whispered over his shoulder. 'Ground rules.'

Ivar offered a dismissive wave for Caitlyn and turned once more to the Professor. 'Speak to me, Brody. Share with us all your tales of the Pooka and Queen Cethlinn.'

'Your spies keep you well informed,' the Professor congratulated him.

'Yes, they do,' the King sneered. 'The Vikings will not be caught by surprise when that wretch of the third realm advances.' He accepted the roared assent of his men.

'Well, that's a relief,' Brody played along, 'my fears for your collection are quite unfounded, then.'

Ivar's brow arched with suspicion. 'What are you babbling about, mud digger? I didn't invite you into the Winter Fort to offer riddles. Speak clearly and without tricks.'

'I speak of your collection of crowns,' the Professor said with a bow. 'If you know of the Pooka's actions last night, you know also that the purpose of his attack was the theft of a crown. It was a crown of gold, ornately decorated and topped with a rough emerald. From my research I could find only one such headpiece. But if you insist it is safe, then so be it.'

'A crown, eh?' Ivar said quizzically. His eyes narrowed mischievously. 'And whose crown might that be?'

Brody was too clever for the trap. 'The crown of your enemy, gained in battle long ago and held by you ever since.'

The King feigned confusion, not ready to end his game just yet. 'I have many enemies,' he said with a smirk and a scratch of beard, 'just as I have many crowns in my collection. Please be clearer.'

Caitlyn rolled her eyes.

Brody selected his words carefully. 'There is one enemy who stands above all others in your history, your Majesty. Many faced him. They sit here with you as a result. Such was his perceived greatness in life that his crown was set with the remains of the emerald stone from the spear of old King Balor. No king ever had such an honour before, or since.'

'Who was this mighty warrior king?' Ivar mused impishly, and he looked to the faces of the Vikings as though for an answer as they chuckled.

Brody struggled to continue.

Caitlyn lost her patience. She jumped to her feet and glared at Ivar through the fire. 'It was Brian Boru,' she declared boldly, 'there, I said it, Brian Boru.' The shield wall thundered its furious objection and pressed closer until she spun towards it. 'Stop that!' she barked and, amazingly, the noise subsided to confused silence. She rounded on the King again, ignoring Brody's horrified look on the way. 'The Professor believes the Pooka stole Brian Boru's crown last night to get the emerald stone from it. We don't know for sure, and we don't know why, only that it is part of some plan to harm the mortal and spirit worlds. The only way to know anything for certain is to check if the crown is gone from your collection here in the Winter Fort.' She glanced at Brody as she resumed her seat. 'Is that right?'

'Precisely,' the Professor confirmed with a gasp.

'Good,' Caitlyn folded her arms and stared at Ivar. 'We haven't got time for games.'

Ivar glared back. His features twisted over gritted teeth and he blinked with murderous hate for that name uttered in his presence, and no fewer than three times! The sinews of his neck rose dangerously, and enraged muscles tightened to gnarl fingers into strangling claws. The tankard in his fierce grip shattered and cast its contents as an eruption onto his face and beard. Through tears of ale, Ivar grinned, and the grin gave way to chuckling, and from there to a raucous laughter that shattered the oppressive mood in the hall.

'This one has the spirit of a shield maiden,' the King declared in awe, and the assembly rumbled in agreement. 'Why, Brody, she should lead and you should follow.' The Vikings burst to laughter and hammered their weapons on shields.

'Your Majesty,' Brody fought to be heard above the clamour, 'time is of the essence. If I am right, the other half of the emerald is now in danger.'

Suppressing his laughter and waving for silence, Ivar fixed on Brody. 'You wish to see my collection?'

'I humbly request it,' Brody replied.

'No.'

'But, King Ivar,' Brody protested.

Ivar ignored him in favour of his other guest.

'Do you wish to view my collection, young Caitlyn McCabe?'

She rose. 'I do, your Majesty.'

Ivar flung back his head, driven to laughter once again. 'So be it. Bring torches, escort our guests, throw back the curtain and behold our Viking treasures.'

Burning torches were hurriedly lit from the fire while Ivar's bearers hoisted their royal leader and marched to a drumbeat of fists on the arms of his throne.

The farthest reach of the great hall was gained and there the flickering torches revealed a long curtain of animal hide draped from ceiling to floor to divide one corner of the building from the rest. At a signal from Ivar, the barrier was swept aside, and the light thrust forth to illuminate a table long and broad. Upon it rested a collection of rounded mounds beneath silk coverings, some larger, some smaller, with one taller than all the rest.

'Well done,' the Professor whispered to Caitlyn.

'Behold,' King Ivar announced dramatically and drew a hand over the first mound. The silk covering was drawn off. Caitlyn felt a surge of alarm for a skull which retained the wispy remnants of a beard and bore a crown of thin spikes. 'King Brega,' Ivar announced to the gathering and the Vikings growled their appreciation. He gestured once again, and a further covering was lifted. A crowned skull with missing teeth offered its death grin to all. 'King Donal.' Once more a waved hand, once more a lifted covering, this from the tallest mound. A bony dome grimaced from beneath the pointed headdress of a churchman. 'Bishop Lorcan,' Ivar boomed, and the Vikings laughed uproariously. 'And at last,' the King said, with a pause to allow for rising anticipation, 'King Brian Boru.'

The covering was whipped from the skeleton mound, revealing the late King's tight grimace and sightless stare, and the polished dome of his head made naked by the absence of his kingly crown.

Ivar's howl was that of a wounded beast. Its agonising power sent him reeling back in his throne and forward over his dead legs. The sound caused torches to flutter and the ranked shields to retreat a step. Speechless in his rage, the King clawed all about for the thief, for a weapon, for revenge. The hall shook to the power of his fury.

'Your Majesty,' Brody called to him through his grief, 'King Ivar. You must listen to me.'

'Who has done this?' Ivar bellowed at his warriors. 'I want him found. I want his skin! I want his head for my collection! I want him tied to a mooring post for rising tides and a million crabs!' With each instruction, a massive fist beat on crippled legs.

'Please listen,' Brody implored. 'I know who did this, and I will give him to you if you help me.'

Ivar fought to suppress his boiling anger. 'You know who is responsible? Tell me, Brody. I demand it.'

'I will, I give you my word. But you must help me, and time is short. Give me ten warriors to prevent another theft that is yet to happen. After that, and when I have questioned the crown thief, you can have him. I give you my word.'

Ivar looked to Caitlyn for her confirmation.

'I'll make sure,' she promised.

'You will have *twenty* men,' Ivar proclaimed over bunched fists and his Vikings roared in agreement. 'Name the time and place, Brody.'

'The time is now,' Brody said to the gathering. 'The place is the History Museum.'

THIRTY-THREE

Through the chaos of the Winter Fort, Caitlyn and the Professor hurried back to the car.

'I only hope we're not too late,' Brody said as he weaved his way through Vikings who charged to obey the orders of their King. Phantom chickens squawked and flapped in protest amid the madness while ghostly pigs squealed their own alarms through the din of a settlement called to arms.

'Too late for what?' Caitlyn demanded as they passed once again through the huge gates and sought through the mist for Marcus.

Brody paused to catch his breath as he continued to probe the fog.

'Until just now I merely had suspicions of the Pooka's true intentions,' he explained. 'The stealing of a crown meant nothing, a puzzle to be solved.' He dug into his pocket for the precious stone. 'But the emerald stone was the clue. If the crown was Brian Boru's, the emerald was from the spear of Balor, and that is what the Pooka sought, not the crown itself. He failed last night, so he will surely try for the other half of the stone tonight. There's Marcus.'

'At the museum,' Caitlyn added to the Professor's deductions.

'Precisely,' Brody said. Ushering Caitlyn towards the vehicle, he addressed Dr Marcus. 'Directly to the museum, and don't forget, Marcus, there are no speed limits in the spirit realm.'

Caitlyn leapt into her seat behind the Professor and, as the car set off, she watched him consider the emerald in his hand.

'What's wrong, Professor?' she asked.

Brody smiled sadly. 'My life has been dedicated to uncovering treasures,' he said, 'yet I am forced again and again to hide the greatest of them. I have to find a good hiding place for this, another secret to keep.'

'Why does Queen Cethlinn want it?' Caitlyn asked.

'That part of the puzzle remains,' Brody admitted.

৯৯ ৯৯ ৯৯

The Wraith gained the gates of the History Museum in a shrieking skid of brakes.

Caitlyn breathed a sigh of relief at the end of the breakneck journey from spirit realm to mortal city and she stepped gratefully to the kerb. She screwed up her face against a foul cloud of burned rubber rising past a hissing engine.

'Well done, Marcus,' the Professor said. He hastily consulted his pocket watch. 'Position yourself quickly to the rear. You can expect to see Ivar's men arriving shortly.'

'Will do, Professor,' Marcus responded. He sent the car into a sliding departure.

Brody strode towards the museum, fishing into his pocket as he went. He produced a large key which slipped easily into the gate lock and turned with an efficient click. He spied Caitlyn's inquiring look. 'A perk of my position,' he said. 'I supplied most of the best artefacts in here.'

He led the way, crossing the short path to the museum doors and beyond by use of the same key, until they stood in the dark and hushed lobby of the museum.

'Where are we going?' Caitlyn asked, her voice automatically dropping to match the pressing quiet of the empty building.

By way of answer, Brody took a short step to one side to reach a display of information pamphlets by the reception desk. He plucked a booklet free and thrust it to her. 'Page fifteen,' he offered helpfully and moved stealthily on.

Caitlyn followed, thumbing quickly to the appropriate page. She did her best in the dim light to perceive the text.

'The Chronicles of Ireland,' she read aloud, recalling at once the bejewelled volume bound in elk hide in Brody's office.

'One of a pair,' Brody whispered in reminding her. He proceeded cautiously, leading with his walking-stick as he checked every corner, every suspicious shadow until they reached a broad staircase coursing up. 'Examine the picture.'

Caitlyn peered hard, tilting the brochure this way and that to capture what light was available. The revealed picture showed the museum's copy of the Chronicles in its glass display, tiny bulbs arranged to draw out the glory of the many jewels clustered about the large central stone of deepest green.

'The other half of Balor's emerald,' she gasped.

'One floor up, in the Early Christian exhibition,' Brody added as he proceeded to the stairs.

They crept through the darkened museum, nimbly avoiding shafts of moonlight which angled to touch polished floors. With softened footsteps on the wooden boards, they slid behind display cases and pillars to reach the gallery dedicated to an exhibition of ancient texts.

They heard the thief already at work as they entered.

Standing by the case containing the Chronicles, the black form was made a deeper silhouette by the tiny spotlights of the display. As Caitlyn and the Professor craned to see, a hand passed into the light and touched the case, centimetres from the sparkling emerald, and traced a perfect circle on the glass with a razor-like fingernail. The hand withdrew and the palm turned uppermost to receive the cleanly cut panel that fell away. Fingers snaked eagerly to prise the emerald from its setting.

Brody stepped from hiding and slid his cane sword free.

'That's far enough, Pooka,' he ordered sternly.

The Morrigan turned her smirking features to him.

'Hello, Professor,' the warrior said and smiled at the paling of his face. Her hand slipped to deposit the emerald into a belt bag and travelled on to rest on her sword. With heightened senses her attention was drawn from Brody and she took a step to the left, eyeing past him to the doorway and the sight of Caitlyn there. 'Caitlyn McCabe,' she said, her voice dripping with menace as she examined the girl's face deeply. 'Who *are* you?'

The question was a diversion. The Morrigan's arm shot forward with lightning speed. Fingers holding the circle of glass released it spinning onto the air. The projectile sang across the space of the gallery and, a mere second after Caitlyn ducked, it exploded against the doorframe where her head had been.

Brody slashed furiously at the air to divert the Morrigan. 'Give me the stone,' he demanded.

The Morrigan examined his weapon and laughed softly. 'You're not going to stop me with that,' she mocked him and drew her broadsword from its sheath to cut a moonlight beam.

'The point is not to stop you,' the Professor informed her, grateful to hear at last the thunder of running feet in the corridors about. 'I just wanted to delay you.'

The Vikings spilled into the gallery from all sides, shields raised instantly to block all exits. Swords and axes extended dangerously.

Unperturbed, the Morrigan calmly assessed Brody and the ranked warriors. 'I count twenty-one,' she said. 'Seven each for each of me.' The Morrigan winked malevolently at Caitlyn. 'Watch this,' she commanded.

'Oh no,' Brody despaired.

Caitlyn looked on as the warrior woman stepped back, sword ready, and in a moment appeared to shimmer unnaturally beneath the spotlights. Caitlyn blinked against it, her brain addled and seeking in vain for explanation as the Morrigan became two, and in another shimmering instant, three versions of herself. Three warriors stood back-to-back, offering three swords to her enemies.

'Let's go,' said the Morrigans freed by the power of the goddess.

The Vikings roared into their charge.

Battle was joined in an echoing peal of blades

through the room. The Morrigan fought on all sides at once, equally determined, and lethal in all directions. Viking swords were met and parried fiercely, shields battered aside, and the first phantom warrior fell victim to her skills.

Caitlyn watched as a Viking, run through by a Morrigan thrust, staggered under the blow and toppled, becoming in his fall a vapour which faded so rapidly that mere tendrils of smoke struck the floor. The same held for the next victim. Blasted to the wall by a savage strike, the Viking vanished in an instant and was gone to the great beyond in wisps of spectral mist twisting in the moonlight.

The Morrigan howled with unrestrained joy through the heat of battle and for the weapons arrayed against her, and her cry was joined by the shrieks of her sisters as they continued to strike all around. Swords cleaved, axes shattered, shields were sundered by her power. Another Viking was struck, the cut passing effortlessly through him to catch the display case. Glass exploded to splinters of flickering light and the precious contents plunged to the floor, the ancient book splaying open as it was buried in the ruin.

Slowly but steadily, the Morrigan beat a path from the gallery, sweeping the remnants of her enemy ahead and making way for her twin allies to follow. The Vikings fell, phantom after phantom, in the drive and pursuit, fighting to the last but vainly to prevent the thief's escape. With a bare handful of warriors remaining, the Morrigan broke the ranks and gained the stairs, the lead fighter leaping to the marble balustrade to scorn her enemies. She cast a triumphant smile to Professor Brody. And, at the last, as the Morrigan re-sheathed her sword, and eased backwards, still protected by her 'others', she saved a final gaze for Caitlyn. Stepping into space, she blew a poisoned kiss and plummeted, followed rapidly by one and then the last Morrigan.

'No,' Brody cried, and he raced for the stairs. He peered into the dim space below in search of the Morrigans, catching sight of motion at the foot of the stairs. The figure there, in the act of mounting the steps, looked up and the face of Dr Marcus was revealed by the moonlight.

'Which way did she go?' Brody demanded frantically.

Marcus cast up his hands in confusion. 'I saw no-one.'

ஃ ஃ ஃ

Brody worked gingerly to retrieve the precious Chronicles from the mound of glass and wood. Thankfully, the damage to the artefact was limited but he sighed forlornly on the vacant space so recently occupied by the emerald stone. Tracing his fingers over the blank cover, he felt the weight of Caitlyn's stare at his back.

'Questions,' he guessed, rising to face her. 'She is called the Morrigan. An ancient warrior, a goddess of war, she is drawn to battle, any battle, to satisfy her lust for fighting. The Morrigan is loyal to none but herself, a mercenary who joins with whoever is offering the best opportunity for conflict and the chance to use her unique talent. Clearly she is working for Cethlinn in expectation of a battle to come.'

'She knew my name,' Caitlyn said and met the Professor's inquiring look. 'Why did she know my name?'

Brody shrugged as he moved the book to safety. 'A mortal newly arrived in the spirit world, a girl with the gift of sight, you were bound to come to attention quickly.'

'She tried to kill me,' Caitlyn added, noting how her reasoning unsettled the Professor.

Again, he affected a shrug. 'Queen Cethlinn is clearly taking no chances when she is so close to her goal. Anyone not on her side is a threat, you included.' He walked away, carrying the treasure to another gallery.

Caitlyn watched him go and was left with the memory of words so recently spoken. 'Another secret to keep,' she repeated, wondering just how many of his own Brody possessed.

THIRTY-FOUR

'Directly to Hell, if you please, Marcus,' the Professor said from the back seat.

'What?' Caitlyn said with alarm. She was thrown back as the car pulled from the kerb.

Brushing speckles of glass from his trousers, the Professor reached to produce a map from his pocket. He tapped a guiding finger on the black and white reproduction of old Dublin. 'Hell,' he repeated and shifted in his seat to face her. 'The old city had many notorious districts in its history, a handful of which survive in the spirit realm, just like the Winter Fort. These were neighbourhoods reserved for Dublin's poorest inhabitants, and more than a few desperate villains. The most infamous of the districts is a war-ren of alleyways and dwellings so grim that Dubliners long ago named it Hell.' He grinned and handed the map to Caitlyn. 'Don't worry, we won't find Lucifer there, though I do think he'd like it.'

Caitlyn studied the map, noting the swirling artistry of the date imprinted at the top, 1652. She examined the multitude of curving, intersecting lines of the city which splayed out in a web of roads and laneways to connect with bridges spanning the Liffey. The river's natural path to the sea appeared as a sensible straight line in comparison to the disordered workings of the city's streetscape. Routes tumbled and coiled to the edges of the map, and in a bottom corner, Caitlyn saw how they led to an even more chaotic knot of streets, over which the same artistic hand had traced the single word: Hell.

'What will we find in Hell?' she asked, and the question sounded ridiculous to her.

Brody peered out at the city lights flashing past. 'After the night's excitement we still seek the one spirit who can best explain things.'

'Buck Whaley,' Caitlyn deduced.

'Precisely. Since the events at the Half Moon Inn, he has gone into hiding while the spirit realm remains in tumult over the appearance of the Pooka. I was forced to begin a wide search for him, employing individuals who have helped me in the past. This evening, I received word from two of them, a pirate with knowledge and a blind man who sees more than anyone in this city.' He caught Caitlyn's confused frown and smiled. 'We go in search of Zozimus and Zekerman.'

The drive, more sedate than the earlier charge for the museum, brought the car in short time to the western edge of the old city, there to pass through ever narrowing streets until the vehicle coursed along with barely a space between the mirrors and the crowding walls. Marcus was expert at the wheel and carried his passengers safely to their destination, braking softly in a blank and unlit courtyard.

The space, more a pit than a functional space, was devoid of all features save two. There was the narrow access by which the travellers had arrived while an even tighter alleyway lay directly ahead. Hung above this grim passage was a crude sign in chipped wood bearing a single word, 'Hell'. Above this an etched representation of the Devil, complete with horns and pointed beard, grinned on the visitors.

'On we go,' the Professor announced confidently. He exited, his walking-stick clicking on the cobbles.

They proceeded to the swift rhythm of the stick into the twisting darkness, moving alley to alley on a path too meandering to commit to memory. Steps down, sharp corners, steps up, all came so rapidly upon each other as to confuse the senses, though the Professor led as one at ease with his surroundings, never once requiring a pause for bearings, nor to ask directions of the many inky figures who watched and whispered in the surrounding recesses.

Another set of steps emerged from the gloom, this one rising to a sweeping bend. When followed, the path gave exit to a vast and central area at the heart of the neighbourhood. Caitlyn followed Brody into a chaos of dwellings in seeming competition with one another for the limited area available. Not an inch of space could be glimpsed between the structures, and barely a patch of sky showed where the rooftops leaned precariously together over the streets below. In those streets, the ragged inhabitants moved quickly and furtively as though in fear of discovery. Those who did not seek the shadows maintained a constant watch over shoulders along their paths, changing direction sharply to avoid the new arrivals.

'Where to now?' Caitlyn asked, scanning the area with dread.

'We need go no further,' the Professor reassured her, 'we'd never find our men in this maze, anyhow. No, they will come to us.'

By way of proof, the Professor stretched forth his walking-stick and offered three crisp strikes of the tip to the pavement. After a brief silence he repeated the action, *tap tap tap* against the stone, and waited another short period before once again *tap tap tapping*.

Tap tap tap, came the distant response.

'Was that an echo?' Caitlyn asked.

The Professor shook his head. 'That,' he said, 'is Zozimus.'

A blind man in ragged clothes advanced along the middle of the street. *Tap tap tap* came the striking of the stick he held in one hand, while from the other, a long leash trailed to the neck of a slavering hound which paced its master's shuffling progress.

Tap tap tap, Brody offered one last time.

'Good evening, Professor,' the sightless man said in reply. He turned his head on the air. 'You have a fellow traveller with you tonight.' His head inclined knowingly towards Caitlyn.

'Zozimus,' Brody said, 'may I introduce Caitlyn McCabe.'

The ragged man caught a breath of wonder. 'Caitlyn McCabe,' he repeated the name as though it was a reverence to his lips. 'Oh, my dear, what a joyous night this is.' He reached out to offer a hand of greeting and felt the unease in hers. 'You're nervous of old Dragon, aren't you?' he chuckled and patted his watchdog. 'No need, no need, my dear. Dragon here is a faithful friend, and the best tracker in the three realms.'

'Second best,' a voice of protest sounded, and all turned to watch a thin figure step from a doorway. Sharp of feature, the man approached, casting suspicious glances left and right as his did so, until he stood before the group in his tattered pirate robes.

'Caitlyn,' Brody nodded to the latest arrival, 'this is Zekerman.'

239

Zekerman the pirate did not extend a hand of greeting but kept both close to the crossed pistols and sabre he wore in his belt while he offered a curt nod.

'Where have you been?' Zozimus chided his companion.

'Bin keepin' tabs on our man the Buck, ain't I?' Zekerman grumbled.

'You found him?' the Professor asked expectantly.

'Dragon found him,' Zozimus declared proudly.

'Yeah, whatevah,' Zekerman shot back. 'I've been watchin' all day, givin' myself backache 'iding in bushes and ditches, I don't mind tellin' ya.'

'A ghost with backache,' Zozimus chuckled, 'I doubt it.'

'Thus far I am not hearing information worthy of payment,' Brody interrupted.

Zozimus rapped his stick on the kerb for attention. 'What Zekerman is trying to say is that he has been watching Buck Whaley's hideout ever since Dragon tracked the rapscallion there earlier.'

'And now,' the pirate butted in to add, ' 'e's all set to move. 'is pals from the 'ellfire Club 'ave a coach ready to smuggle 'im out of Dublin. Got 'im a nice castle to 'aunt somewhere in the countryside.'

'Where is he at this moment?' Brody demanded.

'Leavin' 'is club to 'ead for the city's western gate,' Zekerman stated. 'I daresay if 'e gets that far, even Dragon won't track 'im.'

The Professor's mind worked fast. His stick beat a frantic rhythm in time with his plotting. He turned sharply to his informants.

'The route to the western gate passes Skinner's Row,' he said quickly. 'How soon can you locate the highwayman Cassidy?'

Zozimus and Zekerman offered vague and non-committing shrugs.

'Depends on the remuneration, I s'pose,' Zekerman mused for effect.

'Rattling coins do speed weary bones,' Zozimus concurred.

'Double the usual rate,' Brody said without hesitation, 'if Buck Whaley is stopped.'

'Most excellent,' Zekerman gushed.

'Not a penny if we miss that coach,' the Professor added darkly. The spirits raced off at once to commence the search as Brody turned to Caitlyn. 'I'll add to the search,' he explained. 'Wait here, no argument, I will be quicker alone and will return in a matter of minutes.' He was gone before she could reply.

Reluctantly alone, Caitlyn looked uneasily about, wary of her desolate surroundings and her solitary presence in it.

After barely a few minutes in this neighbourhood she already sensed the discomforting atmosphere communicated by the lightless windows and jostling structures. She felt tiny and alien, unwelcome to the spirit that was Hell itself.

In glancing guardedly about, Caitlyn was drawn all at once to a figure who had been sitting nearby all along. At a place down a grim block and seated quietly at the top of a railed flight of steps, was little Mia. Drawn by curiosity, and more than grateful to see a familiar face, Caitlyn edged her way towards the girl.

Engaged in closely scanning the street of drifting spirits, Mia did not spot Caitlyn until she had reached the foot of the steps. Her concentration broke instantly to a smile of ready welcome.

'Hi,' Caitlyn said.

'You came back,' Mia beamed.

'Sure. Can I sit with you?'

The delighted girl shifted to make space.

'I'm happy you came back,' Mia said. 'I thought the Pooka might have scared you away for good. He's nasty.'

'No,' Caitlyn waved off the notion, 'it'll take more than that to scare me away.'

Mia's smile widened. 'Good.'

'What are you doing here?' Caitlyn ventured.

Mia patted her stone seat. 'This is my step. It's where I fell asleep with my mother. When she comes back it'll be the first place she looks, I'm sure.' She offered her hopeful eyes to Caitlyn. 'That is unless you can help me find her first. Can you do that?'

Caitlyn took the girl's hand in her own 'What have you heard about me, Mia? The last time you told me how you listened when the Professor talked about me. What did he say?'

'It's rude to listen to private talk, isn't it?' Mia said sheepishly.

'Not this time,' Caitlyn reassured her. 'Tell me.'

Mia concentrated on the memory, drawing up the words as precisely as she could.

'The fire in you is enough to save the whole world or else destroy it. The time will come to choose a side and when you do, that choice will decide everything.' She mused over the words and nodded firmly. 'Yes, that's what he said.'

Confounded, Caitlyn absorbed the words without understanding and found no logical place for them in herself. She squeezed the little spirit's hand earnestly.

'If I can find a way to help you, Mia,' she said, 'I will, I promise.'

'We should go,' Brody said curtly, his arrival at the bottom of the steps a surprise to the girls. He rested on his cane as he observed them keenly.

'I can help,' Mia whispered to Caitlyn.

'Time is against us,' Brody said to Caitlyn and he walked on.

Caitlyn descended and as she walked after the

Professor, she turned and gestured for Mia to follow with a playful wink.

'What was Mia talking about?' Brody asked, trying too hard to make the query sound an idle one.

'Her mother,' Caitlyn said without hesitation.

I can keep secrets too, Professor.

THIRTY-FIVE

The carriage hurtled through the spirit realm.

Wheel spokes whirled to invisibility as the vehicle clattered over the roadway behind four surging horses. Bouncing on its on springs and sliding precariously through corners at break-neck pace, the carriage sent startled phantoms running from its path. Foul insults for the road hog were swatted away by the driver's cracking whip and his roared commands to the horses straining in their harness.

A sudden bend in the road challenged the coach to its limits, the deep curve enough to lift two wheels from the ground and bring alarmed whinnying from the horses as they dragged on their hooves. The driver rose in his seat and clasped with bunched fists on the reins as he fought for control. A shuddering contact of sparks marked the return of wheels to road and the manic journey continued.

The road straightened and met a series of dips and rises, an undulating path to be experienced gently on approaching the city's western gate. To the speeding carriage, the landscape took on the character and danger of a storm-tossed ocean. Troughs plunged to create fresh acceleration in the wheels before giving way to mighty swells from which the carriage launched in defiance of gravity. Each landing after became a shattering, skidding contact to test the skills of the driver to the full.

The western gate loomed, the portal gaping beyond a final rise. The whip cracked harder in pursuit of the prize and the carriage sailed forth as the roadway reappeared.

The way was blocked by a caped rider on his mount.

'Staaaand and deliver!' the pistol-bearing highwayman bellowed from his silken mask.

Hooves dragged afire, horses shrieked, and the coach wheels jammed to a rattling stop. The body of the carriage rocked violently where it came to rest, askew in the road.

For a time, the stand-off was marked by complete silence. Driver and rider regarded one another darkly through steam rising from the backs of the exhausted horses. At last, and from within the carriage, a big-wigged head poked through a window.

'What in blundering blazes is the meaning of this?' the figure demanded arrogantly.

'Lord Santry,' the highwayman greeted the phantom happily. 'My compliments to you on this fine evening.'

'Cassidy,' the wigged Santry spat back, 'is that you, Cassidy, you blasted rogue?'

'None other,' Captain Cassidy said, delighted by the recognition. He swung a booted leg over his saddle and dropped nimbly to the road.

Lord Santry responded by pushing furiously on his door to exit the coach in a flurry of gilded frock coat and white stockings.

'What in the name of the Devil's trousers are you playing at, sah?' he blustered. His posh tones rendered 'sir' as 'sah'.

'Highway robbery, of course,' Cassidy said.

Santry's ghostly features actually managed to grow crimson with rage. 'This is preposterous, preposterous, I say. How dare you, sah. Why, I shall see you hanged a second time for this outrage.'

Captain Cassidy's pistol exploded with smoke and light, the muzzle flash sufficient to capture the destruction of Lord Santry's wig in a storm of horsehair and powder.

'Pray, silence, sir.' the highwayman said politely, and he levelled his second pistol to reinforce the request. 'Tell me, do, who else accompanies you on your journey? Are your fellow knaves of the Hellfire Club aboard?'

'No,' Santry grumbled from ruin of his wig. 'I have personal business beyond the city.' He dug into a pocket of his waistcoat under Cassidy's watchful eye and produced a leather purse. 'Here, this is what you want, you villain. Take it and get gone, blast you.'

Sackimum Brody and Caitlyn emerged from the darkness.

'You are *not* alone, though, are you, my good Lord?' the Professor challenged. His words caused a brief and frightened commotion within the coach, betraying the presence of a hidden other.

'You call me a liar, sah?' Santry tried, summoning the last of his confidence.

'Come out, Buck Whaley,' Brody demanded.

A moment's hesitation followed before Buck Whaley emerged from the carriage, his face grim and bold as he led with a pistol at the ready. Pointing the weapon at the unflinching Brody, he offered a cruel smile.

'Beware, teacher,' he scoffed, 'you go too far in tangling with the Hellfire Club.'

'It is you who has gone too far, Whaley,' Brody said. Almost casually, he *tap-tap-tapped* his walking-stick.

Tap tap tap, came the reply, and *tap tap tap* again as Zozimus was led into the light by Dragon, the pair leading in turn the Viking horde to surround the rest.

Whaley faltered, his pistol a dead weight in his hand as he backed uselessly towards the coach to cower behind Lord Santry. 'No,' he croaked, 'no. Brody, take me into custody. I demand your protection. You cannot surrender me to these barbarians.'

The Vikings growled in unison at the insult.

Brody shrugged, playing on Whaley's fears. 'You broke Viking law,' he explained softly. 'It is for King Ivar to judge you.'

'No,' Whaley shrilled, 'not that, anything but Viking justice. I will tell you whatever you want to hear, anything. Bring me before Lord Norbury.'

Brody was silent, appearing to consider the offer. He walked a brief circle, stroking his chin for effect. He offered a sly wink to Caitlyn when no-one else could see and rounded on Whaley once again.

'To the Night Court.'

THIRTY-SIX

The iron door crashed open. Viking guards entered and flung their tumbling prisoner to the cell. The door slammed shut and Buck Whaley lay in blackness.

Curled upon the dusty floor, he wept pitifully, for his sins and for himself. The sound of his tears, snivelling and hollow within the walls did nothing to hold back the din of the Viking horde above, bellowing their hellish chorus of revenge in the court. He listened to their howls, their angry demands for justice filled with lurid promises of vile torture, and he held himself and sobbed.

Was this the reward for helping the ancients? Where was the glittering prize of riches he had been promised by Queen Cethlinn's messenger, the exchange of a single dull crown for treasures beyond measure? Whaley blinked through tears in search of a golden vision and found instead this bleak imitation of a Glasnevin tomb.

It wasn't fair.

At least he was in the Night Court. He took some small comfort in that knowledge. He had beaten Lord Norbury in duels and humiliated him at the card table, but far better to be thrown upon his dour mercy than the bloodthirsty imaginings of the Vikings whose roars still drifted through the stone ceiling.

'Ah, poor Buck Whaley,' a voice whispered from the dark.

Whaley recoiled from the words, scurrying for a corner with a mewling cry. 'Who's there?' he whimpered

'You deserve better than thisss.'

'Pooka? Pooka! It is you.' Whaley came to his knees and reached in search of his accomplice. 'Did they catch you too?'

'Don't be so foolisssh.' Cat's eyes glimmered in the cell's far corner.

Buck Whaley shed tears of joy. 'You came to rescue me.'

'Perhapsss.'

'Perhaps? Why perhaps, what does that mean? You can't leave me here.'

'Lower your tone,' the Pooka warned.

'I helped you,' Whaley protested fiercely, 'I helped you and I am consigned to this dank place because of that. I am owed.'

'And Queen Cethlinn seeks to reward you.'

'Then spirit me away. Take me to safety in the third realm.'

'One more service for my Queen and I will,' the Pooka said.

'Name it,' Whaley said. He shuffled forward on his

knees to listen.

'You will soon be taken before the court,' the Pooka explained, 'there to be questioned by Brody.' His monstrous face drew forward. 'You will tell him everything.'

Whaley blinked through confused tears. 'I don't understand.'

'You will tell him everything, and more besssidesss. Brody will ask why I wanted the crown and the emerald. You will answer that the crown was nothing, but its emerald was all. Because it is through the emerald Queen Cethlinn can see what she desires to gain, through the gem she can see where it liesss.'

'And afterwards you will free me,' Whaley said, his mind filling in that all-important detail. 'You will come to the Glasnevin tombs and free me.'

The Pooka ignored him. 'To convince the court,' he went on, 'you will offer a name. You will utter the name of Dr Devlin. He is proof of the Queen's power.'

'Dr Devlin,' Whaley repeated obediently. 'And then you will rescue me.'

'Do all I ask of you and you will not enter the tombsss,' the Pooka assured him.

Overcome with relief, Whaley fell back on his heels. 'O, thank you, Pooka, thank you.'

Bustling activity outside caught Whaley's attention and he looked to the door. Stomping feet and the jangle of keys announced the arrival of his guards. The iron door flew aside to admit waves of light and Whaley looked for his saviour only to find he was alone in his cell.

⚭ ⚭ ⚭

Ivar the Boneless raaaaaged!

At first sight of the prisoner's entrance to the courtroom, the King led his Vikings in thunderous roars and shield-beating. From his moving throne Ivar offered wordless howls of animalistic fury for his captive. Under his cruel direction, sharpened axes were presented for Whaley's wide-eyed consideration as he worked every terrified fibre of his being to keep from fainting. Only the ropes that bound him and the guards holding them prevented the phantom from toppling helplessly to the floor of the dock.

On the fringes of the tumult, Caitlyn and the Professor watched and waited for the start of proceedings. Glancing above the throng, Caitlyn saw the appearance of Mia's excited face over the rail of the empty gallery.

A flare of light from the bench signalled the arrival of Lord Norbury to his towering chair. With a sneer of disapproval for the Viking presence in his court he snatched up his gavel and hammered repeatedly in demanding 'ORDER!'

The chaos subsided, but only when King Ivar raised

his arms for silence.

'I will warn you once, Ivar,' Norbury declared through gritted teeth. 'You will keep your troops quiet in my court or I will find a place in the cells for you.'

The Vikings offered a jeering 'Ooooooh' while King Ivar bowed with a smirk of fake respect.

'Now then,' Lord Norbury grumbled, 'the court is in special session at the request of the Vikings. The case is one of theft, of the crown of King Brian Boru.' Hisses emanated from behind shields. 'The accused, Buck Whaley, who I always knew would be in my dock one night, will be questioned on the matter. I call Professor Sackimum Brody.'

The Professor took his cue. Leaving his stick in Caitlyn's care, he made his way through the assembled Vikings to stand between King Ivar and the prisoner.

'With your Majesty's permission,' he said for courtesy's sake, 'I have questions for Whaley.'

Ivar sighed and waved limply. 'Yap yap yap,' he mocked. 'Be quick, Brody, there's tormenting to be done.' His words were greeted by a fresh clamour of cheers.

'Silence,' the glowering judge reminded everyone.

'Whaley,' the Professor said, but his call failed to draw the prisoner's terrified gaze from a freshly sharpened axe held dangerously close to his face. 'Buck Whaley, look at me!'

With supreme effort, Whaley turned to Brody. 'Get

me out of this, Brody,' he begged pitifully. 'I'll gift you anything.' With a sudden flash of inspiration, he added quickly, 'The Pooka's gold, I'll give it to you, all of it.'

'The Pooka gave you gold,' the Professor repeated softly.

'Yes, yes, so much. I thought I should be blinded by its light.'

'Was that your reward for stealing the crown of King...?' the Professor stopped himself in time.

'Yes, the crown. He said he desired it. But the third realm could not be blamed for the theft, so I was to be rewarded should I be the one to take it.'

The admission brought a tide of angry grumbling and shield rattling.

'What did he say of the crown. Why did he want it?'

Whaley appeared to think hard. 'At first, he said little, only that he desired its possession. But when he came again, he said more. He revealed it was Queen Cethlinn who demanded its theft.'

Brody took a step closer to the information he sought.

'Why did *she* want the crown?'

'She did not want the crown,' the prisoner revealed. 'She wanted the emerald, the gem that was torn away and lost at the Half Moon.'

Brody stiffened. 'For what purpose?'

'To see,' Whaley explained. 'The Queen possesses

the gift of sight. The Pooka told me she only need touch the jewel to see all, just as Dr Devlin discovered.'

'What did you say?' Ivar demanded. 'Brody, what is he talking about?'

Brody did not answer. Lost in the darkest recesses of his mind where the name Devlin had cast him, he searched fearfully through rooms of learning and shelves of memory for the import of Whaley's testimony, dreading the answer even as he sought it. He returned to the moment as abruptly as he had left it, drawn by Lord Norbury's voice.

'Are there any further questions, Brody?' the judge asked impatiently.

'No, my Lord,' the Professor said distractedly. He withdrew with a polite nod and hastened to Caitlyn, signalling for her to make for the door as the judge's address to the prisoner followed them.

'Buck Whaley,' Norbury's judgement boomed, 'your confession to the court is accepted. You are hereby fined sixteen shillings, to cover the gambling debts you owe me. As for your crime of theft, committed on Viking lands, you are consigned to Viking custody. May God have mercy on your soul.'

The gavel banged, the Vikings roared, and Buck Whaley's shrieks of protest were drowned out.

'What was that all about?' Caitlyn asked, falling into rapid step with the Professor.

'Dr Devlin,' Brody whispered, and Caitlyn was unsure if he was answering her or mouthing a fear too great to hold.

'Professor!' she snapped at him. 'What's the matter with you? Who is Dr Devlin?'

Brody paused, working hard to collect his thoughts.

'He is a spirit with knowledge,' he said vaguely, 'terrible knowledge.' He made to stride on.

Caitlyn caught his arm, forcing him again to face her.

'You're afraid of him,' she said, reading his drawn features.

'No,' the Professor breathed. 'I am not afraid of Devlin, but I *am* afraid of what he will tell us.'

He marched away, fleeing her questions.

⅋ ⅋ ⅋

From his hidden perch on the Night Court roof, the Pooka watched closely.

There, emerging below, he spotted Brody, and read in the man's rapid steps a measure of the urgency he hoped to see. Buck Whaley must have played his part well. The Pooka allowed a smile of pointed teeth to break at his lips and he turned his attention to the progress of the Professor's young apprentice. He sized up the girl, wondering idly about her and her gift of seeing in the spirit world. She must be one in a million or more, he reasoned, and he studied this young curiosity with keen regard, seeking clues in her movements, and her features when she turned to the light.

A roaring confusion below distracted the Pooka. He dismissed the girl to peer instead on the fate of Buck Whaley.

Hauled along, the unfortunate Buck was conveyed from the court by a troop of exultant Vikings towards the Winter Fort. Their charging passage was announced by deafening war cries and Whaley's own repeated shrieks of 'Pooka! Pooka, save me!'

The Pooka, who believed nothing was more delicious than a broken promise, threw back his head to cast hissing laughter at the moon.

THIRTY-SEVEN

'Come along,' Brody urged as he quickly entered the Wraith, 'we have no time to lose. Marcus, take us to the university at once.'

Caitlyn was thrown back in her seat as the car surged from the kerb and swung into a sliding u-turn.

'Questions,' the Professor muttered knowingly.

'Where do I start?' Caitlyn complained as she slid helplessly about to the vehicle's careering motion.

'Indeed,' Brody could only agree, and that seemed to trouble him deeply. 'There are so many more questions than before. Faster, Marcus, faster.'

'We're at top speed already, Professor,' Marcus assured him over the engine's howl. He threw the car into a fresh and unnerving slide to avoid a phantom omnibus. Top hats and bonnets poked through open windows to regard the progress of the speeding vehicle.

An unsettling recollection came to Caitlyn, even as the car continued to jar and jolt her bones.

'Buck Whaley said Cethlinn can see where Balor's spear is just by touching the emerald. Can she really do that?'

'That we will soon discover,' Brody promised. Despite the urgency of their flight, he gave in to a sly smile. 'If only she realised it doesn't even take magic,' he said distantly to himself. 'The spear is so well hidden everyone can see it everyday.'

Ignoring Caitlyn's state of confusion, he tapped feverish fingers on the head of his cane in time to his racing thoughts.

The gateway of Trinity College gaped to receive the car's fishtailing approach. Marcus regained control in time to send the Wraith smoothly through and onto the cobbled square and a shriek of brakes resounded against the buildings about.

The passenger's alighted quickly, their feet touching earth to the first chime of the university clock. Drawn by the musical sound, Caitlyn looked to see the tips of the golden hands join in signalling the midnight hour.

'Good, good,' Brody said, quickly checking the blue-faced clock against his pocket watch. He turned his gaze on Caitlyn. 'To the Long Room,' he instructed.

THIRTY-EIGHT

Caitlyn pushed after the Professor through swinging doors and stopped in her tracks. The gasp she issued rolled from her to the mammoth heart of the space that was the Long Room.

Cathedral-like in scale, the university's old library rose and stretched to grand dimensions before Caitlyn's vision. To its far and vaulted ceiling, bookcases of darkest wood climbed so high it appeared they must surely topple, one against the other to the farthest distance. Only the weight of innumerable leather volumes ranked on the shelves prevented this from happening, it seemed.

Caitlyn hurried to follow the Professor where he moved through the imposing room, conscious of her footsteps tapping loudly through the cavernous quiet. From plinths set at shelf-ends, decorative busts appeared to turn at the sound, and alabaster features tracked Caitlyn in sightless contemplation. The whitened faces added to those of spirit students in candlelit alcoves who looked up from their eternal research to whisper and nudge sharply at her presence.

The mutterings were curtailed by a terse demand for 'Hush!' and a spectral figure swept up. Bedecked in tailed coat and short wig, he greeted Caitlyn and Brody with a courteous bow.

'Welcome as always, Professor Brody,' he said. 'May I be of assistance to you this evening?'

'Good evening, Pembrig,' Brody replied. 'You may indeed. Do you have your keys for the restricted volumes?'

Pembrig smiled indulgently and tapped a hand to his waistcoat pocket.

'I should be failing in my duties as curator if I did not.'

'Good,' Brody said. 'Would you bring the Book of Cethlinn to me at once, please?'

Pembrig blinked, astonished by the request.

'The Book of ...?' his voice failed as he sought urgently about for eavesdroppers.

'Please,' the Professor repeated.

'Of course, Professor, at once,' Pembrig said. He hastened dutifully to his task.

The Professor led on.

Across the dark boards they walked, progressing directly between the endless volumes, all the while followed by those alabaster eyes. Unsettled by the bizarre attention, Caitlyn kept her focus straight ahead, and on the Professor as he reached a doorway. This panelled barrier was built into the surrounding architecture of stacked books and was topped with a sign declaring 'Restricted Access'.

Past the loudly creaking door, a flight of rough stone steps descended and brought them to lower reaches. Here a short corridor travelled to yet another arched door. Caitlyn spotted a sliding panel set into the portal.

The Professor drew up his walking-stick and rapped three times on the wood.

The panel rasped open to reveal staring half-features, thick browed, bearded and serious.

'Password,' the framed face growled.

Brody offered a tired sigh. 'Blackpitts, it's me. You know it's me.'

'Then you know the password,' the unwavering Blackpitts replied.

Brody groaned. 'Trick or treat.'

'That's the one,' the doorman happily confirmed and slammed the panel. A moment later, the turning of a heavy lock rattled through the corridor and the door was hauled open.

Caitlyn entered and hesitated in the frame, overwhelmed by the room within.

No less gigantic than the library above, the room existed as a dungeon for books. Similar cases dominated the space, but the dusty volumes here sat behind heavy chains and stout locks, their words constrained, forbidden. No spirits wandered in idle contemplation of the books here, no light shone to aid academic research. The shelves held their prisoners firmly in cages stretching far off to a place where two long tables stood side by side. Even at a distance, Caitlyn saw one was piled with all manner of books and documents while the other, apparently empty, was the scene of a hushed conversation between three ghostly forms huddled about it.

The door banged shut and Caitlyn jumped. She stepped forward under the frowning supervision of Blackpitts. His meaty hands tucked into his belt and close to the massive wooden truncheon he wore there.

'What is this place?' Caitlyn asked of Brody. Her voice travelled back to her from hidden depths.

'This,' the Professor's voice echoed, 'is the Reserve Room. This is everything. On these shelves are books gathered from across all realms and all ages. They contain folklore, myth, magic, alchemy, all the knowledge of the ancients.' He swept up his stick to draw Caitlyn's attention to the book-laden table. 'There sits the total of everything known of King Balor and his spear. There are maps and stories and diaries, etchings and history. Together they have served to keep the weapon from Cethlinn's grasp for many years.'

Caitlyn approached the paper stacks. She took in an array of documents, not knowing where to focus her attention, hardly daring to touch parchments of ancient fragility. All at once she paused, seeing beyond volumes and scattered pages to a photograph lying partially hidden in their midst. She recognised the image copy of her father with his two companions at Newgrange. Professor Brody smiled with his stained knees and Professor Gilbert wore his yellow flower. Barry McCabe's broad smile shone up at her.

'You collected all of this,' Caitlyn guessed, tugging at the print.

'Yes,' the Professor confirmed. 'It's everything I required in coming to know the mind of the wicked Queen, and to predict her schemes.' He paused wistfully. 'At least I thought it was everything.'

'Is there more?' Caitlyn asked as her hands passed over the documents.

'Look at the photograph again,' the Professor suggested, and Caitlyn returned to the three faces. 'Here are three figures at the very heart of the story of Balor's spear, and the one weapon to match its power.'

'The Sword of Lug,' Caitlyn said automatically from the memory of her own research.

'The sword of King Lug,' Brody agreed. 'It was found alongside Balor's spear in the dig at Newgrange. After your father turned to his mentors, Professor Gilbert and I, for help, I took charge of the spear and hid it from the world. I left no clues, no maps for Cethlinn or the Pooka to follow. Even today I alone know its location.'

'Why didn't you just destroy it?' Caitlyn asked.

Brody smiled. 'You forget how the spear was forged and how much wicked magic was poured into it. Only the sword of King Lug with its equal share of magic can destroy King Balor's spear.'

Caitlyn's mind worked fast. 'But you don't know where the sword is now, do you?'

'No.' The Professor admitted awkwardly.

Caitlyn tapped a finger to the picture. 'The sword was Professor Gilbert's part of the plan,' she deduced. 'He hid it. And then...'

'Alexander Gilbert, born 1953, died 2009,' Brody recited glumly. 'Unfortunately, I only learned of the sword's true capacity one year later.'

'He died without telling you where the sword is hidden,' Caitlyn said.

'Correct. Our own plan worked against us. The Professor did, however, leave a clue to help in the event of his passing.'

Brody pointed to the other table and led the way to the figures gathered about.

Caitlyn recognised at once Laetitia Pilkington in the company of two big-wigged gentlemen, the one slim and sharp of feature, the other barrel-chested and ruddy faced.

'My darling Caitlyn,' Laetitia said fondly. 'If you persist in distracting Sackimum from me we shall have words.' She flashed a smile and flirtatious wink.

The Professor blushed. 'Caitlyn, allow me to introduce Miss Pilkington's companions. This is Robert Boyle, 2nd Earl of Cork, philosopher and scientist.'

The sharp-nosed gentleman bowed politely. 'Charmed, Miss Caitlyn.'

'This,' Brody continued, 'is Dean Jonathan Swift, writer and churchman.'

'*Gulliver's Travels*,' Caitlyn said happily. 'I've read your book.'

Dean Swift beamed with delight. 'Am I still popular?'

'Yes, sir,' Caitlyn said.

'I told you she was polite,' Laetitia said to the others.

Brody cut in. 'Our three friends are the shrewdest wordsmiths in the spirit realm. Together they have been working to decipher the one clue left by Professor Gilbert that leads to the Sword of Lug.' He pointed to the table and the single sheet of paper on it.

Caitlyn drew nearer to view the document.

Dried up and cracked with time, the fragile sheet contained a series of written lines. These had been penned in a neat hand over a surface now curled like a claw, as though the paper itself feared to lose grip on the precious message it held.

'How long have you been working on it?' she asked, noting the stains of age spreading from different parts of the document.

'Eight years,' Laetitia said with a weary sigh.

Caitlyn read.

My four o'clock song,
Is an ancient lament,
Recited in hope,
Against wicked intent.
Balor the King,
Is felled by the blade,
Lying in time,
In a soft-tended glade.
Silent in waiting,
Jubilant in sun,
All resting yet,
Longing battle be done.
And shades pass the hours,
Pressing time to a rock,
And offering their flowers to hail four o'clock.

'The poem is not drawn from any known work or poet,' Brody explained. 'It is Professor Gilbert's own composition. The handwriting has been verified as his and the paper came from his personal stock.'

'The trail begins and ends with him alone,' Laetitia said with a frustrated wave of her fan.

'If I may,' the phantom Earl Boyle interjected, 'have we completely exhausted our investigations of the unusual rhyming style?'

Dean Swift buried his face in a hand. 'Oh, Boyle, not this again.'

'Please,' the Earl implored, 'the disjointed style of the final stanza, it must surely be a marker for us. 'Lament' and 'intent', 'blade' and 'glade', 'sun' and 'done', the timing and rhythm are so standard.'

Laetitia groaned and finished Boyle's argument for him. 'Yes, and then 'rock' and 'clock', the rhymes are out of sequence, out of flow. We've been over this a hundred times, nay, a thousand.'

'Sentence length and word count,' Swift blustered, 'I maintain this to be crucial to the code. All else is folly.'

'Content, gentlemen,' Laetitia reminded them pointedly, 'the question is one of the poem's content.'

The wordsmiths fell back to debating as Caitlyn and Brody looked on. The distraction was enough to cover Pembrig's soft approach with the thick book he carried. He offered a polite cough to attract attention.

'The Book of Cethlinn,' he said simply.

Arguing ceased and all eyes turned with concern to Pembrig. The Professor moved quietly to accept the weighty tome from him.

'What are you doing, Sackimum?' Laetitia demanded. 'That book is forbidden.'

'But necessary,' he added. He walked to the table of documents and laid the volume among them. From his pocket he removed the emerald stone and placed it by the book.

Dean Swift considered book and jewel grimly. Earl Boyle reached to touch the emerald and drew back his hand with distaste from the book's cover.

'Professor, explain yourself, sir,' Swift said.

Brody did, revealing all that had transpired and all that had been discovered at the Winter Fort and Night Court since the chaos of the Half Moon Inn.

'Were it not for Caitlyn,' he concluded, 'we would not have the emerald to allow for our next step.'

'What *is* the next step?' Laetitia asked with a suspicious glance to the Book of Cethlinn.

Brody steeled himself for the reaction that must surely come. 'In order to confirm Buck Whaley's claim that Cethlinn can use her half of the emerald to see the spear, I must test that power. I will visit Dr Devlin.'

As one the spirits cried out in protest. Aghast at the Professor's plan they railed against it, questioning his sanity and vowing to prevent the book's removal from the library.

'This is a step too far!' Boyle spluttered. 'You should have no dealings with that sorcerer Devlin.'

'Folly,' Swift declared, 'from beginning to end, folly!'

'Sackimum, what are you thinking?' Laetitia gasped. 'The Night Court would never allow such a course.'

'Which is why I have not told the court,' Brody confided in her.

The objecting voices raised higher as Caitlyn watched. At her elbow she heard the curator Pembrig release a tired sigh.

'This could go on all night,' he said, catching her eye.

'I don't understand,' Caitlyn said.

'Oh, it's quite simple,' Pembrig replied. 'The spirit they are arguing about, Dr Ernest Devlin, is the authority on Queen Cethlinn's magic. There is simply no-one better informed on that subject. He spent his life cataloguing her spells. The book you see is the culmination of his work. But through that work the Doctor became tempted by the very magic he uncovered, and he took to dabbling with dark powers. In the winter of 1911, he was found dead in his room at the university. His body was lying in a circle of strange markings with the Book of Cethlinn open beside it. A spell had gone so powerfully wrong. Those who discovered the body said the Doctor's face was frozen to a look of sheer terror.'

Caitlyn shivered.

'That's not the worst part,' Pembrig continued. 'A week after his funeral, Dr Devlin returned. His phantom was spotted within the library precincts, apparently searching for his book. Students both mortal and spirit became unsettled, and then the spells began again. There were unexplained accidents, clocks chimed out of time and the portraits in the dining hall wept blood. It was terrible.

'When he was finally tracked down, once more conjuring in his chalked circle, Dr Devlin was dealt with most firmly by the Night Court, and the university at last found peace.'

'What happened to him?' Caitlyn asked, sensing the answer already.

'He was cast into the Glasnevin tombs,' Pembrig said, 'under sentence of forever and a day.'

'And that is our destination,' Professor Brody interjected. He stood before them, the Book of Cethlinn in his hands. 'I have just one or two items to collect, and then we will be under way.'

'I'll help you,' Laetitia said, appearing behind.

'You can't come,' Brody said, a little too firmly.

'I beg your pardon,' Laetitia responded, the polite words doing nothing to mask the rising fire in her challenge. 'If you think you are to be trusted alone on this mad scheme, you are wrong.'

Brody flustered. 'But my dear, the tombs, why, they...,'

'Don't you dare, don't you dare say the tombs are no place for a woman.'

'I wasn't, no, of course I wasn't going to say that.' He faltered under Laetitia's piercing glare.

'I'll get the car,' Caitlyn offered with a grin.

'No,' Brody said quickly, grateful for the diversion. 'We must be discreet. We cannot risk the car being spotted at the tombs. We will travel another way.'

THIRTY-NINE

The streets sang to the clatter-rattle of the ghost tram's passing.

Bouncing along on hard wooden seats, Caitlyn, the Professor and Laetitia sat in silence and tried to ignore the pair of drunken phantoms near the back who filled the carriage with their loud singing.

'The Auld Triangle...,' one offered heartily.

'...Ah-went Jingle Jangle,' the other rejoined.

'All along the banks,' together, and with a mighty pause, 'of the Rooooyalll Canaaaaaal!'

The pair collapsed in a merry tittering heap as the spectral conductor made his way between the seats. 'All stops Phibsboro, Cabra 'n' Finglas. Tickets, please, tickets.' The stout spirit halted by Caitlyn, rocking to the motion of the tram. 'Tickets, please, Miss.'

'I don't have a ticket,' Caitlyn admitted.

'No problem a-t'all, Miss,' the conductor replied merrily and from a dispenser worn at his waist he drew a stiff paper ticket. 'And two more for the lovely lady and her gentleman,' he said and thumbed the machine again.

Laetitia sniffed, still annoyed at Brody as she accepted the conductor's offering.

'Tickets, please,' the man said again to Caitlyn, who, confounded by the bizarre behaviour, handed over the ticket just received. 'Very good, all in order,' he said with a broad smile. He used his punch to validate the paper and gave it back. With a smile he made off to approach the drunken passengers who offered a new song in place of tickets.

'And it's no nay never, no nay never no morrr-rre, will I play the Wild Rover, no nevvvveerrrrr, a-no morrrrrre.'

Caitlyn looked at the book in Brody's arms. 'What are you going to do, Professor?'

Brody stiffened in his seat and gripped the Book of Cethlinn tighter. 'It is time we stopped fumbling about in the dark after the Pooka,' he said. 'So far, we have followed the trickster's path, and the clues he left with the rake Buck Whaley. But how can we trust anything the demon leaves us? It is time for some certainty.'

'You're going to let Dr Devlin conjure from his book, aren't you?'

'One spell only,' the Professor assured, 'and under my strict supervision.'

'Madness,' Laetitia said. 'In any event, why would he help us?'

'You have never been to the tombs, have you, my

dear?' Brody guessed. He tapped a hand to his pocket. 'I have brought a gift that will mean the world to Dr Devlin. He will help.'

'It is still madness,' Laetitia said. 'I would rather see you enter the third realm and face Cethlinn herself than follow this path.'

'I would if I could,' Brody insisted quietly.

Caitlyn frowned. 'Why can't you?'

'The secret ways to the third realm were forgotten long ago,' the Professor said. 'The shifting of worlds closed paths and broke bridges.'

'No spirit or mortal has entered the ancient realm since 1077,' Laetitia added. 'That was when the Knight Fitzgerald, on a gallant quest, stumbled upon a route and fell into Cethlinn's lair. His diary in the Reserve Room makes for grim reading.' She caught a sharp look of warning from Brody and fell silent.

Ding ding, the tram bell clanged.

'Glasnevin Cemetery,' the conductor announced, clinging to the rail as the vehicle rumbled to its stop.

The drunken passengers sang dourly. 'I aaam stretched on your grave and will lie there... foreverrrrrrrrr.'

The singing drifted after Caitlyn as she stepped from the tram to join the others. With a silvery chime of farewell, the vehicle clattered on and Glasnevin cemetery was revealed.

Through high gates black and spiked, the cemetery grounds flowed along avenues flanked by silhouetted trees. The place was a midnight sea punctuated by whitened headstones. Celtic crosses, Grecian urns and protecting angels arrayed the night, topping markers of all dimensions. From simple stones on man-size plots to carved memorials reaching for the heavens, all manner of gravestone stood behind the gates. Yet even the most gloriously ornate monument, designed in mortal vanity to rise over its neighbours, failed to challenge the greatest of all. Rising between the stone ranks and dwarfing them, a mighty round tower that was the cemetery's own marker soared to block the moon's path. Caitlyn turned in wonder to the upper reaches of the tower and a thin, light-less window there. She shuddered at the thought of some ghostly occupant watching from the darkness beyond the glass.

'State your business,' a voice demanded gruffly from the gloom.

Gazes were drawn from the tower to the shine of a lantern by which a bent figure became visible beyond the gates.

'Gatekeeper Gannon,' the Professor said, 'good evening.'

The gatekeeper's eyes shone wet and wide in the lamp light.

'Professor Brody,' he said flatly, 'at this hour? This can't be good.'

The night filled with a song of metal as Gannon produced his keys and used one to bring a dry squeal from the gates' lock. The barrier inched heavily aside to admit the visitors.

Once inside, the Professor caught Caitlyn's attention. 'The tombs lie beneath the tower,' he said quietly.

'State your business,' Gannon repeated, resecuring the gate noisily.

'I...,' the Professor began, '...we, rather, are here to speak with one of the entombed.'

'Prisoner's name,' the gatekeeper said, and despite his phantom existence, he yawned indifferently.

Brody hesitated. 'Dr Devlin.'

Gannon's yawn hiccupped as his head snapped about. 'Dr Devlin! Dr Devlin?' He met the gaze of each visitor as he spluttered and fixed on Caitlyn. 'Are you sure?'

Caitlyn shrugged.

'Quite sure,' Brody reassured him.

'Well, all right then.' He led the way, mumbling doubtfully along the way. 'This is very strange altogether, never heard the like of it, not in my time.'

Falling in step behind Brody and the gatekeeper, Laetitia whispered to Caitlyn.

'If anything happens,' she breathed, 'promise me

you will get away. You must not take risks. We cannot lose you now.'

'What do you mean?' Caitlyn probed Laetitia's concerned face and caught a flicker there. She had said more than intended.

'Just promise me,' the lady said and pressed on.

In the very shadow of the tower the group arrived at a broad flight of descending steps. The way led to the depths of a dry moat running about the base of the monument where the light of the moon fell and revealed another gate of stout black iron. Gannon wearily fished once more for his keys, and holding his lantern high, he led the way down.

The barrier hauled aside on moaning hinges and the gatekeeper turned to his guests with a signal for them to follow. His lamp swung to illuminate numerous metal doors lining the wall of the moat.

Professor Brody politely made room for the others before stepping past the gate. His shoe crunched on the gravel path.

'Broooooooody.'

The whisper rose mournfully behind a door.

'It's Brooooody.'

Wails of anguish erupted from the tombs' hollow recesses at the news. Dust clouds wafted from beneath the portals and carried a phantom chorus of pleas and curses to fill the moat.

'They remember you, Professor,' Gannon said, and he allowed himself a cruel grin. In an instant the smile vanished, and the spirit stepped to the nearest tomb to strike his keys loudly against the metal. 'Quiet down here!' he commanded sourly.

The howling faded to the tombs' distant reaches.

The party made its way on and followed the gently curving path until at last Gannon raised his lantern again to illuminate a number set over a paint-flecked door.

'Seventeen,' he quoted and brought out his keys once more. He fumbled awkwardly through the set, mumbling to himself. 'I can't recall which one it is,' he admitted. 'I don't believe Dr Devlin's ever had visitors. Ah, here we are.' He held up a stout key eaten by rust. 'Let's see if we can get this oul' lock working.'

Inserting the key into its receiver, Gannon unleashed a hellish grating of metal on metal as he worked to free the door's mechanism. Grunting through the effort, he laid both hands to the work and rounded his shoulders to it until, with an unsettling crack and spring, the lock gave, and the door popped free. A cloud of rank air hissed through the gap to assail everyone. Laetitia fanned urgently.

Gannon curled his fingers to the door and hauled back, gritting his teeth as he dragged the barrier aside to a fresh bout of metallic hell-song. Satisfied with his work, the gatekeeper backed away and cast a wary look into the tomb. 'All yours, Professor,' he said and retreated.

The Professor straightened, gathering himself for the encounter to come, and with a glance for Laetitia he stepped forward and framed himself in the open doorway.

'Dr Devlin,' he said into the blackness. His voice travelled flatly through the space. 'Dr Devlin, I have come to speak with you.'

At a spot just past the edge of seeing, a misshapen figure shifted, betraying the movement in a dragging of chains.

Laetitia's hand reached Caitlyn's and squeezed.

When it came, the voice of the prisoner was a dried-up grating of winter leaves.

'Visitors,' it croaked. 'Come.'

FORTY

The tomb smelled of creeping rot.

The visitors eased inside, remaining close to the open doorway while vision adjusted as well as possible to the sucking gloom. Even then the farthest parts of the tomb and the figure waiting there remained shrouded from all sight.

Caitlyn looked on a single coffin, dust-covered where it lay by one wall. She took an unconscious step to her right to increase her distance from it. The motion brought chuckles dribbling from the dark.

'Don't fret, youngster,' Dr Devlin said through his laughter, 'my roommate won't bite you.'

Professor Brody coughed softly to attract Dr Devlin's attention. 'Do you know who I am, Dr Devlin?' he asked.

'I know you, Brody,' the voice agreed, 'all here know you. You are the subject of curses every night among the tomb-cast of Glasnevin.'

'I have brought a gift for you,' the Professor said. From his jacket pocket he drew a slender candle and held it for all to see.

Chains rattled and a sharp breath of desire came with the sound.

'Light it,' Devlin urged. 'Let me see it flicker.'

Brody moved to kneel by the coffin and placed the candle on it. Producing next a box of matches he struck one and brought sparking light to wick. A dancing tallow glow flowered against the blackness. 'For you,' he assured the prisoner and stood back.

Amid a violent jangle of metal bonds, Dr Devlin drew into the light. Oblivious to Laetitia's horrified gaze at his coming, he shuffled his bony frame towards the gift of fire and clawed for it with filthy, broken nails. The illumination slipped between his skeletal fingers and played over decaying rags that hung about his shrunken body. And though he gibbered happily, the light failed to catch what joy might be in his face. A century's worth of neglected hair snaked so fully about his head it obscured all but a pair of orbs given life by the tiny flame.

'It's so beautiful,' the prisoner sighed tearfully, 'it feels so warm.'

Devlin's gaze turned from the candle and he peered by its light across the faces of his guests. He offered each a black-toothed smile of gratitude until he came to Caitlyn. With a blink, his smile twisted as he beheld a fresh source of curiosity and fascination. The prisoner abandoned his gift to pad noisily towards the girl as she stiffened.

'Your hair,' he breathed, daring to reach, not daring to touch, 'it's so wonderful. Children's hair makes the best pillows.' He froze at a new and captivating sight. 'Heterochromia,' he gasped. His head swivelled maniacally between Caitlyn's eyes. 'Sapphire and emerald set in a single, precious face, so exceptional and rare. I have seen it, somewhere, just once before.' His fingernails clicked noisily on his teeth as he struggled to recall.

Professor Brody moved sharply and thrust Dr Devlin's book before him.

Devlin recoiled with an animal shriek. Terrified to speechlessness, he fell back in a riot of chains, kicking and scrambling to the comfort of his precious light.

'I need your assistance,' Brody explained, stepping forward over the blubbering spirit.

'No, no,' Devlin cried. He waved dirty claws against sight of the book. 'Too much magic can make you mad.'

'I have more candles,' the Professor teased him softly. 'When this one burns down, you will have more.'

Temptation and fear battled across the furrows of Devlin's face.

'I was chained here for what you ask me to do,' he shot spitefully at Brody.

'One spell only,' Brody said.

'Just one?' Devlin probed. 'One spell for many candles?'

'One for many.'

Devlin's fingers wriggled as he weighed magic and darkness. 'Show me,' he said.

Brody spread the pages as he reached to his coat pocket. Revealing the broken emerald, he laid it on the book.

'What is this?' Devlin asked as he tapped suspiciously on the glassy surface.

'That you do not need to know,' Brody said, 'only what it might let you see.'

Devlin did not argue. He read hastily, blinking hard after so many years without light. 'I need chalk.'

Prepared, Brody offered him a fresh white stick.

'I need room,' Devlin demanded. He shooed his guests aside with a rattle-jangle of cuffed arms.

The preparation was long and Dr Devlin feverish in tracing the necessary patterns. The floor and walls of his grubby cell became slowly covered with strange and alien tracings. He was followed in his work by the Professor who watched every move, even as he conferred with Laetitia in whispers.

On the edge of all, Caitlyn fought against the slow boredom of waiting. She stretched against tightening limbs and blinked, her eyes tired from following Devlin's growing designs. She looked to the candle on the coffin and saw the burning wax had already reduced by half. She could sit there and rest her feet while she waited, she knew, but there was *no way* she was going to sit on a coffin. There was just one alternative. Despite the revulsion she felt for Devlin and his dreary chamber, Caitlyn stepped closer to a wall and leaned against it, grateful for the instant support it offered her back. She allowed herself a relieved breath and felt her brain unwind.

The moment allowed her inner sense to break through with its warning.

Like a voice that had been there all along, it whispered through the corridors of her mind and carried electric prickles to the roots of her hair. Caitlyn drew back her silent breath and absorbed the ominous shift she felt. It was a premonition without language, experienced as an instinct beyond mortal senses, and it turned her head slowly to the far end of the tomb and the defiant dark hanging there.

Untouched by candle flicker, the permanent veil of black remained impenetrable to sight. Caitlyn scanned it deeply, probing hard for more than it offered while she struggled to discern more of the feeling within herself and the alarm it conveyed.

'It's ready,' Dr Devlin announced, his shrill tone of excitement breaking the moment.

All looked upon what Devlin had created. From his

kneeling place, crude and angled patterns stretched in all directions. Some ran straight and alone to end at chalked arrowheads which seemed to point towards destinations unknowable. Still others curved to meet one another or to touch smaller circles holding symbols of freakish design. The spaces between lines were also sites of bizarre markings, otherworld scrawls of a forbidden language.

'Give me the jewel,' Devlin commanded. He reached with one spindly hand to accept it. He reached again. 'The book.'

'I will hold the book,' Brody said firmly.

'So be it,' Devlin shrugged, 'it makes no difference to the magic.'

Without warning, the prisoner cast his shackled hands wide and began. On rasping breaths, he drew forth low whispers and conversed with himself behind the matted curtain of his hair.

'Dorchadas,' the sorcerer intoned in the old language, summoning the deepest shades of night. He pointed fearfully to one symbol among many. 'Olc,' he breathed, as though in dread of the evil he named. 'Fís cosc,' he demanded and thrust a fist to his own heart as the recipient of forbidden knowledge. He fixed Caitlyn with orbs that all at once twinkled with more than candle fire. 'Eagla,' he said through a crooked smile and sought her fear to complete the spell.

With her gaze locked on Devlin's, Caitlyn sensed the first response to his conjuring at the edges of her vision. On all sides of the tomb, she saw movement growing from cracks in the brickwork. Dust fell in thin streams, and puffed up from the floor, pushed by something that clicked and scrabbled after. Caitlyn heard Laetitia's gasp and looked.

The insects of the night came crawling.

They poured from the walls and fell from on high in their hundreds to join an audible movement of skittering. The mass advanced in a tumbling wave across the floor and over Caitlyn's feet and ankles. Driven on the wind of Dr Devlin's mad laughter, the insects surged, their march a rolling exodus from him, a flood towards the door of the tomb and the escape route from evil magic lying behind.

Chuckling still, Dr Devlin ignored the crawlers that lingered in his hair and called to a place beyond the night. 'Cuilleach Cethlinn, Queen of magic, show mine eyes what I seek.' He drew up the emerald to his face and peered at his candle through verdant depths. Hypnotised by refracted light, he drew rigid, suspended in glowing green as he scanned the glassy world through timeless layers. The links that bound him at last clinked to betray his reanimation, and Devlin issued a startled gasp.

'What is it?' Brody demanded.

Devlin opened his mouth to speak but the voice that came was no longer his. From his lips a wizened tone filled the crypt from a place beyond its walls. 'So old it is,' it croaked, 'a spectacle from ancient times. I see, I seeeeee.'

'Tell me what you see,' Brody said, holding his nerve.

'Time,' Devlin's witch-voice cracked. 'I see time in great measure, from past to present. It follows a distinct path, straight and true, like a...like an arrow. No! Like a spear!'

Laetitia flicked her fan as a guard against the word.

'More,' the Professor commanded.

'It *is* a spear,' Devlin's possessor confirmed. 'The spear that has been sought in the past and present, I see it. No longer hidden, I have found it!'

Devlin toppled in a cascade of chains. Landing heavily within the chalked borders of his magic, he lay there, babbling senselessly as he released the emerald from his grip. The stone slid across the floor and struck Caitlyn's foot. She bent at once to pick it up, recalling with a touch her same action in the Half Moon Inn. How curious it was the stone should reach her this way a second time.

The Professor slammed Queen Cethlinn's book and stepped back from the prone Devlin. 'We should go,' he said.

As Laetitia followed Brody's hurried exit from the tomb, Caitlyn paused just long enough to look on the prisoner one last time. The ragged figure lay in his chains, oblivious to all and apparently in the grip of an unsettling dream that jerked his head and limbs. The scraping of the tomb door sent her to the dwindling exit. It crashed shut behind her.

Dr Devlin dropped his act and let the candle catch his grimy smile. To the sound of his door lock resealing, he peeked to the rear of his cell.

'How did I perform?' he asked quietly.

'Excellently, Doctor,' the Pooka said, emerging from his hiding place. His cat eyes twinkled with relish. 'You played your part well. My Queen will be very pleasssed.'

'That is all I desire,' Devlin fawned. He rattled his chains deliberately, 'that and my freedom.'

The Pooka smiled. 'Soon, Doctor,' he assured the prisoner, 'sssoon. When we have the spear, and the Fomorian army marches in triumph, Queen Cethlinn will herself break the chains that bind you.' He watched Devlin swell with joyful anticipation. 'What did you see within the ssstone?' he added idly.

'Tell her Majesty that she is wise and correct,' Devlin replied. 'The broken jewel was useless for the spell. I saw nothing but Sackimum Brody's stupid face seeking answers.'

The Pooka beamed. 'Then but one final part of the plan remainsss.'

FORTY-ONE

Dr Matthew Remington James was so terribly, terribly afraid.

Seated alone in the dim sanctuary of his tent, he waited, reacting sharply to every windblown shift of canvas, bracing his nerves for the next flap and flutter as sweat tickled the back of his neck.

It was just a cold tickle of sweat, wasn't it?

He leapt from his seat with a cry and whirled around, flicking on the torch he clung to as his only defence. He slashed its pale beam to and fro to push away crushing gloom and the creeping spirits he imagined in their hundreds. The light fell harmlessly, finding just kit boxes and tools and his folding table with its maps and notes. As he struggled to control his racing heart, the wind fingered idly at page edges and sent ripples chuckling along the tent's back wall.

It had been like this for hours. Ever since dusk, when he had ordered the diggers out of the trench and off the site, he had sat alone, waiting in hope for the dawn and dreading what might come across the quiet fields instead.

The diggers had found the man's body in the trench at dusk.

Was it a man, truly? What man ever existed with such dimensions as the giant in the trench? What man's face had conveyed such burning rage and malignant evil as that which had stared on James when he had been called to come, come quickly?

The baleful one-eyed face returned to his mind and he retreated from the vision, brushing it away with the same hand as swept the tent door aside. Better to wait for the dawn outside, he reasoned, where he could breathe and glimpse the first rays of the sun.

Daylight was hours away yet. The dig site and its empty tents lay shrouded in night veils while overhead the constellation Orion hunted the moon towards the western horizon. Directly beneath the chase sat Newgrange, the mound's white walls shining in reaction to the lunar kiss, its granite flecks shimmering like captured stars.

A shrill cry came and went on the air and James spun towards it with a cry of his own. His shredded nerves delayed his recognising the shriek of a fox, nothing more and miles away across the fields.

Where was the dawn?

The wind rose again, drumming on the tents to set them quaking. It tumbled with a moan into the gaps between and swirled in search of a new target, easily finding James where he stood in the open. Gusts swept up and buffeted him into a reluctant turn and held him there as his torch caught and showed what the wind wanted him to see.

The diggers had worked to protect the find against the elements, staking a canvas sheet across the long trench where it, he, lay. But the work had been hasty in the failing light and one hammered peg had pulled free. The mischievous wind quickly detected the weakness and tugged fiercely, releasing a corner of sheet to reveal the gaping trench and the rungs of a ladder protruding from it.

Under the moonlight the square-cut hole looked like a grave. And isn't that what it is, really, with that giant body down there, silently raging?

Dr James tried to back away from the abyss, but the wind jostled him impatiently and sent the freed canvas billowing. The ladder shook and clashed against the rim of the dig and his imagination sparked to a vision of something monstrous climbing its rungs from the depths.

As quickly as it rose, the wind died away once more. The ladder stilled, the canvas fell, and the trench yawned deep and wide.

He followed a careful arc around the hole and gripped his light tightly against the fears it might show. Approaching the stray corner of covering he reached for it, intending to pull it back into place. He would secure the peg and protect the find against damage. Any harm to it was unthinkable.

She would not be pleased. With a shudder, James swept his torch about the site to chase the Banshee's face from the borders of his mind.

But what if damage had already been done? Feeling the sheet in his hand, James wondered how long it had been free and the trench open to the tearing wind? He turned his light down to search. The slab of night below consumed the beam and offered nothing. The find was a distance from the breach in the covering, farther along the straight cut in the earth, but was it far enough for safety? James kneaded the sheet doubtfully between his fingers, trapped between his fears of the woman above and the man below.

In a moment of clarity, he flung the canvas aside and stepped onto the ladder. His need to be sure outweighed the hours of doubt that would follow him back to his tent. He worked briskly down the rungs before clouds of fear could assail him again. He touched the trench floor and swung his torch to the corridor of clay stretching away. The light caught the first plume of his cold breath as it wafted up to the canvas roof.

It was an act of will for him to release his hold on the ladder, a conscious effort to begin his journey along the cut floor. The walls were not really closing in, he asserted and with a touch to one root-covered surface, but it certainly felt that way the more he progressed.

A flapping loud and urgent overhead halted him, and he ducked as he cast up his torch beam. The canvas rippled violently. James cursed the wind. He levelled his light.

The face of the one-eyed man glared on Dr James.

Coming so unexpectedly to the buried man, James started and almost lost his grip on the torch. The resulting play of light served to lend an unnatural animation to the grotesquely bearded features. Lips curled to a long-ago frozen howl and appeared ready to howl again.

Upright in his grave, the one-eyed man stood half in, half out of the earthen wall containing him, framed by it where the excavators had stopped digging as though in fear of releasing his immense and terrible form. Thus suspended, amid a cape whose rolling was stopped by cloying dirt, the man's hands seemed to claw against the final thin layer of clay, his entire body straining to be free of stout roots entwining arms and legs. Similarly, thick stems gnarled about the man's head, and Dr James could not decide whether nature had imprisoned this figure or crowned him King.

The wind moaned softly across the lips of the dead and Dr James decided abruptly that he did not care about the answer to his speculating. Distance from the one-eyed man was of greater importance and he turned hurriedly to go. The wind mocked him with a ripple of canvas, and he cast an angry glance upwards. He saw the still form beyond the covering, silhouetted against the moon.

The wind carried the softest weeping to him.

The torchlight died at the sound, allowing exultant darkness to flow coldly through the trench. Dr James shrank from it all until his back struck a wall. Jabbing fingers of vegetation raked his clothing where he slid along, propelled by a voice desperate to be heard but drowning in fear. *The ladder*, it urged, *get to the ladder.*

'I did what you told me to do,' he tried, his words drying up even as he directed them to the shadow overhead. 'I dug in the right place.' He watched as the silhouette moved, angling itself to drift towards the end of the trench, that end where the ladder stood. Her tearful anguish spilled through the frigid air.

Dr James made to speak again, to implore an end to his torture, but in his search for pleading words, a new and terrible query intruded on his scattered mind. When the shape above had begun to move, why did the sound of weeping not follow? The understanding it prompted in him raised the hairs along his arms. The unending sound of crying was not above. It was behind him.

Dr James turned and faced the Banshee.

She had come to fill the space between him and the one-eyed man, and her own shimmering eye of green was lurid in the blackness. It swam to pierce the heart of Dr James as she wept for him, and she offered nothing with her hands but death as she advanced.

He fell from her, his head shaking to deny what she promised with her tears. His words and screams gagged together in protest. *The ladder.* The image of his last desperate hope flared starkly through the horrific vision and he spun from the Banshee and ran. At full flight he heard the ripping of his jacket and shirt an instant before sensing the cold passage of the sword through his chest. James looked from blade to its bearer, staring in awe at the warrior woman who had descended the ladder to offer her sword, and a sneer for his passing.

The Morrigan withdrew her dripping weapon and let Dr James crash to earth, amused at the lifeless sound. Re-sheathing the blade, she offered a contemptuous glance for the Banshee and stepped aside to reveal the coming of Queen Cethlinn.

FORTY-TWO

'Is it him? Is it really him?'

Despite her regal bearing, Cethlinn could not suppress the tremor in her voice, the sound of desire ten thousand years strong. Only through wilful self-control did she hold her place and not rush headlong to behold her lord.

'It is him,' the Banshee confirmed.

Cethlinn grew dizzy at the words and lost breath at their truth. It is him, she told herself, and felt the warmth of it. At last, at long last, her stolen joy was returned. The one who was her world and would make her the Queen of worlds waited just beyond. She struggled to bring forth his name, the very promise of the sound on her lips making her light-headed.

'Balor.'

The canvas roof shivered though the wind remained silent.

'Majesty,' the Morrigan said. She offered Cethlinn a cloth bag.

'No-one comes near,' Cethlinn instructed as she gripped the offering, 'no-one.'

Thus commanded, the Morrigan bowed and retreated. With a shimmering of her form, one became three and the triple warriors departed to take up their posts.

Cethlinn stepped forward and was surprised at the Banshee's failure to immediately move aside. She met that emerald gaze behind black hair and faced down the depthless hate it carried.

'Stay and watch or get gone, Aoife,' she hissed past her wrinkling scar, 'but if you try to stop me, I will gift you an eternity of tortures.'

The Banshee fixed her scorn on the Queen and withdrew, receding into the darkness until, with a last green twinkling, she completed it.

Cethlinn advanced but slowly along the trench. She probed the murky path, seeking for the glimpse that must surely stop her heart, just as that first time, generations ago across the crowded meeting hall at Croghan. That sight of him, tall and proud among the other warriors, cruel and more ambitious than all the rest, had shaken her very soul, and in an instant bound her dreams to his. She would have this Fomorian and all they could take together. That had been her vow in a moment's rush when he turned to look at her.

The grotesque soil mask of the one-eyed King broke the gloom to look upon her once more. Captivated, she faltered, her heart pounding in reply to a world of frozen promises.

She would have him again.

All things required were in the bag. She knelt and pulled feverishly at the cloth to reach for the contents. As she worked, he loomed over her, his stricken roar urging her to begin her conjurations.

'These gifts I bring, my wayward King,' she whispered precisely in drawing out the first gift. 'Wood struck by lightning.' She held it up for his clay filled sight and placed it carefully at his feet. The wind grew disturbed. 'Blood drawn from a graveyard owl,' she said, and produced a vial. She uncorked it and poured sticky fluid through her fingers and across the wood to the sound of rippling canvas. 'Finger bones from a hangman hanged,' she offered with a clicking scatter to the mix. She rubbed her dripping hands above the fiendish ingredients and, as the sheet whipped back to wash her King's face in moonlight, she held her palms to the prisoner. 'A Queen's bloody hands,' she recited breathlessly over the wind and from the heart of her spell, 'hands that have killed in your name. They seek for you in deepest black, hands to reach and pull you back, hands to shape what should not be. Defy the dead, return to me.'

The wind gasped to fearful silence.

The first groan came, agonising from deep in the earth. Through a mouth stopped up with dirt, it rose from its grave in the prisoner's throat and forced its way up, pushing clay in dribbling gouts past those suspended lips. Tremors followed and formed cracks through the confining soil as a growing fury rolled in all directions. Cethlinn cowered as the groan became a cry and the cry increased to a howl until the trench filled with all the rage and hate it conveyed. The encompassing soil could no longer withstand, and it sundered, releasing one hand, and after it the other. Reanimated fingers clawed by instinct to pull at twisted stems and set free the rest. Hauling through a cascade of earth, Balor and his battle roar tumbled forth.

For a time, there was nothing but the King's confusion. With his eye made as blind as its partner by cloying dirt, he knelt afraid beneath his crown of roots and sent fingers on the air and over the cut walls of the trench. He heard at last the sound of her jubilant breathing and tested it with his touch.

'Husband,' Cethlinn dared whisper.

There was recognition in his dusty gasp, hope in the hands that reached for her.

'My Queen,' he uttered when his touch found her.

They reunited in a kiss of ecstasy and earth. Moist lips swam to his, freeing the clay to streak over her cheeks and neck. Her bloodied hands blessed his eye with vision and smeared his face even as his fingers slathered mud on her shoulders and ran thickly through her hair.

The horrified moon fled between clouds.

ઝ ઝ ઝ

Afterwards, she drew the rain and led him through it.

Under glowering Newgrange, Balor turned his face to the sky and received the cloudburst, flexing every freed sinew until the last of his confinement washed away. His eye socket filled to overflowing and sent deluges to wash his beard and cleanse his parched throat.

'Does it please my King?' Cethlinn asked attentively.

'Beyond description,' he said, refreshed. 'So many times I listened to the rain on the earth above, its taste never reaching my lips in the depths.' He looked on her, seeing for the first time the angry scar she wore. 'You have suffered too.'

She shuddered to his touch. 'Only through losing you,' she said.

'Our enemies were cruel. They will know cruelty.'

The Morrigans approached on three sides and bowed to the returned King.

'Welcome, Majesty,' they chorused.

Balor examined the warriors' swords with relish. 'You are ready for battle,' he said.

'More than ready,' the Morrigan agreed. 'It has been too quiet a time.'

Balor leered. 'We'll soon put paid to that.'

FORTY-THREE

Caitlyn screwed her eyes shut against the intruder.

Wound up under the blissful warmth of the duvet, she contested its arrival, willed it gone, and longed for power to make it happen. *It couldn't be here already*, she grumbled inwardly, *it's not fair*.

But it was and would not be denied. Navigating the gaps in her bedding, the dawn came creeping to find her and sent its tickling beams to end all hope of more sleep.

Caitlyn groaned and surrendered to reality. 'Too early,' she croaked and sat up amid a tangle of hair.

The morning blazed exultantly, and she cursed it along with late nights and Sackimum Brody.

'You up, love?' the call came jauntily from below.

'Yes,' she replied weakly.

'Grand. Will it be tea and toast or fried eggs in milk?'

Her stomach rolled. 'Toast,' she managed.

'And the magic word is...?' Gran prompted.

Caitlyn thought of a few, and some in outrageous combinations.

'Please,' she replied instead.

Shower, toast, kiss goodbye, front door, all happened in a groggy progression and the funk of too few hours of sleep. It clung to her until well over halfway to school. Even then the journey did not become a merry jaunt, but the sun was higher and kinder, and a fresh breeze cut steadily through her internal haze. She swept back her hair to receive the morning's balm and lifted her face to it.

The school gates did nothing to enhance the day, but by the time she reached them, Caitlyn felt ready to get through the deskbound hours. After that, she determined, all the gods and ghosts in all the realms could wait while she caught up on her sleep.

Danny was waiting and trying to look like he wasn't as she passed into the schoolyard. She responded to his furtive wave with a nod that served at the same time to bring her fringe in place over one eye. She eased towards him casually, but watchfully too. No school bullies loomed on the horizon just yet.

'Hey,' he said, and it was immediately clear he had more to say.

'Hi,' she said.

'Up late?' he asked.

She started. Really, did she look that shattered? 'What?'

'Up late, studying for the test?'

'*What?*' Caitlyn's heart sank in freezing waters.

'The third-year history test is this morning. You remember, Mister Flood posted it last week.'

'Oh. My. God.' The schoolyard heaved beneath her feet and set her stomach churning. She must even have staggered because Danny reached as though to steady her. She jerked back from him.

'Hey, don't worry,' he soothed, 'it's a no-brainer.'

'Were *you* up late studying?' she challenged him.

'Well, yeah, but it's history, come on, I had to cram. You didn't, not for this one.' He caught her quizzical frown. 'Look, it's a test set by Miss Farrell, a week after the trip to Newgrange. I'll bet you a lunch in Dario's all the questions will be on ancient Ireland, with maybe a couple on boy bands of the last decade thrown in for the no-hopers.'

She burst to laughing despite everything and almost touched his arm, almost.

'Lunch at Dario's,' she accepted his offer.

'Easy bet,' he smiled, 'you'll blast this one.' He waited a second and then seized the moment with a deep breath. 'I was wondering if I could ask you something.'

'Sure,' she said lightly, and braced for it.

'Well,' he said, consciously slow, 'end of term is coming.'

The end-of-term dance too, she nearly said.

'It is,' she replied, matter-of-factly.

'Well, I was wondering,' he made to explain and midway through he stopped, diverted and confused by something he spotted behind her. 'Why is that man watching us?'

Caitlyn followed Danny's gaze towards the gates to where Professor Brody stood by the Wraith, leaning with a sombre air on his cane.

'I think I have to go,' Caitlyn said, reading the Professor's dark mood at once. She stepped away from Danny.

'Really?' Danny asked. He cast a concerned look towards the Professor. 'Who is he?'

She stepped close again, almost to touching.

'Come dance with me and I'll tell you,' she whispered and meant it.

She left him there, nodding mutely through a smile, and joined the Professor at the kerb.

'No school today,' Brody said simply. He opened the door for her.

'The spear?' she guessed.

'Safe for now,' he replied as Marcus gunned the engine. 'But there has been a development. Dr James was murdered at Newgrange last night.'

Murdered at Newgrange.

In an instant she was six again. She was hauling at box lids to reveal vivid colours, pumpkin lights and ghostly silhouettes. She heard the doorbell's chime and watched paper skeletons fall like leaves.

The roar of a passing motorcycle jolted Caitlyn from her memories and she entered the car.

A short time later the city thinned as the car whispered north. Marcus fixed his gaze on the route and was silent, as was the Professor at Caitlyn's side but for an occasional and loud sipping he offered the takeaway cup at his lips. The drinking vessel was so at odds with the character of the Professor that Caitlyn frowned on seeing it.

'What is that?' she asked.

'It's supposed to be coffee,' Brody responded with a curled lip of distaste. 'Really, Marcus, where did you source this concoction?'

'The vending machine by the student lounge,' Marcus said. 'You said we were pressed for time.'

The Professor sipped again and gagged. Surrendering all hope of flavour, he set the cup aside. The action presented Caitlyn with a clear view of his fatigued and drawn features.

'You didn't get much sleep,' she deduced.

'I fell asleep at my desk,' he explained, adding distantly, 'I was dreaming of cat's eyes.' The unsettling recollection prompted him to pinch the bridge of his nose as though to dispel it. 'The call from Newgrange came at an unearthly hour also.'

Murdered at Newgrange.

'What happened?' Caitlyn asked, propping herself against the seat as the car eased into the off-ramp curve.

The Professor laced his fingers. 'What we know at this point is that late in the afternoon yesterday students working with Dr James unearthed a significant find. They described it as a statue of some kind, a giant man in a crown of branches.'

'The Lost King,' Caitlyn said at once.

'It would seem so,' Brody agreed. 'But as soon as the excavators made their discovery known Dr James ordered everyone to finish working and clear the site. He would remain to make notes and sketches, he told them. Some students believed at the time this was James's way of claiming the glory of the find for himself, nothing unsurprising in that. This morning when they arrived, however, they found the Doctor's body. As for the "statue", well, you can guess at that.'

'Gone,' she said.

'Released,' the Professor said.

'It looks like this is as far as we go,' Marcus called back. Slowing the vehicle, he drew attention to the length of blue and white police tape stretching across the road and the stony-faced officer manning the cordon. Past this, and sparkling in response to the morning, Newgrange waited.

Caitlyn and the Professor walked the rest of the way. After brief introductions and identifications to the policeman, the tape was raised, and they traced the path on and upwards towards the mound. With every step the structure loomed larger until it seemed to Caitlyn that Newgrange was advancing to fall on them from the crest. She stared at the rectangular lightbox above the doorway. It stared right back.

'Do you see?'

Brody's voice brought her attention away and to the east where their elevated position offered sight across a cluster of tents. She followed where the Professor walked for a better view of the dig site.

Less than a minute later it lay fully below. They gazed on a scene of intense activity. Between the small encampment and a long cut trench, police officers bustled to and fro in their investigations. Groups met in consultation and to question a small group of students huddled on the edge of the area. Others engaged in a joint effort at the trench itself. As Caitlyn and Brody watched, officers hauled a covered stretcher free of the trench to distressed cries from the students.

'I want you to remain here, Caitlyn,' the Professor said. 'You don't need to see this.'

Caitlyn made to protest but before she could speak Brody walked away without looking back. In a rush of anger, she determined to follow, to march right past the Professor in defiance of his command. The moment was lost as she watched the stretcher set down and saw a dead hand flop from beneath its covering sheet.

'There's a better view from up here anyhow,' she muttered sourly after Brody.

The Professor had by now reached the hedgerow enclosing the encampment and passed through a narrow gap in the foliage. Caitlyn looked on as he introduced himself to a detective and was led to the trench whose depths shifted between shadow and light under clouds racing across the face of the sun. The driving wind swept over Caitlyn's back and on down the hillside where it plucked at the tent tops and deadened all sound at the site but for a distant scraping. Caitlyn frowned at metal drawing repeatedly against stone but could not find the source anywhere across the dig.

Maybe it was coming from the trench, she reasoned, where Brody was peering down, perhaps on officers seeking clues to an incident they would never understand. The sound died away, falling with the wind only to rise quickly again. The harsh scraping came on a renewed gust that shoved at her back. Caitlyn realised then the noise was not carrying from the site but from behind, and she turned to locate it.

In a shallow trench a short distance from her position, a man scraped the earth with a trowel. With his back angled to her he worked the tool rhythmically to clear an exposed layer of interlocked stones. Caitlyn blinked at the sight, struggling to account for how she had missed this figure on the climb to the crest. Had the Professor missed him too? They must have passed within metres of the dig, but they had not seen or heard the man. Yet here he was labouring away in the clear morning light. Caitlyn continued to watch as the man's efforts prompted another thought in her. Why was he still digging when all activity in the camp had been stopped?

The digger paused, long enough to stretch his weary back. He set his trowel aside in exchange for a hand brush and the motion afforded Caitlyn the briefest glimpse of his young profile.

The tingle to the roots of Caitlyn's hair was as nothing to the burst within her chest.

'Daddy?'

FORTY-FOUR

The ghost of Barry McCabe returned to his work.

Oblivious to all but his remarkable find, he brushed the dust from the stones and picked roots from between. Nothing could divert him from it, not the blazing sun or the tumbling clouds, not Caitlyn where she circled in front of him.

'Daddy,' she said again through her amazement, but again he did not hear. Falling to her knees and into his direct eye-line she tracked his motions to be seen. 'Daddy, it's Caitlyn, it's me.' But the work continued unabated and he neither saw nor heard her, and she understood at once that he couldn't. The whole scene, she realised, and not just her father, was a phantom memory. Like the funeral procession for King Lug, this was an event replaying.

Newgrange sent an eager wind to her back.

Her father's hair was ruffled by it, an unruly tossing he ignored in the moment, and Caitlyn unconsciously reached out, intending to sweep it from the elements buffeting the strong lines of his face.

The earth gave way, becoming a clattering descent of loose stones and Barry McCabe was pitched violently forward into the chasm suddenly opened at his knees. His cry came in time with Caitlyn's, and she watched him fall away. She scrambled for the edge of the collapse to peer down into the dusty subterranean pitch for signs of him.

She detected movement below, at a place where sunlight failed beyond the pile of collapsed stone. Her father was moving slowly there among the shadows. Without hesitation, she swung her legs over the edge of the hole and eased gingerly down, her feet straining to reach the summit of heaped debris. Loose rock threatened to shift beneath her weight and when she released her grip, she surfed on a brief avalanche to the base of the fall. She waved against a choking dust storm to relocate her father.

He pushed to his feet in a broad tunnel stretching from him to unseen depths. The corridor was of hand-cut blocks, curving to keep to the rounded shape of the hillside and the circular architecture of Newgrange. McCabe dug excitedly through his pockets for his torch. Its light flared to play on walls enriched with knotted carvings which swirled the length of the passage and on past the distant bend.

'Dr McCabe!' The voice came from above, concerned and searching. 'Are you all right? It's Professor Gilbert. Do you need help?'

Caitlyn glanced towards the hole and saw head and shoulders silhouetted against the sky. A buttonhole flower was vivid yellow in the light.

McCabe laughed through the dust. 'I'm fine, Professor. I've found something.'

'I'll fetch a rope,' Gilbert offered, 'and Professor Brody.'

'I'll explore,' Barry McCabe replied happily, but the figure overhead had already gone. Guided by his torch, he set off along the mysterious way and Caitlyn followed.

They travelled along smooth stones, but over what distance Caitlyn could not tell in the sunless confines. On and on the wall-art led, its snaking flow enticing them further into the earth, a gentle decline perceptible beneath their feet as the air grew stale and colder.

The passageway ended in a gasp of wonder from McCabe. He drew up, almost staggering back from what he beheld.

Caitlyn peered through the gloom and was dumbfounded.

In a recess of vibrant decoration, the spear of Balor and the sword of Lug glimmered together. Set on a stone altar, the weapons crossed each other in a display of eternal contest. At their intersection they were bound in a bracket of triple rings, their power to harm symbolically confined by the three realms. In revealing torchlight, the etched blade flared, and the spear's jewelled tip twinkled, impervious to rust and the decay of time.

Barry McCabe moved forward in a hypnotised stagger towards the treasures. He reached for them but feared to touch what his fingers might discover to be nothing but a teasing mirage. With a joyous cry he fell to his knees, dragged down by instinctive reverence for these weapons of antiquity and humbled by the scale of his discovery. He examined quickly and expertly the text along the blade and attempted to decipher the jagged curses on the spear. He noted closely the damage to its haft where some inlaid stone had been torn away from others surrounding. Then and only then did he allow himself to draw breath and offer up a smile of understanding.

Caitlyn watched her father's happiness, captivated more by it than any glittering treasure. The only need she had for gold and shining stones was to use their light to view the animation of his face and the full life in his eyes.

The woman's shadow rose to kill all joy.

Deep black and angular, it eclipsed the weapons' glow. Its touch set torchlight blinking, so the Banshee's arrival was a flickering advance. She filled the corridor and gazed with emerald gleam on the trespasser and the fearful astonishment he offered her.

Caitlyn's voice was dry with fear. 'Daddy,' she whispered harshly, 'Dad, get up.'

But Barry McCabe did not hear across time and space as the Banshee glided with stealthy poise. The blade she drew should have prompted him to motion, its icy touch against his neck even more. But the winking light caught the angle of her cheek where it framed a single eye moistened with paralysing fury and rooted him.

'No,' Caitlyn said against it, and louder, 'No!'

'No!' she cried to the patch of sunlit grass, her tears coming under the open sky where Newgrange hulked impassively. The wind caught her voice and flung it away as a useless thing.

Only the returning Brody heard, and he followed her gaze to the undisturbed ground. He remembered the past she had witnessed.

'You saw them,' he concluded quietly.

'I saw my Dad,' she said without revealing her tears.

'Then you saw where it all began.'

'I saw how he died,' she replied angrily. 'And I saw who killed him.'

She walked away from Brody and carried her vengeance with her.

FORTY-FIVE

They drove back in oppressive silence.

Once or twice the Professor made to speak, intending to prompt a discussion of matters as they stood, but Caitlyn ignored him. She didn't want to hear any more about spears or Pookas or haunted realms. It was all pain and death, and she hated it and its ghosts and gods with their ambition and betrayal. Most of all she hated seeing it with a vivid gift that could change nothing.

The car slowed and she saw the school fence and the class block behind. It was normal, everyday, boring, a relief.

'Don't come tonight,' she said, exiting swiftly.

'Caitlyn,' the Professor said, and there was everything in the way he said it.

She faced him. 'I'll be back,' she said. 'Just, don't come tonight.'

'Time is not on our side,' he tried, but saw her face unchanged and he relented. 'Call when you are ready, Marcus will come.' With a polite nod he closed the door and the car departed.

She blinked the Professor's face away and allowed her ears to fill with the clamour of the school yard at recess. She gave herself over to it gratefully, the din chasing almost everything else from her mind as she stepped through the gates.

Bustling activity to one side of the yard meant that her return went unobserved by the other students. Some unfolding nonsense near the bike shelters had drawn excited crowds so that all backs were turned as she aimed towards the main building. She would find Danny, she determined, and talk to him, but not about the dance. She didn't want to dance anymore.

A howl erupted from the gathered students, prompted by some outrageous spectacle their ranks hid from sight. She wilfully ignored it as she mounted the school steps and pulled up sharply where Mia shimmered in her way. The little spirit looked at Caitlyn with gravest concern.

'Mia,' Caitlyn said, surprised, 'what's wrong?'

Mia pointed towards the exuberant throng. 'The boy you like is in big trouble.'

Caitlyn spun back. Her high position on the steps afforded a view across the jostling heads and to the clearing at the heart of the whooping mob. That was where Danny stood, his pale features set as he watched Luke Goslin circling him with vicious intent.

Caitlyn cleared the steps in a bound and she sprinted

for the wall of massed students. Elbowing through, she pushed to the front, deafened by the chants and shouts of outrage for the action at the centre.

'Say it again!' Luke Goslin challenged with a finger jab towards Danny's face. 'Say it!' Here Luke sprang forward and shoved with both hands against his opponent's chest. Only Danny's anticipation of the move, his stepping back with it, prevented him from sprawling to the ground. 'Go on,' Luke Goslin spat through his rising aggression, 'tell everyone what you said to my girlfriend. Go on!'

Debbie Walsh. Caitlyn scanned the multitude of faces quickly and found her. Flanked as ever by the Kelly twins, the girl grinned malevolently, tittering with delight at her champion, and at Danny's suffering. When the boy did not speak in answer to Luke Goslin's jibes, she did.

'He made fun of my hair, Luke,' she said in wounded tones.

'Yeah,' the outraged Luke Goslin said. 'You have a smart mouth, don't you, Magic Man?' His fist bunched tight. 'You need something to shut it up.'

'Do it, Luke,' Debbie Walsh squealed hungrily. Her eyes flared in expectation.

Danny closed his fists for the attack to come but the movement was awkward and slight.

Caitlyn launched forward. 'Don't you dare,' she

shouted at Luke Goslin. Her intervention brought fresh cheering from the crowd. She closed on the boys, aiming fiercely for the space between.

The pull on her hair was no less fierce and she was swept painfully back as the volume of whooping soared to deafening levels. Her head twisted unnaturally, and Caitlyn saw Debbie Walsh's cruel face above her own, screwed to a malicious joy.

'Where are you going, freak?' Debbie Walsh demanded with a renewed twist of hair for control, and just for the pleasure of it, before returning her attention to Luke Goslin. 'Well?' she barked. 'What are you waiting for?'

The cry Caitlyn released was anguished, fired by blinding pain. It travelled up and past gritted teeth, and on its way, it became something else. Transformed to an animalistic tone, it forced silence on the crowd and drove them back from what was rising through Caitlyn's pain. Her cry became a snarl which fed on agony and stored-up frustration. In an instant it was a shriek of rage, piercing against bullies, against harm to those she cared for.

Against being touched.

Caitlyn twisted, ignoring the sting in her scalp and drove fiercely against her opponent's grip. The motion caught Debbie Walsh by surprise and in the moment of distraction, the girl found her hand pulled behind her as Caitlyn ducked and swept up, at last breaking her hold. The crowd gasped, but Caitlyn wasn't nearly done yet. Coiling the offending arm back, hard, she whipped a hand to clasp Debbie Walsh's perfectly pampered head. Fingers sought skin, smearing greasily through foundation and lipstick as Caitlyn pulled her cheek to cheek.

'Do you want to see something freaky?' she whispered to the bully.

Debbie Walsh had no choice. She saw. The mortal world ran like melting paint, and she saw, and received everything Caitlyn offered.

Gone were the howling students and in their place scabrous hags congregated to laugh at her plight through tobacco smoke and blackened teeth. Their cackles increased at the sight of a masked hangman twisting his knot in eager anticipation of Debbie Walsh's neck. The gruesome figure made to approach, but his path was blocked by plague victims, crawling and begging towards her across the blackened earth. Mangy dogs stood on a splintered coffin and slavered for their portion until driven off by a bucking of the lid and a mottled hand which probed the air. A little girl, big-eyed and pretty, worked furiously to pull her face into as many frightful contortions as she could manage. And besides all, a sight which brought pitiful groans of terror from Debbie Walsh, was that of

Grandmother Walsh standing in her funeral clothes and wagging one scolding finger.

Caitlyn released her enemy when she felt the girl's legs buckle. With guilty satisfaction she stepped back and looked down on Debbie Walsh blubbering on the school yard.

The astonished mob crashed in on itself. With exultant cries for the momentous event of seeing Debbie Walsh bested, students stampeded past Caitlyn and between Danny and Luke Goslin to bear witness to the bully's downfall. Without moving, Caitlyn abruptly found herself at the back of the milling crowd. She retreated from it, breathless, jubilant, her heart racing. She laughed giddily at the strength she had unleashed. From the throng about Debbie Walsh, an exclaimed 'she's peed her pants!' drew howls of ecstatic disgust from the whole school.

From nowhere Danny was at Caitlyn's side, his excited words unheard in her moment of joy. Realising she was grinning like an idiot, Caitlyn fought to calm the storm surge of emotion within and focused on his lips.

'Have you ever skipped school?' he asked.

'Today would be a first,' she admitted.

'Let's go.'

Out the gates they fled together, and into school legend.

FORTY-SIX

Their destination was agreed on the run and without words.

Joyously they ran to Rosehill, tearing through undergrowth with abandon, skipping and tripping along hidden paths until the grand hall resounded to their uncontrolled laughter.

Struggling for breath, Caitlyn turned her face up to the open roof and felt sunlight and freedom wash over her face as she drew in gulps of air past still rising chuckles. These were prompted by Danny's apparent inability to say anything but 'incredible' over and over.

'It was incredible,' he gushed again, and he worked with feverish hands to contain the moment and the scene replaying in his mind, 'incredible'.

'It was something,' she agreed, watching with open amusement where he marched excitedly back and forth over ruined tiles.

'Something?' he thrilled. 'That was more than something. You just wiped the floor with Debbie Walsh. Don't you know what that means?'

'I think you're dying to tell me.' Caitlyn smiled and she stepped between the shafts of light streaming through Rosehill's empty windows.

Danny's fingers skittered in the effort to explain all, to pull the chaos of words and ideas competing behind his lips into more than a babbling torrent. With supreme will he calmed himself and faced her.

'It means everything,' he proclaimed loudly. Ravens took to chattering flight high above as though to bring his message to the world. 'You beat the school bully in front of the *whole school*.'

'I did, didn't I?' she said, pleased with herself and she shielded a guilty laugh with a hand.

'Incredible,' Danny said for the umpteenth time and he stared in wonder at her, and perhaps for a little longer than he intended.

'What?' she asked self-consciously through a smile.

'I'm trying to work it out,' he confessed. 'What did you do? How did you freak her out like that?'

Caitlyn shrugged, her smile becoming awkward as she scrambled for a lie she didn't want to offer. 'It was just shock at my reaction,' she tried. She caught his narrowing eyes and saw he wasn't convinced.

'You're a real puzzle, Caitlyn McCabe, do you know that?' he said.

'Oh,' she played along with a wink, 'you mean I'm mysterious.'

He smiled with her, and then, before he could catch them, the words were on the air. 'That's what I like about you.'

He wilted under her gaze.

'Wait, no,' he flustered, 'I didn't mean to say that, I mean, what I meant, what I mean is, I like you as a person, I don't mean, well I do, but hell, it's just that I think there are things I can do with you that I can't with others and oh, God, that's not what I mean, you know what I mean. Don't you?' He trailed off, hoping for more than the terrible silence descending on Rosehill.

'Truth or dare,' she challenged him, looking at his face, but not looking at his eyes.

'Truth?' he guessed.

'Dare,' she said and meant it.

It was decided in the way Rosehill had been chosen, unspoken, agreed and understood silently between them. She waited for him as he crossed the floor, drawing tentatively close to her where she stood at the centre of the hall. Stepping into the sunlight containing her, he offered his arm to her waist and met the emerald and sapphire sparkle of her eyes looking to his. He saw hopes and desires reflected, and as he bent for her lips he understood as she did that words only get in the way.

Her touch transformed everything.

The barriers crumbled before it and Rosehill flourished anew, its great hall dazzling and bedecked for lovers. Under the candlelit gaze of portraits, the orchestra led the ball and dancers swept in graceful motion to its time, filling the panelled room with the exultation of forever. Ball gowns flowered where straight-backed gentlemen in tailored attire guided ladies through musical rhythms to elegant pirouettes across polished tiles. Chandeliers flared from the buttressed ceiling to splash crystal brilliance on coloured streamers bursting from the gallery and stairs repaired, flung by spirits masked and jubilant.

Celebrated and toasted with sparkling champagne, Caitlyn and Danny clung together and were oblivious, lost in that space between worlds contained in a kiss.

ॐ ॐ ॐ

At dusk she led him by the hand to the balcony, steadying him in his first overawed tripping through the spirit world.

Danny looked and was overwhelmed, shrinking at first from phantoms drifting near and then trusting to her guidance and the sights she granted him. In the shadow of Rosehill, they held closely together for more than vision. In the tended gardens below, partygoers shimmered to and fro among beds of black roses inclining to the moon. From the ballroom, the orchestra offered a gentle timbre to the still air.

'Is it always like this?' Danny gasped.

'Yeah,' she said happily.

'Now I understand why you come here. It's all just...'

'Incredible?' she offered with a chuckle.

'Thank you for showing me,' he whispered.

She clung to his warmth and breathed the glorious night. And as she did she saw the watcher beyond the glass. Phantom Danny peered at them with an air of approval washing his pale features.

'Why do *you* come here?' she probed gently, only to feel tightening arms and Danny's overlong silence.

'Don't spoil it,' he said at last. He gestured to bring her attention to a nearby table laden with delicacies for the feast. As they watched, a chocolate-smeared Mia popped up and impishly pilfered more cakes while a servant's back was turned.

Caitlyn accepted the distraction and smiled at the little spirit's antics. 'No more questions,' she promised Danny.

Questions. She heard the Professor's voice in the word. There had been too many questions since his appearance in her life, questions in need of answers but left unanswered, questions on questions. She was fed up with them all. Hadn't she been happy enough without them, wasn't she happy now, in her corner of the spirit world without Brody's interference, with Rosehill a blissful oasis against intruding mysteries?

Questionsss.

Danny mistook her shiver and shielded her from the night chill as she caught the memory of that other voice, sneering from the rooftops. *You are so far behind the game,* it mocked, *with all your questionsss.* She looked over Rosehill's spectral partygoers and heard the Pooka's foretelling through the wistful strains of the orchestra. *The King is coming and the Fomorians with him. They will take everything.*

And with fresh perception, she recalled the strangest words of all.

Puzzles and poetry won't save your world.

She spun from Danny's arms, clasping his hand tightly as she faced him.

'Puzzles,' she blurted, 'you like puzzles.'

'Yes,' he said. His brow arched quizzically at her behaviour.

'Do you like poetry?'

'What, seriously?'

Her mind raced ahead of her lips. 'There's a poem and a puzzle, there's a puzzle, in a poem, and a sword,' she read the concern for her sanity in his features. 'I have to go. We...I have to get you a glove, we have to go, right away.'

'Okay,' he agreed nonplussed. 'Where are we going?'

But she ignored him and released his hand to race ahead. Glorious Rosehill faded.

The party was over.

FORTY-SEVEN

Sleep held a fitful grip on Sackimum Brody.

At his paper-strewn desk and in the quiet left by Marcus's departure, a deep fatigue he had kept in check these past few days finally overtook him. With nothing to distract, it lulled him to a nodding state even as he struggled to hold on to waking thoughts. Plans in his heavy head became mere wisps, unable to prevent his eyes from closing as they drifted to the corners of his mind, there to blend gently with memories and produce soft...

Dreamsss.

The Professor's head snapped up and he became alert to threats. His hand reached unconsciously for the desk and the cane he had set strategically close. The room about him lay still, its shadows between display cases nothing more than pressings of the moon through the windows. The skull of Ivar the Boneless mocked his restlessness with shining teeth.

Brody drew out his pocket watch. Flipping the case, he was dismayed to see the passage of barely fifteen minutes since Marcus had left in answer to Caitlyn's excited call. Doubting the timepiece, he rose and stepped to the windows. From there he looked to the university clock, its illuminated gold hands confirming the accuracy of its tiny cousin. Meanwhile below, discreet vapours held fast in doorways and corners, maintaining their secret vigilance. None of the watching spirits knew what was guarded, only that the Professor had charged them with reporting at once any strange activity within the university grounds.

Satisfied, Brody thumbed the watch cover, shutting it with a click that was altogether too loud in the vaulted hush of the room. It was almost as though the securing of the miniature lock had come in time to one larger, like those of the display cases which snapped harshly whenever opened.

Brody spun around to regard the darkened office once more. The black spaces stood impervious to sight, each one a depthless portal to a hiding place for night villains and...

Thievesss.

The Professor eased forward, skirting deliberately behind his high-backed chair to regain his desk on that side nearest the cane. This he lifted carefully and just as carefully slid its blade free to cut the moonlight.

Useless, the night sniggered.

Brody left the cover of the chair and his heart skipped as a shadow darted by on his right. He looked and discovered it was his own, formed when he stepped into the light from the window. He cursed himself a fool and advanced, the tip of his blade pointing the way to an inky channel directly ahead.

He passed into the maze of glass. Dusty cabinets rose on all sides to obscure and confound. Far more than treasured exhibits, they held the promise of a concealed enemy at every turn, an assassin to be made monstrous behind refracting panes.

'You waste your time, Brody,' the Pooka chuckled through black canyons.

The Professor's sword whistled on the turn.

'You will not have the spear,' he snarled.

The Pooka's laughter rattled the display cases.

'We have it already,' he choked though his merriment. 'Golden in the grasp of the Returned King it is a thing of beauteous dessstruction.'

'Liar,' the Professor spat.

'Look to your hiding place, Brody. It is empty.'

As the Pooka spoke, he rose. Surging up behind a cabinet, his weapon sang free in search of blood.

Brody detected the warped movement and struck out. His sword caught the display, sundering wood and glass, the erupting clamour blending with the Pooka's shriek of murderous rage.

Brody bolted upright in his chair, jolted from his nightmare by the storm of violence. Confused on the border between sleeping and waking, he swept the air with his empty hand, aiming to strike a monstrous face that seemed to follow from his dreaming to a place within a pool of shadow by his chair. He saw his cane still in its place and snatched it up, toppling his chair aside as he slashed against dreams and unseen demons.

We have it already, look to your hiding placcce.

The dream-words-real-words took him, giving sudden impetus to his feet. Brody was driven towards the door. Blade in hand he raced blindly between the exhibits and hauled the barrier open. He took the stairs two by two in a frenzied and unthinking descent until he reached the cold air outside and cut through it to trip across the cobbles of the square. He saw nothing in his stumbling flight, neither mortal nor spirit, nor the headlights of the Wraith from where Caitlyn leapt as though to intercept him. He was deaf to her alarmed calling to him, oblivious to everything in his confusion but the safety of the spear in its everyday hiding place.

It was still there. The Professor looked with addled eyes and saw it was still there. Relief welled up, carried on a single harsh breath that dispelled the last traces of dreaming. But even as it plumed on the night air, Brody perceived the cold reality of the game and he looked fearfully to the shadows.

The Pooka looked back. His cat's eyes watched as they had during Brody's sleeping and from the instant of his waking, watched closely his trail of panic, watched his actions at the heart of the university square, and watched the upturning of his face where he had looked to the spear's hiding place.

'No,' Brody cried in despair against trickery.

The Pooka looked and was breathless at that which he beheld. The university clock tracked to midnight and the Pooka saw the moonlit spear wink in the motion. The sharpened hour hand, long and slender, proudly displayed its shaft of intricate carvings, and the beauty of it drew from the Pooka a gasp of adoration which bloomed to a triumphant howl where he sprang to action.

From beneath his cape, the Pooka's claws flashed to the bricks and hauled his form across and up the university's façade. Dizzyingly fast he scurried higher and higher until the clock was gained. There he coursed about its face like a malignant spider circling its catch and relishing the moment. The spear was grasped and to a grinding protest of stalled cogs was torn from its fixing. The clock died in a scream of ruptured springs and broken gears. To the chaos the Pooka added his howl of jubilation and swept up and over the roof as clock parts crashed to earth.

Marcus was already gunning the Wraith hard as Caitlyn and the Professor dived aboard to meet Danny's stunned gaze.

'Go!' Caitlyn commanded, falling into her seat as the car screeched to motion.

'Don't lose him, Marcus,' Brody urged. 'If the Pooka reaches his path to the third realm, all is lost.'

FORTY-EIGHT

The Silver Wraith roared across the city.

Through streets broad and narrow, the car leapt junctions and slid into corners, fighting for every inch of cobble in pursuit of the Pooka who dashed the roof-tops above.

'West,' Brody called from his vantage point hanging out a passenger window. Beside him, Caitlyn pressed to the glass and struggled to keep the demon's progress in sight. Next to her, Danny stared in wonderment and confusion at the rapid passage of the spirit world.

'He's turning,' Caitlyn warned, 'going right.'

Marcus followed with a violent spin of the wheel. His passengers tumbled through the compartment behind with cries and they scrambled to regain the windows.

Overhead, the Pooka betrayed himself with a giant leap between buildings, the spear flaring with reflected light to catch the driver's eye. Marcus again forced the screeching vehicle into a hair-raising turn. The manoeuvre was completed just in time for the pursuers to see the Pooka's first mistake.

Launching once more between rooftops, the demon misjudged the distance in his headlong rush. He struck heavily, his landing spot splitting to a web of fault-lines and, just as he regained his balance, an avalanche of broken tiles swept down, toppling the helpless Pooka into space and towards a lower roof. As he fell, the thief's grip on the spear was lost.

Marcus applied the brakes hard.

'We have him,' Brody said, half in hope as he extricated himself from the pile of tumbling bodies. With a kick to open a door, he quickly assessed the situation. 'We have to get up there fast. Caitlyn, you come with me. Marcus and...,' he looked quizzically at the unidentified boy.

'Professor, Danny, Danny, Professor,' Caitlyn said rapidly as she swept by.

'Are you armed?' Brody demanded.

'What? No!' Danny exclaimed. He looked where Marcus dived to pop the glove box and produce a pair of ornate flintlock pistols. He thrust one into Danny's hand before the startled boy could argue.

'Stay with Marcus,' the Professor ordered, 'and be ready to continue the pursuit.' He ducked from the car in search of Caitlyn.

She was pointing the way. 'Professor,' she cried, gesturing to a grimy fire escape. The ladder hugged the side of the building which had received the Pooka.

They sprinted towards it.

Brody was quickest and, utilising the handle of his sword, he hauled down the retractable ladder to offer access. The metal struck ground with a reverberating clang and he began to climb, Caitlyn hard behind.

The fire escape led them up its zigzag stages. Feet clattered noisily against the metalwork until Brody slowed as he approached the final set of steps to the roof. Here, at his signal, they advanced more softly and cautiously to gain the top.

The sound of the Pooka's struggles reached them before their first sight of him. He lay at a spot beyond old chimney pots and modern steam ducts, grunting bitterly in the effort to dig free of the mound of tiles that had buried him. Caitlyn and the Professor took in the scene quickly, seeking the spear among the debris but finding no sign. Brody broke cover and raced to stand over the helpless Pooka. He levelled his sword, bringing fear to the demon's face with the gleaming blade.

'Where is it?' Brody demanded angrily. He offered a threatening jab of the weapon to loosen the Pooka's tongue.

Caitlyn sensed the change an instant before the Pooka's monstrous face twisted to a sneering smile. To the roots of her hair the warning tingled like electricity. Too late she turned in answer to her senses but just in time to perceive the spear where it swept into view, a golden arc lighting the night.

The blow was crushing. Caitlyn felt the air driven from her lungs as she and the Professor were hit and sent tumbling along the roof. She heard Brody's cry and the chiming of his fallen sword before all sense was numbed by her landing, hard against a chimney stack.

King Balor of the Fomorians emerged from shadow.

Through swimming layers of vision, Caitlyn watched the terrible figure raise the spear he held. Expertly he spun his regained weapon, at one with its thrumming motion. He exulted in its weight and form as he passed it hand to hand, his gashed face illuminated by splashes of light caught on the whirling tip.

The display ended and the warrior King was satisfied to stand before his fallen enemies and glower. By his side, the Pooka rose to kneeling supplication.

'All hail my glorious King,' he mewled.

'Who are these challengers?' Balor growled. His eye roved over Caitlyn and Brody.

'Those who have worked so hard to keep your Majesty from power,' the Pooka replied eagerly.

Queen Cethlinn offered more. Stepping into view behind her King with the Morrigan by her side, she smiled with a cruel satisfaction. 'Professor Sackimum Brody,' she said, 'meddler and thief, upstart pest.'

Brody met her hateful gaze, unwavering.

'And his apprenticcce,' the Pooka interjected slavishly. He gestured to the fallen girl.

'Caitlyn McCabe,' the Morrigan reported, and with a wink she added, 'kissy kissy.'

'Ah,' Cethlinn exclaimed with feigned joy. She turned a gaze of curiosity on the girl. 'Are we really in the presence of young Caitlyn McCabe, the girl with sight?' She bent for closer examination, her tone becoming grim. 'I wonder, what a freak of nature you are that you see so much?'

From deep within, Caitlyn found a reserve of strength and lashed out. The slap was sharp enough to turn the Queen's head and it drew a gasp of horror from the Pooka.

'You dare?' he shrilled. 'You dare?'

Cethlinn straightened, controlling the fury that rose with her. 'Balor, my love, my King,' she said softly, though with grinding teeth, 'my honour demands redress. Let our enemies witness the power you hold.'

Balor swept up his weapon in answer. With a roar to the sky, he thrust it high as though to pierce the heavens and slashed down to level its tip on Brody. With a tightening grip, the King braced for the power that must come at his command.

Nothing. Silence reigned and the spear hung powerlessly on the air, bringing forth nothing more than looks of confusion between King and Queen.

Brody seized the moment. He rolled to his fallen sword and brought it singing from its resting place.

With a deft movement he contacted with the spear tip and swept it aside, clearing the way for a thrust towards the confounded King. Throwing his weight forward and drove straight for Balor's heart.

Brody's sword found the King's breast, its edge nicking the first layers of material before the Pooka's weapon flew in defence. Sword sang on sword and the attack was blasted aside to leave the Professor exposed to the counter thrust. The Pooka plunged his blade deep into Brody's chest.

Caitlyn's distraught cry burst on the air. The sound sent agonising waves through her injured head. She fought against swimming vision to reach for the stricken Professor where he was driven backwards by the hissing Pooka. With a flailing hand she caught the hem of the demon's cape and tugged as though to halt the scene but failed in a harsh rending of cloth. The opponents reached the edge of the roof and the Professor tottered with no more than a final moment to look to her before he was gone, tumbling towards the oily black waters of the Liffey. The Pooka flung a howl of triumph to the splashing river.

The Morrigan advanced to finish things. With Caitlyn fixed under a look of malevolent determination, the warrior drew her sword and tracked her victim where the girl tried to blend with the chimney bricks and avoid the inevitable.

'Stop!' Cethlinn commanded sharply. She waved the Morrigan aside. 'Why should this be quick when it can be slow?' The Queen offered her command with a snap of fingers.

The night shivered to the weeping approach of the Banshee. The air rippled at her calling and parted in cold waves as her shape bled from darkness. She stood before her controlling Queen, ever shifting but for the straight hair framing that watchful emerald eye.

'Aoife,' Cethlinn offered a false fondness, 'look upon this impudent child who would strike a Queen. Deal with her.' Fingers snapped loudly.

The Banshee did as commanded and turned to look on Caitlyn. Her singular cruel eye stared hard, and as she stared the woman leaned forward, and so much that the angle of her body to the roof beneath became unnaturally sharp. Further yet she inclined until, beyond the point of toppling, she mirrored Caitlyn's prone position and floated on the air towards her. The woman's hair and dress rippled slowly in her wake, and the only sound to come with her gliding approach was the whisper of the dagger she drew.

Caitlyn watched as the horror swept to blot out the stars. Unable to escape, to resist that withering gaze, even to cry out, she clamped her eyes shut against what was coming and shuddered under the Banshee's vacant winter breath. When the woman's voice came, insistent and soft, it ran as ice on Caitlyn's neck.

'Look at me.'

Caitlyn squirmed against the invitation that was a piercing command.

'Look at me.'

This time the whispering was irresistible, and Caitlyn opened her eyes wide in helpless fear. The Banshee peered back from clouds of floating hair and gasped at the sight of sapphire and emerald eyes. Her grip tightened on the dagger to a crack of knuckles.

'What have they done to you, my beautiful darling daughter?'

The Banshee screamed.

The deafening power of her cry was enough to send Aoife back to standing. She whirled in a tumult of splayed hair to pour bottomless depths of hate on Queen Cethlinn with both eyes, eyes blazing green and blue in their fury. With her dagger raised, she swept forward, the very motion shattering spells and propelling Cethlinn back in fright.

'Stop her, Morrigan,' the Queen cried pitifully. She staggered in retreat before the merciless shrieking of her granddaughter.

Aoife anticipated the Morrigan's actions and easily met the warrior's flashing sword. With inhuman strength, the Banshee held against the weapon and struck backhanded at the Morrigan to drive her off. She stepped past her opponent even as one became three in a crashing fall. Shifting the dagger in her grip, Aoife drew back her arm for a strike at the Queen.

Balor's move was faster. He sent the shaft of his spear rebounding against Aoife's head and the attack was ended in a senseless collapse. The Banshee's dagger clattered uselessly across the tiles as the King stepped to his Queen to shield her from further harm. Clinging together, they watched the Morrigans surround Aoife where she struggled defiantly to rise.

Cethlinn wailed in Balor's arms. Fear and anger mixed to create bitter shrieks until the Queen gathered her senses and burst from his embrace to jab a finger of hate towards Caitlyn.

'Kill that *creature*,' she screeched tearfully to the Pooka who stood in voiceless confusion on the edge of the uproar.

'No,' Balor barked. His command drew Cethlinn about in astonishment and she examined his face as it swam with curiosity and possibilities. 'No,' he said again, and he peered on the fallen girl named Caitlyn, the one who was..., 'my great-granddaughter.' A smile flickered beneath the King's beard, fed by a calculating spark behind his eye. 'Spare the girl,' he ordered with a wave of his spear. 'We go.' He dismissed the Pooka and the Morrigans who departed quickly. He offered a reassuring look to his Queen and drew her close.

'What are you thinking?' she asked.

'Do you trust me?' he asked softly, and when words failed her, he said, 'Trust me and we shall have more than a spear in the fight. We cannot lose.'

Cethlinn spared a last glance at Caitlyn as she allowed the King to lead her away. They had taken but a few steps when vengeance overcame reassurance and Cethlinn spun back in fury. Drawing her whip, she cracked its length to the fullest and to coil harshly about Aoife's throat, hauling up that single green eye to focus all its pain.

'Caitlyn,' the Banshee sighed, her voice forlorn. The whip pulled to choking and she was torn back to darkness.

Caitlyn's vision dimmed as she lost the fight against injury and tears. Her arms and legs failed, her voice too as it struggled to cry out and give form to a word at once strange and familiar.

Mother.

FORTY-NINE

She woke to Danny's face.

He was close, attentive, sitting by her where she lay on a couch in an unfamiliar room. A single bulb offered the only light in the windowless space, sufficient to catch his relief at seeing her wake.

'You're okay,' he said as though to convince himself.

'Not really,' she said against bolts of pain at the back of her head. She closed her eyes to the harsh light, and the moment allowed her to detect the array of raised voices beyond the little room. 'Where are we?'

'Back at the university,' he explained, 'under the library. You're safe.'

'Brody,' she said. The flashback exploded in her head and brought fresh waves of agony. She saw once again the Professor's tormented face as he tumbled back from the roof.

'He's gone,' another voice answered. Marcus, red-eyed and grim stepped forward. 'We saw him fall.'

'He knew,' Caitlyn let her anger rise despite the pain, 'he knew about my mother.'

Marcus shook his head quickly. 'He suspected,' he stressed, 'but your father never said. That was to protect you. The Professor guessed the truth but couldn't be sure, even about your gift. Did you see spirits when your mother touched you, or did you see them yourself? When we found that answer, Brody was convinced.'

'He should have told me.'

'How could he?' Marcus protested. 'You are your father's daughter, but you are the Banshee's daughter too. You are Balor's great-granddaughter. How could the Professor know where your loyalty might lie?'

'If he didn't trust me, why did he involve me?'

'Newgrange.'

'What?' she asked and pressed up on her elbows. Her mind spun and Danny reached to ease her to sitting.

'Your visions at Newgrange,' Marcus reminded her. 'Please understand, you don't see spirits there, you see family memories. The funeral procession for King Lug your uncle, and the day your father met your mother. Something at Newgrange wants you to see those things. There is a reason. When the Professor realised that, he decided to reach out before others discovered you,' he faltered, 'before your mother led you to Balor.'

'She wouldn't do that!' Caitlyn snapped bitterly. 'She's Cethlinn's prisoner, she's controlled by her. I saw that on the roof.'

'You're a princess,' Danny mused.

She was not overjoyed at his deduction. 'We don't get to choose our family,' she grumbled.

'I know that,' he replied cryptically.

The raised voices outside came louder, more urgent.

'What is going on out there?' Caitlyn demanded.

'Everyone's here,' Marcus said. 'With the spear returned to Balor's control, it's only a matter of time before his army returns. The spirit world is in a panic. Everyone is looking for answers, and now they know who you really are, well, they're looking to you.'

Caitlyn groaned and fell back. 'I can't do this,' she exclaimed.

'You need some time,' Marcus said. He moved towards the door. 'I'll tell the others.'

The volume rose briefly as Marcus slipped out, and Caitlyn closed her eyes against the din of voices. She covered her face with a hand to hold against the threat of tears.

'I can't do this,' she sighed again helplessly. 'I don't know who I'm supposed to be anymore.' She gripped Danny's hand to save herself from failing.

Danny made a decision. His words were considered, softly spoken. His words were considered, softly spoken.

'Did you know I had a brother? David. We were twins. He was older than me by three minutes and he never let me forget it. We were the same in all the usual ways, only Mum could tell us apart, but we were different in other things. I like puzzles and books, David loved sport, especially running. He was good too, really good, a record-breaker, though he always said it wasn't about that or winning and losing. He told me, "Running isn't running, it's the place I go to work things out." I didn't understand that, so I called him a plank and we fought the way brothers do.

'It was Dad who pushed David into competing. He said not winning was a waste of talent. He told him, "You're a champ and you'll bring home the trophy." And he did. There are piles of medals in our house, all David's, all gold, never silver. Dad wouldn't tolerate that. "In it to win it," he'd say. He had a catchphrase for every race. "Stronger, son, faster, son, beat that clock, do it for your dad, go, go, go."

Danny wrestled with the truth.

'David died five months ago. It was sudden, after another big race. That morning he told me he was looking for a way to tell Dad he wanted to stop competing. He wasn't running for himself anymore and he hated it, but how do you disappoint your Dad? The last thing he said, the very last thing, in the door with his kitbag was, "You like puzzles, Danny, maybe you can work it out for me".

'Later, the doctor tried to explain what had happened to David. He used big medical terms no-one understood, and Mom was all tears and questions, so he tried to make it easier. I remember his words exactly. "There was too much pressure in David's head".'

He gripped Caitlyn's hand and she saved him from failing.

'My Dad still looks for David. When he realises it's just me he gets angry. "Your brother should be here, not you," he says. That's okay. I've learned that when he talks that way, he won't do anything worse. But some days he doesn't talk at all and it *is* worse. That's why I go to Rosehill.'

He set his gaze on Caitlyn's.

'You said we don't get to choose our family. You're right. But they don't get to choose who *you* are.'

She absorbed the words and returned the firmness of his grip as the storm in her head began to recede.

'Help me up,' she said.

⚜ ⚜ ⚜

They passed into a chaos of spirits crammed into the Reserve Room.

Across the vast chamber, ghosts jostled and argued in an atmosphere of intense agitation. Debates raged and anxious questions were hurled back and forth. Challenges were met with fiery words and despair came wailing from countless tongues. On his throne, like a lonely boatman on a stormy sea of heads, Ivar the

Boneless met shaking fists with furious roars. He took time to hurl insults at Lord Norbury who shoved through the milling ranks. No less angry, Laetitia Pilkington stood imprisoned in a crushing ring of defenders, swatting each one repeatedly with her fan. Dean Swift appealed vainly for calm as numerous ghosts offered bizarre and heated interpretations of Professor Gilbert's poem.

Caitlyn rolled her eyes and walked to Brody's table of documents. Using the chair by it as a step, she mounted the boards and surveyed the swarming crowd from her elevated position. The wall of sound assailing her defied any hope that she would be heard in calling for calm. A sharp signal to Captain Cassidy drew the highwayman to her, a whispered instruction placed a flintlock in her hand, and a simple tug of a finger set matters straight.

The pistol's explosion thundered about the room to strike all voices dumb and brought gazes swivelling in blank wonder towards Caitlyn.

'Shut up,' she ordered. She sought with a cold eye for anyone defying her command. The only sound that came was from Mia as she rapped her fists with excited pleasure. Caitlyn watched the spirits gather round, maintaining a serious countenance to mask her racing thoughts. What was she meant to do now? What could she possibly say? 'Questions,' she recited and tried not to smile at the irony of it, 'you have questions.'

'Is it true?' Lord Norbury called as he came nearer. 'Is it true Queen Cethlinn has regained the spear?'

Caitlyn braced. 'Yes,' she announced to horrified gasps and cries of 'doomed' and 'lost'.

'What about Sackimum?' Laetitia called with dread quailing in her voice.

Caitlyn confirmed the lady's worst fears with a shake of her head and watched tears concealed quickly by a fan. She faced the gathering once more.

'The Pooka killed Brody,' she said, 'but only because the spear didn't work. Balor tried to use it, but something went wrong.'

'Balor!' someone shrieked. 'You saw King Balor.' The name raised further exclamations of despair.

'Listen to me!' Caitlyn shouted them down. 'The King needs the spear for his power and right now that power is not there. I don't know why, but it gives us time to prepare for what's coming.'

'How much time?' a shrill voice demanded. 'How can we prepare against Balor and his army? How can you hope to defeat them?'

The throng faced Caitlyn, standing as one and seeking answers from her. Caught by the challenge she looked over them in silence, from one to the other, the ghosts of all time, of all forms, united in doubt and fear.

A small hand was raised on the edge of the crowd and eyes followed Caitlyn's gaze to it.

Mia cleared her throat to be heard.

'Are you *really* the Banshee's daughter?' she asked solemnly.

Caitlyn blinked as heads turned back for the answer.

'Yes,' she said boldly, 'yes I am, and if you use the time we have left, I will defeat Balor and his army.'

'What's to be done?' King Ivar asked, relishing the thought of battle.

Caitlyn spoke quickly, firmly. 'King Ivar and Lord Norbury will recruit warriors and plan a defence of the spirit realm.'

The Vikings howled their approval.

'Marcus, go straight to the Glasnevin tombs, question Dr Devlin. I want to know how long it will take Cethlinn to repair the spear.'

Marcus understood and pushed through the crowd.

'Laetitia, Boyle, Swift, this is Danny, he's going to need help with Professor Gilbert's poem.'

Laetitia shooed her pesky guards aside and smiled proudly on Caitlyn.

'Pembrig, you have a book here called the Diary of the Knight Fitzgerald?' The librarian nodded in agreement. 'Bring it to me. Mia.' The little spirit jumped up to offer a soldierly salute. 'Find Zozimus and his dog, bring them here. Don't offer him coins or gold. Tell him the Banshee's daughter commands it.'

FIFTY

A storm was coming.

Everyone in the throne room felt its rising. With each step the Queen took in her relentless pacing, they waited in breathless hope of avoiding the tempest's imminent fury. The Pooka watched her from the shadows, the witch servants likewise at their guard about the kneeling Banshee. The Morrigan leaned at the fireplace and surveyed all with a knowing smirk. On his throne, spear in hand like a sceptre of rule, King Balor tracked his wife's movements back and forth, not daring to speak as he anticipated the storm surge, exhilarated by its coming.

The rage broke from Cethlinn as a shriek of violence for the world above. She became a wounded thing howling to the farthest recesses of her domain. She screamed to breathlessness and the passing of her voice left behind the sound of knuckles cracking to vengeful fists.

'A daughter,' she hissed in revolted disbelief. She turned her steps abruptly towards the prisoner. 'You had a daughter, conceived in secret and born in some dark corner, a loathsome, sneaking thing best hidden from all the realms, and from me.' Cethlinn took a grim satisfaction from the anger in the Banshee's eye for her words. But next a thought surfaced to wipe the Queen's mirth away. 'Who is the wretch's father?'

Aoife's eye twinkled with a smiling malice.

'He was a mortal man.'

Cethlinn tightened against the obscenity of it. In an instant she drew back a hand and with a fresh howl she slapped the truth from her granddaughter's lips.

'You did this to spite me,' she wailed and raised her hand once more. 'Name him. I order you to name him. I will send my servants to bleed his craven heart.'

'He was the man of Newgrange who found the sword and the spear,' Aoife proclaimed unabashed. 'He was worthy of both. You were too slow to stop him and you are too slow to punish him now. My husband's life was stolen years ago.' With a gaze that promised worse than slow death, Aoife glared on the astonished Pooka and sent him snivelling from the room.

'Daughter will join father,' Cethlinn vowed. 'The Morrigan will see to it.'

'She will not,' Balor interjected. He struck his spear to the floor to reinforce his will and faced down his wife's anger. 'Banshee Daughter will not be touched. There are more important matters to attend.'

Cethlinn rushed to him. 'Husband,' she implored, 'you do not understand. The girl threatens everything by her birth. It is dangerous, an unnatural thing, it is...,' she struggled for words until Aoife mischievously helped.

'...destiny,' the Banshee whispered.

Stung by her granddaughter's defiance, the Queen stared into Balor's disfigured face.

'Let me show you what is at stake,' she offered. She stepped back to lead him.

႙ ႙ ႙

Cethlinn's burning torch showed the way where she drew her King along the webbed corridors of the third realm. She moved deliberately, navigating the long route amid ruins and rock falls, the better to sway his heart. When he hesitated with a gasp, she was kind and took his hand, comforting him past the smashed statues of his forebears. She felt his grip tighten beneath the sundered tapestries of his great victories over the Clann Dé Danu. She soothed his cries of grief when they came to the empty chests of his treasury. She led him across the floor of the fallen, a meandering course between ruptured shields and Fomorian bones. With calculated ease she played the light over sightless sockets, exposing the frozen anguish of the dead in their last sacrifice for their King. When at last the way turned upwards, he stumbled blindly against the incline and again she was at his side, attentive until he was ready to go on.

They emerged into the chill air of a night wood. An owl hooted its alarm at the sudden appearance of the royal couple and took to ghostly flight. The beating of its wings pulled Balor from his sullen reverie and he looked about in confusion at the setting.

'Where are we?' he asked.

'You'll see,' she promised him, 'come.'

The tree line was gained, and it released them to a high hillside. The vista ahead was a steep descent to a broad river plain running between hills towards the open sea.

'I know this place,' he said with studied eye. 'I see there the black pool of Dubh Linn.'

'Take my hand, husband,' she requested lightly.

He reached for her and looked again as her touch pulled aside the veil between worlds.

The river plain erupted to light. The mortal plain was swept to a treasure chest of golden flares, a landing place for fallen stars. Towers of glass rose along the banks of the river and mapped its flow with their internal fire. Yet more lights moved across the vision, innumerable spots coupled white and red as they swept along roadways towards the city. None of the lights found Dubh Linn. In an instant its dark depths had been overlaid by a black castle from a different age. Overhead, the sky was cut to the roar of a giant beast on fixed glimmering wings. Balor shuddered beneath its mechanical power and held his spear in defence as he followed the craft's descent towards the place that had become Dublin.

'There is so much to take,' he gasped overawed.

'All this and the vengeance you are owed,' Cethlinn said, 'when I reinvigorate the spear.'

'You must do it at once,' he insisted.

Cethlinn faced her King. 'There can be no Queen but me.'

He pulled her close. 'None but you,' he vowed.

'The girl.'

Balor smiled. 'You have the gift of vision, my sweet Majesty,' he said, 'but there is something even you do not see. Trust me, Caitlyn is of value to our plans.'

He quit her side and the vision died.

The loss of light obscured the storm renewed in Cethlinn's face. She struggled against it, resisting her anger's demand to be unleashed. She drove the nails of bunched fists to her palms until the pain eased her spirit. With hitching breath, the Queen shifted her focus to a nearby presence.

'Bring her.'

She watched her servants lead Aoife in bonds from the shadows. Cethlinn stared on the prisoner. 'Are you smiling in there?' she asked bitterly of that hidden face. 'Do you dare to believe your daughter is safe?'

'Not while you live,' the Banshee hissed.

Cethlinn did not rise to the bait. Instead, she circled and offered her plans in a poisoned whisper at Aoife's ear.

'As always, I must protect your grandfather from himself,' she said. 'He is headstrong. It must be a family curse. For his sake I must act against his commands and be subtle in my actions.'

'You cannot compel me to harm Caitlyn. No magic is that strong.'

'No,' Cethlinn sneered, 'but I have yet power enough to slow her down, to distract her. I hold magic sufficient to command you, my wayward granddaughter, to harm someone else, someone she cares for.' Fingers snapped, and the shackles clattered free as the Queen whispered to all the hate in the Banshee's green eye. 'Fail me this time, disobey me more, and I promise Caitlyn will know all the suffering I have to offer the world.'

FIFTY-ONE

'No way,' Danny protested, 'you can't do it.' His alarm echoed to the lofty ceiling of the Reserve Room, restored to peace after the crowd's departure.

Caitlyn bristled at his statement and the command implicit in it. She glanced up sharply from the book Pembrig held open for her and shot Danny a fierce look. 'Who says I can't?' she snapped.

The boy floundered, lost for words. He looked to the others, from Dr Marcus to Laetitia, for support in his argument.

'I agree with Danny,' Marcus said. Rising from his place behind the piled-up desk he approached and implored Caitlyn to see sense. 'Any thought of going into Cethlinn's lair is madness. If the Professor were here, he would say as much.'

'The suggestion that you attempt this is folly,' Laetitia tried. 'Caitlyn, you are far too valuable to risk on a doomed venture.'

'They're right,' Danny said.

'You're meant to be solving a puzzle,' Caitlyn reminded him icily. She was instantly stung by his wounded face. 'She's my mother,' she argued softly, desperate for understanding.

'Yes, and you should be reunited,' Laetitia agreed, 'no-one stands against that. But surely this must be *after* the sword is in your hands and we defeat Balor.'

'We need her,' Caitlyn countered, ignoring their doubtful expressions. 'Balor has the spear, and he has Cethlinn. So far, we have nothing, a poem that maybe leads to the sword, maybe. But it was Aoife who made the sword for King Lug, the Professor told me that. Maybe she has the power to do it again, and maybe even enough power to challenge Cethlinn. We need her.'

'That's a lot of maybes,' Marcus said. 'How do you even know we can trust her?'

Caitlyn fumed at the question but fought to keep her voice steady. 'I saw what I saw. Aoife is under Cethlinn's control.'

'Then,' Marcus mused, 'in addition to finding your way through the ancient realm and facing the combined might of Cethlinn and Balor, you also have to break the spell that binds your mother to the Queen.'

'It's been broken once already,' Caitlyn said, her mind flashing back to the Banshee's defiance on the rooftop. 'She broke it for me.'

'All right,' Marcus said and held up his hands in surrender. 'But you are forgetting one important element that makes all this arguing pointless. You don't have a way into the ancient realm, so where do you begin?'

'I have a way,' she replied as she returned to her studies.

Marcus frowned and glanced to the book in Pembrig's hands. 'Not with the Knight Fitzgerald's diary you don't. If I recall, Pembrig, the text doesn't reveal the entrance discovered by the knight on his quest.'

'Quite correct, Doctor,' Pembrig concurred. 'The diary records Sir Roger's entry to the third realm via a portal known as the Silken Door but fails to disclose the location. The omission was intentional on Sir Roger's part, to prevent others falling into the clutches of Queen Cethlinn and suffering as he did. The diary is quite graphic in this regard. Also, I feel compelled to add, Miss Caitlyn, the knight warns that he faced 'grim challenges' on his journey.'

'And got past them all,' she shot back with a finger tap to the pages.

'Only to suffer the worst tortures the Fomorian Queen could inflict,' Laetitia reminded with a shiver.

Marcus folded his arms and offered Caitlyn a dubious look. 'I am still intrigued to know how you plan to find your way into the third realm.'

The answer to his query came in a sharp knock on the Reserve Room door. The company turned to watch as Blackpitts jumped up and waddled his meaty frame to the hatch. He slid it aside to examine the caller. Mia's voice without offered a chirpy 'Trick or Treat' and the portal was hauled open to admit the little spirit and those she had fetched along.

Zozimus, led by Dragon the panting hound, entered.

'God bless all here,' Zozimus offered to his unseen hosts.

Caitlyn looked knowingly at Marcus as she approached the new arrivals and paused to gently rub Dragon's head. When she turned back, she held before her a tattered piece of cloth pulled from a pocket. 'I tore this from the Pooka's cloak when he killed the Professor,' she said. 'Zozimus says Dragon is the best tracker in the spirit world.'

'None better,' the phantom declared proudly.

'We follow the Pooka's scent,' Caitlyn said. 'He's my way into the ancient realm.'

⚜ ⚜ ⚜

The Wraith coursed its lonely way through the city, following the path of the Liffey. The reflected moon sank there and shimmered like a drowning ghost.

The night held to an eerie silence as the car slid past and for the first time Caitlyn looked and did not see in the spirit world. No shade walked the gloom, no spirit lovers stood on bridges, not a single ghost light shone from the cityscape's inky silhouette. Twilight reigned supreme.

'I don't think my glove is working,' Danny said as he peered at the outside world.

'It's working,' Caitlyn said, leaving him to solve the mystery.

Dublin's departed were hiding, in the dark and from it and the ancient fear it promised. The only visible ghosts now were Mia and Zozimus who stroked Dragon's coat as the faithful dog hung his head from the car window in search of a scent.

Caitlyn watched the hound closely for signs of reaction to the cloth she had offered its nose. As she watched, she felt Mia's gentle prodding at her elbow. The girl clearly had a secret to share.

'I have something for you,' she whispered when Caitlyn bent close.

'Oh yes?' Caitlyn said.

Cautious of the others, Mia reached to draw out a steely dagger, huge in her tiny hands. She pressed it quickly to Caitlyn. 'When they were helping you on the roof,' she explained quietly, 'I found this. It's your mother's.'

Caitlyn weighed the knife in her hand and examined it keenly, from bone handle to its blade of swirled etchings. She curled her fingers tightly on the grip as though to feel her mother's touch and played the moonlight along its length in search of the weapon's memories. The knife shone dangerously.

'I'll feel better with this,' she assured her friend.

Dragon barked. His call was a deep rumbling on the air and he followed it from sitting to an urgent scratching on the car's door, seeking exit in pursuit of prey. He conveyed his frustration with another throaty bark.

'Stop here,' Zozimus instructed, his hands already fumbling for the door handle.

With wheels still rolling to the kerb, Dragon led with a bound from the vehicle. Straining at his leash, he hauled Zozimus helplessly along ahead of the others where they scrambled to behold their destination towering before them.

Dublin Castle hulked forbidding black against the speckled sky. Rising to hunch its battlements, the building flung disjointed shadows into the path of those who dared approach. In echoing tones, the structure captured Dragon's barking and amplified the sound as it bared its gate of iron teeth against intrusion.

'This is starting to make sense,' Marcus said as he hastened to follow Dragon's route to the gateway. 'We should have seen it before.'

'Why?' Danny asked.

Caitlyn was quickest to answer.

'Because the castle sits over the Black Pool, and everything you see in the spirit world, everything in the mortal world came afterwards. The Black Pool was here even before Cethlinn and Balor. It makes sense for the Pooka to follow a path more ancient than he is.'

'Is there a way to reach it?' Danny said over Dragon's barking. He tested the unyielding gate.

'There is a way,' Marcus revealed. 'It's called the Poddle. It's an underground stream leading from the pool to the Liffey. The castle builders sank a well to tap its water, and the well is still here.'

'It's no good to us if we can't get inside,' Zozimus stated the obvious.

'Don't worry,' Marcus said, 'The spirit in charge is an old friend of the Professor.' He pointed through the bars at a form shifting across the darkened courtyard.

Rider and horse approached at a ceremonial pace, the spirit beast advancing with practised steps in bearing its shimmering charge. For his part the rider was a figure tall in the saddle and resplendent in a frilled and medal-heavy jacket surmounted by a fur-trimmed cape of ermine. He swept a feathered hat grandly from his head as he drew near, the better to display his immaculately groomed short wig and ribbons.

'Good evening,' said the spirit with velvety elocution.

'Hello, Charles,' Marcus called. He faced the others. 'That is Charles Lennox, Duke of Richmond and Lord Lieutenant of Ireland in the 19th Century.'

'Dr Marcus. Is that you?' the rider asked with joy.

'I believe it is. But pray, who else do you bring, and why on this of all nights. Do you not know that Balor walks abroad in search of tasty victims?'

'That's why I'm here,' Marcus said. 'I have Caitlyn McCabe with me, on an urgent and dangerous mission.'

Lennox gasped, impressed. 'Caitlyn McCabe, why did you not say? Rollicking stuff, I shall open the gates at once.'

Marcus offered a grateful smile but whispered to Caitlyn from the corner of his mouth. 'This could take a bit of time.'

So began the Duke of Richmond's struggle to dismount. With focused concentration of tongue between lips and a straining effort, the phantom leaned close to his mount's neck and dragged a wary leg across its rump, his cape becoming a major impediment through the motion. To increasingly jerky motions and commands of 'steady, steady', the Duke clung to the reins and freed himself from the saddle to begin the attempt at earthbound descent. As a foot tapped frantically in search of the ground the Duke's centre of gravity shifted and he finally plunged down in an undignified heap of frills and fur.

'What the hell was that?' Danny gasped.

'He's not good with horses,' Marcus said. 'In fact, he died after falling from one.'

'I'm fine, I'm fine,' Lennox pronounced as he surged

up and worked to regain some decorum. Smoothing his wig, he moved to the gate. 'A pleasure to meet you, Miss McCabe,' he said with a strained smile as he slid the lock free.

'Still trying to ride, I see,' Marcus said as the group slipped into the castle.

'But of course,' the Duke said happily. He winked at the others. 'They said I was mad for trying and when I died, they named a lunatic asylum after me. But I'll show them. Now, state your business.'

'We need to reach the old Poddle well,' Caitlyn said.

'Aha, indeed,' Lennox replied thoughtfully. 'Well, the castle is yours to access. Marcus knows the way.' He secured the gate and stepped to his horse. 'I will continue my rounds. It is time for great caution against old enemies.'

The Duke seized the reins, placed a foot into a stirrup and hauled upwards, only for the weight of his costume to topple him earthwards again, this time with his foot still locked into its place. Tired of all, the horse snorted impatiently and began to walk away, dragging the hapless Duke slowly behind in a spreading trail of cape.

'Do you need help?' Caitlyn called in alarm.

'No, no, all under control, thank you,' Lennox shouted back. With one hand on his wig, the other stretching for a dangling rein, the Duke was pulled away.

Prompted by a shrug from Marcus, Caitlyn set off after Dragon and the others.

They moved swiftly through the castle precincts, along cloistered walks and on through rooms and corridors until descending steps spiralled the way to hollow places beneath the complex. The space gave volume to Dragon's excited panting and doubled the sound of their footsteps. The subterranean world responded likewise to their presence and offered a sound of its own, one that came from the arches and pillars to whisper of flowing water.

'This way,' Zozimus said as he was yanked into a hard left turn. The rest followed eagerly only to pull up sharply. The way ahead with its song of water was barred firmly against them. Just ahead and out of reach, the brick circle of the Poddle well stood behind a chained gate, imprisoned in the gloom of a stone chamber.

Zozimus ran his fingers over the aged lock and chain securing the barrier. 'Rusted,' he noted. 'There'll be no getting past this.' He tried to calm Dragon who snorted and pawed at the bars.

Marcus turned from the well. 'This is for the best, Caitlyn,' he said. 'Please, let's turn back.'

Caitlyn's answer was as swift as it was violent. In a single stroke she produced the Banshee's dagger and swept it against the metal links. The chain jangled to the floor like a dead snake. Flexing her grip on the knife, she faced Marcus defiantly, a single green eye visible between strands of fallen hair.

Time itself seemed to freeze. Through the silence and creeping primal fear, Marcus heard his foot drag on the stone floor as he took an involuntary step back from that glaring eye. Dragon whined and sank behind Zozimus.

Caitlyn broke the moment and pushed on, casting the gate open in her advance on the well. Her hands grew cold where they pressed against the brickwork and she peered in. She was surprised to find the water flowing within reach below.

'How deep?' Danny asked at her side. 'How far to the Black Pool?'

'It's not deep,' Marcus said, 'but I don't know how far it is to reach the pool.'

'Then how do we know Caitlyn can make it?' Danny's tone cracked nervously.

'I'll make it,' she said, already clambering across the wall. She eased herself down, gasping as the chill water washed over her ankles. Steeling herself, she lowered further. She released her grip and crashed the surface, momentarily vanishing. She sprang up again, once more gasping against the cold shock. Danny caught her reaching hands.

'You don't know how far you have to swim,' he said through his fear.

She worked hard to summon courage enough for the two of them. 'No further than a medieval knight in full armour,' she quipped and watched his face contorting with doubt and anxiety. 'Truth,' she challenged him.

'I only just found you,' he said.

She hauled up and surged into him with a kiss.

'I'm coming back, I promise.'

Caitlyn let go and fell to a spray of white water and was gone.

FIFTY-TWO

Freezing water crushed and pushed.

Caitlyn clawed through a dark tunnel that contained the Poddle, her breath held tight in the face of the racing current. Hands and feet scrabbled blindly for purchase against slimy bricks as they fought to drag her on. She battled through her own swirling hair which had become sinuous and blinding in the water's churning. Misplaced fingers slipped and for a terrifying instant the gains she had made seemed lost. Feet saved the day as she was swept backwards, splaying to catch uneven outcrops of stone, and halting the retreat. With pounding heart and the first spark of burning tension in her lungs, Caitlyn sprang forward to clamber with desperate fury for her goal.

All at once she reached a place of calm. The dragging flow ended in a moment and the fearful confines of the tunnel gave way to quiet water. Caitlyn turned rapidly upwards, every fibre begging for air, each limb kicking and straining to its limits in reaching for the surface.

She erupted in spray and with a great inward cry of release. Her lungs scorched for new breath and she fell back on the waves she had formed, dimly aware of a great expanse of water beyond her clearing vision. Blinking against droplets, Caitlyn looked to beheld the vast cavern of the Dubh Linn.

Colossal in scale, the cave stretched immeasurably from her on all sides, the pool's endless shoreline coursing far beyond sight. From its unseen limits, the cave reared up to become an overarching roof laden with stalactites huge and dripping, renewing the pool with echoing drops of new water filtered from the world above. As Caitlyn gazed on, the cave offered from its staggering depths a leviathan's moan of welcome on a breeze that rippled to chill her skin.

Overawed by the cavern's scale, Caitlyn backed away from it until her feet struck the foreshore. She rose unsteadily, entranced, and examined all before her without watching where she placed her feet.

To a dry clack and clatter, the ground shifted dangerously, and Caitlyn staggered. She cast out a hand as she fell, and it rolled across human bones. She cried out and reeled back, arms flailing. Wherever she looked, wherever she stepped, there were bones. The shoreline was covered with them.

A soft titter from the dark behind brought her spinning about.

There was a mermaid reclining on the water's edge.
A mermaid.

Caitlyn staggered again and the watching girl chuckled and combed her hair with a skeleton hand plucked from the pile. Her smile glistened sharply beneath obsidian eyes that followed Caitlyn's struggle for balance.

'Hello,' the resting girl said with a flirtatious tone.

'A mermaid,' Caitlyn blurted.

'No,' the girl replied with a flick of tail and a wave of her bony comb, 'we are the Merrow.'

We.

They arrived through the softest breaking of water about Caitlyn. Dark heads encircled to look on her with the same hungry orbs as their sister's.

Caitlyn snatched for her dagger and displayed its dangerous edge to the reclining Merrow. The creature's response was a soft laugh that flittered away through the cave's vastness.

'No need for that, Caitlyn McCabe,' she chastised gently, 'we know who you are. We would invite you for dinner,' and how those black eyes twinkled at that, 'but it would only bring the Banshee's vengeance on us, and we do not want that. You may pass, and safely.' She caught Caitlyn's look of doubt and was quick to draw the skeleton hand against her chest, tittering mischievously again. 'Cross my heart,' she added with a moist wink.

'Thank you,' Caitlyn said uncertainly. The water rippled and, one by one, the Merrow sank back to the depths.

The girl on the foreshore pointed far off. 'That's the way,' she instructed. 'But do be careful. Maelmorda the cursed King is waiting, and he *doesn't* know who you are. He might not even care.'

Warily, Caitlyn eased back to deeper waters. Anticipating a clasping of fingers at her ankles she held tight to her dagger as she pushed to gain the centre of the pool. The way was long and hard, but her fear of the sucking depths drove her on to stroke beyond normal endurance, hauling the distant shore ever closer as she maintained her watch for hungry pursuers.

At last, and with no small measure of relief, she felt the pool's edge rise to her feet. She rooted herself and waded ashore to a rock that was a welcome seat while she recovered. She allowed her breath to regain its easier rhythm and regarded her surroundings.

The land here was thankfully unlike the Merrows' bone yard. In place of a shoreline of skeletal remains were moss-covered rocks of all shapes and sizes. The landscape promised arduous clambering and twisted ankles. But what was the destination?

Caitlyn squinted into the gloom. At first, she saw nothing but the cave's thick veil of permanent night. But as she worked harder to see, the cave groaned deeply once more. She felt a cold breeze wash past her and on across the rocky surface. It reached a place on the border of stone and shadow, where something moved under the eerie breath. It was a subtle movement, an almost imperceptible shifting, as though fabric floated on the air.

Caitlyn set off. Using a distant pinnacle of rock to fix her target, she scrambled along, pausing frequently to catch her breath and assess the dangers underfoot. Slowly her efforts brought the guiding pinnacle closer until she reached for it as a last support. Here she halted to examine the mammoth goal surrendered from the dark, recognising it at once from its name she had read.

The Silken Door rose high and wide. Sculpted from the living rock, the imposing portal reared to pierce the high gloom within a carved frame of Celtic knots. Their tumbling flow from the distant apex demanded an adoring eye, and Caitlyn was compelled to look, but only briefly. An altogether different creation demanded her equal attention and she peered on it with rising dread. Overhanging the huge door, wrought by tireless weaving, was a massive curtain of spider webs. Caitlyn started as the dusty veil rippled visibly, just as before, though this time the motion was not in answer to a restless cave-breath. This time the silken layer was disturbed from underneath, by a many-legged scuttling close to the door's handle.

Caitlyn swallowed hard against a scurry of fear along her back. She held her knife against its unseen cause, knowing that she must inevitably reach with her free and unguarded hand to move beyond it. With clamped lips she eased gingerly towards the silk.

The scuttling stopped. That was worse, so much worse. The webs hung on a sigh of waiting and Caitlyn felt the first hanging strands brush her forefingers.

The eruption came in an avalanche of stone behind her. A hidden figure broke cover and rose from among the rocks. Trailing a moss-stained cape, the misshapen form lumbered as a rock come to life, but with a dizzying agility in drawing his huge sword to challenge Caitlyn. Her dagger was a mere sliver by comparison, her form tiny before the growing giant who lunged into the attack.

She ducked the first blow, rolling aside beneath a hum of sharpened metal and quickly regained her feet. Moving to mirror her attacker's rapid turn, she strained to see his face but found it hidden by strands of beads hanging from his helmet. Each one bore tiny cuts Caitlyn recognised in a flash as the ogham lettering of the ancients. Tattooed hands offered a second thrust and Caitlyn leapt back with little room to spare as the crashing blade sent sparks flying from the rocks at her feet. The brief light caught pale lips beyond the mask, drawn apart to a snarl of yellow teeth as the warrior wound up for yet another blow.

Caitlyn paused. The tingling from deep within to the roots of her hair told her to. There was time enough, she somehow realised, time enough. She read the coming attack in the signs her opponent offered. His shoulders flexed, betraying the intention to draw his blade high, just as that step back on one foot foretold a shift of balance for the strike. She perceived the angle and the moment of launch in an instant and was already moving when it began. She offered the flying sword nothing but empty space and rolled forward to spring up inside the weapon's arc. Her blade touched dangerously to the neck beyond the mask and her attacker froze on the knife's edge.

'You are Maelmorda?' she guessed. 'You are the cursed King.'

The voice of the stayed warrior hissed defiantly. 'The same,' it said with a glowering between the beads, 'cursed for treachery against Queen Cethlinn. I am keeper of the Silken Door until time runs back. You are trespassing.'

Caitlyn peered unwaveringly to meet the warrior's stare. 'I have the right to go into the ancient realm,' she informed him boldly.

Eyes made cloudy by permanent night narrowed in doubt behind the ogham lines. The pale Maelmorda leaned slowly forward despite the razor threat that held him. Beads clicked to the motion and the huge sword rasped dangerously on the stones. Caitlyn pressed her weapon more firmly to his exposed throat, but he ignored her action to bring his broad face ever closer to hers. Almost to touching, he abruptly sniffed, examining the scent of her clothes, her skin, her hair.

'You are mortal,' he sneered with contempt. His sword dared lift slowly from its resting place.

'Try again,' she commanded, and this time as he leaned in with reeking breath, she offered words unshakeable and true. 'I am born of Aoife, descendant of Cethlinn, successor to the crown of Balor. I am the Banshee's daughter, and if you do not let me pass, I will weep for you.'

Maelmorda's blade grew heavy and the eyes upon him too much to bear. With a gasp that fled in terror between the rocks he drew sharply from her. 'It is true,' he told himself breathlessly, confirming it with dim vision, 'eyes of earth and sky, and the blood of all tribes in your heart.' The cursed King hastened to bend his massive frame in a respectful bow. 'The way is yours.'

Caitlyn took a cautious step back, withdrawing slowly her readied dagger.

'What lies behind that door?' she demanded.

King Maelmorda faced the portal with dreadful memory and pointed blindly to it. 'The Queen's fiercest guard waits there in the dark,' he warned, 'most terrible in form, raised in shadow and cruelty by Cethlinn, cursed with eternal vigilance and forever hungry. If you go beyond the door you must face Catcallach.'

Caitlyn breathed through her fear. 'Then I must,' she said. She offered a nod of thanks to Maelmorda and stepped away.

'Wait,' he urged, 'Banshee Daughter, wait.' He opened his arms to her. 'Have mercy on the cursed of Queen Cethlinn. For want of battle I should have joined the kings of old in the hereafter millennia since, but for petty vengeance I linger.' Spindly fingers gestured to her blade. 'Release me as only you can, Banshee Daughter.'

She drew back in horror at his request. 'I can't do that,' she cried, 'I won't.'

Maelmorda sagged, forlorn behind his mask. 'I linger,' he cried into his hands. 'I should have died in battle.'

Something other than pity, a whispering calculation in her head, brought Caitlyn to return and stand over the weeping King, and a reasoning she did not yet understand impelled her to lay a hand on his shoulder.

'When I deal with Cethlinn you'll be free,' she vowed.

Shamed by his tears, he turned away and let her go.

The webs of the Silken Door scuttled at her approach, alarming undulations closing from every corner of the frame. She resumed her place and reached once more with an unsteady hand. Just as before, the first tentative contact brought a sudden halt but for a deep and predatory breathing under the veil. Bracing against unseen terrors, Caitlyn dipped her hand through clinging layers in search of the door handle.

A sudden touch of cold hardness under her fingers sent a cry racing to her throat. She stifled it, tightening her lips to keep it at bay, and watched the quivering mounds beneath the silk inch nearer. She quickly identified the feel of metal, long and curving to the shape of a pitted handle. She grasped it and leaned down. The lock protested in a rusty grating and then to a shattering crunch of tumblers. The door swung from her as the silk veil bloomed and shuddered to a breath from the cavernous deep.

Through the billowing, Caitlyn spotted a declining staircase. She used the back of her hand to ease the silk aside for a better view. Steps hewn from the surrounding rock led the way from her to foul air and chuckling echoes. She ducked through the webs, mindful of creeping things, and placed a foot to the head of the stairway, listening as the underworld drew a horrified breath at her presence.

She followed it down.

Along the rough and twisting spine of the third realm she descended, craning in anticipation of hidden traps around each curve. She sought clues to her destination in faded carvings that ran across every surface but the ancient language cleaving to the backs of epic beasts and serpents offered her nothing but fearful imaginings.

She slowed into a final turn and eased carefully towards the bottom step, shifting to one side to hug the wall as it gave over to a short corridor.

Caitlyn chilled at the sight of cat's jaws yawning monstrously wide.

Whether through perverse artistry or wicked intent, carving hands had framed the doorway ahead with the face of a gigantic feline. Raging eyes peered from a barrier that was simultaneously a doorway and a devouring mouth with giant teeth bared in frightful readiness to consume the traveller.

Caitlyn stepped from cover and walked under the monstrous gaze to draw close to the door. Careful to listen first for any sounds beyond the wood, she engaged the lock and pushed the door open.

The place of many doors she entered was a scene of utter destruction. The evidence of unspeakable violence lay everywhere, transforming a once beautiful room to a shrine of barbarism. Decorated walls that curved away had been slashed and hammered, their artistry smeared over by vile and familiar graffiti. From the blade of Dr James, Caitlyn recognised the handiwork of the Fomorians. The same obscene hands had torn down and brutalised the many statues that once lined the chamber. The floor was a wasteland of marble remnants that crunched beneath her feet where Caitlyn moved further to the heart of the room, drawn by a single undamaged item there.

It was a harp. Standing tall and regal in silence, the instrument was untouched by the carnage visited on the rest of the room. Dark and delicately sleek, it remained unblemished by settling dust too, allowing ornate carvings to shine richly from polished wood. Within the frame, strings still held taut against the ravages of time. It was beautiful, Caitlyn mused, but could its beauty alone be the reason the vandals in their frenzy had spared it?

A scratching sound reached her. Alarmed, she took a second too long in identifying the source, a shifting of rusted hinges and the soft click of a lock. By the time she turned, all doors stood uniformly shut against her.

She hurried back to the barrier by which she had entered, only to find it devoid of a handle on this side. With increasing dismay, she looked from door to door, finding the same truth on each smooth surface.

She was trapped, sealed in the room of ruin.

FIFTY-THREE

Caitlyn came to the end of her examination of the final door. She cursed under her breath.

Despite a long and detailed search, she had not found any hidden latches or subtle clues to make this last door any different to the previous eleven she had examined. There was simply no obvious way out of the chamber.

The initial alarm she felt at stumbling so blindly into the trap gave way to frustration and she beat a fist against the unyielding barrier. The strike ran hollow about the chamber. On the other side of the wood, it boomed far off to hidden spaces.

She cursed again at wasted time and stepped back towards the centre of the room, the only sound that of her feet crunching over shattered stone as she moved to consider the harp again.

Looking over the instrument, she pondered its unsullied perfection and set this against the surrounding debris. She pictured the onslaught of barbarian hands and the fury with which they had laid waste to all but this centrepiece.

'Why?' she asked aloud and jumped at the resounding of her voice overhead. 'Why did they not hurt you?' She reached gently to test the surface of the thick wood and found it wonderfully smooth under her fingers. Had it been too beautiful to damage, she wondered again. That was hardly the answer, and she rejected the notion. The statutes that once adorned the room were clearly beautiful too, yet they had suffered raging blows unchecked by any respect for their artistry. The harp, it seemed, was something else entirely to the attackers, protected from harm, a forbidden object, maybe, or something... 'useful to them,' she deduced aloud.

Perhaps the hidden latch she sought was here. Heartened by the idea, she sent her hands further over the ornate surfaces. She pressed on raised swirls and tried to turn circular patterns, but all to no avail. The harp stood impervious.

Not ready to concede defeat, Caitlyn travelled down the triangular frame. What if, she speculated, the doors she could see were meant as a distraction from a door she could not? What if the real door lay under the harp itself? But no, the instrument stood on a solid base of circular stone, cold beneath her hand as she slapped it with renewed frustration.

'Some help you are,' she muttered to the harp as she stood again. Probing her brain for inspiration, she sent a finger to flick dismissively at a random string. The note produced by the act came flawlessly to her ear, and the light it inspired threw her shadow to the wall.

'Wait, what?'

There had been a light, sharp and brief, yet undeniable. Caitlyn glanced quickly about. The room stood unchanged on all sides. There was no doubt, however. She had clearly seen her shadow cast by some flaring source. From the angle of travel, she figured, that source was behind her. She spun with heightened focus, her ears detecting as before the grinding of hinges and the click of a receiving lock. One of the doors had been open! Her brain made rapid connections. When primed by the harp's note an unseen lock had released just long enough to offer admission. That had to be it.

Caitlyn whirled back to the harp and its multiplicity of strings. Her eyes roved in confusion over the net of possibilities, seeking to reacquire the note, the key she had tripped. Hazarding a guess, she plucked a string and the attempt gained nothing more than another crystal note, this one more sonorous than the last. She moved on to the next, picking it lightly to no greater reward. Despair impelled her to further strokes, one rapidly after another, and then to a whole finger sequence to fill the chamber with angelic chords. Light flashed in answer to the music.

Caitlyn was ready for it and turned. A door hung open in line with the harp's leading edge, and the once plain surface of the barrier was decorated with a marker of flaring magic light. Caitlyn saw the image of three crossed arrows, downward pointing and tied together. Beyond the illuminated door, a stone passage stretched off to darkness.

She leapt for the barrier even as it began to swing back to the fading of its activating note. Her hand caught the edge and stayed its progress easily, and she prepared to step through. A gust of foul air from the depths swept to greet her, and something in it stopped her committing to the path. She perceived a warning cry within herself against haste, which had seen her trapped once already. With tickling senses, she released the door and watched it slip back to its lock.

'Too easy,' her inner voice told her, 'far too easy.' As the arrows faded to invisibility, she turned back to the harp.

One secret note hidden among many was meant to be a clever trick, she reasoned. One opening door set among twelve was designed to be a challenging mystery. How much of a mystery, though? She had found the solution relatively easily, heavy-handedly, in fact. She looked again at the positioning of the arrow door, and how it was set in a direct line with the pointing of the harp. That, she thought, was not clever at all.

Something about the set-up was wrong. There were simply too many parts to this puzzle for such an obvious solution. With hands on hips, Caitlyn pondered over the instrument and tracked slowly around it. She looked to each wooden door along her path, and with every step, a new solution rose to suggest itself. There wasn't just one note for one door, she realised, there were many doors and one note for each.

She strode to the harp and with a single bold finger traced every string from first to last. A wave of air rolled as the room filled with wondrous sound. Again, the light arrows flowered to the entrancing call, and the same door swung to offer its path. The remaining portals held fast.

Caitlyn's disappointment grated with the closing of the door.

She withdrew, wary of the harp's allure, its sensuous distraction. The debris crunched underfoot. She turned up to the chamber roof and searched for fresh clues in the rotunda above. Next, she looked down to the instrument's base, searching across the tiles. She found nothing but a polished circle in keeping with the flow of the room, an island in a sea of rubble.

Circles. She stepped through one of her own making as her mind leapt in acknowledging the room's deliberate shape. She turned round, and round again to send the doors spinning by. She drew up short and walked to the harp, spurred by a spontaneous inkling. Placing herself in the position a player would occupy, she tested the weight of the wood against a new theory. Abruptly she threw her shoulder to the thick spine of the instrument and pushed hard, her hands reaching in the same instant for the strings.

Random chords melded with grinding stones to create a hellish tune as the harp began to turn on its base. To Caitlyn's grunting efforts, the leading edge shifted past the door of arrows to align with the next door as she continued to stroke note upon note.

She watched as the door flared in answer to its musical key! Fiery signage on the wood displayed lines etched to jagged mountain tops, and Caitlyn thrilled to the solution illuminated.

The harp was a compass.

The image faded as she propelled the harp on, bringing it in line with the next door, this one reacting to flare with the outline of a skull with crossed bones beneath. She pushed harder, erasing the skeletal smile in favour of the next offering. Caitlyn watched as a crown burned brightly, a crown of three tips, each tip fashioned to enclose a Celtic swirl. There was no guessing. Caitlyn knew without doubt it was the crown of a regent of the third realm.

The music faded under a hand stilled by amazement and the unlocked door threatened to swing back.

Caitlyn plucked again to bring the headpiece to dazzling and she raced for the portal. She peered into a tunnel winding and hot, and its burning draughts confirmed her choice. This was the path to the cauldron of a sorceress queen.

Caitlyn smiled in triumph and found herself wishing Danny was here to witness her cleverness. Something in the raising of his name caused her smile to falter and she looked back sharply into the circular chamber. Warm gusts from the doorway rolled to create a spiralling cloud of dust among the wreckage. Its form and dancing shift seemed to Caitlyn like a spirit tripping through the room. She watched with morbid fascination and for the first time she was unsettled by the idea of ghosts. She fled into the tunnel and pulled the door firmly against grim notions.

FIFTY-FOUR

She quickly began to doubt her route. Narrow as it was, low and confining, the tunnel was also home to a lifetime's worth of fluttering cobwebs, undisturbed until she reached out to push through. Considering her dusty hands with disgust, she realised she was the first to come this way in countless years. Not even the Pooka had used this passage in his journeying between worlds. She paused at the knowledge and was on the point of turning back when warm air surged again and cast wispy tendrils of web to her shoulders and cheek. Their dry touch promised answers to their shifting at the end of this grim tunnel and held her from retreating. Repulsed at the sensation on her skin, Caitlyn swept at cobwebs and doubts. She pressed on.

A last all-covering layer of web succumbed to Caitlyn's blade and admitted her to a broader space. Stepping through, she found she was in a corridor of ordered architecture. Neat flagstones ran to her left and right, walls cut smoothly through the rock and climbed to a high ceiling from which lantern bowls, empty of fuel, hung from rusted chains.

She stretched her back after the constricting tunnel and considered the way. On either side the passage snaked to blackness while the walls around offered no signposting for the visitor. She looked to the floor in the hope of discerning footprints in the dust, but the effort was for nothing. Only the flow of warm air remained true. She tested it on her face, turning fully around to perceive its direction of flow. Coming to rest with the air caressing her cheeks, she stepped into the breeze and continued.

The darkness receded ahead, peeling back in fright at her presence until it spilled through a wide doorway and bled up to a sculpted roof, there to await her entry. Caitlyn eased to the doorpost and looked inside, catching her breath at the sight.

The chamber beyond was an immense tomb. Lying at its heart beneath a craggy roof, an ornate stone sarcophagus was flanked by four lesser coffins. The burial spoke at once of a fierce and terrible personage who demanded sacrifice even in death. The evidence lay on all sides of the monument. Frozen in the motion of clawing its walls, a chaos of headless skeletons piled up and strained for what lay out of reach on the lid. Their skulls had been set there to a grisly mound dominated by another, this one crowned and resting in loathsome glory.

Repulsed, Caitlyn forced herself to look beyond the fearful burial to the far side of the tomb. Directly opposite her doorway, and cut in exact replication, was the only other path from the crypt. She fixed on the spot and set off.

The sockets of the dead leered with eternal jealousy on her every step and demanded with hypnotic insistence that she return their staring. Caitlyn met sightless eyes with a shiver for toothy grins, and as she looked her attention fell to a rough carving on the facing end of the central sarcophagus.

Beneath the original crossed lines of ogham, someone had spent time and effort to decipher the ancient words. The translation was set between stacked bones in a crude etching. Caitlyn pictured the Knight Fitzgerald on this very spot, hundreds of years ago, hacking at the stone with feverish haste to inform later travellers of his find.

Dúlachán: The Headless King.

Caitlyn stepped back from the title, overawed by the terror of it. What was this realm, her frenzied mind wondered? What terrible kind of world was she the successor to?

Scccraatch.

In the silence of the tomb her senses sped to the noise, dry and slow among its deep recesses.

Scccraatch.

She whirled about, frantically searching, and her feet disturbed a scattering of bones to a jarring dry rattle. She froze, straining to the returned silence for more.

The tomb growled. It was a fearsome, deep-throated rumbling as from the bowels of the earth, but from a source much, much closer. Caitlyn held a steadying breath and scanned for its origin. The tomb mocked her with emptiness on all sides. She was alone but for the unending glee of skulls.

Scccraatch.

She zeroed in on the sound at last, tracking it past the head of the sarcophagus. At a place on the floor just beyond, a tiny cloud of dust rose to dance on the air. She watched closely and witnessed as the cloud was renewed, fed by a tumbling of tiny stones *scccraatched* from overhead. Caitlyn fought her fear and turned upwards.

Catcallach the witch's black cat peered back with enormous yellow eyes.

Impossibly inverted, monstrously gigantic, the feline clung to the ceiling, its maw held to a murderous snarl. Saliva from its jaws over-spilled the upturned muzzle to drip towards the floor. The cat's huge orbs became slits as they met Caitlyn's and a massive tongue slicked hungrily over razored teeth.

Caitlyn ran. Almost tripping on crossed bones, she hurled herself before Catcallach's pursuing screech and aimed for the far doorway. She glanced back as she ran and saw the beast chasing after. Across the roof, Catcallach shrieked and galloped into Caitlyn's eye-line, descending to where ceiling became chamber wall. Just as easily as it had hung to the roof, Catcallach clawed the wall and followed its arc in racing to flank its prey. With inconceivable dexterity, the mangy cat leapt along the brickwork, slavering and hissing as it competed to reach the doorway before Caitlyn.

With arms pummelling and legs pounding, Caitlyn sprang from her feet, diving for the exit. The air through which she passed filled with the giant cat's fetid breath and the space behind her heels became clashing teeth as she tumbled through the portal. The floor rushed up and Caitlyn crashed down, ignoring the pain of contact to scramble quickly up and on.

Catcallach was an instant behind. The cat squirmed its bulk through the doorway and threw its furious voice after the sprinting girl. Chasing a short way along the floor, it once again threw itself effortlessly to a wall and next to the other, never once breaking stride in its unnatural and closing pursuit.

Caitlyn dared look back even as she reached to her belt. The monster was almost at her shoulder, the moment of attack was a split second away. At full speed she wheeled around, hauling her feet clear of the floor and her dagger free from her belt. She swept the blade hard against the nightmare vision of teeth as it passed overhead and rolled beneath a storm of stinking fur.

Caitlyn's determined cry blended with Catcallach's shrieked of agony as they descended to an uncontrolled tumble. Dust from the cat's landing swirled up in this new chamber hunter and prey had entered. Caitlyn was momentarily aware of towering pillars, of two great statues, one headless, and a pair of huge doors between the pillars. And then her vision filled again with Catcallach where the beast shook itself off and faced her. Its massive tongue licked to clear blood from a wounded muzzle and Catcallach's eyes rolled at the taste. Caitlyn clutched her dripping knife and watched the cat tense for another strike.

The chamber shook to its roar and the charge began. Paws thundered across the floor as the creature's jaws drew wide. Caitlyn held forth her weapon and braced.

Catcallach went into a final bound, gathering its rear legs nimbly in readiness for a leap at its target. In mid-stride the manoeuvre faltered, the launching flanks tensed against the jump and paws dug hard against the stones. The cat came to a skittering halt, its spiteful features washing over with doubt.

Transfixed by the melting of Catcallach's ferocity, Caitlyn did not see the Morrigan until her three forms burst from the shadows. Swords at the ready, the warriors advanced past Caitlyn and drove the cat into retreat with triple threats and curses. Nor did Caitlyn sense the witches until it was too late. Bony cold hands snaked to envelop her arms and face.

The light died.

FIFTY-FIVE

King Balor was waiting.

Between the mighty statues of Aoife and Lug beheaded, he held himself imperious, a hand to his sword, his lone eye beneath the crown tracking his great-granddaughter's forced arrival, kicking and struggling all the way. He allowed a smiling moment to regard her efforts, proud of the ferocity she displayed. Then he shaped his damaged features to a feigned confusion.

'What's this?' he asked with a challenging look to the witches. 'What means this guard that lays hands to one of royalty? Release her.' He dismissed the witches with a flick of his fingers.

The witches were replaced by the Morrigan, striding forward with Caitlyn's dagger in hand. 'She had this,' she reported and presented it for the King's consideration.

Balor looked upon the weapon, recognising its true ownership in the carvings along the blade. 'This was Aoife's,' he said. 'Now it is her daughter's. Give it back.'

The Morrigan betrayed her confusion, and an instant spark of disobedience for the King's order. She suppressed all quickly under his amused gaze. Sweeping towards Caitlyn she offered the knife, dangerously close to the girl's neck before deftly reversing it to present the handle.

Caitlyn seized the dagger and offered looks far sharper in return.

Balor smiled again for the girl's defiance. 'There is the daring that brought you through the third realm and home to us,' he said. 'But you must be hungry after you journey.' He called to the dark, 'Bring food and mead at once.'

'Where is my mother?' Caitlyn demanded. Her eyes travelled up to the gigantic statue weeping over the gathering.

The question caught Balor by surprise. He looked to the Morrigan who could only shrug with disinterested ignorance. 'She cannot be far off, I'm sure,' the King offered. 'Perhaps the Queen will tell us.'

'Where is Cethlinn?' Caitlyn asked with suspicious glances about the chamber and to the mighty doors beyond.

'She labours close by,' Balor assured with a smile. 'She will join us shortly.'

A bowing, snivelling figure approached, and Caitlyn recognised the Pooka as he conveyed a tray of delicacies to her. She ignored them to hold his sneering stare.

'This monster only brings poison,' she said.

Balor threw back his head and sent laughter echoing through the chamber. His hands clapped delightedly. 'Truly you are a child of my house, Caitlyn. Ha!' He signalled for the Pooka to get gone as he continued to enjoy the moment of levity.

'I am nothing to you,' Caitlyn snapped. Her anger drove his laughter away.

'Oh, but you are,' he corrected her, the kindness of his tone edged with menace. 'Caitlyn, there are things you do not know, things that have been hidden from you. They can help you recognise your place in the world. It is why you came to us, is it not? Why you faced the fearful devices my Queen laid in your path. You want answers.'

'I want my mother,' she countered.

'Because you want to know who you are,' he shot back and watched the truth betrayed in her face. 'Caitlyn, you are on the cusp of understanding all things.'

'Are you going to teach me?' she scoffed.

'Of course,' he said earnestly, 'who else but I, the one who was there at the very beginning?' He read her doubt easily and scratched his beard as he pondered. 'Tell me, who was your grandmother? No? Name your grandfather. You cannot. You do not know them, so you do not know the fullness of your own story or its importance, but the desire to learn burns fiercely in your heart. I could forge a thousand swords by its heat. You would face a thousand traps and terrors for the simple answer to who, you, are.'

He let silence reign.

'Go on,' she said finally.

With a smile for his own knowing, the King guided Caitlyn's attention to the mighty sarcophagus lying between the statues. His hand drifted over its ornate carvings and to its ogham inscription, and his touch for it was one of loving.

'It says Eithlinn,' he deciphered, 'my daughter.'

'My grandmother,' Caitlyn whispered.

'She was the apple of my eye,' Balor continued. His damaged face shifted to the irony of his words. 'She was born at the turning of the year, a daughter fair of face and fierce of nature, the rock upon whom my kingdom would rest secure. That is what I wanted for her, but she wanted something else.' A renewed anger flickered across the King's features. 'Can you guess?'

'My grandfather,' Caitlyn replied. She caught Balor's nod of regret.

'Cian, a warrior, and worse yet, a prince of the Clann Dé Danu,' he lamented. 'What was I to do? Cethlinn whispered of murder to end the unsuitable match. A Danu prince, in *my* household, how the gods mock us. I forbade it, ordered an end to it. But I was too late.'

'A child was born,' Caitlyn concluded.

'Two children!' the King barked. He gathered himself bitterly. 'Eithlinn gave twins to my realm, a boy and a girl. And through them she gave rebellion.' He touched the ruin of his eye. 'Lug was strong, so strong. Aoife, with eyes Fomorian blue and Danu green, she possessed almost all Cethlinn's abilities. It was she who placed the sword into Lug's hand against me.'

'The sword,' Caitlyn said under her breath.

'Aoife was the means of my exile,' Balor said, and he laughed at a truth he alone saw, 'and now she becomes the source of my renewed greatness.'

'What are you talking about?' Caitlyn demanded.

'I'm talking about *you*, Caitlyn, Fomorian descendant of Eithlinn, Danu heir to Cian, conceived between the mortal and spirit realms. You are all things to all and through you the promise of realms reunited can be fulfilled.'

Caitlyn reeled from the King's dreadful vision.

'You want to use me so you can rule everything,' she gasped.

'The balance between worlds is broken,' Balor sighed, 'I would ask you to restore it.'

She barely heard his weasel words, her ears filling instead with those of another. She heard again Mia's precise little voice.

The fire in you is enough to save the whole world or else destroy it. The time will come to choose a side and when you do, that choice will decide everything.

'Why would I choose this?' Caitlyn demanded angrily.

Balor fixed her. 'You want to save your friends, don't you? Join with me, Caitlyn, and mortals and spirits will follow readily and peacefully, with no need of bloodshed. But if you spurn my offer, so many will suffer, and perish.' The King offered a welcoming hand.

Her friends. Caitlyn drifted to the faces filling her mind, countless and upturned to her in the Reserve Room, looking for their strength in her.

'I won't choose this,' she promised them firmly. She reached for her dagger and pointed it at Balor. 'Where is my mother? Where is Cethlinn, I want to know where my mother is.'

The answer to her demand came from the great doors. With a thunderous rumble they parted, revealing an inferno beyond. Flames roared high in the opening and reached with scorching tongues to draw the portal wider, and from the blazing throne room the tip of Balor's spear appeared, thrusting in the hands of she who carried it back from the fiery depths where she had descended in pursuit of magic. Untouched by the fire storm, Cethlinn walked, though in her gait she laboured, beset by some dragging agony. She grimaced against it, so afflicted that the spear was a terrible weight in her arms. She passed from the fire and trailed with her the visible remnants of her conjuring, streaks of burning light that clung to her wizened features even as she stumbled on failing knees. The sparking illumination ran over her clamped teeth and to the hatred rising in cloudy eyes as they beheld Caitlyn.

'What is she doing here?' Cethlinn growled.

Balor rushed to aid his Queen. 'Caitlyn is returned,' he said soothingly, 'just as I said she would. She was worthy of your challenges and passed all to come home to us.'

The Queen's anguish became unbearable and tore through her to form a shriek of fury and rejection from her lips. She tried to rise up, to conjure a spell against the girl but failed. Her energy and magic were expended. She tumbled back into the arms of her King with a pitiful cry. 'She brings death like her mother, nothing but death.'

'Where is my mother?' Caitlyn demanded again.

Cethlinn smiled at this despite her suffering, and its mockery was worse than any scream. 'Where indeed?' she croaked.

Balor's brow furrowed as he read the look in his lover's face. 'What have you done?' he said, his voice filled with cold doubt.

Cethlinn locked eyes with her great-granddaughter. 'The Banshee is about my work, little girl,' she teased. She laughed hoarsely at a sudden realisation. 'Why, you must have passed one another in the dark.' And then she chuckled harder. 'I sent her to visit Danny.'

Caitlyn recoiled, made hollow as she retreated from madness and cruelty. She turned and bolted, sent into a desperate sprint from the crazed merriment that came cackling after.

FIFTY-SIX

He sighed and read again.

My four o'clock song,
Is an ancient lament,
Recited in hope,
Against wicked intent.
Balor the King,
Is felled by the blade,
Lying in time,
In a soft-tended glade.
Silent in waiting,
Jubilant in sun,
All resting yet,
Longing battle be done.
And shades pass the hours,
Pressing time to a rock,
And offering their flowers to hail four o'clock.

Danny stretched in his chair and groaned aloud as he tried to refocus his mind. He rubbed his overworked eyes and listened to the silence of the Long Room as it mirrored the emptiness in his head, even now after so many hours of reading and reasoning. Hours wasted in searching and failure. He sat helplessly and without answers while Caitlyn drew steadily closer to danger.

Overtaken by frustration at that knowledge, he slapped his hand against the desk. The violence of the strike unsettled the articles before him. The page of poetic lines fluttered with secrets and the framed photograph borrowed from the Reserve Room trembled. Danny watched the smiling figures of Brody, Gilbert and Caitlyn's father topple flat with a clatter. 'What am I missing?' he demanded angrily of them. His question repeated endlessly through the echoing library.

Annoyed at himself and the maddening silence from the books surrounding, he flexed his fingers and refocused his mind. 'Okay,' he said to steady his aching brain, and again, 'Okay' as he set things right for a renewed approach to the poem. First, he realigned the page under his gaze and next reset the fallen picture until those within, with muddied knees and fashionable flower, were smiling directly at him again.

Consciously avoiding Barry McCabe's captured stare, Danny looked hard at the face of Professor Gilbert, whose inspiration he had sought for hours. 'What are you trying to tell me?' he demanded of the beaming man. The response was another flutter of the page between them as it shifted to the softest waft of air. Danny pinned the paper down with a finger. 'Okay,' he repeated, and consulted the lines again, more slowly and deliberately.

He sagged, defeated once more. Through a sudden and fresh bout of annoyance he pushed from the desk with a grinding of his chair over the wooden floor and turned his back to the infuriating poem.

'Time,' he recited sourly, 'four o'clock.' He rounded on the poem, demanding answers. 'What's that even about? Who gives flowers at four o'clock?' The page shifted on another gust and rippled with silent laughter at his efforts.

Danny walked away in exasperation. He needed to escape the poem and the confining atmosphere between the shelves. Walking into the main area of the library he halted, breathing deeply again behind closed eyelids as he searched to calm his tormented brain cells. 'It can't be that difficult,' he grumbled. 'No puzzle is that difficult.'

He opened his eyes to the world of books surrounding him and scanned the voluminous ranks lined high on ordered shelves, a world of learning from A to Z. In between lay B for Blossom, C for Chronograph, R for Rose, T for Time, all the answers to all the questions, F for Four O'Clock Flowers.

He laughed aloud at that.

'What is a Four O'Clock Flower anyway?' he called with despairing laughter to the ceiling. His question came back to him and he paused to allow the words push through clouds of thinking until they reached his lips again. 'What *is* a Four O'Clock Flower?'

Danny stood still as he accommodated the first fragility of a notion pushing from the back of his mind. Gently he shifted his attention between the poem and the silent bookshelves. His head tilted unconsciously, as it always did when he was considering a new angle of attack on a puzzle, and then a bit more as his thinking offered a wispy suggestion. Its trails led to a hint of possibility which drew him, almost sleepwalking back across the boards towards the poem. In his off-kilter position he read, but not lines this time, not even words. No, it was just the letters he focussed on this time, individual letters that he began to isolate one after the other for an entirely different reading.

A step forward became two steps back under the weight of a fresh possibility, and the motion became a turning to bring Danny's vision again to the towering shelves. The alphabetical listings ran from him and drew him forward, at a walk and then a jog, and all at once he was sprinting towards an answer. To the stairs he ran, racing to keep up with thoughts that led the way and demanded confirmation. He ploughed upwards to stop just long enough to scan the board of shelf listings, his choices pulling him in multiple directions at once: B for Botany or F for Flowers? He followed his instincts, tearing along the rows, nearly sliding past the F bank. He gained it, breathing rapidly, his fingers scrabbling across book spines to the arrhythmic hammering of his over-excited heart. There! *Flowers, A-Z.* He grabbed the title, pulled it free and threw open the pages in a single swift motion. He chased the words, swatting useless pages aside in pursuit of the desired entry until he had it, his answer beneath a coloured illustration, presented in black ink alongside its given name in English, and its Latin designation beneath!

Danny stumbled back from the truth of it, the oh-so simple solution, and he laughed aloud in disbelief. His retreat sent him heavily against the opposite shelf and the crash jarred him to his senses. He should double check, he warned. He was right, he knew it, but he needed to confirm with the poem. He set off once again at a charge, carrying the book with him.

He took the stairs two at a time and leapt the final five, hitting the floor already in a headlong run for his place. His feet thundered over the polished floor where he approached the turn, splaying the book open as he reached the desk and slammed it down to reach for the poem. He was right! He saw it, he saw the two words that told all, he saw them in the catalogue entry and just as clearly in Gilbert's text even as a shadow fell like a stain on the page. Danny looked for the source and stopped breathing.

The Banshee stood waiting.

She lingered at the table's far end, shifting languidly on the breeze as she watched. Her green eye held motionless but for a single tear that coursed from its depths.

'Danny,' she whispered.

Ice formed on his bones at her faraway voice.

The Banshee stepped forward, reaching with a flicker of her own imprisoned will to drive finger-nails deep into the table's surface. Curls of wood squealed from deep trenches where she clawed to stagger her progress. She swept up to a shelf with her other hand and drove the dagger it held deep into the spine of a thick book. The blade cleaved slowly through pages and burst to a paper shower before plunging into the adjoining book. The action combined with dragging fingers to delay but not halt the Banshee's tortured advance.

'Danny,' she repeated mournfully and through increasing tears, 'I can't stop this. *Run!*'

He reeled in terror, crashing past the chair to a stumbling blind flight from her. Through agony and crushing despair the Banshee freed her hands and came shrieking after.

Danny regained the main floor, his heart surging as he dived towards the library doors. Through the glass panels he saw the gas lamps on the square and aimed for the reassuring light. Such was his pace he almost ran into the Banshee where she emerged between shelves ahead to turn on him. His soles skidded on the polished floor and he tumbled back, mercifully below the arc of the dagger sweeping for his throat. He rolled over, slapped his palms to the floor and launched away just in time to escape the plunging blade which split a board between his ankles. Fear, overwhelming and total, gave fuel to his race and he careened from the whisper of the Banshee's cloak, darting at the last instant between shelves and just as quickly between a gap in one.

He halted abruptly in the maze of books and pressed his back to the volumes, the better to see any surprise attack from left or right. Through pumping adrenaline, he suppressed dragging gasps for the air his lungs demanded and fought to listen for his attacker past the heartbeat thunder in his ears.

The library became an empty vessel, devoid of movement and sound.

Think, he demanded of himself, *think*. He needed stairways and exits, windows and doors. He flung the eye of his mind to see the entire library at once and mapped what he remembered of his surroundings.

Like a puzzle to be solved, he mentally charted pathways and alternate routes, the challenge bringing renewed vigour to his limbs and hope of escape.

Her weeping snaked for him among the books.

He drew away, sensing her approach from the main floor. He pictured her some three to four shelves away and closing in. He tried to reason through his dread for her rising voice. If he moved quickly, he could reach the end of his row and duck about its rear as she passed. That would clear his path for a fire exit he knew lay farther back. He eased along the volumes and turned.

A pair of staring eyes looked fearfully into his and stilled him.

It was like looking into a mirror. The face peering back was as his own and held in it the same chilled fear he felt. But while his mouth opened to give way to a horrified cry at the sight, David cast a phantom finger to his lips for silence. With a quick signal he led his brother deeper between the stacks.

Danny was led numbly. He struggled and failed to form words as he and his brother crouched together in a recess. Of all the departed, he thought feverishly, all those who could be ghosts to see. He almost buckled at the shock of seeing his own brother.

'I know, I know,' David soothed him while he kept a keen watch about, 'here I am, but there's no time to explain.'

'You were here all along?' Danny half-guessed and his head swam.

'Of course,' David said, wounded by his brother's surprise.

'But why?' Danny blurted.

David shrugged irritably. 'There's no time.'

'Make time,' Danny demanded.

'Because I couldn't leave you, okay?' David rolled his eyes. 'This is so cringe. I couldn't just move on and leave you to face everything.' He cut across Danny's attempt to respond. 'And it's a good thing I did stay. That exit you were thinking of aiming for, she's already there.'

'What do we do?' Danny whispered.

'We surprise her. Straight across the library is the door we want, a hundred-metre dash and we're clear.'

'No, we're not,' Danny protested. 'You're the runner, remember, not me. If I sprint a hundred metres, I'll be shattered, and then what? She'll still catch me. I think she has to.'

David struggled for an alternative plan and despaired. 'Hell, you're the clever one, give me something.'

Danny plotted rapidly. 'You make the run. Draw her off, even for a few seconds and I'll head for the door this side.'

'Can you make it?' David asked doubtfully.

'I might not need to,' Danny said. With a wink he pulled a thick book from the nearest shelf. 'Get ready.'

Back-to-back they prepared.

'Wait,' David said. 'You worked out the poem, didn't you?'

'Yeah, so?'

'So, genius, maybe you should share, just in case.'

'It's an acrostic.'

David sighed. 'See, I don't even know what that means.'

'Go look it up, sporty.'

'Wait!'

'Damn, what now?'

'Caitlyn.'

'What? What about Caitlyn?'

'She's cute, isn't she?'

'Shut your face. And keep your distance.'

David smirked and offered no promises. 'Go!'

The brothers exploded to action.

David surged onto the main floor. Glancing to his right he found the Banshee there, stalking the rows. His onward motion drew her head to a turn of splaying hair, her cape to billowing as she set off in pursuit.

Danny raced the space behind the stacks, feet skimming the boards in taking him to full speed down the alphabetic listings. The green-lit sign of the emergency exit shimmered through the far gloom. He passed F for Freedom, his lungs starting to burn once more, hard past E for Escape, on through D and C and on, on to

B, B for Banshee where she rounded the shelf and met his flight with the full force of her dagger.

Danny was stunned by the force of the blow. He stopped, hanging on the blade, and so close to the Banshee his long outward breath stroked her hair to part the strands. With eyes wide in shock, he looked to a rolling tear and saw his own stunned face reflected. A sound, distant but sharp came and he felt the dagger snap. His legs gave out and he fell to crash against the books. Looking down, he found the broken blade protruding from his shirt, and a pool of dark blood seeping around it.

Banshee weeping filled Danny's ears as they drifted together into darkness.

FIFTY-SEVEN

Caitlyn hurtled through the third realm. Blindly through twisting corridors she ran, stumbling over debris, rebounding off walls, searching frantically for the way back and up, up to the mortal world and to Danny.

The voices sounding through the tunnels added fuel to her flight. Urgent and echoing, she heard the Morrigan insisting *this way*, and *no, thisss way* from the Pooka. Balor's voice bellowed over the others, demanding action and every passage carried his command.

'Find Caitlyn, stop her!'

She leapt a fallen statue and careened towards a junction. Left, or right? There was nothing to aid the choice until, and far off along one whispering corridor, flickering torchlight signalled the coming of the hunters. The choice was made for her and she sprinted from rising voices.

The way opened up. Caitlyn found herself on a rocky outcrop within a natural cavern. The cave climbed dizzyingly high and plunged to unseen fathoms. Across the depths ran the stony remnants of a bridge, the only way forward. Affected in no less measure by the damage visited on the third realm, the path was a thin portion of the original span, a mere thread of a once much wider structure now cleaved and lost to the abyss.

The angry chorus reached her from the passage and Caitlyn spun to it. Dancing light was already coursing about the edges of the stone doorway. She realised with a start she couldn't hope to cross the bridge in time. Desperately she looked for an alternative, finding nothing along the fractured wall and only scant hope in the cover offered by rock piles nearby. She raced to the nearest boulders and ducked.

The burning torch swept from the passage, lighting the Pooka's way. His slit gaze twinkled in the hunt and he paused, seeking prey with eager sniffs of the air. A scent was detected. He eased onto the outcrop to hold his torch higher. By its flaring he probed, looking far off across the shattered bridge and from one side to the other. He rejected the way of the bridge in favour of hiding places among the rocks and turned that way.

Caitlyn heard him coming. Past the rubble barrier to which she pressed tightly, she heard feet crunching to a brief pause, and in that moment the distinct whisper of a sharpened blade drawn from its rest. Caitlyn softly drew her dagger in reply and waited for the attack.

A reverberating clatter shook the cave. From somewhere on high it came. It was the clear sound of a rock disturbed to strike and tumble to the depths. The Pooka's feet scraped harshly where he reacted, and Caitlyn sensed him turn from her place. She perceived his eyes scouring the wall before, *yes*, he identified a way up and his footsteps moved quickly away.

Caitlyn gingerly peered over the boulders and to the heights. In a cleft far above she spied movement, subtle and dark among the rocks there, but could not make out the figure whose actions drew the Pooka farther off.

Caitlyn seized the moment and made for the ruined bridge. As quickly as she dared, she gained the precarious sliver, clamping hands tightly to the wall's rough capstones as she slid a foot to an uneven surface. Loosened stone chips crumbled under her weight and fell, pulling her frightened sight with them to the bottomless dark. Easing forward, she willed her attention up and forward. No more looking down, she vowed. With a keen focus on the task, she traversed hazards lying in wait for her feet and eased over lethal cracks under her hands, cracks that seemed to grow longer and wider with every touch. The abyss received the grating sound of deterioration and magnified it to a hungry rumbling from the earth.

She touched a rough stone, testing it fully before trusting her weight to it. The stone slid abruptly from its fixing and Caitlyn was pulled dangerously forward as it rasped free. The damaged rail beneath struck her hips and only that saved her from toppling. Fighting for balance, she watched the capstone spin to its doom and heard its death rattle against the rocks far below. Alarmed by the thunderous echo, she glanced back in search of the Pooka and hastened on.

Through the receding gloom, Caitlyn saw the bridge widen to a point beyond its collapse and return to its original form where it reached the far side of the cavern. Only a short portion of her precarious track remained until she would reach it. Hand over hand she hauled nearer to safety.

'Do be cautiousss,' the Pooka teased her.

Caitlyn cried out against fright and almost lost her grip. Craning back, she found her pursuer close by. He had taken to the capstones and with steady and casual balance he walked upright along them, hardly glancing down as he cleared the fallen section. She doubled her efforts and threw caution to the pit in favour of an accelerated scramble for the far side. His laughter chased after and all the louder when her foot slipped to near disaster. With a final tensing of every muscle, Caitlyn cleared the ruined sliver at a bound and crashed headlong to the bridge.

The Pooka leapt nimbly behind and with enough power to sail over her and land between her and escape. He stood to confine her on the serrated edge between the bridge and oblivion.

'Such effort,' he mocked, watching as Caitlyn produced her dagger, 'and all for nothing.' He played his own long blade on the air and admired his face reflected. He looked on his prey with contempt. 'You place me in a pickle, Caitlyn McCabe. King Balor wants you returned, to stand and rule by his ssside. But my Queen, she wants you crussshed.' He looked thoughtfully into the abyss. 'Who should I fear mossst?'

'Go ask my mother,' Caitlyn spat.

The Pooka fumed at her daring and the tickle of fear she caused in him. 'I will cast your body into the pit,' he snarled, 'and your heart after.' With a malignant growl of hate he drew his sword high and struck down.

Metal crashed on metal, the contact a clear singing note that rolled to the depths and back again. Caitlyn hissed against the percussion and looked up to where blades crossed at her face, the one vibrating in the hand of the stunned Pooka, the other held by a figure who brought his thin and upright frame from the darkness in time to intercept the killer blow.

The ghost of Sackimum Brody smiled down on her.

'Questions?' he asked with an arched brow.

'Not really,' she gasped.

To the Pooka's frustrated howl the combatants jumped apart and faced off, sword tips chiming. The

Professor moved quickly to place his shimmering form protectively between demon and girl.

'On you go,' he instructed her quickly. 'Find the stairs back. I brought someone to help you.'

The Pooka's raging cry ended all talk and, as he drove furiously at the Professor, Caitlyn turned and raced away.

'I should have killed you a thousand timesss,' the Pooka snarled.

'Now we have a thousand chances,' Brody mocked him with a chuckle.

They hurled themselves into the fight.

∋ ∋ ∋

Chased by echoes of clashing steel, Caitlyn plunged for the doorway from the cavern.

Once more she ran along rubble-strewn corridors, weaving through the ruins. Unlike before, however, she felt beneath her feet the first slight drag of an incline to the route. With a growing anticipation she breathed against the tougher work rate demanded of her legs and powered on.

Another portal loomed. The door that once secured it was rotted to just a few dusty planks hanging forlornly on the hinges. She burst through with senses alive to all possible threats.

The wide chamber was not unlike the room of the harp. Rounded in the same way, this place too housed numerous doors, many bolted, many more suffering the same slow decay as the one just passed. No beauteous harp stood here, and the centre of this space was devoid of adornment. What dominated the attention lay at the far end of the chamber. Commencing at a wide spot some metres from the wall, a broad staircase swept upwards. Formed in massive slabs, the stairway was littered by fallen rocks as it travelled beneath a high arch cut through the earth. The arch held ancient symbols boldly announcing the destination.

'Newgrange,' Caitlyn guessed aloud. She started forward.

The sound of her feet crashed to the limits of the space as she crossed at full speed, every step becoming ten in a storm of echoes. She drew near the first step and altered her pace so that the noise of her sprinting fell and, in its receding, allowed for an altogether different sound to follow. The low angry growl of a gigantic cat rolled at Caitlyn's back.

Catcallach's form stalked from a doorway to regard her over dripping teeth. The raw wound on its muzzle glistened and the memory of the girl still burned in the creature's eyes. It circled at a safe distance this time, beyond the threat of daggers. The feline hissed and crouched on its haunches, watching its prey back farther up the stairs. Filthy hair bristled along its arched back as it placed a paw to the first step and raked claws against the stone. The cat flexed its legs for a mere beat of time and sprang.

Caitlyn dug her feet in and drew her dagger back for the strike. There was no running from this, she realised, just one hopeless chance of landing a blow on target. Catcallach charged to fill her vision with teeth and claws.

The stone that flew was right on target. It bounced against Catcallach's head and pulled the enraged beast up short. In time with Caitlyn, it whirled to identify the attacker.

Mia stood below, tiny and defiant. Mia, Brody's promise of help, who had followed all through the darkness and tracked Caitlyn's every step, shook an angry fist at the monster cat.

'Get lost, smelly!'

Catcallach's furious bellow erupted through the room. It followed its cry, shifting to grip the edge of the staircase for a leap towards the little spirit.

'Mia,' Caitlyn called desperately.

But the girl was already on the move. Retreating towards the nearest doorway, she looked up to Caitlyn. 'Keep going!' she called urgently. 'You're nearly there.'

Catcallach launched. Paws outstretched, the creature left the stairs to hurtle for Mia, dwarfing the child in its dive towards her.

Caitlyn could only watch as the girl stood to face

the approaching teeth before deftly skipping aside and then ducking through the doorway, leaving Catcallach to crash to earth. In the moment of confusion, Caitlyn barrelled up the steps.

Catcallach's screeches assailed her ears as she pounded upwards, the sound overflowing with rage as the beast tried to choose between targets. The decision of its flaming brain was signalled by the renewed tear of claws on the staircase and Caitlyn drove harder.

She passed beneath the arch and looked to the way receding. Countless steps rose towards a similar gateway, far off. Her pounding heart faltered at the sight of so great a distance to cover with Catcallach closing rapidly. A moment later she was renewed, perceiving the optical trick playing out. There was no vast distance across which the creature would outpace her. The stairs were physically narrowing. From their initial great width, they shrank with each step in reaching for the next arch, this one a fraction of the size of the last. Better yet, she could fit easily though but Catcallach surely would not. Caitlyn felt a wave of hot breath on her neck.

She flung herself beneath the arch. Scrambling forward and across steps, she saw Catcallach's shattering contact against the narrowing. She rolled farther as the collision brought a shower of stones and dust from the roof. In its fury the beast was oblivious to the danger and struggled harder to progress, teeth gnashing in its hunger for her. The shower grew to a rumbling and rocks began to break free overhead. Caitlyn looked at the whole world falling and threw up her arms against it. The underworld roared and Catcallach's pitiful howls were swept away on the avalanche.

Time went astray in rolling clouds. The storm ended in a moment, but its echo seemed to last forever, booming slowly away as choking dust settled on new rock piles.

Caitlyn surfaced through the layers of dirt slowly, dragging upwards to be more than a buried memory in this place. She clawed across stones, beset by pain and with senses dulled by a sharp blow to her head. A warm trickle of blood mixed with covering earth to create a muddy stream along her cheek. She ignored it and hauled on, relieved when fingertips reached the limits of the destruction and felt the carved roughness of the stairs. She advanced from prone to kneeling and from there to dizzy standing. She did not look back in search of what had become of Catcallach, focussing instead on the route forward and willing her sluggish feet to take her that way.

The stairs ended. Narrowing to a passage she could touch with outstretched arms the steps ran to an abrupt stop at solid rock. Caitlyn looked with dull confusion at this unexpected termination. Blinking against her rattled senses, she turned to the ceiling so close overhead. A square cut into the stone was clear and within reach. She reached with aching arms and pushed the trapdoor aside.

Clambering up, the last of her strength played out and Caitlyn fell back amid branches and leaves. She smelled the freshness of vegetation and felt a night wind on her face. She turned to its caress, and what she saw brought her clawing from the undergrowth. Despite the fog of pain and exhaustion, she recognised the shadowed hulk sitting upon the hill above. The moon appeared from sundered clouds and shed its ghostly rays on sparkling walls and the lightbox that stared down blindly and indifferent to her return.

Lost between realms, far from her mother, farther still from Danny, she offered Newgrange her tears.

FIFTY-EIGHT

Balor tended his Queen.

With loving care, he carried her through the ranks of the witch guard and placed her weakened body on the throne, carefully arranging her garments as he looked attentively for signs of discomfort.

'My Queen,' he whispered fondly.

Cethlinn smiled through parched lips at her title. 'Queen,' she replied dreamily. With sluggish movements she reached for his torn face. 'Sit by me, husband.'

'Not yet,' he said, mindful of the task ahead, 'but soon.'

She became animated, strengthened by anxiety and she rose heavily in her seat to fix him. 'The spear, did I succeed?'

In answer he smiled and reached for the gleaming weapon, levelling its tip to a far corner of the throne room. The golden tip winked briefly by the light of the fire and all at once through its own light, flaring from within. Power danced crackling as the spear's luminescence surged and in an instant the room overflowed with lightning from the shaft. Balor braced to control the might of the weapon in his hand and the witch guard ducked, overawed at the dazzling power that clawed the far shadows asunder and scorched the walls.

Cethlinn fell back, her joy mustered in a weary sigh.

'You have given me victory,' Balor lauded her and lifted high his spear. 'In return I will sweep our enemies away and give you the world.'

'Three worlds,' she said, and a smile lit her wan features.

He looked on his hungry Queen and bent for a kiss of wizened lips.

The throne room filled with lamenting for cursed lovers, a weeping that chilled through the heat of the fire to announce the coming of the Banshee. Aoife emerged from darkness, aching and forlorn.

'Granddaughter,' Cethlinn cooed with malign glee, and she snapped her fingers.

Aoife trembled visibly beneath her grandmother's power but held against its diminished potency, defying its grip until, and with greater emphasis, Cethlinn snapped her fingers once more to push Aoife to her knees.

'That's better,' the Queen said, breathing hard from her efforts. 'Do not dare hope I spent all my power in restoring the spear, Aoife. I have enough magic yet for you. Speak.'

'My task is complete,' the Banshee reported coldly. With a flick of her hand, she sent her broken dagger chiming at the feet of the royal couple.

Cethlinn looked from the weapon to the Banshee's face. She leaned forward abruptly, her joy melting to wary suspicion. 'Is the boy in the spirit world?' she tested. 'Did you let him linger there to help Caitlyn?'

'My cut was deep,' Aoife said. 'He is not in the spirit realm.'

Cethlinn searched keenly for lies, probing the half-hidden face of her granddaughter for the slightest hint of deceit. Satisfaction came, but slowly. 'Very well,' she said at last and eased painfully back.

The tall doors of the throne room rumbled open to admit the Pooka and the Morrigans.

'Where is Caitlyn?' Balor demanded and the witches hissed for the lack of a prisoner as the group approached.

'She's gone,' the Morrigan said. 'Escaped,' her sisters chorused.

The Pooka squirmed. 'She had help. It was Brody.'

Only Cethlinn saw it, the slim half-smile that crept beneath Aoife's hair. With urgent and tortured effort, she seized Balor's sleeve and pulled him close.

'Begin your march to the sea,' she ordered and cast him off before he could protest, 'summon your troops.' She accepted instead his wordless bow and watched as he strode towards the doors, tall and glorious beneath his spreading cloak, invincible with his gleaming spear. 'Send for me,' she called after. 'I want to watch the mortal world burn.'

FIFTY-NINE

The world swam back into focus. At first there was sudden illumination, sparking harshly before easing to soft lamplight overhead. A portion of ceiling came into relief, its panelling appearing, from this prone angle, to rest directly on the bookshelves towering up on either side. The effect was unsettling, so restricted and confining. It was like being in a grotesquely over-sized coffin. And then Laetitia was there, looking down like an angel.

'Danny,' she said.

'Yes,' he said dimly.

'Thank the heavens,' she exclaimed and almost succumbed to weeping. 'He's here,' she called, and louder, 'here!'

Her voice seemed to come miles from her lips. The concern it held slipped somehow from a place farther off in the library and travelled ahead of footsteps Danny heard rushing closer.

Pembrig was first to arrive. Expertly navigating the pathways of his library in answer to Laetitia's summons, he appeared with a cry of relief at sight of the boy. It was quickly tempered by a look of concern for the split blade still protruding from Danny's shirt-front. He moved quickly to nurse the wound.

David sprinted into view between the book stacks. He fell to his knees by his brother and under the startled gazes of Laetitia and Pembrig.

'His spirit has left his body,' Pembrig cried in fright.

Despite the pain in his gut, Danny laughed. 'Twin brothers,' he said, amused at the librarian's confusion.

'Rest easy,' Laetitia cautioned and, with visible unease she looked on Danny's bloodied shirt.

David struggled to sound reassuring. 'It's going to be okay,' he said, and it was as much for his own ears as his brother's.

'I know,' Danny said with a lopsided grin. He reached for his shirt and over the protestations of the others he eased its bloodied material aside. All looked as he removed a thickly bound book skewered by the Banshee's blade. 'It stopped the worst,' he reassured his brother, 'the cut's not deep.'

'Wondrous young man,' Laetitia exclaimed, overjoyed.

'The clever one,' David repeated and fell back on his knees with relief.

'That's a first-edition *Ulysses*,' Pembrig wailed for

the damaged book. He received a chastising swat of Laetitia's fan.

'Fetch bandages,' she instructed and sent him running with a glare.

'The book,' Danny said, remembering. He began to rise.

'You must not move,' Laetitia cautioned.

'I really must,' he said with gentle insistence and leaned on his brother. 'I have the answer to the poem.'

Laetitia blinked and followed the boys across the library. 'You do? Pray tell.'

Danny hissed against the pain of his wound as he moved. 'Puzzles only ever appear complicated,' Danny explained. 'But after you solve one, it's always "oh yeah, so simple". Professor Gilbert's puzzle was just like that, a simple answer all wrapped up in poetic knots.' He reached for the sheet of poetry as Pembrig returned with medical supplies and proceeded to fuss over Danny's cut.

'It's a cross-rigged poem,' David informed Laetitia, trying to sound smart.

'Acrostic,' Danny corrected him.

'Acrostic,' Laetitia gushed and flung her arms wide in excitement. 'Of course! Why did we not think of that?' She smirked. 'Dean Swift will go mad.'

'*I'm* going to go mad unless you explain this,' David said.

Danny held up the sheet. 'An acrostic poem is one where the first letter of the first word of each line combines with the rest to form a word or sentence hidden by the poet. Gilbert's poem gives two words this way.'

David and Laetitia read the letters quickly to construct growing words from whispers.

'Mirabilis Jalapa,' David recited from the garnered letters. He looked quizzically at his brother. 'What the hell is that?'

'It's Latin,' Laetitia deduced breathlessly.

'Yes, it is,' Danny said. He placed a hand to the book snatched so eagerly from the shelves earlier. 'Mirabilis Jalapa is the scientific name of a South American plant known in English as the Four O'Clock flower.' He gestured to the photograph. 'Dr Gilbert is wearing one, right there. I think this is a pointer to where he hid the sword, in a place marked by Four O'Clock flowers.'

Laetitia shrilled excitedly and with a sudden rush she grabbed Danny and rewarded his cleverness with an exuberant kiss on his lips. Withdrawing abruptly, she hid behind her fan. 'Don't tell Caitlyn I did that,' she instructed, abashed.

David was first to recover from the moment. 'Do we have to go to South America?'

'What?' Danny asked, distracted by the taste of strawberries. 'No. The answer will be closer to home, maybe even here at the university. What we have to do is find where Dr Gilbert planted Four O'Clock flowers.'

David looked doubtfully to his brother. 'How are we supposed to do that?'

'That's easy,' a reassuring and familiar voice said from behind.

The group turned and there the speaker and her companions stood. Dishevelled and tired, Caitlyn managed a smile for Danny, while Professor Brody leaned on his stick and held a large book under his arm. Mia, meanwhile, eyed David warily from the corner of a bookshelf.

'Caitlyn,' Danny gasped. They moved in a single rush to be together. 'Are you okay?'

She nodded and shook her head all at once and held on until he winced.

'You're hurt,' she said.

He smiled. 'I met your mother. I think it went okay.'

Under Laetitia's swimming eyes, Brody carried his book towards the table and accepted her warm embrace.

Mia fixed David with an accusing stare. 'You're not Danny,' she said.

The book banged heavily on the table-top and commanded all attention to the title rising from among colourful floral pictures: A Botanical Catalogue, by Professor Alexander Gilbert.

'We are nearing the end,' Brody told them. 'Balor's spear is renewed, and the Fomorian army will soon answer his call. Thankfully, we have Caitlyn back, and thanks to Danny, we have the weapon needed to meet the threat.'

'I haven't found it yet,' Danny cautioned.

'I think you have,' Brody corrected him. 'While I was listening to your brilliant solution to Professor Gilbert's puzzle, your words struck a chord and sent me looking for this volume.' He turned its pages as he spoke. 'Alexander's passion for flowers is contained here, the travels he undertook in gathering seeds, the hours he spent cultivating them to success, and the homes and organisations to which he donated his famous blooms.' The Professor stooped to read a paragraph found beneath a large illustration. '"Of special significance was the gift of a colourful display of Mirabilis Jalapa to the National Botanical Gardens in time for the restoration of that famed centrepiece admired by all visitors".' He rotated the book for all to see. '"How appropriate it is that Four O'Clock flowers should decorate the refurbished sundial in the Gardens".'

Danny recited quickly from memory. 'Shades pass the hours, pressing time to a rock, and offering their flowers to hail four o'clock.'

The Professor nodded and tapped his fingers on the book. 'You would have found this, Danny, I'm sure, but time weighs so heavily on us now. Balor's march is underway. I have already sent messengers through the spirit realm. The departed will answer, I'm certain, and will hold Balor as long as they can, but the sword of Lug must be recovered at once to allow Caitlyn do what only she can against the mad King.'

All looked to Caitlyn as though in expectation of some profound words.

'Let's get this done,' she said.

SIXTY

The Wraith weaved through the crush of mortal traffic. Amid horns honked and curses hurled, Marcus drove as fast as he dared, slewing the car perilously around each new obstacle. Sliding into a curve, he saw a policeman whip past the window, baton raised and a shrill whistle at his lips. Marcus was relieved to see the officer was a spirit dweller, not one who could give chase through the living world.

'Everyone okay?' he called to the back, throwing the vehicle hard left and right again to leave the rush hour traffic behind.

'Surviving,' Caitlyn said as she and Danny tumbled helplessly to the motion.

The final mission was theirs alone. Dispatched by Brody, they had left him to his planning the last defence of the spirit realm to speed north through the city. Word had gone ahead by spectral messengers to all corners of the night. In the spirit world's hour of need, Caitlyn McCabe would bring help to those who helped her.

Really? As she slid once more across the upholstery, Caitlyn was chased by doubt. What help could she offer, even if the lost sword came into her hand? What was her real part in all that was unfolding? What could she do that her mother had not?

Questions, always questions. The Professor had seen them again in her face, but now, when she needed them more than ever, he did not have answers. Faith, he had told her assuredly, he had faith.

'Nearly at the Gardens,' Marcus promised his tumbling passengers, 'not much longer.' He braced for the crest of a hill and gripped the wheel tightly. In a stomach-dropping moment, the car's wheels left the roadway and the Wraith broke gravity an instant before a juddering return to earth with a mechanical whine and burst of steam. The road ahead became visible through the boiling clouds and Marcus cried out at what he saw. Slamming both feet to the brake pedal he brought the car to a shrieking stop.

Caitlyn and Danny followed Marcus's gaze through the windscreen and gasped at the spectacle before them.

The spirits of Dublin were on the march. Across the breadth of the way the ranks of the departed walked in quiet unison. The spectral wall advanced on the car and flowed around it as the ghosts wound their way slowly on. Some turned to look on the occupants of the car, one or two to offer hopeful smiles for Caitlyn.

Most did not look at all, their faces set with resignation on the path.

'What are they doing?' Caitlyn asked with her voice at a whisper.

'They're answering the Professor's call,' Marcus said. 'They're going to face Balor's army and buy us the time we need.'

Caitlyn looked closer at the faces passing to the fight, all grimly determined in their progress. 'We're wasting time,' she said, unable to look any more.

Marcus followed a slow course through the tide of ghosts.

Minutes later, and beyond the spirit ranks, the car came to a stop again. Marcus killed the engine, and all exited the vehicle to approach tall black gates caught in the headlights' beam.

The serene dark world of the Botanical Gardens lay between the bars. Ferns and petals stood unmoving beneath the veil of night. To the limits of sight, the gardens had been transformed to a dour celebration of ink but for a solitary spot of illumination, a curved reflection of the moon where it struck the distant canopy of the main glasshouse.

'Over we go,' Marcus said. He quickly formed a stirrup with his hands by which Caitlyn and next Danny surmounted the barrier.

The night pressed hard on the trespassers and for a

moment they held back from it and the fears it offered the unwary.

'Which way is it?' Danny asked, squinting into the dark.

'I know the way,' Caitlyn said and led quickly on.

Traversing from pavement to grass, they walked rapidly before the gigantic form of the glasshouse and to a central point on its access path. Here the cultivated precision of straight lawn edges cut to a circle. At its middle stood a short granite column, its top set with the brass plate and sail of a sundial, its base surrounded by dark blooms.

'Four o'clock flowers,' Marcus said and reached for the petals.

Caitlyn moved with Danny to inspect the brass plate, coursing her hand across it to feel the engraved numerals beneath her fingers.

'There are no screws,' Danny muttered, his mind already whirring with possibilities. His inquisitive mind led him to his knees from where he closely examined the underside of the dial's setting.

Caitlyn's fingers flowed to the centre of the dial, her senses drawn to the raised marker, the shark-fin of metal across which moon shadow offered itself to the inlaid hours. In a flash of certainty, she seized the angled portion with both hands and leaned to it, throwing her weight behind. Breathing through the effort, she felt the brass triangle resist and hold fiercely to its setting until, and all at once, the entire dial rotated and grated on its stone base. Watched by Danny and Marcus, Caitlyn heaved on, unscrewing the timepiece until it fell aside to reveal the hollow interior of the column. She peered inside and her breathing stilled.

Caitlyn reached for what she saw, stretching down to clasp and draw it up to the moon, its polished blade feeding on the light as it emerged slowly to sing on the air. Caitlyn's stunned breath misted on the inlay of knotted whirls along the sword's length.

'It has no weight,' she gasped, testing the weapon.

'It has the strength to destroy a King,' an overawed Marcus reminded her.

'What do we do next?' Danny asked.

Caitlyn had no answer. She looked blankly from the sword to Danny and Marcus.

'You could try running,' the Morrigan suggested.

They spun about to find her advancing across the lawns, the raven black of her armour terrible under the moon, the sneer she offered more terrible yet.

'Get behind me,' Marcus ordered. He drew himself up to meet the coming challenge.

The Morrigan laughed at his display, amused at his misplaced confidence. With a casual hand she drew her sword and tested it expertly without breaking stride.

The Sword of Lug reacted.

Caitlyn cried out at the spontaneous motion under her grip, a vibration that travelled from the weapon to drive her arm upwards. Taking an involuntary step forward, she offered the blade to the approaching Morrigan with a confident fluidity she did not control.

The Morrigan blinked and the arrogance in her face washed over with a flicker of doubt. She halted her advance and took up a defensive stance before Caitlyn's bizarre motions.

Caitlyn's blade mirrored its opponent's, sweeping to a point so fixed that Caitlyn believed it would hang there even if she let go. She realised in the same instant that she could not actually release her hold. The sword and she were as one, melded hand to haft, the weapon taking its vitality from her, and, she realised with breathless certainty, offering its sure expertise in return.

'Come on,' she dared to taunt the Morrigan.

The warrior divided before their eyes, shimmering to her three parts. She drew her added swords in a blinking and offered three weapons to Caitlyn's one.

'You will be destroyed, Caitlyn McCabe,' the Morrigans warned in chorus.

Caitlyn set her face against fear as the warriors closed the distance.

An arrow pierced the night. Whistling from on

high, the projectile found the gap between the fighters and struck the earth between, halting the Morrigans' advance.

With jubilant battle roars, Ivar the Boneless and his Viking horde charged from the trees. They swept forward, carrying their King aloft to rampage across manicured lawns under his direction, an impenetrable shield wall of glittering axes and sharpened spears.

The Morrigans fell back, closing their short rank quickly to meet the headlong rush. They howled in return, a chorus of furious defiance in the face of overwhelming odds, and they met the charge. The thunder of combat rolled.

Diverting his bearers towards Caitlyn and the others, Ivar glared down triumphantly on them.

'You have it,' he growled towards the weapon in Caitlyn's hand. 'Good. That gives us a chance, eh?' He glanced briefly to the continuing battle. 'Get gone,' he ordered, 'we'll keep old triple-trouble occupied for as long as we can.' Without pause for reply, the King lent his roar to the others and steered his throne into the fray.

Caitlyn turned and ran. With the battle-hungry sword thrumming in her hand, she led the others off the field and towards the main gates once again.

Marcus sprinted ahead over the final few metres and spun to offer his clasped hands for the return climb. Caitlyn ignored the offer and moved directly to the barrier. With a single sweep she brought her sword hard against the lock and sundered it to an eruption of sparks. She pushed through and headed for the Wraith.

Danny gained on her. 'Where are we going?' he asked as they tumbled into the vehicle.

'North?' Marcus guessed. He brought the car roaring to life.

'Yes,' Caitlyn confirmed. She faced Danny. 'I don't have all the answers I need yet, but I think I know where to get them. We're going back to Newgrange.'

SIXTY-ONE

Balor marched to the sea.

Striding the land along paths between worlds, with the moon alone his constant companion, the King moved with furious intent, every part of his being alive to this momentous night. In his crushing grip the spear led the way, a massive compass point winking with interior fire, its power drawing him on, and eagerly on, towards a distant shore.

Visions brief and faltering came to surround him, and Balor looked with contempt on oblivious mortals beyond the veil of realms, drifting and shifting at their play, shining at their feasts. Their hearty songs reached him as misty echoes through the barriers of space and time. With a rage no longer muted by crushing earth he roared at their existence and their ignorance of the coming storm, and when their mechanical vehicles came flickering towards him, he swept his spear fiercely, cleaving them as smoke.

Occupants of the spirit world he drove in fear before him, railing against their audacity to be anything but slaves, and he showed them the power of the spear, a demonstration in flame and thunderous lightning to illuminate their terror and drown out their cries.

On he marched, blind of eye to the faces of spectral fear, deaf to their supplications. He would listen only after the chaos of war, when the realms reunited in a song of adulation for his name.

The veil thinned once more. Balor found himself walking within a broad tunnel cut through the earth. He recognised the paltry construct of mortals, their way of lights and signage offering passage beneath the earth for wheeled vehicles, and he saw for the first time that the mortals guiding the vehicles towards him were afforded an instant of seeing too. Their shock at his abrupt appearance in their world was communicated with wide eyes and a hauling on steering wheels. Large and small the vehicles blared with alarm through the cavernous space and weaved by, colliding in panic to pluming fire and rolling smoke in his wake. He slipped through the veil once more and, but for the mocking laughter he left behind, he was lost to mortal sense.

Bridges flashed over forests of old, homes appeared and disappeared along paths at once rock hard and then clay soft. Drawn by the spear, the realms merged in a blizzard of images and Balor's head dizzied to over-swimming realities.

Only the river he reached, and the stars above remained true, and the King oriented himself by them. The warrior belt of Bres the slave-keeper he kept to his right hand, its three glittering stars declining the way to the sea. Directly ahead he beheld a W-shaped cluster, named for Conand of the Vengeance, and Balor warmed to the jagged smile it offered for his endeavour. The worlds twisted and bled, and the Fomorian gods glimmered for joy.

He heard it a moment before he crested a rise, the hissing of sea foam where the river reached its mighty destination. Waves crashed onshore in greeting, from black to breaking white, the waters prostrating themselves at his feet and casting a kiss of tangy spray to his lips. Here he faltered, his breath snatched away by recognising fully the scale of what he would unleash. He stayed his hand, but just for an instant as the night searched his empty socket in vain for a measure of pity for the world.

With tremulous expectation, Balor dipped his spear tip to the surf.

The night wind fell to a startled breath and reversed its tack, enfolding the King's cape about him in its hastening from land towards the dark horizon. The diamond light of reflected stars rippled on the surface of the water, their sparkle swept to undulating strands by the air's caress and then by something more. A disturbance deep below agitated the sea to pools of bubbling and then to a boiling. Balor smiled across the tempestuous water.

The first Fomorian long-ship erupted from the maelstrom. Dragon prow and blood-stained sail surged up from the depths to crash down on the surface, its oarsmen already pulling hard to their King's call back from deepest banishment.

Another vessel burst free, and a third, and yet more, an entire Fomorian fleet cast up on all sides by the regurgitating sea. The waters ripped and shattered to countless risings near and far. From one grim hull a war horn gathered the armada to a common bearing and animalistic grunts and tattooed muscles sent the vessels churning for shore.

Balor's laughter rose at the sight and cut through the spray cast by the advancing fleet. It was laughter maniacal and born of a place as dark as the ocean's depths where his army had waited impatiently across the years. The King threw his arms wide as though to embrace all warriors at once and he raised high his spear, its guiding light bringing all ships to him. He felt the sea swell at his knees where the fleet's oars crashed in unison to stay their approach and felt the weight of a thousand hungry eyes on him from darkened hulls stilled and waiting.

'Brothers,' he said, and at first his voice cracked with the emotion for the long lost regained. 'Brothers!

Do you see me, my warriors?' He thrilled to the unified bark of salute which came. He held forth the spear. 'And do you see that which I bring?' The ships over-spilled with howls of celebration. Balor braced himself for the best. 'And do you see what it allows?' Without hesitation, the King stepped onto the water and the black surface held his weight. He walked unhindered and bold across the glassy floor into the shadow of the fleet. 'Brothers,' he called to the dumbfounded silence, 'Fomorian warriors all. You have kept faith with your King and the promise of your Queen. But have you kept your blades sharpened in expectation of this night? Ten thousand years of waiting have come to this, ten thousand years of spirits roaming unchecked and dancing on our defeat. The mortal world has grown fat on spoils that should be ours. They swill our mead and feast at our tables and pay no heed to the Fomorian gods. They have made drinking houses of our temples! But they have grown soft. Not a single warrior walks among them to stem the vengeance we bring to them this night. Across the spirit realm the vapours cower in fear. In the mortal world the children are sleeping. I will bring them nightmares. Who is with me?'

The night erupted to a chanting of blood thirst and vengeance, and to a riot of swords hammering on shields.

Balor showed the way. With a twist of his spear, he indicated the river mouth and marched there, listening to the clamour of disembarking warriors and the sound of feet marching over the water. The troops fell into step, the ranks of meaty and heavy-browed warriors moving in a grunting procession behind their King. His strength surged to bursting and Balor drew his frame to full height at the head of his army renewed. He filled his lungs' capacity against a heady swirl of excitement and issued a pluming growl to make the night fog tremor.

The undulating mist parted, it seemed, in deference to his greatness. It drew back and revealed the smooth stretching of the river ahead, and from bank to bank upon it, the raggle-taggle army of spirits arrayed and waiting for him.

'No farther, King Balor,' a warning voice called, and Sackimum Brody stepped to the front of the mass gathering.

Balor's surprise ebbed slowly to amusement as he beheld his mismatched opposition.

'What's this?' he taunted. 'Have you come in surrender to me?'

'We come to stop you,' Brody corrected him, and the spirits roared in concert.

'Fools!' Balor roared. 'Fools all. Behold the warriors I bring, smell the hunger on them. You would defy us?

Tonight, the balance tips in favour of the old gods and the old ways, when the realms were united under the strength of one ruler. As it once was, it shall be again.'

The Fomorians bellowed their agreement.

'We are already united, and under one leader,' Brody countered boldly.

Balor read between the Professor's words and laughed. 'You mean Caitlyn McCabe? Ha! And where is she, your Queen of last hope?' He scoffed. 'You have no hope but to survive on the scraps we leave you tonight, if you survive at all.'

Sackimum Brody drew his sword. Balor weighed the spear in his grasp.

The weeping came softly on the night wind, and the Banshee's lament floated like smoke through the space between armies and snaked through the ranks to reach nervous ears. Unsettled by it, the opposing warriors looked all around for the source. To a Fomorian's cry of fear, all looked to the high riverbank where Aoife's dark silhouette stood in mourning for them. Her cries became waves of fear cascading through every heart.

To a violent movement, Aoife was pulled to her knees, and the emerging form of Cethlinn was revealed, holding in her hand the whip securing the Banshee's neck. Beside her, the Morrigan arrived, bloodied yet eager for more fighting. The sight of her was more terrible yet and murmured doubts ran through the spirit army.

Cethlinn sought Balor and offered her champion a burning glare.

'Well,' she demanded, 'what are you waiting for?'

Spurred to action by the sight of his Queen, Balor thrust high his spear and issued a battle cry for his army to echo.

Brody swept his sword up and slashed it down to unleash his roaring troops.

The armies charged into the fray.

SIXTY-TWO

'How far?' Caitlyn asked, shouting to be heard over the tortured roar of the engine.

With a determined grip on the shuddering wheel, Marcus scanned the countryside night to either side of the road. 'Not long,' he offered, 'if the car holds out.' He shifted gear and the engine whined in protest.

Caitlyn looked quickly to her watch. 'It's twenty minutes to midnight.'

'Is that important?' Danny asked at her side.

She threw up her arms in frustration. 'I don't know,' she grumbled and looked into his eyes in hope of guidance. 'I still don't know what I'm supposed to do.'

He steadied her with a touch. 'You've done alright so far. And look,' he added, raising the sword, 'you're closer than ever to the answers. Let's just get to Newgrange and see.'

'Questions, answers, answers, questions,' Caitlyn sighed and grasped the weapon.

From the front, Marcus made a curious, quizzical noise. 'Er, what's that?'

Caitlyn and Danny looked to his features reflected in the rear-view mirror, and to his eyes staring past them to the route behind. They turned to the roadway whipping back to blackness and peered deeper into that blackness where even as they watched it seemed to *reorder* itself.

Shifting from a single thick entity of shadow the night offered instead numerous speeding shapes, undulating with motions as frenzied as the demon steeds they rode and yet soft and as flowing as the diaphanous veils overstretching their cruel faces. Four witch riders, and the Pooka who led them, raced into view and closed on the Wraith with poisoned hisses.

The car's rear window burst, casting a diamond shower over the occupants as the first whistling dart passed through. The tiny projectile sang deafeningly against the sword and tumbled to bury itself in a panel dangerously close to Caitlyn's head. The car veered wildly and Marcus momentarily lost control.

'Faster,' Danny urged desperately at Marcus's ear. With a cry he fell back, pulled roughly aside by Caitlyn as another dart slashed through the vehicle, this time to slice the upholstery where the boy had been a second before.

'Glove box,' Marcus reminded everyone urgently, 'glove box!'

Without question, Danny dived over the seatback

and scrabbled at the catch in the driver's panel. The little door it held sprang open and the twin flintlock pistols clattered free. Straining to reach, Danny's fingers clasped one and then a second pistol. He drew upright, and just in time to see a witch rider take fresh aim from beyond the passenger window.

Glass exploded and Danny flinched against shards peppering his face. Unseeing, he felt the car shift violently at the same time as a pained cry from Marcus reached him. A hand reached and snatched one pistol away.

Caitlyn fired point blank at the witch rider. Smoke and fire rolled to a hellish scream and the demon was lost to sight. There was no time for celebration as Caitlyn looked where the remaining riders gained steadily behind even as she felt the car's creeping deceleration.

'Why are we slowing?' she cried.

'Marcus,' Danny replied as he tumbled fully into the front seat.

Caitlyn dumped the spent pistol and leapt to see. The sight of blood seeping about the witch's dart in Marcus's leg drew a startled hiss from her and she looked to his face which was drawn to shock and pain. Forcing herself to turn away, Caitlyn grabbed for the second pistol and drew a steadying breath. 'Get us moving,' she ordered and spun back.

The next dart was already in flight. As Caitlyn lev-elled her gun and used both hands to haul back the hammer, she saw a pale hand outstretching and the wink of metal flung through the gloom. She fought the urge to duck and locked her muscles for the shot, sensing the dart's passage through her billowing hair as she held firm. The pistol crashed, muzzle fire illu-minating all, and Caitlyn was afforded a nightmare vision of grizzled faces beyond the veils. A rider was struck from her saddle by the pistol ball and its rolling thunder. The sound gave way to that of the engine's howl as Marcus groaned and forced his injured leg down hard on the accelerator.

With cruel strokes the Pooka drove his mount harder in pursuit, lashing the animal to maintain and then close the space to the rear of the car. To inhuman shrieks he spurred the beast on and guided it danger-ously alongside, drawing his sword as he neared.

Caitlyn dived aside as the demon's blade screeched into the vehicle, piercing its metal all too easily. The sword was quickly withdrawn only to cut through an instant later in another place, jabbing and prob-ing for her. She rolled from danger and fell across her sword, its metal thrumming beneath her. The sword's energy was intense against her, and at once she felt its emboldening power, its inspiring strength.

Caitlyn rose up to meet the next Pooka thrust. His

blade presented through a shower of metal sparks and her own met the challenge in a swinging defence, her cry of effort coming a second ahead of the metal strike.

Energy immense and staggering flowed within the car as Caitlyn's sword met its opponent and sundered the lesser blade. Blinding light and buffeting wind issued from the point of contact and swelled through the vehicle. Refusing to be confined, the storm punched through all windows at once and sent one door tumbling away to the night. Through a shielding hand, Caitlyn was afforded the briefest glimpse of the Pooka's horrified face as he and his horse were lifted and swept away like leaves on the wind.

The remaining riders screamed and whipped their steeds on. On clattering hooves they carried their increased rage and closed on the struggling Wraith. Bony hands reached in preparation for fresh darts and steered mounts for simultaneous attacks left and right where they gained on the groaning car.

'Ha –ha –haaaa!' came the highwayman's cry, boisterous and flamboyant. Between the witches Captain Cassidy rode, his horse powering at full speed and through the gap they made. He offered hands already filled with pistols primed, arms flung wide as he fired at both witches. The air filled with shrieks and through powder clouds the demon horses charged on with empty saddles. 'Go!' Cassidy called after as he drew to a sliding halt. 'None shall follow, Miss Caitlyn. This highway is mine!' For added dramatic effect, the spirit reared up his horse and swung his hat in joyous salute for the receding car.

Relieved, Caitlyn clawed through the shattered interior. She found Danny tending to Marcus's wound as the injured man tried to maintain focus on the road ahead through plumes of steam billowing from the car's tortured engine.

'Can we make it?' she asked.

Marcus smiled despite his torment. 'We already have,' he said and pointed.

Between the trees, moonlight and quartz revealed the destination. Resplendent in the night, the walls of Newgrange drew the stars' attention to glitter like a beacon of hope. From the heart of glowing splendour, the shadowed lightbox gazed dispassionately on the approaching Wraith.

The stricken car eased at last to rest and fell to smoking silence. Caitlyn and Danny hurried to exit, watched coldly by the mound.

'I guess we have to go up there,' Danny said doubtfully. He surveyed the hulking structure and the pale track weaving to it between standing stones and rising mist.

'Not we,' Caitlyn said, 'just me. You have to stay with Marcus.'

His brow furrowed in confusion. 'Why? You said you don't know what to do. I should go with you, just in case.'

She silenced him with a kiss. Hard and hopeful she held him, one arm to him, one to the sword at her side.

'I *don't* know,' she agreed, 'but those times I learned things here, I was alone. I think that's part of it. You have to stay here.'

Without letting him respond, she pulled away and plunged for the track.

SIXTY-THREE

The mist crept in to greet the trespasser. Round it rolled, testing Caitlyn's skin with smoky tendrils, dampening her hair with wispy caresses. Coiling plumes found animation about her breath and swam to merge eagerly with its brief warmth. With impish intent the fog danced hypnotically across her vision to obscure the way forward even as it weaved thickening strands to seal the way back.

Pressing forward, Caitlyn felt the sword lighten in her grip and rise against potential threats within the miasma. All was lost to vision but a few metres of path ahead and, to either side, the standing stones. They were giants, dourly watching behind the swirling curtain.

A black shape came sudden and bursting. Bearing its cackle on fluttering wings, the creature surged up to Caitlyn's face. She blinked against beating feathers until the raven wheeled aside and flapped away in panic. The harsh caw of its escape through the murk dwindled to a spectral warning from the night's depths. Caitlyn flung silent curses after the bird and moved on behind the sword's piercing tip.

Perseverance was rewarded where the mist began to tumble back in receding layers. First the end of the track and the altar stone were exposed and in the next instant the sullen doorway of Newgrange pressed forward just metres beyond. Caitlyn hesitated and peered reluctantly to the carved rectangular eye of Newgrange gazing from on high.

Shifting the sword, she looked from the overbearing structure to the altar's cascade of swirls. She sought blindly for clues and hoped desperately for a response to the sword's arrival in this place.

'I'm here,' she called at last only to hear her voice flung back by the uncaring night. She was plagued again by doubts as she sought within for the next step to a ritual of which she was ignorant. 'I am the daughter of Aoife,' she tried, 'I am the heir to King Lug. I have brought his sword as proof.'

Newgrange remained silently indifferent.

Caitlyn flexed her fingers against a growing frustration for the passage of vital minutes as a battle unfolded far away.

'I'm here!' she tried with her voice more determined. She raised the sword this time but again received nothing more than the monument's imperious disregard. 'What do you want from me?' she howled, and her despair crashed uselessly against the walls of Newgrange.

The place of visions offered nothing, no more clues, no further guidance. Caitlyn stood helplessly in a silence that moved to refill the space left by her echoing voice. In that space of returning calm, her mind perceived an inkling of possibility and she seized on it. Perhaps, she reasoned, it fell to her to fill the void left by the waiting world.

She looked to the uplifted sword in her grip, in her sole possession, and felt the first tingle of conviction that it was for her to make the next move while Newgrange awaited her command. She examined the polished surface of the blade closely and saw the memory of that move. With eyes reflected she saw again the priestess who had led the funeral of King Lug, millennia ago. She had taken the same sword and raised it before she...

Caitlyn dipped the sword's edge to the altar and drew it along the stone to a harsh scraping of sparks. The blade-song drifted to the monument's unyielding countenance as she waited for a response.

Newgrange was hushed.

Caitlyn sank under the crushing silence. Defeated and robbed of all ideas she surrendered to it and lowered her sword. The night became a place without hope, soundless but for the far-off and urgent whinnying of a horse intruding on her grief. The only motion was the rolling fog as it made a slinking retreat from that far-off sound. Its movement allowed the moon's rays to play against the edges of the lightbox, but the moon had already set behind the distant hills and the horse's cry and now others rising were not so far away after all. Puzzled, Caitlyn turned her face up and saw light grow from a twinkling to a pulsing illumination which gave furious life to the eye of Newgrange. She watched as it surged brighter, not without but from within, from the very heart of the monument, and saw how it crept to enliven the quartz walls to sparkling and to a growing drone matched eagerly by the sword in her hand. She had time for a single breath before the captured sun-risings of ten thousand solstices poured from the lightbox in search of her.

The sword of Lug blazed as the blast of light pierced Caitlyn's eyes, holding her as it swam through the prisms of green and blue to her very being. With the blinding illumination came vision and understanding, clear beyond measure, all the burning knowledge of the ancients stored up just for her. In a moment ten thousand years in waiting, all doubts were blown from the ends of her whipping hair and there were no more questions. The sword of Lug chimed a mighty war song, and everything was forged anew in the cascading fires of Newgrange. Their flames seared white-hot through Caitlyn's veins and filled her mind with scorching knowledge as another vision rose. Through the storm of light and learning, she saw the great army that came at her command.

ॐ ॐ ॐ

Danny and Marcus cowered under the roaring storm. Curled up within the Wraith, they shielded themselves against the hammering onslaught of wind and light. Hands pressed in protecting their ears from a charging violence that howled across the land and shook the earth as it hurtled away to the south. And then, as quickly as it had risen, the storm was gone, from chaos to silence in a moment's blinking. Danny bounded for the shattered doorway but was caught on the way by his injured companion.

'You mustn't,' Marcus warned with a grimace of pain. 'Caitlyn will be all right.'

The boy broke easily from the man's weakened grasp. 'You don't know that,' he cried and sprinted for the hillside.

The track Danny sought was no more. He tripped and fell over wet clods where once the path to Caitlyn had led. In its place and all around for as far as he could see, the ground was a torn ruin, the green earth gouged up by the passing of some colossal force that had galloped amid the storm. He clawed through the muddy destruction, fighting for purchase as he moved desperately upwards.

Through settling mist, he reached the altar stone and fell against it, exhausted as he searched for her. Across the devastated ground he looked to Newgrange rising above and was offered nothing to ease his pain.

Caitlyn was gone.

SIXTY-FOUR

'Hold them!' Sackimum Brody shouted through the din of battle. 'Hold them!'

The fighting raged to overwhelm the senses with dizzying onslaughts and cries amid clashing arms. The spirits flung themselves recklessly into the struggle against growling Fomorian ranks, battering back against the advance with no thought for their own numbers which steadily decreased in silvery eruptions all along the battlefront.

Looking on all, Brody felt a cold stab of despair, but the feeling was abruptly driven off by the sight of a lone Fomorian charging him down. The Professor quickly took up his stance, presenting his sword for the attack. The enemy, as lumbering and stupid as his comrades, charged on, throwing high his arms and the huge axe he carried. It was a simple matter for Brody to strike the exposed warrior with a single expert thrust.

The Professor stood over the fallen warrior and took stock, ignoring a volley of arrows that cut the air around him. On the right flank, the Vikings held firm under King Ivar's roared encouragement, more than a match for the Fomorians, but too few, far too few to hold for much longer. To his left, meanwhile, helmeted Normans slashed and hacked at the enemy but were visibly losing ground. Between, the rag-tag line of spirits continued the fight with determination and curses, sticks and fists, their number dwindling fast.

Brody knew he was watching a losing battle. Scanning again across the line, his gaze came to the far riverbank and caught the jubilant features of Cethlinn where she watched the fight. With a sharp jerk on her whip, he saw the Queen haul up Aoife's tortured eye to watch too.

A lone cry caught his attention and Brody looked in horror where Laetitia stood isolated from the rest before a Fomorian warrior who stomped hungrily towards her, sword ready. Brody charged.

Standing her ground against the towering brute, Laetitia flung up her fan with a gasp. 'Sir,' she implored, 'you surely do not raise your sword to a lady?'

Confounded by her appeal, the Fomorian hesitated, his sluggish thinking betrayed in a wondering grunt. Laetitia seized the moment and ended his bemusement with a concealed dagger to his heart.

Brody arrived at a run to level his sword on the falling warrior. 'Laetitia...,' he began.

'Don't you dare,' she snapped, 'don't tell me to stand behind you, Sackimum, don't tell me to seek safety. I won't leave you. Do you hear me? I won't.'

He smiled on her. 'I don't want you to leave,' he assured gently. 'Laetitia, without you beside me, what have I left to fight for?'

'Oh, Sackimum,' she choked, and reached for him.

The Viking rank burst under a strike of power and light. Fighters spun flailing through the air before it. Ivar raged with broken sword against his falling and Balor led his Fomorians through the breach with crackling spear. Swords and axes closed round Brody and Laetitia, and the cruellest spear of all pointed to the Professor's defiant face.

'Enough of this nonsense,' Balor snarled. His spear tip sparked in reaction to his anger. 'Tell them to surrender.'

'Surrender to you?' Brody asked, aghast. 'To become slaves? We will not.'

'You are without hope,' Balor scoffed, 'you are without your last hope. Where is Caitlyn now when you need her most?' He smiled down on the Professor, but briefly. 'One last time, surrender.'

Balor's spear tip floated closer, humming with the promise of untold agonies.

For a moment Brody wavered, caught in the glow of that frightful weapon. By its light he saw the losing battle, the many spirits flaring to the great beyond in a last desperate attack. Its light played across the stained Fomorian weapons and sparkled in Balor's triumphant eye. It tumbled to the surface of the river, there to catch a multitude of ripples so suddenly and strangely forming under some vibrating force drumming along the body of the Liffey. Sackimum saw it and understood. With renewed defiance he met Balor's face, and with a knowing smile he said, 'Goodbye, your Majesty.'

The battle became insignificant to the approaching storm. Its growing intensity was sufficient to stay weapons and draw gazes to the darkened slopes where the black river led. Those who did not look there looked instead to their feet in search of the tremors they felt between the ripples. A far greater mystery to all eyes was that of the sun apparently rising in the west, a golden white blast of light which signalled the coming of Caitlyn's army.

The Clann Dé Danu rode charged across the crashing earth, war banners streaming and helmets gleaming in the luminescence that rose from itself. Horses whinnied in their innumerable thousands and drove on, carrying the women and men of arms towards the fray in thundering ranks behind the one who led them.

Caitlyn rode at the head of her vast force, fierce in the saddle, her eyes glinting with the inner light of ancient knowing she carried. In her hand the sword of

Lug vibrated in a battle song of anticipation while her cape streamed from shimmering battle garments. Her hair was knotted in the old way, the better to display her war-paint, black drawn to tears in honour of her mother.

And for those about to die.

Countless blades chimed in reply to their leader's song and Caitlyn ordered the charge with a sweeping. The glittering army of the gods crashed as a flood and fell upon the Fomorian horde.

The sounds of collision echoed through the realms, rolling to a tempest of flashing metal and voices amplified to ferocity and anguish. The advance guard of Fomorians was swept ahead of the charge, propelled by it, and warriors were thrown over the heads of their comrades and cast back to the waves.

From the midst of the battle, and at Caitlyn's signal, some of the galloping warriors passed on, streaming through sundered lines towards the Fomorian ships. Points of light, quick and flickering appeared from the massed army as archers took aim from their speeding mounts. As one they released a volley to double the stars. A rain of fire cascaded onto the defenceless vessels and the reflecting sea ran orange as the fleet burned on open waters.

Illuminated by the blazes, Fomorian despair increased and threatened to overwhelm the fighters until Balor drove through his own ranks and swung forth his spear. In a blast of power, horses and riders were struck cruelly aside to create a space around which the King offered a rallying point for his troops and a baleful eye for any who dared retreat now. His troops fought towards him and assembled as Balor spared a glance for his great-granddaughter where she dismounted to face him.

'Impressive,' he cast at her, 'but no worse than I faced the last time.'

Caitlyn smiled. 'You lost the last time. Now you'll lose again.'

Something in Caitlyn's voice, coupled with the daring in her face, drew Balor's hard scrutiny and he perceived the change in her being and the challenge in the smile she offered him. He played his spear over the raging battlefield for her to see. 'You believe you can win, little girl?' he scoffed. 'But for you, I see nothing new here.'

Caitlyn lowered her sword tip to the water. 'Keep watching,' she ordered.

The blade pierced the surface of the river and Balor and his warriors watched the run of tiny ripples from it. They saw too the strange movements beneath the surface in answer to the sword and looked here and there at forms undulating through the deep water. Fomorian brows furrowed at the sight of women dancing beneath their feet.

The Merrow burst up. Between the gathered Fomorians they rose on powering tails and reached hungrily with sharpened nails to clasp unprepared fighters. With shrieks of terror one Fomorian after another was hauled to the choking depths as the rest panicked and broke ranks.

Pursued from below and above, the stricken army ran in all directions, some blindly to the waiting swords of Danu warriors, others to the spirits who re-entered the fight with emboldened cheers. One group of invaders fled to the riverbank, clambering for safety across a rocky outcrop from snatching Merrow. Their goal was Queen Cethlinn's place where she stood horrified at the shifting battle. Safety was almost within reach when Maelmorda gave up his hiding place among the rocks. His giant frame halted the Fomorian flight and his sword put paid to their last hope with savage strokes.

With a cry for fading dreams, Cethlinn stood transfixed, watching as her army was overcome on all sides. 'Do something,' she implored no-one, anyone. Through the heat of her rage, she sensed a face turning in response. She found Aoife's upturned eye and peered unwillingly deep into its emerald truth.

The Banshee's promise was a whisper slashing through the tumult.

'I will weep for you, Grandmother.'

From the heart of fear the Queen struck out, offering a back-handed scream for the Banshee's defiance. The action re-focused her mind and she peered on the unfolding carnage, seeking a new strategy. She saw Caitlyn staring back.

Caitlyn's eyes blazed with fury at her mother's injury and offered waves of hate for the Queen. With crushing fingers, she raised her ringing sword to a waiting band of Danu.

'Boghdóirí,' she called to her archers in the old tongue and pointed to her mother, 'mo mháthair.'

Arrows loosed over the combatants and streamed towards those gathered on the bank. Cethlinn gasped as the Morrigan closed in and elbowed her towards the river. The warrior ducked after. Aoife remained alone and perfectly still. She tracked the arrows' flight with an air of calm as though having all the time in the world to examine the coming wave.

The projectiles arced down, closing on her until, with a single assured motion, Aoife raised her tied hands and allowed a lone arrow to split her bonds while the rest peppered the earth all around. The Banshee rose and with a pitiless cry for her enemies she entered the fight.

From the base of the riverbank where she tumbled, Cethlinn heard the wailing and reeled from it. She scrambled between jostling legs, desperate to escape as she saw Aoife gather up a fallen sword in pursuit. She whimpered for herself and tried in vain to summon a final vestige of the power she had lavished on the spear. The Banshee closed in, her half-face over-filled with vengeance, and she raised her weapon. It wheeled down, a killer stroke set for Cethlinn's neck and the Queen screamed. Her cry mixed with the sounds of battle and the metallic chime from the Morrigan's sword as she checked the attack.

'Enough whining,' the Morrigan taunted. She divided in three to deliver her challenge as one. 'Let's do this.'

Cethlinn shielded her ears from a deafening peal of swords.

Through the noise, Balor sought his fallen Queen. Hacking at those in his way, Danu and Fomorian alike, he advanced on the spot where he had seen her tumble, cold fear drawing him on to her unknown fate. But try as he might, he could not locate Cethlinn amid the surge and he struck out in frustration, clearing a space to renew the search. Caitlyn stepped boldly into the arena he created.

'Give up, Balor,' she snarled, 'one last chance.'

He looked on her sadly, almost fondly. 'You won't even call me Great-Grandfather, will you?'

'I'll never do that,' she snapped.

'You don't get to choose your family, Caitlyn,' he chastised her. 'I'm your family.'

'You're right,' she agreed, 'but you don't get to choose who *I* am.'

Sword and spear drew level.

'We could have achieved so much together,' the King lamented.

They flew at one another. The crash of ancient enemies was shattering to the senses, a bone-jarring eruption of wind and light as the magic of blade and tip struck and repelled one another. Warriors on all sides were caught and hurled aside on waves of power while those who held were forced to ride the water's turbulent roll.

Caitlyn stood firm at the dying of the light. She breathed hard and focused on Balor where he stepped back in wonder at her first attack and with a smile of pride for his royal descendent. The smile did nothing to conceal his sly moving of the spear for a new attack. Caitlyn braced for its coming.

She met and equalled the multi-pronged charge he brought. High and low she swept, trusting to her blade's swift strikes and blending with them to repulse her opponent's flurry of blows. And though she fell back ahead of Balor's expert motions, she watched all the while his growing frustration, his path towards anger uncontrolled until at last he stepped back and offered her a bellow of vexation. She watched him in his anger, how he hefted the spear and drew it back, ready to separate himself from his weapon in a moment of blind unthinking. The sword of Lug throbbed in readiness. The King's arm flew.

Queen Cethlinn surged up behind Caitlyn. With a scream tortured by hate she raised a dripping dagger high.

Caitlyn spun to the attack. She faced tear-stained eyes awash with murder, and as the dagger began its downward course she was almost held by their hypnotic sheen, almost. A sudden twinkling on her sword's leading edge, a glittering reflection of the spear tip in flight, pulled her loose. Caitlyn followed the only course open to her. She knelt before Queen Cethlinn.

The spear passed through the space remaining, through Caitlyn's flared hair, and gathered the Queen to itself. Returning all her fiery magic, the weapon cut deep and drove her backwards across the glass-like surface of the river. Grasping against the weapon, she stood a moment, long enough to match the astonishment in her King's face. Still trying to say his name, she collapsed among the warriors.

'The Queen is dead!' the cry went up. It reached the phantom combatants who echoed it, uttering its joy as the fight continued. It reached Professor Brody as he fought on and began to drive back his opponents with renewed vigour. The news was taken up loudly by Ivar the Boneless and turned to a battle cry, by Lord Norbury in his imposition of death sentences all round, by Zekerman, and Zozimus who set Dragon snarling against terrified warriors, and by Pembrig in his daring advance on the shrinking enemy.

Only the Banshee remained silent. With no tears to waste for the fallen Queen she faced down the Morrigans, daring them to launch another onslaught against her. Countless strikes had already failed but their lust for victory remained undimmed even as the cries of joy increased.

'You think it's over?' the Morrigan smirked. She thrust her chin towards Balor as he rushed to his fallen Queen. 'We're not finished yet.'

Balor fell to his knees by Cethlinn. In agony he reached for her lifeless form, drawing her close as though to find a hint of life remaining in her scarred face. Death mocked his hopes and his furious mistake in her prone form. To her dead lips he placed a kiss, and then to her stilled voice he offered his own. It came as the slow rising of animalistic rage, born of anguish and promising the world a scorching revenge. Its power swelled his chest and forced back his head to escape between twisted lips. The howl that issued forth carried all the hate he felt for a world without his Queen.

Balor took up his spear and turned in search of Caitlyn.

She stood unwavering before him.

He offered nothing less than consuming fury and advanced on her with his spear aglow. The weapon spat power in all directions. Bolts of magic crackled on the water in search of her where she kept her stance. She moved only when he aimed a stream of deadly magic directly and then merely to turn her blade to reflect and deflect simultaneously. The impotence of the attack infuriated Balor the more and he quickened his advance, seeking nothing but her destruction, her utter obliteration.

Caitlyn trusted her weapon. Close by her cheek, she listened to it and the meditative hum it offered so softly to the coming storm. The calming force held her hand and kept her still against the warnings from within herself. She stood in the path of a savage force and recklessly exposed her racing heart to it. The sword bade her watch in the time remaining, closely, keenly, for the instant the King's roaring display would become the attack itself.

She saw it in Balor's shoulder first. As he raced forward, the muscles there twitched upwards, betraying the motion of raising the spear. The shoulder moved and the arm bearing the spear began to shift, drawing not up but back. The thrust, now reaching to tighten the King's wrist would be straight and low towards her torso. The motion followed the vision a mere heartbeat later.

Caitlyn brought up her sword. Too early to fend off

the spear, she drew the flat of the blade into its path and steadied herself behind the thin shield she had created. She caught Balor's look of contempt for her effort and the increased momentum he gave his thrust. Only then, only when the King was fully behind his drive and committed to it, did she shift her defence. It was swift and subtle, and it made all the difference. The spear tip had reached its full and irreversible drive when she turned her sword.

From full flat to razor's edge, Caitlyn twisted the blade and leaned in. With impossible precision, blade and tip met at their narrowest points to a searing diamond flare, its brilliance dappled with sparks cast from the unmoving sword and golden shards where Balor's spear began to render in two.

The weapon fractured along its full length, the fissure at its tip meandering rapidly through the shaft and bursting through the surface in all directions. A blizzard of etched metal tumbled through the explosion. Balor, plummeting headlong in his charge, screwed up his eye against it. In that unseeing instant he ran through the tempest and fully onto Caitlyn's sword.

The King's rage gasped and bubbled at his lips. The vital fuel it gave him was replaced so quickly by shock he buckled onto Caitlyn's hands at the sword. Those eyes of green and blue swam to his and he watched how they softened from previous anger to something he struggled at first to recognise, so little of it did he possess himself. With an ember of clarity, he accepted the pity his great-granddaughter offered and reached for it, stalling abruptly where his hand trembled between conflicting impulses to stroke or claw her face. In the grip of indecision, he passed away and brushed her cheek in a crimson blessing. The King fell to rest and bowed kneeling before his heir.

Caitlyn watched in wonder at the softening of Balor's features. The light fading from that single eye stayed on her to the last. What remained was a sound that she struggled at first to identify. It rose slowly between them, pushing steadily against the silence that had come to envelop their shared moment, and it grew to a chorus of many voices, all cheering at once for Balor's defeat.

It dragged Caitlyn sharply back to the moment and she ran in search of her mother.

SIXTY-FIVE

The chiming of swords led the way through riverbank trees.

To a rapid metallic rhythm, the Banshee and Morrigans locked in spinning combat. Swords became pulses of reflected starlight in a lethal dance of breathless strikes and angry thrusts. A Morrigan was driven aside only to be replaced by its other, this one no less ferocious but no more successful against the Banshee's dizzying form, and she too was sent reeling.

Tireless Aoife fought. After years of captivity she was unbound to a raging energy she offered her opponents, one after another and even together. When the Morrigans struck in unison her blade met all in whirling defiance of their skill, punishing three as easily as one. On between the trees, and to a singing of blades, Aoife led the dance of death.

She read the Morrigan's faces and perceived the nodded agreement they shared for a fresh strategy. It came as a timed assault, each warrior charging a split second after the other. Aoife blasted one to the left, one to her right and lashed down towards the head of the third, forcing her enemy's sword to rise in blocking the strike. Banshee and Morrigan blades met and briefly held. The moment was enough for the Morrigan to free a hand and catch Aoife's wrist in a fierce grip.

'Got you,' she sneered between raised arms as her sisters echoed, 'got you.'

Aoife saw the charges from left and right. Glittering tips drove towards her exposed body. But through it all she saw something else. Emerging from the darkened trees, she beheld Caitlyn, slicing through the shadows to come on at full speed. Empty fists pumped the air until she reached, not for the sword sheathed at her back but for that which she carried within her garments, the weapon she had been gifted and now came to return. Caitlyn's hand flew and her mother's dagger cut the night.

The Morrigan looked on in horror at the whistling knife and how Aoife expertly snatched the handle mid-flight. Her touch was so deft the blade's motion was uninterrupted as it drove deeply into its target. The warrior gasped against the burning thrust, her breath driven hard before its power, and to a taste of blood on her lips. Distantly she heard swords scrape the earth, suddenly too heavy to wield. She looked at the faces of her sisters in their twisting agony, and when she peered astonished into the Banshee's eyes, she saw her own perfectly reflected in a single tear slipping over one pale cheek.

The Morrigans exploded. In a chorus of screams the warriors burst to a swirling cloud. Caitlyn threw a hand up against the flapping multitude that formed it, a storm of ravens, each one a portion of the Morrigan's rage in its urgent cawing. The birds cried and rolled and dived in collective fury until escape was found and they spilled away, cackling into the forest to leave peace washing after them.

The storm cleared, and in the silence left behind, eyes of green and blue beheld.

Recognition and affection replaced all else and Caitlyn rushed to her mother, uniting with her in the goal of embracing warmth and a rage of heartbeats against the hush.

Caitlyn searched her mother's face and Aoife knew what she was looking for.

'No more tears,' she said.

Caitlyn smiled and held fiercely, clinging to the heat of belonging until nothing else mattered. Questions and tests and injuries and learning melted before the fire of a bond reforming and she happily let it all drift away. Only that soft tingling to the roots of her hair remained, the sense which could never be dulled, and its gentle insistence brought her gaze to probe the trees. Between the leaves in sheltering gloom, a pair of wide and hopeful eyes looked back.

'Mia.'

The little spirit approached cautiously, uncertain of her place and wary yet of the Banshee. She looked from the black-haired figure to her friend.

'You found your mother,' she whispered.

'Yes, I did,' Caitlyn said.

'What does it feel like?'

Caitlyn could only smile. 'I can't describe it in words,' she said and caught the longing for more in the little girl's face. 'I can only show you.'

From the boundless store of knowledge gifted by the light of Newgrange, Caitlyn opened her palms as a book and offered them to the startled Mia.

'Really?' the girl said.

'Really,' Caitlyn assured. 'I have the answers we both wanted. And a promise is a promise. She's waiting.'

The girl reached forward gingerly. She angled her hands to hover a moment at Caitlyn's and then touched them. With the first soft contact, the power that was now Caitlyn's to command blossomed.

It pulsed from fingers and grew between palms as a sun's dawning. The opening of the way forward shone brilliantly at Caitlyn's effortless behest. Rays of illumination poured from the breach and washed the night forest from sight. Amid its crystal shimmering Caitlyn held fast and watched only what was left to see, Mia's widening gaze as the little spirit searched earnestly, and in the instant before the light burst to obscure even that, Caitlyn caught the change from flickering smile to a breathless recognition. Then sound alone remained. Mia's laughter came tinkling back, resounding through the limitless space beyond realms until it met and joined with another exultant voice.

Caitlyn held the portal just long enough for her own portion of joy. Then the light tumbled back as she closed her empty hands.

'Thank you, Mia,' she whispered to the trees.

Caitlyn rose and saw those who had been watching. On all sides they had gathered, warriors and spirits united as overawed witnesses to her power. Professor Brody looked on proudly as did Laetitia, clinging to his arm. On the shoulders of his triumphant Vikings, Ivar the Boneless winked and chuckled silently at the battle's outcome, while Lord Norbury raised his sword in salute. Through the ranks, Danny helped the limping Marcus, elbowing his way forward to smile at her.

Caitlyn dashed forward and pulled him to a kiss, deep and oblivious.

The Banshee watched with emerald eye.

'My mother,' Caitlyn giggled.

'We've met,' Danny said with a sheepish nod.

Professor Brody addressed the gathering.

'Queen Aoife of the third realm,' he proclaimed with a bow, his action and words echoed heartily by the rest. He turned with a wry smile. 'Caitlyn McCabe, princess of the house of Aoife, champion of all realms.'

The cheers rose to deafening.

⚘ ⚘ ⚘

They rode together from the site of victory. Leaving the minstrel Zozimus to lead the music, and Brody and Laetitia at their dancing, daughter and mother slipped from the spectral celebrations and rode the misty paths of the river valley. They followed the coastline where the last of the Fomorian ships still burned on the water and turned inland to the ways that ran between realms. They basked in the city's golden lustre until, and at last, they moved quietly between trees and looked to a lighted window.

Gran was in her kitchen, working a hot pan and happily singing, 'Sizzlers...are doing it for themselves!'

Caitlyn allowed herself a smile as Aoife wrinkled her nose for the scent of cooking reaching them.

'What is that?' Aoife whispered, aghast.

'Gran's favourite,' Caitlyn said, 'fried banana omelette.'

They chuckled together amid the leaves.

'Will she understand how much has changed for you?' Aoife asked.

Caitlyn considered, nodded. 'I'll help her. I'll hold her hand.'

'To see what you see?'

'Yes,' Caitlyn said distantly.

'What *do* you see?' her mother pressed.

Caitlyn drew a breath for the question. In her mind's eye she peered not to the house light but once more into the fierce glow at Newgrange and the scale of vision it had seared into her. Words seemed insufficient.

'I see everything,' she tried, 'every spirit, every ancient and mortal in the three realms. I see them all. If I close my eyes, I hear their stories and songs, and rhymes in ancient words and, somehow, I can understand them. I know every path between the realms. I knew this one would bring me home even before we took it. And more than that, I know the last path, the one that leads beyond. And I know how to help others find it.' Breathless, she faced Aoife. 'Is that what you see?'

'I see you,' the Banshee said. 'That's how I see everything.'

Caitlyn was warmed by her mother's smile. 'What do we do now?'

'We rebuild,' Aoife declared, 'we renew and make things as they once were. The palaces of the ancient realm and all the bridges between worlds will be restored. Together we'll carry the light back to Newgrange.' She winked. 'We're going to be busy.'

'I'll barely have time for school,' Caitlyn joked.

The Banshee gazed fondly into the emerald and sapphire glow of her daughter's eyes. 'I don't even know what they can teach you now,' she conceded. 'You've learned everything that's important.'

'No, not everything,' Caitlyn said, and she searched her mother's face. 'Tell me about my Dad.'

16th September 2018